The Aerialist

The Aerialist

A NOVEL BY

RICHARD SCHMITT

SEWANEE WRITERS' SERIES / THE OVERLOOK PRESS

SEWANEE WRITERS' SERIES/THE OVERLOOK PRESS
First published in the United States in 2000 by
The Overlook Press, Peter Mayer Publishers, Inc.
Lewis Hollow Road
Woodstock, NY 12498
www.overlookpress.com

Portions of this book have appeared, in different form, in the following
publications: "Leaving Venice, Florida" in *Mississippi Review* and *New Stories
of The South: The Years' Best, 1999*, "Alberta Hufstetler" in *Puerto del Sol*,
"Curtainman," "Tentman," and "Ben" in the *Marboro Review*,
"Twenty-four-hour Man," Even the Cats," "Raymond and Bertha,"
and "Trainman" in *Flyway*.

"Like A Rolling Stone" words and lyrics by Bob Dylan, copyright © 1965
by Warner Bros., Inc. Copyright renewed 1993 by Special Rider Music. All rights
reserved. International copyright secured.Used by permission

Library of Congress Cataloging-in-Publication Data

Schmitt, Richard.
The aerialist / Richard Schmitt.
p. cm.
1. Circus performers—Fiction. 2. Venice (Fla.)—Fiction.
3. Aerialists—Fiction. 4. Young men—Fiction. 5. Circus—Fiction. I. Title.
PS3569.C5166 A68 2000   813'.6—dc21   00-058489

Book design and type formatting by Bernard Schleifer
Manufactured in the United States of America
First Edition
1 3 5 7 9 8 6 4 2
ISBN 1-58567-070-7

For Benny

ACKNOWLEDGMENTS

I am grateful to the Sewanee Writers' Series made possible by the Walter E. Dakin Memorial Fund established by the estate of Tennessee Williams. I'm indebted to many people who made contributions to the manuscript at various stages, including Andrea Barrett, Stephen Dobyns, Mary Engel, Richard Gabriel, Ehud Havazelet, Bob Jones, Rick Wallenda, my wife Valerie, and my daughter Chelsea. To Peter Turchi for his tireless dedication to this book, and Padgett Powell for his endless promotion of my work, I extend my most sincere gratitude. Special thanks to John and Kris Carter for, among other things, the word processor.

The Aerialist

Twenty-Four-Hour Man

Running contrary, crosscut to the grain of regular habits: your evening news, your family dinner, retiring at a decent hour. Running at night when regular people are tucked away, stoplights blinking yellow, streets shining wetblack from streetlights and sweepers, the Twenty-four-hour Man staples red cardboard arrows to telephone poles. He uses a stepladder and a staple gun to set the arrows just out of reach of school-bus-waiting kids, weekend yard-sale people, religious nuts with paper proclamations; he sets them at precise angles which speak the subtle tongue of his people. He is the one who points the way.

Local cops crawl by in their patrol cars. The cackle of their scanners carries for six 3-A.M. blocks. Suspect is a heavyset man near the railway station. He has papers to prove his intentions. The papers of a person of cross-purposes. He carries documents from sponsors, the chamber of commerce, the city commissioner, maybe the mayor himself. The cops eyeball his staple gun, heavy duty, ten- or twelve-gauge staples. They consider crowd control, overtime pay, elephants running amok.

On the car seat with the arrows and the stapler and a role of duct tape for metal poles, the Twenty-four-hour Man has some old French fries and a two-liter jug of Coke. He has posters, rolls of tickets, bags of yellow rope-off ribbon, and a piece of foam rubber to sleep on at rest stops. He has more than a hundred city maps in the back of his Ford Country Squire. He is a nobleman of the road. An attendant of the country. An unlanded gentleman of logistics. He makes strange places familiar to his people who follow him. Not that they are of the same purpose; they are not. He has no peer in the town, and none on the road.

Some early-bird followers catch him; they cross paths by chance, some clowns driving overland. They pass him, faces pressed to the windshield, watching for the next arrow while he's still on the one that's gotten them this far. Fools! Wormhunters, gunjumpers, budnippers. Flying in advance of the advance man. Why don't they sleep at night? He watches them pass, then come driving back the other way, lost. Now they see him, the only car on the road. Soft springs in the back. Alabama tag scraping the asphalt. A car seasoned by miles of concave road; edges rounded by each rut and turn; each gear-grinding uphill crawl, each screeched-to-a-stop close call, and thousands of hard-swerve cranks of the wheel, stomps on the gas, jams on the brake pedal, have produced sophisticated shaping refinements no assembly-line designer could have foreseen. A car with faded stick-on wood paneling, a roof rack with two spare tires, remnants of a tarp shredded by wind, and some boxes tied up with string. The clowns see him and say, Who is that guy? They know he's not from the town, but they haven't seen him before. He goes on, driving to the place where he will put the next arrow.

In some towns he has used the same poles for years, guiding old-timer and first-of-May alike over the road to the lot so they won't need a map or have to stop and talk to townies. If he moves too fast, something might happen to the arrows, his people will be lost, and he'll catch hell from the home office. They couldn't find the lot in Saginaw: a rival show put posters over them. Arrows blew down in Chicago. Poughkeepsie passed an ordinance against signs on telephone poles. If he finds himself too far ahead he slows down, takes a motel one night, drops coins in the Magic-Fingers bed, watches a movie on TV.

You never see this man stuck in traffic. Sometimes he watches from the highway when his work is done. You see him by the side of the road. The baggy-clothes guy leaning against his car without the hood up, his hands in his pockets, or smoking a cigarette, with all the time in the world, all the world in his head. He works for you too, you town people, you regular folks. You don't want his followers lost in your town. But he has no arrows for you. You follow your own direction and he depends on that. He knows when your main arteries will be clogged, when you will be choked on fumes rushing to your job, when you have retired home for your evening news, your family dinner, expiring at a decent hour. Why you do these things he cannot recall. It does not matter to him. He knows the next town; he knows who his people are, and where he will lead them.

Leaving Venice, Florida

Dave and me sat in Betty's Elephant Car Cafe a couple years after quitting high school in '69, couple months after Dave left New England, couple of weeks after I'd hitched down in the dead of winter. We sat at the counter on chrome stools covered with cracked red vinyl. We weren't talking much because it was early and the night before Dave told me he was sick. Said he'd been to a doctor in Sarasota. They wanted to cut him open. To look around, they said. Nothing serious. But it sounded serious the way he said it. He wanted me to go with him to the hospital, because we were friends, because he had no one else, because he was scared. He didn't say all that, but I knew.

"Dave," I said, "I'm no good at hospitals."

Behind the counter Betty, a retired circus trouper, now waitress and cook, fixed us a pair of Ring Two Specials—poached eggs on toast with grits or homefries for $1.45. Dave hadn't said anything about being sick on the phone. Said he had a car-cleaning business in Venice, Florida. I was doing nothing but freezing in New England; working at shit jobs, switching roommates every month. Dave said I'd be a full partner. I pictured palm trees, girls in bikinis, large drinks with flowers in them. Turned out car cleaning wasn't big business, and Venice was a bus stop, but I didn't hold it against Dave since we were old friends.

The bell over the door sounded and two guys walked in. One tall with a handlebar mustache, the other tiny, thin skin over sharp bones. They took stools at the counter. Big guy ordered a Center Ring Scramble—three eggs with onions and black olives mixed up in an iron skillet for $1.65. The rat-faced guy had water. Big guy told Betty he was looking for a car wash. She glanced at Dave.

"That your van?" the guy said to us.

I spun my stool to face the plate-glass window. Parked next to Dave's van with the plastic magnetized sign on the side—Dave's Auto Detailing—was a white Buick Riviera. Big guy said his dog had been hit by a car; died on the way to the vet. He needed to have bloodstains removed from the interior.

"Is it a white interior?" Dave asked.

"It was white," big guy said.

Dave went outside with the big guy while I sat sipping coffee and eyeballing the rat-faced guy. He continuously flicked his thumb against the filter of his cigarette and glared at me. I thought I'd seen him the night before, climbing out of a dumpster behind the Showfolks Lounge. There were only three bars in town, and Dave and me were kicked out of two of them. Only place we could go was the Showfolks. None of the places had large drinks with flowers in them.

When Dave and the big guy came back, Dave was holding two one-hundred-dollar bills. Big guy said he'd drive the Riviera down to the shop; we could keep it overnight as long as we parked it inside. They left without eating and that was the last I saw of them.

On the way to the shop we were in high spirits holding over a month's rent on a single job so we stopped at Jax Liquors to restock the beer cooler and bought a quart of Canadian Mist.

Dave said the carpet looked like burnt toast. "Had to be a big dog to produce that kind of crust," he shouted over a Bob Dylan tape. Dave's van had an eight track and four big house speakers. "Had to be a big gutted dog." We howled *How does it feel . . .* down to Dave's shop, which was an end unit in a strip of garages, an open space with water for $150 a month: cement floor, rolldown door, slab of tarmac out front. It was a neighborhood of transmission joints, self-storage areas, welding shops, places vacated by people after dark. Except us. Dave pulled his van inside at night and slept in it. I had a sleeping bag and the benchseat of a Chevy pickup. We were only a block from the police station so we pulled the door down after dark and kept quiet, or walked to the Showfolks, or drove out of there in the van, which we didn't like to do because coming and going after hours attracted attention. Dave was sure we'd be taken for burglars. Dave was also sure the landlord did not intend that the units be used as homes.

The Riviera was parked in the sun outside the shop. Blood caked on the floor in smooth cracked wafers like a dried-up mud flat. "Must have been a huge dog," Dave said. He unbolted the leather seats front and back, then pulled the carpet out. The steel floor was wet with blood. I wanted to run the hose inside the car but there was no way to drain it so I took off my sneakers and shirt and squatted inside the shell and squeegeed the muck from side to side with a dustpan. When I had a panful I scooped it up and tossed it out the door. Dave sprayed the carpet and seats with bleach, scrubbed with a long-handled brush, hosed a pink river down the driveway. I sloshed rinse water around inside the car and sucked it up with the wet-and-dry vacuum. We took regular cigarette breaks, sitting in our wet shorts on plastic lawn chairs with the cooler between us, listening to Dylan, chasing beer with sips from the whiskey bottle. By late afternoon the floor was clean and the carpet dried on a line strung across one side of the garage.

"Dave," I said, "there is no dog that big."

We sat watching our neighbors pull down their doors and

drive off. They had homes to go to. Regular middle-class houses with lawn around them and carpet in the living room, homes like we'd grown up in, like I'd run away from. Closing time at the shop was hard because we had no place to go. We could head for the bar or pretend to be working late. The sun was low in the sky when we got it into our heads that it would be a great idea to drive the Riviera down to the beach. "What the hell," Dave said, "we got chairs." So we set the cooler in the car between the lawn chairs and Dave rolled two huge joints, locked the van inside the shop, took his box of tapes, and backed the Riviera down the driveway. Dave drove pretty well but had to take the corners real slow otherwise the chairs shifted around. He had the wheel to hang onto but I fell over twice before turning my chair sideways and locking onto the door with my elbows out the window.

We drove down Main Street past the police station and the Showfolks Lounge with music blasting through the Riviera's speakers and on out of town where there were no cars. We drove over the intracoastal waterway bridge and took a dirt road through the scrub pines and palmetto bushes by the circus winterquarters to a stretch of pristine shoreline. In the mid-eighties, after Venice had grown, the place became a notorious nude beach with cops dragging naked women over the sand and men without a stitch on waving their arms and yelling. But when Dave and I drove between the dunes of sugarsand and sawgrass, down to the water, it was wild and unknown.

We sat on the hood with our backs to the windshield in the best part of the Florida day with the sun spreading out into the gulf and the sky in the west gone the color of pink champagne. Low waves smacked the sand over Dylan singing *How does it feel* into the breeze that kept the mosquitoes moving and the joint burning even when we forgot about it and held it too long between our fingers. And lions were roaring. It must have been feeding time at the winterquarters. Lions or something like lions huffed loudly over *to be without a home,* and we were stoned enough to wonder what they wanted. Did they roar for horse hocks or rib cages? Or did they eat some kind of Purina Lion Chow? Dave said a large part of his small intestines might have to be cut out. "What do they do with that stuff?" he wanted to know. "What do hospitals do with people's parts?"

"Dave," I said, "hospitals make me sick." But he wouldn't stop talking about his small intestines and with those damn lions roaring *a complete unknown* all I could think about was catgut. Catgut wooden tennis rackets Dave and me used when we were kids. My dad had them in the basement. They must have been made in the 40s, catgut strings and warped wooden frames. Dave and me used them in the road between our houses *with no direction home* until the catgut fell loose and broken and the shellac on the frames dried and flaked away like old skin. Dave said chemo made your hair fall out. Said he'd never have kids. *Like a rolling stone.*

We stayed on the beach sitting and not talking much until dark, until there was an inch of backwash left in the whiskey bottle that neither of us intended to drink but would not throw away. We'd smoked both joints but still had beer, which we used to try to get normal enough to drive back to the shop. We drove between the dunes with the lights off following the moonlit road. The lions were quiet. I imagined them gnawing on wormy bones and decided right then, old friends or not, I wasn't going to any damn hospital.

We saw the winterquarters lit up like a small city a mile or so across a war zone of palmetto bushes. Reaching the main road Dave switched on the headlights and turned the car toward town. I had my chair facing the door with my arms and head out the window so I didn't see what happened, but somehow Dave lost control of his lawnchair and crashed to the floor. He held onto the wheel with one hand. The car turned sideways to the road, fishtailed hard, and the two of us, with chairs and cooler, clattered backward. When the rear wheels hit the sandy ditch the car stalled out and came to a halt buried to the frame. The rear wheels were stuck in the ditch with the front wheels on the pavement. We crawled uphill toward the door, stashed the beer in the bushes, and walked around the car for a long time, shaking our heads, saying, if only we had front-wheel drive or a couple of stout boards and some rocks and a place to stand or a tractor with nine guys and a rope. We were miles from town and nobody drove this road unless they were going to the winterquarters. There was nothing except the drawbridge, the dark pines, the low palmettos. No houses, no sounds, and no lights, except across an expanse of low scrubland, the circus gleaming in the dark like a planet.

"What we need is an elephant," I said.

"Hey!" Dave said. "We can walk over there. They've got stuff to pull us out."

"Elephants?"

"Someone should stay here," he said.

"You stay here, I'll go."

"I don't even have a license," he said. "What if a cop comes?"

"You're the proprietor of a business, Dave. Say someone stole the car and you walked here and found it." He held his head and walked around in the road. I wanted to bed down in the ditch and sleep, but I knew he'd start walking if I didn't, and I saw for the first time a change roll over his body. Blood took leave of his face and he gripped his midsection with both arms as if to wring pain from his body like a sponge. It was at least a mile to the winterquarters. "Dave," I said, "I'll walk over there."

I began walking up the middle of the road. The bridge was a hump with a glass booth. A telephone. I thought about breaking the glass. Who would I call? The police? A tow truck? The hospital? I'd say a man in need of surgery was stranded on the winterquarters road, then hide in the woods and watch them carry Dave away. Again I felt the urge to hide under a palmetto bush and sleep. But I went on up the middle of the road, looking back at the white car halfway across one lane, front wheels on the pavement, back end buried to the frame. It was too dark to see Dave.

Past the bridge I left the road and walked on a swath of trampled sand that ran through the palmettos. I walked slowly, watching for snakes in the harsh light streaking from the winterquarters. I came to a dirt parking lot next to a building that looked like an aircraft hangar. Behind the building was an open area the size of a football field surrounded by a chainlink fence topped with three strands of barbed wire. Low buildings, animal stalls, and aluminum trailers backed up to the fence. Farthest from the main building were two large green tents. People moved about on foot and drove strange blue vehicles pulling brightly painted wagons. I heard voices. Next to the main building was a guardhouse and gate. A short stocky figure in a guard's hat dragged one leg behind him as he paced in the road under a vapor lamp attached to a telephone pole. Later I learned this was Backdoor Jack, and had I approached him that night, things would not have worked out.

I moved away from the guardhouse, keeping to the shadows, until I came to a break in the fence behind one of the green tents. A man in coveralls rolled a wheelbarrow of steaming cannonballs across a makeshift bridge, planks over vile liquid, to a manure pile. I was no expert on crap, and, not thinking clearly, I suspected whatever let loose crap of those proportions had to be big. I suspected elephants.

I slipped through the gap in the fence and followed the wheelbarrow man along hardpacked dirt between tents. They were old damp-smelling canvas tents surrounded by trenches of seeping juice the color and consistency of used motor oil. Around front I mixed with busy people. No one challenged me. An old guy sat on an overturned bucket. I sidled up to him. He held a Coke can with both hands.

"Lookin' to get on?" he said.

"Maybe."

"Hilmer's the man."

"He around?"

"Somewhere." He took a sip off the Coke can. This didn't seem like the guy I needed to help me get the car off the road, so I moved inside the tent flap.

Elephants. Massive. Silent, active, and close. They were chained side by side, swinging their trunks and whipping their clublike tails, rocking their heads back and forth, lifting one foot then the other, repeating each step in turn like some demented dance. I saw their eyes on me, acute, not missing a beat of their dance. Then there was a compact man wearing tight bluejeans and knee-high turquoise boots, no shirt, and teeth like Chiclets. Chiclets chewing gum right out of the box. He had bleached blond hair over his shoulders and he said, "Ja? Ja? What do you want?" He looked like a picture torn from a glossy magazine and tossed to the gutter. All I could think of was George Armstrong Custer.

"The guy out front," I said, "he said I might get on."

"You been on bulls?"

"Bulls?"

"We're loading out," he said, "tell Martin to set you up." He was gone before I had a chance to say I knew Elephant Car Betty.

I cut back through the tent flap to the bucket-sitting guy with the Coke can.

"You Martin?"

"You get on?"

"I guess so."

"Been on bulls?"

I didn't answer. It took me three days to figure out for sure that elephants were called bulls.

"Got a hook?" he said.

"Hook?"

"How 'bout a smoke?"

"I got nothing," I said. The guy leaned so far forward I thought he would fall on his face, then hocked a blood red gob of spit between a pair of cracked wingtips with curled toes. He tilted the bucket to one side, reached underneath and brought out a bottle of Everclear, unscrewed the cap, and tipped the bottle to the Coke can. He put the bottle back and slowly stood, flatfooted and swaying, like he was riding a subway. When he had his bearings, he turned and ambled off toward one of the aluminum buildings, waving me after him with his Coke can.

The building was crowded with men and women packing stuff into boxes and bags, leather stuff, nylon, canvas, and rubber stuff, with brass rings and silver chains, steel buckles and studded straps. Elephant stuff. Martin rummaged for a club and handed it over. "Yours while you're here," he said. "You leave, you leave it." It was a sledgehammer handle wrapped in black electrical tape. Embedded in one end was a vicious looking steel hook, a bullhook.

It might have been the bullhook that really altered things. I hadn't forgotten Dave, but for the moment I felt swept along, as if my plans had died when I slipped through that fence. I never had a plan anyway, never had a plan in my life that wasn't born out of necessity or desperation. I felt as though I'd fallen into a fast moving river. I was buoyed up, carried off. A strange collaboration of circumstances had given me a part. Playing it seemed the only thing to do.

Outside, I wandered around carrying the bullhook, trying to look on-duty, expecting someone to tell me what to do. No one did. I rolled bulltubs to wagons. When the wagons were full and the doors clamped shut, someone roared up in one of those blue vehicles, "unimugs" Martin called them. They had large steel pinhole hitches on both ends, two steering wheels and a revolving driver's seat. Their sole function was to push or pull. Dave would be impressed if I showed up with one of these things. I held the tongues of the wagons for the drivers to back into and tried to catch their attention, but they backed up fast, dropped the pin into the hole without leaving their seats. One driver nodded, so I stepped up to his steering wheel and said, "I have a problem." He drove off fast.

The center of activity was the brightly lit building across the lot. Two sliding doors big enough to roll planes through were open, and inside a jungle of ropes and cables hung from the ceiling and gray canvas bags cluttered the arena floor. People lifted, carried, pointed, and pulled. Shouts rose and died. Steel poles clanged and clattered as men grimed with sweat slid them into wagons and slammed the doors. The wagons were immediately taken up by unimugs and towed around the corner and out the gate where Backdoor Jack stood. I watched from under the seats and tried to think straight. I decided Dave should come here. We'd work on bulls and to hell with that white car. But Dave had baggage. His van, his wet-and-dry, a hospital appointment, something growing in his gut. People hustled about eyeballing me standing under the seats with a bullhook so I went back to the elephant tent. It was close to midnight. The only person sitting was the old Coke-can guy, Martin, so I slid up to him and tried to get information. "What time do we knock off?" He stared at me through eyeslits like pencil lines and took a hit off his Coke can.

The blond guy, Hilmer, grabbed my arm. "You come here." He dragged me behind him into the tent. "Next town you see Huffy," he said. "Huffy in the pie car. Tell him you're on bulls." He took my bullhook, handed me a pitchfork, and I spent the rest of the night scraping soiled straw from beneath elephants. I watched and copied the other guys. You timed your work to the elephant's dance, dodging swinging tails and trunks. When the left front leg came up you grabbed a sodden forkful and backed off, then the right rear, the right front, and so on. They seemed okay with me, but their eyes left no doubt: they knew I had no idea what a bull was.

Before we finished, Hilmer came in yelling. Everyone put up the forks and began unchaining feet. The chains were shackled on a rear leg and each shackle had a pin that had to be unscrewed. This happened fast with a lot of loud jabbering by Hilmer. Within minutes the bulls moved out of the tent. Each delicate trunk took the tail of the one preceding it. They moved with strong snorts of breath on round padded feet and lined up facing an identical group from the adjoining tent. The men stood between them. Even Martin was on his feet, bullhook in one hand, Coke can in the other. I mimicked the other guys, trying hard not to do anything stupid in the proximity of forty loose elephants and a dozen men with clubs.

I wondered where we were going, but it didn't occur to me until later, after I'd seen the train, that all of us—elephants and their stuff, unimugs and wagons, worlds of people, animals and things that I had no notion of but had somehow become caught up in—were leaving Venice, Florida.

Hilmer hollered and both lines of elephants moved at once. I moved as the guys near me moved. We walked at the left hind leg. We carried our clubs prominent. The beasts were not to break the trunktail hookup, that was gospel; if one let go of the tail our job was to hook the inside back leg and say, *Tail!* If the tail wasn't picked up immediately, the role of the bullhand was to take a full roundhouse swing with the club and bury the hook in the leg. This took something more of an adjustment than I'd been able to muster that night, but luckily the beasts were compliant, they knew their role, fell readily into it, and did not test mine.

The impetus of the movement, the focal point, was Hilmer. Each man and beast watched Hilmer and he watched everyone. He moved along the line and spoke in a way I could not at first understand, spoke in what I thought was a foreign tongue, but once we'd gone through the gate, past Backdoor Jack, and out onto the same sandy path I'd taken across the palmetto field, I heard what he was saying were the names of the elephants. He wasn't talking to us but to them. Moving slightly faster than the herd, he cooed the name of each beast. They had regular girl names: Ellen, Jenny, Cindy. He said their names slowly and affectionately and he looked each one in the eye as if they had his personal assurance that everything was under control, that they would be fine, that there was nothing to worry about. That reassured me too. I saw that in this world bull and bullhand were not that different, both had a place, both were taken care of. I nurtured a state of helplessness about Dave, pushing guilt behind fantasy, and felt better the more confusing things became. The world had shifted and I was caught in the afterwind. I went with it because it was the easiest thing to do, because it was what I always did.

The eastern sky had gone peach over the black horizon. At the rate we moved we'd pass the car in broad daylight. I could bail out of line. I knew that. I could simply stop walking, hand my bullhook to Martin as he went by, and everything would be the same as the night before. Nothing would stop the line, that much was clear. If I fell down dead they'd walk on over me. But nothing else was clear to me. I didn't want to stop. I wanted to walk to Africa. I wanted to be a bullhand whatever that meant, not on a whim but because it called out to me. A voice I didn't know, yet recognized, said go this way. And I went because I didn't want to clean bloody car floors, sleep in garages, or wait in hospitals for my friend to keel over and not get up. The problem was not the car, or even Dave. But rather, could I abandon a dying man? I felt like I could. In fact a dying man felt like the best kind to abandon. Dave would understand that. Only a captain goes down with the ship, and clearly I was no captain.

We made it onto the road as the sun broke over the treeline and the inland waterway began to steam. From the drawbridge I saw the car. The herd padded silently in pairs straight down the double yellow. As we got close to the car I hunkered tight against my elephant's leg, moving with her, and as we passed I peeked back under the tail and saw Dave's face in one of the windows, his eyes wide as binocular lenses. He never saw me.

Shortly after, we turned onto a dirt road and came upon a white train parked in the woods. Brilliant white. Freshly painted white. With large red and blue letters on the sides. It sat there waiting for us. For me. I was stunned. Never in my life would I have considered the idea that there was a white train in the world.

Even the Cats

The blessing of the backlot is very important to the Mexicans. They set up a makeshift altar on Sunday morning, a wooden prop box covered with a special white cloth, they secure a priest from some-where, and he says Mass at the backcurtain before the show. They kneel on the cement floor that is covered with track rubber so the horses and elephants don't slip. The priest stands with his back to the blue and white striped curtain and casts the blessing out over the rubber that runs off to the left all the way to ringstock. The closed curtain is backdrop to the monstrance, the exposition of the eucharistic host—the priest holding it high above his congregation. All ten of them.

The blessing goes out over them, the men in their old-country suits, the little girls in white lace dresses, the darkeyed women with doilies pinned to their hair, and it wafts down the wide hallways in both directions, around the stiltwalkers' stilts and twenty-foot stepladder that sit just inside the curtain next to the Rubbermaid poop barrel with the broom, aluminum shovel, and brown-paper bale of sawdust for when an elephant takes a piss, then over the two wardrobes: costume boxes pushed together forming separate dressing rooms for ladies and men—no roof—so the hallowed air floats into the open space where people cavort buck naked. No, they simply dress and undress, most of them wear bathrobes and underwear, but still the air is sanctified in case of cavorting. The priest is the exterminator, spreading holy mist for vermin, keeping the place pure whether anyone likes it or not.

The blessing travels past the no-speeka-de-Engleesh shoeman sitting at his table fixing elk-hide soles to soft leather uppers, the sewing lady stitching sequins to Spandex, the rack with the workingmen's clean coveralls, and into clown alley, historically a holy place anointed in greasepaint, baby powder, and good intentions—clowns raise the dead every day—and down the hallway where big shots preen privately in small dressing rooms. There are names on the doors, some as elaborate as Connalessia, others plain like Nock.

The blessing finds the animals: follow the gray rubber road past the clown car, the pony cart, the kiddy train, the terrible cannon which sends men heavenward—sometimes to meet their god—past the pie car dinner wagon, called Junior after its big brother on the train, to the elephants and horses and three odd camels and a goat in separate chainlines with their ropes and wheelbarrows and water buckets and tack wagon with the door swung wide, the wagon full of horseshoe nails and bullhooks, bridles, halters and soft smells of corn and oats and waste, to the pyramids of hay bales and straw bedding, inside of which workingmen carve tunnels and caves with their bodies, naptaking crannies where they burrow between numbers to hide and read cowboy books.

The blessing finds even the cats in their cages, hidden away as best as possible, but sniffed out easily if you know their sharp smell. Even the cats, roped off from the world—not their world—with warning signs saying Danger, saying Keep Away, saying there is some evil here for the unblessed, for the stupid. Fire extinguishers and pitchforks surround the cages in case the blessing doesn't make it this far, or doesn't work. The Mexicans have faith. But the others . . . ?

In the name of the Father . . . the white tiger raises her head and *sniffs. And of the Son . . . two elephants trumpet in unison. And of the Holy Spirit . . . a lion roars at the Benediction. And the performers walking on the backlot, taking no chances, bow their heads passing the backcurtain.*

Old Friends, New Places

Teardown night in Shreveport, cold and rainy, we packed into the pie car to eat while the train was being slammed together. Rollo, the transportation boss, had fired the diesel mechanic and was whining to Huffy about not having one, so I mentioned my friend Dave. It was a spontaneous thing; I felt guilty leaving Dave in Venice. I said Dave was a diesel mechanic, which wasn't exactly true. Dave could tinker most things into temporary operation, but he'd never worked on big generators like the show used to provide electricity for the train.

I'd been on the show a month and had switched from bull-handler to butcher. Strawbosses like Rollo wouldn't usually talk to butchers. In movies guys like Rollo were called roustabouts and butchers were concessionaires, but we didn't use those words. We called them workingmen, they called us butchers, and the line between us was clear. Since I'd been on bulls Rollo listened to me about Dave, and Huffy okayed him being flown in. Dave didn't have a phone but Rollo said he'd call Elephant Car Betty, see if we could get Dave into the next town.

People looked at me different after that. Big guys on transportation with tattoos and Fu Manchu mustaches nodded to me in the pie car line where I stood waiting for food. Huffy paced the center aisle eyeballing me squinty-eyed through cigarette smoke. He shook his head up and down slightly, as if he'd decided something I'd find out later. He was not a dwarf but he had the elongated dwarflike body, bowed ape legs, belly hanging over his belt, stubby arms and club head, both eyeballs bulged like wall-eye marbles and one aimed off into space like a loose headlamp. Huffy was a troll, an ogre, a gnome, and to 150 riggers, animal people, ringcurb guys, wardrobe boys, transportation men, and train porters, Huffy was the paymaster, the hirer and firer, the distributor of dukie books, the hangover antagonizer, the finger-pointer. He was The Bossman. And he hated me because I was too good to shovel shit on bulls, at least that was his first reason, later he'd come up with a list.

Butchers had their own boss and sat at the back of the pie car. Where you sat was determined by where you worked. Up front near the counter was the booth for Pie Car Bill, Huffy, and Rollo, who couldn't fit his oversize gut into a booth but sat sideways on the vinyl-covered bench, his back to the thick plate-glass window, with one elbow on the table and his feet across the narrow aisle. Bob Furr might be up there, the assistant show manager, who was part Cherokee from Oklahoma. And his sidekick Radar, who nobody knew anything about except that he was called Radar because he had an ancient Salvation Army hearing aid: plastic box hooked to his belt with a wire run up the underside of his shirt to a flesh-colored plug stuck into his ear. Say something to him he'd give the box a slap and say, "What?" You'd say, "Forget it." He'd whap the box again. "What?" There was no way to get in a line like: Where you from?

Across the aisle from the bosses sat the old trainman and his smelly dog. Then the big guys with tattoos, riggers or ringstock guys. Performers were independent contractors and sat wherever. Members of the New York Wheels, basketball playing unicyclists from Harlem, sometimes sat in the back with us, or up front in Huffy's booth if they wanted to make a point. Huffy didn't sit much anyway. He paced the aisle glaring at people and blowing cigarette smoke on their food.

I'd just taken a bite of a grilled ham and cheese sandwich when Huffy walked up to the booth where I sat with Pierre, a Puerto Rican souvenir-stand operator from Queens. We were eating and watching the trainyard through the window. Huffy's squinting-from-smoke face came even with mine just as a yard engine slammed into us and the ham and cheese got shoved up my nose. It was hot off the grill and the yellow cheese stuck burning to my upper lip like napalm. Huffy stared with his cock-eyed eyeballs—I think he had a glass eye. He was unaffected by the cannonshot which jolted the train. The cigarette in his mouth bobbed up and down and dropped ashes onto the floor. "This friend of yours better be good," he said. He puffed a cloud of smoke into my face and walked off, leading with his pregnant gut, nodding his giant bald head with that one haywire eyeball roaming.

Pierre laughed, at the molten cheese or the threat of Huffy, I couldn't tell. "You're screwed if your friend's a chump," he said.

"I don't know why I opened my mouth." I told Pierre that Dave was an old friend I'd run out on.

"You owe him anything?"

"Nothing like that," I said. "It's just that nobody knows me here, and I like that."

"You're afraid he'll cramp your style."

"I just don't want daily reminders."

"Where you from? Long Island?"

"I want to forget that place."

"What place?"

"Forget it."

Pierre said that as a mechanic Dave wouldn't be living in the butcher car. The butcher car was a famous caravan car. A closed car, a door at only one end, and the last car before the stocks.

Ringstock people couldn't walk through the butcher car to the stocks where they lived, but had to jump off and run along the ground. The butcher car vestibule deadended a mile-long passageway beginning at the pie car which was just behind the private cars and the engines. Six of us lived in the butcher car: Eddie and Rodrigo, Chicanos from L.A., a fat guy named Frank who never said where he was from, and Bula from Harlem, friend of the Wheels. There were eight bunks but two of them had the foam mattresses removed and were used as storage shelves. The floor was orange linoleum. There was an old red refrigerator and a small green stove but nobody used them. Our door, a thick slider with a padlock, was brightly painted with the name of the show. The vestibule, black steel and silver deckplate, which we shared with the Wheels unicycle troupe, was the premiere party spot on runs. We had a ghettoblaster, day-glo painted walls, peace and black power symbols, blacklights, and a stenciled Mr. ZigZag. We hung out on the runs with the top half of the Dutch doors latched back and the wild air from anywhere slamming in. Only serious party people made the trek to our vestibule. We offered fat joints and jugs of psychedelic wine. When the train paused in the middle of nowhere, animal people would scramble over the closed half of the vestibule door—scare the bejesus out of us—and make their way across our vestibule, down the narrow aisle through the New York Wheels car, the stinky Bulgarian car, the Polish car where vodka flowed, the sweet smelling showgirls car, the clown car that was tricky to get through—the clowns being devious practical jokers—the Hungarian car full of giant men who drank yellow wine and slapped you hard on the back, the midget car where everything was built low and lightweight, another caravan car where workingmen slept in bunks, through the screaming generator car, to the pie car.

The night of the Shreveport to Galveston run was cold and wet. Pierre shut the upper doors on both sides of the vestibule, and Buzzi of the Wheels hauled out his guitar and wailed away—

he was a Hendrix freak. One of his unicycle partners, Rulfo, pounded a pair of bongo drums. Keywash came out with his saxophone, and Bula wearing black glasses did his impression of Stevie Wonder. The unicycle guys nicknamed everyone on the show except big shots who had two names: Louis Morgan, Sigfried Heinemann, Lalo Cadonna, Rudy and Diana Sabastian. There were only a few two-namers and they stayed in the private cars up by the engine. There were many one-namers: Cowboy, Baldy, Shorty, Highrise, Ziggy, and at least a dozen guys called Indian or Cherokee. Some people had only initials: TC, BJ, HQ. And some had titles, like Pie Car Bill and Backdoor Jack. At first I didn't know all the people who crowded onto the vestibule, but it didn't matter, I got to know them. Show people scorned town people, until you joined, then it was as if you'd always been there, as if we were the whole world reeling and rocking on that vestibule, drinking and smoking our way south into Texas.

Late morning I woke in my bunk and knew that we were in the yard. I couldn't see out—the windows in the butcher car were painted white—but yardrails were always new and we rolled so slow, smooth, until the moving disappeared. Roll, stop, roll to a stop so softly I couldn't feel it. Pierre was at the sink with his head under the faucet. Frank was in the can grunting and farting. I took my rolled bluejeans from under my head and pulled them on and fell out through the curtain and into my sneakers. Pierre came from the sink with a towel over his head. "It snowed," he said.

"Snow in Texas?"

"It will kill the house."

I put on my hooded sweatshirt, snapped up the front, and went through the slider onto the vestibule. It was empty, the doors open, slush on the deckplate. Wind drove frozen rain, what New Englanders call sleet, through the vestibule. I turned my back on the wind, unzipped my jeans, and pissed out onto the railbed. We were barely moving, the yard deserted in the silent gray morning. I could have stood there gently rocking for a year or two with that warm pissing feeling steaming out onto the frozen rocks and my bunk just inside if I wanted to go back.

The station, a quarter mile ahead, had a tin roof over a cement platform. Along the tracks a few show trucks were parked with the windows fogged, overlanders asleep on the seats. Bob Furr and Radar stood on the platform with a yard guy, all three held walkie talkies; the old trainman carried the gigantic wrench he used to tap the city waterlines. I saw Huffy walking with Dave. They moved off the platform toward the pie car. An odd couple. Dave tall and thin hunched inside a tan corduroy coat, shoulder length brown hair, bluejeans, a pair of two-doller boatshoes. About six inches of thick wrist and basketball-palming hands hung from too-short coat sleeves. He hated that, often complained he couldn't find clothes that fit him. Huffy wore a topcoat, scarf, and wool hat. He craned his neck up at Dave and tried to light a cigarette in the wind. Eager to talk to Dave, I jumped to the railbed and walked over the frozen rocks to the pie car. By the time I got there Huffy stood at the counter talking to Pie Car Bill.

"Your mechanic showed up," I said to Huffy.

"Another Yankee," Bill said. Bill was from New England like Dave and me.

Dave lived across the street from me in Rhode Island when I was eleven, but he wasn't a friend of mine until I saw him kneeling in a church pew at my mother's funeral. Dave was Protestant and didn't have the kneeling right. I don't know why he was there, curiosity maybe, first time in a Catholic Church. He looked scared and I remember hoping I looked at least as scared because, after all, that was my mom going into the ground. Kneeling there I suppose Dave considered the consequences of being motherless because all Dave had was a mother. His dad was gone; "separated" was the word used in our neighborhood. We became friends based on the single parent thing, and the funeral thing. We became best friends. At times we fantasized that we were brothers, that my dad married his mom and we lived happily ever after. But that's not what happened.

"I sent your friend down to 143," Huffy said.

Car 143 was a catchall of strawbosses, porters, girl clowns, ticket guys, and elite workingmen. Rollo and Pie Car Bill lived in 143 and that was where the old mechanic had lived. Dave was going to have a private room, a prize among workingmen and butchers. Bosses and performers snagged staterooms, and there were double staterooms for couples. Big shots like Huffy lived in private cars, a half-dozen rooms with the walls taken down between them, and Louis Morgan, the show manager, had an entire traincar. Dave had a roomette, the bottom rung of rooms. But roomettes were still rooms, with a locking door, a window, a fold-down bed, and walls to hang pictures on. You stood in the aisle to lower the bed and when it was down there was no floor-space, you jumped into bed and slid the door closed, or kept it open a crack so you could see who walked by. Dave was figuring these things out as I came up the aisle behind him. He'd lowered the bed and was wrestling with his ratty brown suitcase, shiny brown like it was laminated, cracked across the sides and chipped at the corners. There were latches but Dave must not have trusted them because the case was covered with duct tape. He'd already cut through the tape and dumped out his stuff onto the bed.

"Dave," I said.

He turned the case on end, rested it on his foot and leaned back against the wall. "There you are," he said. We were both grinning when we shook hands. "What the hey," he said. I don't know where Dave picked up that expression but he used to yell it across the street between my house and his, and I remember him shouting it out the window of his first car, and yelling it in the echoey hallways of our high school, but it never sounded strange until I heard it in car 143.

"Where's your room?" he asked.

"Butcher car," I said.

"Butcher car?"

"I'm a butcher."

"What do I do with this suitcase?"

"You don't need stuff like that here."

Dave set down his case, unlatched the bed, and pushed it into the wall with his clothes on it. He stood in the room with his palms pressed against opposite walls. "A phone booth," he said.

"A place to live," I said.

Dave didn't ask me why I'd disappeared in Venice, and I didn't ask him what happened after I left. That's the way our friendship worked; we avoided tension and expectation. Things were accepted, understood or not. Over the next few weeks the story came out, usually when we were drinking, how I'd been shanghaied by Gypsies, stuffed into a rubber bag and beaten senseless, then chained nude to the floor of the bullcar. We told outrageous lies to avoid unpleasant truths. Dave knew I'd run out on him for the same reason we always ran out on situations that became "too heavy," which meant we might have to face some responsibility, even worse, do some work. Dave said the Buick Riviera had belonged to dope dealers. He'd left it where we ran it off the road, walked most of the way back to Venice, and never did make it to the hospital. We had in common an overwhelming urge to avoid responsibility and work at any cost, and since we both understood that, there were no hard feelings about me vanishing in Venice.

Dave did seem a bit grudgy about the roomette, and about the job I'd gotten him. From the beginning he didn't get along with Rollo. Dave had one of those long last names that ended in *ski*. The type of name that made everyone say: You must be Polish. Rollo didn't say that. Rollo's real name was Bert Bensieble. He spoke English in gruff choppy sentences, had a barrel chest and a huge half-moon gut that hung over his narrow waist. He was the kind of guy you didn't get in front of because he was always walking too fast, leaning over that gut, arms rowing the air, making way for the day he would clutch his chest and pitch forward onto his face. Rollo did everything fast, and Dave was your slow methodical type. Rollo waddled ahead, looking back at Dave and shouting, but Dave never hurried. He'd take a puff on his cigarette, and keep strolling at the same pace. "Dead diesel engines don't go no place," he said.

Rollo figured Dave wasn't a real mechanic. But it didn't take Dave long to understand the generators, and to know that Huffy was The Man to get on the good side of. Dave worked around the train fixing stuff for Huffy and Pie Car Bill who was short tempered and broke everything. I'd come in from the show at night and see Dave behind the pie-car counter splicing an electrical cord or fixing the toaster or drink dispenser, which Bill had smashed. Dave was a train guy. He didn't miss the show like I would have. He didn't cramp my style, as Pierre said, but he never did give up that ratty suitcase. He often talked about what people back in New England would say about the show. I never thought about that unless he brought it up, and he brought it up too much.

The first time he saw me running the seats for Pierre he laughed like hell. "How can you do that?" he asked. I wore a red and white striped smock with large blue pockets across the front. I was on floss that day and held a big red board of it over my head. I sold whatever was going good. If Sno-Cones were going good, I jumped on Cones. Plastic rayguns, astrolites, programs, blowup toys, I sold them all. Texas was mostly a floss state. With the board held high I pounded the cement steps to the music of every number, sweated out Openings, intermissions, and Finales charging up and down the rows yelling, "Candy! Cotton candy!" The goal was to unload a board of twenty-five at two bucks each before the sugar liquefied red and gooey and the airy fluffs shriveled on the paper cones into something that resembled matted sheep wool. "How much you get?" Dave asked.

"Five bucks a board."

"That's crazy."

"That's what it is," I said.

He shook his head, looked at me like I was nuts, and went back to the train. Dave just didn't get the running game. He never understood that butchers were part of the show. Our smocks were our costumes, we wore special paper butcher hats, we sang the opening numbers. We were the first and last things the people saw at the circus. The kids pointed and screeched, parents scowled and shook their heads, heads I could turn, even while they tried to look around me. *Hey!* I'd bellow as the band took a breath. *Candytime!* And when they looked I dumped candy on the kids who would die before giving it back. I turned their heads from the flying man, distracted them from the contorted woman, snatched their eyes from the dancing dwarf, the snake charmer, the lion-trainer's head in the fat cat's mouth. I pulled their eyes anytime I wanted. Being visible was power, a feeling I'd never felt, and having felt it never wanted to give up.

I'd walk to the center of a crowded tier aisle, stand there without moving or saying a word, then turn slowly and run my eyes over the people packed shoulder to shoulder. They'd be looking at *me*, expectation on their faces, wanting something from *me*. I'd hold up an astrolite, a raygun, a Dumbo on a stick, as if to say, *you* want one of *these?* I'd look away. By the time I walked over to them they'd buy five. In a good town I'd make fifty bucks a day. But I didn't think of it as a job; I did it because the show was the world to me, always different yet always there, and running the seats was part of the show. I knew, even then, I wanted a bigger part.

Dave didn't care about the show. Dave was on a lark, an adventure. By the time we'd crossed Galveston, Waco, Houston, San Antonio, and Laredo off the route card, he was sitting up front in the pie car with Huffy. When Rollo complained about him, Huffy just shook his bald head, shrugged his shoulders, blew smoke, and strolled away. I didn't see Dave during the day, but at night we generally closed down the nearest bar to the train. On runs we drank in the pie car or hung out on the butcher-car vestibule heading each week south to the bordertowns.

Pierre said Brownsville was one of those towns where something always happened. Immigration officers often raided the show there. A year ago one of Pierre's butcher girls was found dead in the river. The train and the building were within walking distance to the border. Each night after the show we walked in a group: Dave and me, and Pierre, Frank the morning farter, Eddie and Rodrigo, assorted butchers and workingmen. We walked over the bridge through the turnstiles, past the guard booths, the begging children, into Matamoros where the streets, still warm from the day, were jammed with tourists drinking tequila, shopping for cheap leather goods, and searching for a rumored "donkey show."

The attraction of bordertowns for us was available and affordable sex. The fleecing of sex-starved punks revolved around cabdrivers. We'd pile into a cab and be taken to a strip joint full of whores who would give the cabby a kickback. The women, various ages and shapes, bled us for drinks. When we'd spent our limit they'd take us into rooms to get the rest of our money. We were suckers and knew it, but they were cheap and we didn't care. For some reason the oldest and fattest were attracted to me.

In one place Dave found a young girl, at least one that could accurately be called a girl, and left me with a fat grandmother sitting on my lap. This woman was no taller than Huffy and no more attractive. She wore a red satinlike sleeveless dress that was so tight and short I saw her girdle when she sat on my lap. A girdle! I was five-foot-ten, a hundred fifty pounds, she felt like a boulder in my lap. Pinned like a spent wrestler, I couldn't weasel out from under her. She had me in a headlock and kept squirming her great slippery butt into my crotch. Dave strolled with his arm around a girl young enough to be this hag's granddaughter. A girl too good looking for this place. She held a drink in each hand for Dave. He smirked and pointed at me, laughed at my frustration. The old whore stuck her tongue in my ear. Her painted lips felt like sticky worms on my neck. She repeated two sentences: "I love you, baby. Buy me a drink."

I made hand signals. "I'm broke," I said. "No dinero." She kneaded my pockets, jabbered in Spanish, and reached between my legs trying to grab hold of something down there, but my balls were squashed flat against the wooden chair. When I wouldn't put out for drinks she hollered in Spanish across the table to Pierre, and he asked me with a straight face if I was ready to go to her room. Dave disappeared with the young girl. I said, "Tell her I have to go take a good shit for myself." That was something I heard Dave say. He was one of those people who announced his toilet intentions. I put on an urgent face. "That's right," I said, "tell her I have to take a shit, then I'll be ready." The woman got up scowling and moved across the room tugging down her dress and shaking her legs one at a time like a cat trying to get water off its feet. I bolted for the door. Later I felt sorry for her. Maybe she had no better way to live. How would she survive old age? Helplessness I understood.

I wandered the streets. Poked into stalls of woven blankets, leather coats. Tried on a black velvet sombrero garnished with plastic beads and tassels. From a vendor I bought a burrito filled with something that resembled used coffee grounds. There was garbage in the gutter, heads of cabbage, pools of coagulated grease, cantaloupe rinds. Garbage smells and bad feelings. What bothered me more than not getting laid was how Dave, without trying, stumbled into a perfect fit everywhere. I found him a job, he got in good with the boss. We crossed the border, he found the only good-looking girl in the bar. I'd be in the pie car tomorrow with a hangover, tentatively downing some watery scrambled eggs, he'd plop into my booth and say, "I just took a wicked shit, Gar." He persisted to call me Gar, short for Gary, as if we were still little kids.

Pierre came walking down the middle of the street. "They've all gone with girls," he said. "Eddie, Rodrigo, even fat Frank." We went onto the main strip, looking for a new bar, and came to a place where Pierre made an arrangement with two good-looking girls who were willing to do a single room. The place was a rooming house with a downstairs bar. We were not paying for the girls, but for the room. These "rooms" cost fifteen dollars.

Since the girls agreed to share, we only had to put out $7.50 each. It was a small room with a single narrow bed. We used it sideways, stretched out on our backs shoulder to shoulder while the girls did their work on top of us. They were very professional and had us drained and nodding on the bed in minutes. While the girls took turns squatting on the porcelain sink in the corner, scooping water up between their legs with their hands, someone pounded on the door and kicked us out.

Next morning having just missed breakfast in the pie car, I sat in a booth eating a grilled ham and cheese when Huffy came in saying, "The fuck's your friend? Didn't show up for work. Rollo wants to shitcan his ass."

I went down to 143. Huffy had unlocked Dave's door and he hadn't been there. I figured he'd been thrown in jail across the border and I'd need Pierre's help. But Pierre would have none of it. "The man's an adult," he said. "He can take care of himself." Of course Dave could take care of himself in New England or Florida or even Texas, but I wasn't sure about Mexico, and I wasn't sure what to do, but I knew I'd better go back over and look for him because I didn't like the thought of explaining to his mother that the last time I saw him was with a teen-age whore in Mexico.

I walked to the bridge and stopped at the tiny police station just across the river. A couple of distracted cops said they had no Americans in the tank and suggested I talk to cabdrivers. I walked around but didn't see many cabs. In daylight the town smelled bad and looked worse, a place no one who came there at night should ever see.

I found the bar where I'd last seen Dave. The doors were shut against the sunlight and I was afraid to go in. But it was either that or continue aimlessly. I pulled open the door and stepped inside. It was so dark I couldn't see anything. I knew where the bar was and walked toward it trying to avoid bumping into tables and chairs. The place was empty except for the bartender, whom I recognized from the night before, and a woman I didn't.

I told them my problem and like everyone else they seemed to have heard it before. They mumbled and shrugged, the woman dismissed me with a wave of her hand. "No here," she said.

The bartender said if anyone passed out cold they put them out the back way.

"The back way?"

He pointed. "The back," he said. They threw the drunks out the back door, but no back door was visible so I went out front and circled around. I walked down a couple of bars and cut through an alley.

Behind the strip was a dump lot. There were clumps of grass mixed with tall weeds, foot-pounded paths leading around piles of smoldering trash, rusted vehicles and kitchen appliances, broken bar stools and tables, barrels full of cans and bottles, flattened cardboard boxes. A guy wearing a dirty apron set a paper dish down on the ground and stepped back from a herd of timid cats. Two men who didn't look like they had the strength to move sat on cinderblocks watching the cats eat. Maybe a hundred yards from the buildings a dirt road crossed the lot and beyond that was a neighborhood of scrap shacks, plywood, tar paper, tin roofs, leading down to the river.

Staying a safe distance from the road and the unhealthy strip of buildings, I moved along until I thought I must be behind the bar. At some point I began following a dog up a footpath. The dog was a rib cage wrapped in skin, meager patches of gray fur on his head and lower legs. He seemed to be checking regular sites, lifting his leg, moving on. Then he veered into the weeds and stopped. His bony back arched, head down, then he turned sideways to whatever he was sniffing and lifted his leg. A bare foot came up kicking at but missing the dog. The animal leaped away and continued up the path. I would have moved off without looking further, because to look further I had to wade into the weeds, which I did not want to do but I did because I was an American in Mexico and I was sure that the dog-kicking-but-missing foot was sticking out of a genuine pair of American bluejeans. They were. It was Dave.

Misshapen, headwhacked, shoeless, pukestained, penniless, shit-canned, dogpissed Dave from New England, USA. He was on his back with his arms over his face trying to hide from the sun.

They'd taken everything off him except his pants and shirt and would have taken those except Dave was taller than most people in Matamoros. He wasn't beat up, although his head hurt enough that he might have been blackjacked, but the fact that he couldn't remember a thing after his second drink led us to suspect he'd been ambushed by altered alcohol. "A mickey," Huffy told us later, "chloral hydrate. They're known for that down there. If you black out after the first couple of drinks, you've been mickeywhacked."

It was a long painful walk back without shoes. "Who would steal those cheapass boat shoes you had?" I said. "And size twelve!" He couldn't talk. I helped him to the main drag, and we took a cab to the border but then had to walk two miles to the train, the last hundred yards over cinderbed stones that hurt even through sneaker soles. Smelly as he was I dumped him into his room and went off to the building to shower and do the show.

I didn't see him until the next morning when I was going along the railbed to the pie car. Dave was struggling over the rocks in a pair of plastic flip flops he'd brought from Florida. It wasn't flip flop weather and he was shivering without a jacket. "Rollo fired me," he said.

"What are you going to do?" He shrugged. I had a picture in my head of Dave taking up residence in Texas and getting beat up by cowboys every night. "Talk to Huffy," I said, "he'll give you something else." Transportation was never right for Dave and I felt bad about getting him into it. We went to the pie car, sat in a booth, and I bought him breakfast.

"Got a day's pay coming," he said. "Could hitch back home."

When Dave said "back home" he meant New England. "I'll never go there," I said. He looked at me like he thought I was joking, like I was full of shit, like I had no choice in the matter. But I spoke then to let him know how serious I was. "I'm happy here," I said. He was doing a messy job of eating a bowl of Rice Krispies, and he looked at me while I repeated what I said. He knew by the time that bowl of cereal was gone that, no matter what else happened, I was staying at the show.

A wardrobe guy named Big John came in and hovered over our table. John was a wide open queen and had taken a liking to Dave. Called him Davie. "Heard Rollo shitcanned your butt," he said. Big John said he'd just switched from wardrobe to train porter and thought Dave might grab the wardrobe job. Wardrobe was traditionally a place that employed gays. Dave didn't know that. He liked the idea. We figured Huffy would give him the job since Huffy liked Dave, not in the same way John did, but he would want to keep Dave around. I didn't say anything and we went to look for Huffy.

Two hours before the show I was upstairs helping Pierre set up his stand when Dave came grinning down the hall. "You're looking at the new wardrobe boss," he said.

"Huffy gave it to you?"

"You too," he said. "They need two guys in wardrobe. I told Huffy you'd do it."

Pierre rolled his eyes. "Let me think about it," I said. Dave said there was nothing to think about. Said I was foolish to run the seats yelling *Candy*.

"Sno-Cones," Pierre said, "this town is strictly Sno-Cones."

After Dave left, Pierre said wardrobe was one of the easiest jobs on the show.

"Will everyone think I'm a faggot if I take it?"

"It's always been that way."

After intermission I went down to wardrobe, a room fabricated by huge costume boxes pressed together and surrounded by tall blue curtains, an enclave, maybe thirty-five by twenty feet. When everyone came in to get dressed it was chaos, but only for a few minutes, then wardrobe was the calmest place on the show. The job was ridiculously easy. We stood around watching overly fit men get undressed and dressed. I saw why it attracted gays. Dave still didn't get that, and it wasn't until I took the job and worked there a day that Dave came up to me and whispered, "Do you know there are people around here who think we're fairies?"

"Fairies?"

"You know," he said, looking around. "Queers." He seemed truly stunned by the idea. For a second he looked like he did when we were little, always the last to get anything. After he figured out that wardrobe men were thought to be gay, he took to wearing cowboy boots and hanging out with a tough guy named Cuts. He tried to remember to talk in his deep voice when everyone came in to get dressed, and he repeated over and over the embarrassing story of how I screwed the fat grandmother the night he was robbed. He had an original influx of memory about that, recalling for everyone the ins and outs of the young girl he had before some louse knocked him in the head. I didn't deny any of it. I should have. But it was important to get laid. That was why we crossed the river each night. I was stuck admitting I didn't get anything or saying I jumped on someone's grandmother. So I didn't say anything. I let him run his mouth and assume I screwed the old bag.

But I quit going over the border with him after that. I'd go with Pierre or whoever wasn't going with Dave. Until the final night. We'd been in Brownsville five days, and teardown night we were loaded out of the building around ten. I met Pierre by the backdoor and we decided to make a final trip across the river. This was foolhardy since there was a chance of missing the train, but it was not unheard of, performers who had little or no teardown work often went out to eat or to a movie on teardown night. The train took hours to load and hook up. Then we had to wait for an open line. When you travel by railroad you don't take off whenever you want, you go when you receive clearance, and since we were a private train and not considered high priority like Amtrak or a mail train, we generally had to wait until the early hours of the morning. The problem was that they moved the train around for loading and hooking up. We never knew exactly where the train would be moved to or when.

It was my last night in the butcher car, and I wanted to spend the run there with Pierre and the other guys. Since I was a wardrobe guy now I'd be moving to the workingmen's car. Dave too, Huffy said, next town. I strolled with Pierre toward the border with no intention of staying late. We thought we would pick up a bottle for the run and head back and hang out on the vestibule. We came to the river, dark evil liquid under white arc lights, a cement wall on the U.S. side, mud and tarpaper shacks on the other. "Imagine drowning in that water," Pierre said, looking down from the bridge, and he told the story of the butcher girl found floating the year before. Kids the color of the brown water called to us from under the bridge, begging cigarettes and centavos with straw baskets atop wooden poles. They covered the Mexican side, lined up with their hands out. We couldn't give to all of them so we didn't give to any.

As we crossed the bridge Dave came running up behind us talking loud about where to buy weed for the run. This wasn't smart and Pierre told Dave not to say anything to anyone about dope. We skirted the main street, walked away from the border, past open bar doors, ignoring the whores waving us in. We wanted something different, something new. That was the nature of teardown night. After a week in a place we were striving for change. We'd given up on anything like a donkey show; that was cabdriver bullshit.

We came to a residential area where the road turned to dirt and there were no streetlights. There were what looked like cafes built into the front of small ramshackle houses; family-run joints for the locals, places the cabdrivers and shopkeepers went to get away from tourists. "The real Mexico," Dave said, "where they keep the good stuff."

We picked a place because it had a neon Black Label sign, and moved slowly through a wire-fence gate, between two rusted Volkswagens sinking into the weeds, toward a screen door framed in yellow and blue stucco. The doorway was low and Pierre and Dave had to stoop. Inside the small barroom a half-dozen guys stood with their backs to the bar watching us, a few sat nose to nose in booths along one wall. There were no barstools or tables. The loudest sound in the room was our feet crossing the gritty wideboard floor. Down the middle of the room were thick roughcut posts with bark still on them. Under the only light was a pool table, and in a corner one of those bowling games where you slide a steel puck down a wooden lane to fold up plastic pins. We ordered from a heavyset bartender in street clothes, no apron or anything, and carried a number of drinks and beers over to a booth where I sat with Pierre while Dave went off to investigate how he might play a game of pool.

Pierre was not a heavy drinker, and with the arrival of Dave I was unsettled enough to not feel like drinking either. We sipped beer and talked Pierre's favorite subject, which was how he worked in Shea stadium for some bigshot concession boss. You've heard of so and so—he'd say the name he knew I'd never heard except from him. Pros in Shea stadium are called vendors and Pierre sold hot dogs there and so on. I didn't really give a shit about it but he liked to repeat the story so I listened and nodded my head and sipped my beer and kept one eye on Dave. He came over with a pool stick, bent over the table, and downed a shot of tequila. "I put some feelers out," he whispered, putting his thumb and forefinger together.

"Dave," I said, "remember where we are." He scowled, then laughed and staggered off. Heads turned from the bar. "We might have to drag him out of here," I said.

"The man's an adult," Pierre said. "You're not his babysitter."

A woman appeared, collected glasses, spoke to Pierre in Spanish, went back to the bar. I saw her mutter to the bartender and go through a door behind the bar. Dave came back with his arm around a small Mexican. "Pedro," Dave said. "My friend Pedro." Dave was talking like Tarzan: "Me Dave. You Pedro." The guy nodded his head and grinned, doing a poor job of pretending we were all in the midst of some festive occasion. Dave grabbed drinks off the table and sloshed them down his shirt, talked openly about weed, walked up to strangers, slapped them on the back, shouted stuff like *mi amigo!* Sometimes he screwed up and said *comrade*, which was the term used in the same situation with Eastern Europeans.

Around midnight it was time to go. For my benefit Pierre went over to the pool table where Dave and a group of locals were playing for money. Pierre spoke loud in Spanish. That set the locals back, caught them by surprise. Pierre was a large man and could be intimidating. The locals looked sheepish and none answered him back. Dave and Pierre were not good friends and I saw Dave wave Pierre off. He walked toward the door and said, "Forget about him. Let's go."

Dave looked from across the room and I pointed to the door and headwagged him. He gave me a pitying look and turned back to the table. I walked over and told him he was going to miss the train. He was like a little kid saying *just one more game*, whispering in my face, "I'm making some good mooch here."

"I'm not missing the train," I said. "I'll go without you." He scoffed and turned his back on me. Not that he didn't believe I would leave, he just didn't care. I went up to the bar, bought a bottle of tequila for the run, and without looking back followed Pierre out the door and through the streets to the river, crossed over, and walked to the train.

It was hooked up, breathing, buzzing, hissing from the engines, awaiting clearance just off the main line. The old trainman and his smelly dog stood alone on the platform. Pierre went to bed but I stayed on the vestibule sharing the tequila that was no novelty after a month in Texas. Buzzi sat on the floor in the dark playing his guitar without the amp. Down the hall in the Wheels' car someone blew notes on a saxophone, same three notes over and over. In the pie car a nightlong poker game was just beginning. In the showgirls' car performers labored atop girls so beautiful I was struck dumb in their presence.

Bulgarians ate large smelly food. Down in the stockcars animal people sat with their beasts and masturbated in bunks without curtains.

Texas in winter is quiet and sad, but I was safe with the feeling I'd come to value most about the show: the soft rolling away, the feeling of being carried, cared for, kept. It was shocking how new it felt every time.

We came out of Florida in January following the route card and good weather across the panhandle to Alabama, Mississippi, Louisiana, Texas. After New Mexico, Arizona, Colorado, and Utah, we'd sweep back across the high plain: Amarillo, Lubbock, Tulsa, Oklahoma City, Wichita Falls, Dallas-Fort Worth, Abilene, and down to El Paso. The route seldom made logistical sense. A lot depended on building availability, and weather—nobody wanted to play Kalamazoo in March. In early spring we'd make a run across the desert to California, and we'd spend the summer moving up the pacific coast to Canada. I anticipated this, looked forward to it more than anything I could remember. I couldn't wait to get to the next town, and I began to wonder if Dave was going to be with us.

I'd grown up with Dave, loved him the way you love your hometown. But home was a word that had slipped away from me. My hometown held no fond memories. I'd left that place ten years ago when I came home from school to find my mother dead in her bed. And I'd had no place since, until this shifting world of strangers that did not seem strange to me came reserved with a place I felt safe, a place I belonged, my spot of earth. Dave belonged to a place I had abandoned, a place that had abandoned me, and if he wanted to get fucked up in Mexico that was too bad. I hoped he didn't, but, if he did, the last thing I could do was anything about it.

I stayed on the vestibule until everyone had gone to bed and the train began to move. It rolled so slowly at first you didn't feel it. A post floats by, you hear a click, feel a slight sway, your blood quickens a bit, your body becomes something different than it was just a moment before. There was reason to think I might see Dave running for the train, his long form blacker than night, blinking across the fires dotting the riverside. He might be passed out in his room already, or looking out over another half-closed door. From any vestibule the angle of vision is very narrow. Dave's room in 143 was a half-mile from where I stood. He'd make it back and I'd see him in the next town, and if he didn't, the next town would be there anyway, and the town after that, and the town after that.

Tentmen

On the runs Pie Car Bill locks the vestibule doors and plays poker with Huffy, Backdoor Jack, Rollo, Radar, and Shorty the prop boss. They drink whiskey, smoke cigarettes, and argue about the tent days. Only Huffy and Backdoor Jack were actually on the show in the tent days. Rollo says he's been on European tent shows, and Pie Car Bill claims to have worked for madman Crawford Diego, owner of the tightest tent in America.

Diego carries a pistol, Bill says. He'll kill anyone who messes with his tent.

Heard he tried to shoot down the wind one time, Huffy says. You guys in?

God, is that man scared of wind, Bill says. Surrounds his tent with tractor-trailers every town. In Iowa City a clown parked his pickup in the wrong place, Diego drove a forklift through the side of the truck, lifted it out of the way. They all chuckle. Diego loves that tent.

It's his bread and butter, Huffy says. You in, Bill?

I'm in.

Americans don't know tents, Rollo says. In Europe we have tents.

Oh, bullshit, Huffy says, dealing the cards.

Steel wheels click over railends, the pie car sways gently through the night, the men talk serious tents. Not pup tents or umbrella tents or those save-your-soul behind K-Mart tents. Those aren't tents; there is no art in bringing them to life. Look at the geometry. The roof lines loose and drooping, the walls sagging in the dirt. A sadsack state of affairs, a child's game of stake-out-a-sheet-in-the-backyard, a wimp of wind comes up and they're gone. These guys talk tents that hold thousands of people and come to life in ten hours of strenuous twenty-man labor. They talk living and breathing tents. Tents that contain in the fibers of canvas and plastic and nylon rope the lifeblood of certain people. The blood of tentmen.

I work ten year for Bruno Ralston in Switzerland, Rollo says. Mr. Bruno set up in a typhoon. During the show he walk the roof so tight he bounce a football on it.

He means a soccer ball, Bill says.

That's bullshit, Shorty says. Ain't no way to set up in a typhoon.

They don't even have typhoons in Switzerland, Bill says.

Mr. Bruno learned by the Bedouin of Arabia, very windy there.

The who? Radar says.

Draw a damn card, Huffy says, and pass that bottle over here, Jack.

Ain't never heard of no A-rab circus, Shorty says.

Everyone knows the best tents are made right here in America, Jack yells at Radar. At Sarasota Tent and Sail. John Ringling his-self went there for tents.

I suppose you saw him, Radar says.

Damn right. Before you was ever born.

I'm out, Bill says, dumping his cards. Huff, you got a light?

Before you was out of diapers, Jack yells at Radar.

Sure, Radar says.

*You people in? Huffy says passing his Zippo and the cards to
Bill. You in, Radar?*

*I was on this show when there was three trains, and the tent
took a hundred men and twenty elephants to set up.*

What? Radar says, whapping his hearing box.

Are you in? Huffy says, looking at Radar.

*There were five thousand stakes. All of Hartford, Connecticut,
fit inside.*

Deal, Bill, Huffy says.

Ain't Hartford where the tent burned that time? Shorty says.

*Course it was, Radar says, throwing a five on the pot. And Jack
was there. Right, Jack?*

Damn right I was—

Passing buckets of water to John Ringling.

*Bill lights a butt, sucks the coal redhot, releases smoke through
his nose, looks at Huffy.*

Are you people playing cards or what? Huffy says.

There was so much smoke the sun was blacked out, Jack says.

And the icecaps started melting, Radar says. Right, Jack?

How'd that fire start? Shorty asks.

Mrs. O'Leary's cow kicked over a lamp, Radar says.

That was the Chicago fire, Bill says, starting to shuffle.

Jack was at that one too, weren't you, Jack? Radar says.

Fuck you.

You're talking out your ass.

I was there!

You're dreaming.

Bullshit.

Fuck you.

*Huffy pounds on the table with his fist and yells, Shut up and
play cards or I'm quitting!*

*Things quiet down for a couple hands. Shorty goes behind the
counter for a beer. Mark it down, Bill says. Shorty makes a mark
in the beer book. Someone slides the bottle of Old Fitzgerald to
Huffy and they play and drink quietly until it begins again.*

I heard in Tokyo they set up a stakeless tent once, Bill says.

Was Bull Genders, wasn't it? Rollo says.

Some earthquake scientists designed it and hired Bull to set it up. Heard Bull took one look at the plans and told them it wouldn't fly.

Bull's one of the best tentmen in Australia, Jack says.

Well, he was wrong about the stakeless wonder not flying.

What happened? Shorty asks.

They wanted him to set up on a lot surrounded by skyscrapers. About the time the top was up a bad wind got to circling the lot—two for me, Huff—anyway, some newspaper people were there, and this tricky wind sucked the stakeless wonder skyward like a corkscrew popping a wine bottle. It whirled straight up to the ninety-sixth floor of the surrounding buildings and sent the diners in the rooftop restaurants stampeding in panic. Thought it was a Mars attack.

Let's see it, Bill, Huffy says.

Four queens.

Shit, Shorty says.

It was in all the papers.

So what happened? Jack says, throwing down two pair. Slide the ashtray over here.

Well the thing was like an umbrella in the wind. Filled with uplifting air the stakeless wonder got free of the city, caught a prevailing wind, and sailed out over the ocean like Swift's flying island.

Like what? Radar says.

Ain't no such thing, Shorty says.

Never heard of Gulliver's Travels? Bill says, pulling the pot to his corner of the table.

Who? Rollo says.

He was on the road for years.

Bill's one of them smart fuckers, Jack says, he's been to college.

Like them tent designers, Shorty says. They all chuckle, and Bill finishes the story.

The stakeless wonder got halfway to Hawaii before the air force sent out a couple of fighter planes to shoot it down.

They wag their heads. Jack shuffles. Leave it to college boys to screw up a perfect mousetrap.

Think that's weird, Radar says, some brains in Arizona tried to put a world inside a tent, a miniworld. Biosphere, they called it.

I heard that, Bill says.

Didn't work. They fucked up the ventilation, the walls started sweating, everything poisoned everything else. They all shake their heads again and agree that only showfolks like Crawford Diego, Bruno Ralston, or Bull Genders would know how to put an entire world inside a tent.

A Big Thing

Walking from wardrobe to the pie car junior I bumped into Hilmer and Rudy beating the shit out of each other by the back-curtain. They lurched around, locked onto each other's costume, and landed blows with their fists. I was knocked off my feet. Flat on my back I watched Rudy's wife, Diana, wearing a blue sequined bodice, fishnet stockings, and jeweled spikeheels, try to pull them apart. Both men wore boots.

Hilmer had a gold bathrobe over his gladiator suit and Rudy wore a white leather motorcycle outfit. I rolled to one side, jumped up, and saw the muscles arc across the top of Diana's thighs as she strained to separate her husbands. Well, they weren't both her husbands then; she was divorced from Hilmer. I heard a sharp crack and saw Hilmer's cheek go shiny red. He grunted and cursed in German. Rudy, who was a bit younger than Hilmer, used the word *old* in his cursing: *old* motherfucker. Fucking *old* fart. Diana said *whoa, whoa, whoa,* which may have had to do with her vocation. Diana was an equestrienne.

It was intermission so everyone was in the bathroom or buying food or smoking cigarettes. Rudy had closed the first half with his motorcycle, and Hilmer was on with his cats following the break. Performance Director Sigfried Heinemann saw the fight and came running. He had a styrofoam cup of coffee in one hand and a donut on a paper plate in the other. The hot coffee sloshed over his hand and onto his tuxedo shoes. He hopped around frantic for a place to put down his food. When the donut slid off the plate and rolled under a wagon he set the coffee on the cement floor and charged into the fray. He grabbed Rudy and they toppled onto the concrete. Diana, who was a big woman, secured Hilmer in a hammerlock. They gulped air, red-faced and sweating. Rudy's costume was torn and Hilmer had blood down the front of his bathrobe. Rudy and Sigfried, up from the floor, brushed away bits of straw and dried elephant dung. Diana let Hilmer go and Sigfried guided him through the backcurtain toward the cat cage.

Back in wardrobe I told the story to Dave, a unicycle rider named Oaks who was reading a book, and Tino the Rumanian who was stretched out on a table in his underpants. A lull in the show after intermission, Hilmer's twenty-minute cat act, and some aerial fillers to give the workingmen time to strike the cat cage, made it a quiet time in wardrobe. Dave picked up a red, white, and blue basketball and began beating it against the floor. I embellished the fight story, speculated that Diana was the spark igniting the fight. "Hilmer's still porking her beans," Dave said.

"Rudy's a queer," Tino said.

"I heard he's impotent," Oaks said.

"Who wouldn't be," I said, "having to satisfy that woman?"

With my back to the curtained doorway I saw Dave go wide-eyed. I turned to face Diana. She'd swept in through the curtains disregarding the fact that this was *men's* wardrobe where there might be actual men standing around in their underwear or even stark naked. She held Rudy's costume over her arm. Born in America of longtime German showfolks, Diana was big boned, big everything, blond hair piled and stacked high in curls and loops and held in place with jeweled barrettes. Standing two feet from her was like standing at the edge of a cliff, I wanted to back up, but I was drawn to look.

"My husband's costume," she said. I looked into her face and my brain turned to hash. I looked down at the floor. Her legs were as long as forever and ended in the dangerous blue V of her costume cut high over her hips. "It's been torn," she said. I looked at Rudy's costume. "You will have it repaired?" I made some mewling sounds, managed a yes. Yes, I would do it. I'd have sat barebutted on hot coals if she asked me to. I risked a glance at her face. Gray eyes, multifaceted like jewels. She had a slight smile on her lips. Big lips, big eyes, big everything. I gathered the costume into my arms and my fingers grazed her forearm. The woman gave off heat waves. I felt like I was melting into a puddle of something she wouldn't want to get on her shoe. "Thank you," she said, and swished out through the curtains.

The costume being leather I took it to the old shoeman and waited by his table while he handsewed the seam with waxed thread. Then I went looking for the dressing room. Sigfried Heinemann assigned dressing rooms on setup days by putting strips of masking tape on the doors and printing the names in black magic marker. At the end of a hallway I found a door marked Rudy and Diana Sabastian. Rudy swung the door aside and stood there in an untied bathrobe and a pair of white underpants and clear plastic shower shoes. A bathroom door hung open across the room. Rudy looked confrontational, like maybe he hadn't calmed down from the fight, but his hair was wet and I smelled soap. He had narrow cool eyes and he looked directly into my face. Many people took his attitude to be aggressive and resented it. He had the top aerial act on the show and was widely disliked by his fellow performers. Rudy was viciously hated by Hilmer, who, besides being Diana's ex-husband, was a bigshot animal trainer. "Hello," Rudy said. "My costume. That was fast." He held out his arms. "Thank you very much." He was overly polite, and some people took this as pompousness, but as a workingman I found it refreshing to be spoken to civilly.

"The new wardrobe boy," Diana said to him. She sat sideways to the door at a dressing table pushed against one wall. She leaned close to a mirror and applied a thin black line to her lower lip. She had on what she wore under her costumes: a pair of thick flesh-colored pantyhose with a pair of fishnet stockings over them, and a formidable white brassiere. It was a workhorse bra, designed for big bust support, must have been a quadruple E cup, battle-axe nurses wore these in war zones. Heavy-duty straps dug into her shoulders. The strip across the back was four inches wide with a half-dozen of those hook-and-eye fasteners. The bra completely encased her breasts and wasn't nearly as revealing as your average swimsuit. The effect was very clinical: still, she was in her underwear, so I tried to keep my eyes on Rudy.

"What's your name?"

"Gary," I said. "Gary Ruden."

"We need someone to handle our stuff," he said. "Twenty bucks a town if you want it."

"Sure," I said, not knowing what *it* was. Turned out the show wardrobe had to travel in the official wardrobe boxes. A rule. But big shots like Rudy and Diana didn't want to dress in wardrobe, so they collected their stuff on setup and returned it on teardown. My job was to lug their stuff between wardrobe and their dressing room. Each town Rudy gave me twenty bucks. In this way I came to know Rudy and got to see Diana in her underwear twice a week, which was worth more than twenty bucks.

The difference between Rudy and other performers was that Rudy would treat you like a human being. Hilmer didn't pay anyone to carry his costumes; he simply ordered them to do it. I first saw Rudy's act back in Saint Pete, Florida. I was scraping crap from under an elephant named Laura when I heard a rumble like a train rolling through the building. The people were pounding the floor and hollering. I looked at old-timer Martin and raised my eyebrows. "The bike," he said, taking a sip from his Coke can, "they go nuts for it." The Globe of Death was a round steel cage, maybe a twenty-foot radius. Inside on a dirt bike Rudy roared around while the cage was pulled up in the air spinning like a planet. He went upside down, sideways, let go of the handlebars and stood on the seat. At the end of the act he'd circle just above, and parallel to, the equator of the globe while the lower hemisphere dropped away. Two hydraulic shafts on the outside of the globe lowered the bottom section to the floor. While workingmen carried it off, Rudy continued around the top of the globe forty feet up with nothing beneath. Momentum kept him stuck to the wall of the globe. If he slowed at all, or the bike stalled, he'd drop straight to the cement floor.

A vital quality of a daredevil act is the appearance that the performer is doomed, that he's in over his head, no way out. That's how Rudy appeared in the top half of the globe, going around two feet from the edge. The band stopped. The house lights came up. The only sound was the haphazard popping of the two-stroke Yamaha. The ringmaster appealed to God to let the people know that something had to happen. When Rudy felt the tension peak he'd turn upward and full throttle the bike over the top of the cage. For a moment the people had an unobstructed view of him upside down with his head turned back facing them. Then he shot straight down the side and out into space. Some people had spotted the ramp, which had been rolled underneath, some hadn't. It didn't matter. When Rudy hit the ramp after free falling thirty feet, rode it to the floor and roared down the track with one arm raised over his head, the sense of relief in the arena was audible. The people pounded approval with their hands and feet. No act received the response Rudy did. Every day I'd sneak off from the bulls to see the act. I was fascinated by the people's reaction. I stood as close as possible to feel the lights and hear them scream and pound for Rudy. It was a greedy feeling—I wanted it—I pretended they screamed for me.

Of course I didn't tell anyone that. The division between performer and workingman was clear, and breaching class lines was noticed immediately. Most workingmen were secretly attracted to parts of the show and to the idea that they too could perform if whatever it took to do so would shift in their favor. They pretended it was a matter of choice, but I felt that *need* had more to do with it. Practice was a way of life for performers. As workingmen, we watched them practice before, between, after, and sometimes during the shows. In remote parts of the building, under stairwells, in the backlot, on railroad platforms, practice went on day and night. When nobody was looking we all tried our hand at juggling three balls or balancing a straw broom on our forehead. Workingman practice was discouraged but it was impossible to stop.

One of the clowns set up his low wire, two-foot A-frames, near the animals and he didn't care who used it. I'd watched the workingmen tromp across it in their workboots like apes in a ballet company. I wouldn't go near it when anyone was around, but one day when no one was looking I stepped up onto the wire and went wobbly across without falling. That surprised me. So I did it again. Something ignited. The wire was live. Some charge, current, connection was plugged in. I went across again, and again, and when I fell I stepped back on and walked, and while I was walking I couldn't stop thinking *I can do this*. I said it to myself, I said it to the wire, I said it out loud, but not too loud. Such a feeling I couldn't remember, and I didn't want it to go away.

I walked the next day, and the day after, and the next town, and every time I walked that wire felt good, like it was something I should do. Workingmen saw me and shrugged, as if they could do it too, if they wanted to, if they didn't have better things to do. I tried to be careful about who saw me, but the tendency is to show off, the tendency is to become greedy and careless. One day Hilmer came up quietly and cracked me across the chest with his bullhook, knocking me from the wire. He stood over me and pointed to the line of bulls. "Your work is over there. The rake, the fork, those are your tools. Not this," he said, pointing to the wire.

After that I didn't play on the wire unless I knew where Hilmer was. Once I'd quit bulls it didn't matter what I did in front of him, but Hilmer introduced me to the notion that as a workingman I should not be looking beyond my station. A notion carried further by Huffy who gave me trouble after he found out I had aspirations. Huffy didn't mind violent alcoholics, useless winos, thieves, or demented people, but he hated anyone with aspirations. If you were a workingman and he saw you juggling three apples, he hated you for life. Luckily, Huffy rarely visited the buildings or came back by the animals.

Rudy and Diana were often around the horse stable. In a southwestern town, Phoenix maybe, or Albuquerque, I was going back and forth on the wire before the show and I heard, "Bend your knees. You can't walk a wire stiff as a tree." It was Rudy passing with Diana. As they walked toward the horses Rudy looked back and said, "You'll never do it in those tennis shoes, rubber is no good for wirewalking." This was different, I was used to scorn from performers, this was advice from the top performer on the show.

Rudy didn't give me formal help, but often he'd pause to say, "Your arms are too low" or "Look further ahead." Once he handed me the address in La Crosse, Wisconsin, of a place that made special elkhide shoes. His approval gave me the courage to try harder in the face of ridicule. He helped me scrape together a low rig of my own. I swiped cable from one of the buildings, and Rudy gave me an old turnbuckle to tighten it. I hid the rig in a wardrobe box on the runs and set it up each town in out-of-the-way places. Huffy knew I was practicing and waited for a chance to attack. In Salt Lake the rig turned up missing. I systematically searched the lot, every square foot. I found a suitcase full of clothes under the seats, a few odd shoes, a pair of soiled underwear, some used rubbers, five dollars and sixty-three cents. Behind the horse tent I found a bag of cowboy books, in a wagon a cache of stolen souvenirs—butchers ripped off the show and sold the stuff for pocket money—and finally, with the lot nearly loaded out, I found my rig buried in the elephant muck pile.

When Huffy saw that rig set up in the next town it was open warfare. My days were numbered. I began setting the wire up close to the horse stable so he couldn't steal it. I'd use one of their wagons to anchor it. At times Rudy would step onto the wire and recite circusisms: "When you start attracting attention you know you're making progress" or "If they're not talking about you you're doing something wrong." He couldn't make it across the wire without falling, and that gave me the biggest boost of all. Rudy Sabastian couldn't walk a wire and I could, at least a low wire.

I became physically stronger, but it was difficult to judge when I would be able to walk up high. There was a highwire act in the show, some Colombians who would stroll by laughing while I practiced. "Try that at forty feet," they'd say.

Rudy said quit worrying about highwires. "You keep on, it seems like nothing is happening, then one day you'll notice a big change." He said I'd never build an act as a workingman. "Things are against you here. If you're serious, go to Sarasota, put in a year."

One day I was concentrating on a difficult jump, doing it over and over, trying to resist the urge to drop my arms on land-ing, when the horse guys brought out a mare. One guy pinched her nose with a twitch while another tied up her left front leg with a rope. They wrapped her tail, held it aside, and scrubbed her backside with warm soapy water. "Not too much," Diana said, "you'll ruin her scent." A guy named Indian led the black beast called Angus that Diana rode in Opening. She spoke to him as he saw the mare and reared up. I stepped off the wire to watch. Diana sidled up next to him with a bucket over her arm, reached between his back legs and took hold of his foot-and-a-half-long member. She scrubbed it with a soapy sponge while he snorted and bucked, lifting Indian clean off the ground by a chain that ran through the stallion's mouth and hooked to a ring on his halter. Diana spoke to Angus and sloshed rinse water over his stiff pole. It was half pink and half black and thick as the fat end of a baseball bat. Then she stepped back, said "do it," and Indian let Angus mount the mare. I moved closer.

They loosed the mare's leg rope so she had four feet on the ground. Angus lunged into her and pumped away. When Diana said "whoa," the guy holding the mare turned her sideways, causing Angus to sprong out of her. His front legs still hooked over her back he drove his hips and pumped as if he were inside her. Diana reached underneath, grabbed his penis with both hands, and pointed it into a stainless steel bucket with a plastic liner. "Hold the bucket up" she hollered to the groom leaning under the horse from the other side. Cheek and shoulder pressed against the stallion's rib cage, she pulled at him with both hands, careful to keep the cauliflower-size head pointed into the bucket.

Diana wore what she always wore between shows, short silk robe tied around her waist with a sash, double-layer leggings and industrial-strength bra. I knew this stuff would be stained with horse sweat and she'd be giving it to me for cleaning. Her make-up was blurred from moisture. Sticking to one side of her face I saw a myriad tiny black Angus hairs. Without warning Angus slipped off the mare and his front shoes hit the asphalt. Diana, Indian, and the bucket guy moved with him, not missing a beat. She pumped her arms the length of him. "Come on Angus," she said, "fire it for God's sake." Then the horse grunted and gouts of yellow semen squirted into the bucket. "That a boy," she said, the log in her hands reduced to a rubber hose, the stallion deflated. Diana drew her hands down the slimy thing stem to tip, squeezing out the final drops, until it hung down like a dead snake. The twitch was taken off the mare and the horses were led away.

Who would think such a thing could be seen behind a city's civic center? At night, in my bunk, I saw Diana blow with the side of her mouth the strands of blond hair falling across her face as she strained against the side of the sweaty stallion. I saw the white breasts in the gaping robe, I watched her bare arms working beneath his belly, and I imagined her doing to me what she did to him. During the day in the dressing room I examined her hands. I saw her scraping the stuff from her fingers on the edge of the bucket, sweeping back her hair with her forearm, breathing with her mouth open.

When she brought the sweatstained bathrobe into wardrobe Oaks was reading a book in his corner, Dave was stretched out on his back on the table, Tino the Rumanian sat on a folding chair polishing his shoes. Diana took no notice of them. "Have you anything going to the cleaners?" she said.

"Next town."

She held the robe by her fingernails. "If you don't mind," she said, "it's been soiled."

"Yes, I saw," I said. My relationship with Diana was still, in spite of the Angus act, maybe because of it, formal. I was still in awe of her, but in a different way than when we first met. I pretended we were intimate, making up things she never said to tell the workingmen. I bragged that I saw her naked when I went to the dressing room, which was not true. She always wore the robe, or the utilitarian underwear that was not at all revealing. But on her anything was erotic. She could zip herself up in a sleeping bag and still turn heads. It was the flashing eyes, the suggestive smile, the big everything, the things she said.

"You saw the semen collection?"

"What do you do with that stuff?"

"Ship it to Florida, where we keep some mares."

"Messy business," I said.

She turned to go, then turned back. She looked at Dave, her slight smile more pronounced than usual. "If that sort of thing interests you guys," she said, "I'll let you know next time we plan to collect." Without waiting for a response she swished through the curtains, fluttering her fingers, and left me standing there rolling the words "you guys" over in my mind. I looked around, but nobody was paying attention. "You guys?" I said. "What does she mean by that?" There was no denying the way she cast her eyes around the wardrobe when she said "you guys" as if we were part of some clique, and the way she raised her eyebrows, fluttered her fingertips and swung her hip through the curtains. Diana thought we were gay. She thought I was gay. The realization that I'd been admitted to her dressing room solely because she figured me harmless, a man unaffected by the sight of a beautiful woman in her underwear, caused a reticent male beast to awaken in my mind and begin pawing the ground.

I didn't think Rudy thought I was gay, but I couldn't be sure; he didn't spend enough time around wardrobe to know that things had changed. From then on when he stopped to help me practice I'd talk about girls and make derogatory remarks about gays even though there were gay people on the show whom I had nothing against. It was much weirder to be, say, Bulgarian, than it was to be gay. I tried to impress Rudy by calling his enemy Hilmer a fucking faggot. I'm sure Rudy didn't relate these things to his wife. Rudy didn't seem to have Diana on his mind as much as I did. In the dressing room they seldom talked or laughed. Never a chuckle or wry remark passed between them. They seemed more working partners than marriage partners. Maybe those rumors about Rudy were true. Maybe he had trouble making the old lady sing the high notes. When he was in the dressing room the atmosphere was businesslike. I went in and out as fast as possible. There wasn't room for three people anyway with the dressing table, two wardrobe trunks that opened like closets, two chairs, and a narrow whip box. I couldn't fathom what it would be like to be intimate with a woman who owned a whole box of whips—whips of every color.

Sure, I eyeballed Diana sitting at her makeup table, who wouldn't? If she thought I was harmless I might as well take advantage. I took to arriving when Rudy was gone, when she was applying makeup or removing it, or when she was in the shower. I'd walk to the far side of the room and look into the bathroom where her tights and gigantic bras hung over the shower stall. I'd ask questions about her act, or skincream, or stallions, anything to get her talking so I could stand next to the dressing table and peek into the gaps of her robe. If it was setup, she'd have on the heavy-duty underwear, but on teardown I wouldn't arrive until she had removed that stuff and sat in her silk robe with nothing underneath. At night I expanded my fantasies to include the role of gay dresser. Like kings and queens have people to help them get dressed, I imagined being Diana's personal breast hefter, pantyhose puller, snap fastener, strap buckler, semen provider.

I practiced on the wire and made slow progress. In Denver Rudy crashed his bike on the ramp and broke his leg. He couldn't work so he asked me to help Diana with the dressing room. "You have to load in the trunks, the whip box, makeup table on setup, and make sure it all goes to the wagons on teardown. Don't trust the prop guys, those bastards will lose stuff."

He handed me a hundred bucks and made himself scarce. I saw him every few days. I set my wire up in the horse stable and worked on it day after day. Diana was around working and sometimes watching. I consistently pulled off a jump known as "the split." When I knew Diana was paying attention I'd fire off a half-dozen of these. I was much better with someone watching. Not only her; anyone who watches a performing artist contributes to the quality of what they are witnessing. There is a transference of energy from performer to audience and back again. She watched me jump and land solid with confidence, and while she watched, something passed between us. I worked out hard for this audience of one, and she stayed watching long after she needed to. "You're coming along," she said.

You never know what performers know. I wouldn't have thought Diana knew anything about wirewalking, but one teardown night we were alone in her dressing room. Rudy was back to work but decided he liked not bothering with the dressing-room stuff. He was taking down his rigging, and I'd lugged his trunk away and was waiting for Diana to finish showering and packing her stuff. She came out of the bathroom wrapped in a white towel. She left wet footprints on the rubber tiles. "I'll be back when you're ready," I said and turned to go, but she started talking.

"Did you know I was married to a wirewalker?"

"Before Hilmer?"

She nodded, took her seat, and began combing her wet hair with a gap-toothed comb. I saw clearly the dark roots where her hair had grown out. The water slid off in clumps and sunk into the terrycloth towel wrapped across her breasts.

"Who was he?" I said.

"Gino Mendoza."

"You were married to Gino Mendoza?"

"Years ago. In Europe."

"Were you married to him in Munich?"

"Yes."

I didn't know what to say because Gino Mendoza was a famous wirewalker killed in Munich performing a trick nobody else did, a swinging trick he'd originated himself.

"He was a brave boy," she said, "and we were very young."

Gino Mendoza was a legend among wirewalkers, some said the best wirewalker ever. "Who trained him?" I asked.

"He worked on his own," she said, staring into the mirror, the comb still. "You can't believe how hard he worked." She turned to me. "Not yet anyway." She rose and stepped over to the door. With her back to me she opened the towel and wrapped it tighter around her body. Then she turned and faced me. "In time you will learn, if you stick with it, what it is to be a wirewalker." We were close, an arm length between us. She said, "Why do you want to do it?"

"I don't know. I found that I could."

"Yes, well, that's the way it is, isn't it? Something happens and you work on it."

I wanted to know about Mendoza. "How long did he practice? Did he practice high or low?"

She released a breath and looked impatient. "There is a big difference between what you do now and what happens in a show," she said. "Many are adequate down low who cannot get off the platform at forty feet." She leaned back against the door, resting one hand on the handle, her other arm hooked over her head squeezing out the wet ends of her hair. Barefoot and slouched the way she was, we were the same height. "You have to do it where it counts, at the right time, for the right reason. If you do, you'll have traveled a great distance; you'll be a different person."

I looked at her white underarm, the crease where the towel rolled over her breast and tucked into itself, merely an inch or two held it in place. I reached for the small brass deadbolt knob on the door, it was close to her ear, and turned it to lock. Then I turned it back. I was aware of her eyes on me—it wasn't like my heart was pounding or anything—aware too that more than one thing was happening, and had been happening since I started walking on that wire. *You work on the same thing over and over and then one day you notice a big change.*

Outside in the hallway people were yelling, rolling boxes, pushing trunks, dragging canvas bags along the floor. They were moving fast, looking forward, but in the dressing room we were suspended. I guessed by now Diana knew I wasn't gay. I raised my eyes to look at her and continued to click the lock one direction then the other. I still had trouble looking into her face and could easily get lost in her eyes that never stopped moving even when they were calm. But I looked anyway. I stared, concentrated on the effect, if any, my lock game was having on her. She met my gaze, wide open. "It's a big thing," she said at last. "Do you think you are brave enough to do it?"

In the arena men lowered rigging, packed wagons, coiled ropes and cables. Rudy was out there somewhere; he could be just outside the door. We knew that. And at some point, before I dropped my hand from the door, unlocked, and she moved away, we both knew we could have done whatever we wanted, and would have, right there on the tile floor in her wet footprints if I hadn't said, "I don't know."

"Well," she said, moving away from me, "that is the thing you must find out."

The truth was I already knew. She'd told me what I needed to know. Sometimes knowing you can do something is the same as doing it. And sometimes it isn't. I knew when I left her dressing room that night that she had helped me more than Rudy had.

In the next town, after setup, I rigged my wire back by the horses, put on my wireshoes and warmed up. During the quiet time before the show when everyone takes a break, I went into the empty arena, climbed the incline to the highwire and walked across. Just once across. Then I stood on the platform trying to breathe and stop shaking. I didn't look around, I didn't think, I didn't imagine anything. Then I crossed the wire again, climbed down the ladder, and went back to practice.

Curtainman

Opening night in Tulsa, Curtainman checks his Rubbermaid crap barrel to make sure it's roomy enough for the Spec crap, then stands with his back to the curtain, ready to draw it back when the director blows the whistle. Spec is crowded with people and animals parading through the curtain just before intermission. Curtainman opens and closes the curtain, that's his function, and he keeps the curtain area crap free. He has a fifty-pound bag of sawdust, two brooms, and a wide aluminum shovel with which he scoops piles of horse shit, logs of elephant shit, sometimes tiny poodle shits, and always the Camel's hard balls rolling about in the dark. He hates those camels. They don't stop to shit like every other beast, he says. Camels go like they've got a goddamned desert to cross, shitting marbles all the way.

Painted faces press the curtain. Curtainman is packed among the performers. He hears what they say, things that worry them, who they talk about. He sees showgirls tug at their underclothes and pull their breasts up with the palm of their hand. The clowns wear gloves and brightly colored coats with cloth-covered buttons the size of dinner plates.

Stilt the stiltman shoulders his way through the crowd to his ladder sitting just inside the curtain. With each hand he holds twenty-foot-long pantlegs rolled above his knees like giant bagels. He climbs his ladder without letting go of his pantlegs, straps on his two-by-four legs, stands and lets the pantlegs drop. He lifts one leg then the other for balance. Stilt looks down on pink heads, purple heads, bushy red and orange heads. Showgirls in flowing plumes, clowns in towering coneheads. One man has long golden locks swept back like a mane, another, bald as a cue ball, holds a pack of toy poodles on lines: rhinestone collars set off their curly white heads. Horse heads are fidgety, camel heads chew cud, striped tiger heads stare behind bars, and a big gray elephant head rocks and bobs like a harbor buoy. Directly below Stilt is Curtainman's dirty blond head. Curtainman has never gotten used to a guy with twenty-foot legs standing over him. Trapped against the curtain he nervously eyes Stilt. If that fucker falls . . .

Two minutes! Two minutes! Heinemann in his black tuxedo, a chrome whistle the size of a doorknob around his neck, plows through the curtain knocking Curtainman aside. Gottdammit, Curtain, he says. He doesn't know Curtainman's name so he calls him Curtain.

The performers are quiet, painted faces taking deep breaths, anticipating the whistle. Then there is a sound like the opening of a fire hydrant. Everyone starts yelling and pushing and jumping back from Alfred, the only male elephant on the show. His giant penis is wagging back and forth and bouncing a torrent of yellow piss off the cement floor.

Curtain hurries to the bag of sawdust. He hasn't been a curtainman long and has no experience with pissing elephants. He grips the bag with both hands and drags it to Alfred who is standing in a massive, fast spreading, pool of urine. Everyone is whining and holding their nose and saying goddammit and looking at their piss-splattered shoes. Everyone except the bullhandler who stands unconcerned in the puddle, his canvas sneakers soaked, his blue coveralls darkstained to the knee. Alfred is flowing strong and

Curtain has trouble opening the bag of sawdust. They got about a forty-gallon bladder, the bullhandler says. Finally Curtain pulls out his knife and stabs the bag and sawdust explodes all over him. Performers are gagging and coughing and saying goddammit and then the whistle blows and the director starts shouting Curtain! Curtain! Curtain panics and tries to run but the piss has crept under his leather boots. He slips and falls to his knees. Clowns push the curtain back and make way for Stilt who ducks under the curtain cable and takes fifteen-foot strides down the backtrack. Alfred, forty gallons lighter, is ready to go. Curtain scrambles out of the way.

While they are out walking and waving Curtain spreads saw-dust in a sodden twenty-foot circle. The cement floor is covered with thick rubber mats, and the piss has gotten underneath and traveled around. After the show Curtain will have to turn back the mats to let the cement dry. It will take half the night to shovel up the wet sawdust.

Stilt walks big, waving and smiling, dodging ropes and cables, watching for ground obstacles. Once a season or so he catches the tip of a stilt on a wrinkle of track rubber and goes down like a sawed-through timber, breaking his arm or nose. He has forgotten the elephant piss when he returns to his ladder. He later told Curtain he was thinking about his wife and son who live in Sarasota during the school year. He wants his kid educated so he'll have options. Not that the kid doesn't have a future as a stiltwalk-er, the three of them are great in the summer walking together, the wife on sixteen-foot stilts and the son on ten-footers. A real daddy-longlegs family. They are enroute from Sarasota to Tulsa, and that, not elephant piss, is what Stilt has on his mind.

He ducks under the curtain cable, plants one stilt, and reaches for the ladder. But the rubber mat slides on the piss soaked floor and the stilt goes out from under him. Once that happens there is no getting the twenty-foot stilt back under his body. He grabs the only thing within reach. Curtain has a full shovelful of sodden sawdust when he hears the grommets pop one, two, three. He looks up to see Stilt toppling toward him like the crown of a lopped-off redwood. Curtain drops the shovel, raises his arms—he knew it was coming to this—and the sun explodes in his head. They both go down into the mess of golden sawdust.

Curtain is famous after that, working with a broken collarbone and a concussion. The director is easier on him, learns that his name is Gregory; he does not shout at him so much. Stilt has a broken wrist for a few towns and the following year gets it written into his contract that he doesn't have to work when an elephant takes a piss. Gregory the Curtainman becomes part of Tulsa, even years after he vanishes from the show up in Canada and nobody remembers his name, they still, when Tulsa comes around, say, remember . . .

Pie Car Bill

After the show about a hundred of us went back to the train to eat. Not everyone ate in the pie car. Bulgarians cooked in their rooms, stinking up whole sections of the train, butchers roasted steaks outside on Hibachi grills, animal people ate with their animals, smooth-skinned trapeze artists took showgirls out to eat. I ate in the pie car. I liked the performer/workingman mash packed into the Pullman dining car remodeled to serve a lot of people fast. A narrow aisle ran from the vestibule along one side of the car to the serving counter and a few foam and Formica booths beyond. Down the other end Huffy had a little paneled and barred paymaster office.

I was wedged in line between unicycle riders Buzzi and Rulfo. Dave was behind Buzzi, and behind Dave was a long line of hungry people. Rulfo studied the menu hanging on the back wall over the grill. He'd been on the show for years and the menu had changed little, but he studied it anyway. On the other side of the counter Pie Car Bill was bent at the waist with hunched-up shoulders like his body might swallow his head. To make eye contact with Rulfo, Bill cranked his no-neck sideways, mashed his fingers on the counter, not knuckle-walker style, but splayed out like fat boiled sausages, and buttressed his massive upper body with hairy elbows stuck out at ninety-degree angles. Pie Car Bill was very big. The pie car was very little. Small men would not have to crouch or squeeze to work behind the serving counter; their backsides would not bump the hot oven. A half-dozen Orientals could easily crawl around behind the counter without collision, and did, until Bill took over to the relief of everyone who ate in the pie car. "Fucking rice every night," Bill told me. Bill had been in Vietnam and did not like rice. He lumbered, bumped, grunted, cursed, kicked the trashcan, and swore he'd blow the show any day. But Bill was as much a part of the pie car as the pie car was of the train. He had two Polish guys as helpers. One showed up that night. The no-show Polish guy was down in his room drunk.

"What do you want?" Bill said to Rulfo. There was a narrow cupboard over the counter full of cups and glasses. On our side of the cupboard was a chalkboard that read: SPECIAL SPAGHETTI & CLAM SAUCE—$3.25. Rulfo was about six foot three, so the chalkboard stared him in the face.

"What's the special, Bill?" Rulfo said without bending down. Bill was straining to get low enough to see under the cupboard. He wanted to see Rulfo's face. Bill had to see people's lips move because he was hard of hearing from the noisy Vietnam War. He might have seen Rulfo's lips easier if he could bend his knees, but Bill had not been a squatter since his involvement in the sport of football. "The hiker," he'd say. "I was the fucking hiker." The sport of football resulted in his knees being ruined, resulting in him getting bounced out of college, resulting in him being drafted into the army in 1968, even with the bad knees. I can't squat, Bill told them, I'll get my head blown off. You're a no-neck bastard, they said, and shipped him off to Vietnam to be deafened. But Bill wasn't a bastard. He had God-fearing parents in a suburb of Providence, Rhode Island. I know because I grew up in the town where Bill was a high-school football star. Everyone knew Bill Doyle in our town. I was in junior high when Bill, a happy galumping jock, was shipped to Vietnam, and had quit school by the time he came home a deafened drug-using homosexual. A piece of molten metal whizzing through the jungle came to sizzling rest in Bill's left buttock. The shard—could be anything: broken glass, rusted nails, piece of flattened fish tin— was lodged too deep to dig out, and it gave Bill some misery. Not only physical, some other kind. Bill went away the best neighborhood Santa Claus anyone could want and came home liable to punch someone in a gay bar.

Bill remembered that burning shard every time he reached for his wallet to show someone the picture of himself in uniform; the flat spot sliced from his butt happened to be the size and shape of your average billfold. When he bent stiffly at the waist to look across the serving counter his wallet didn't bulge out like on most men; his wallet had a neatly carved niche, a pocket scooped from his body, as if just for that purpose. In spite of the pain, and the way it ended, Bill was proud of the time he served. He kept medals in a sock in his room.

"The special is spaghetti," Bill said to Rulfo. "Spaghetti and red clam. You want it?"

I didn't recognize Bill when I saw him on the train in Florida. He was heavy, unshaven, two front teeth knocked out. But after I heard him talk, and heard him called Bill, I said, "Aren't you Bill Doyle from Barrington, Rhode Island?" I was trying to get in good with a show veteran, and Bill appreciated someone from home who knew who he was. He was a regular show grunt having been around for two seasons, and having the pie car was like being Huffy's right hand.

Bill was in his bent-up-not-squatting-looking-through-the-pie-car-window-waiting-for-the-order position, and Rulfo seemed to be considering the special.

"You want it or not?" Bill said.

"Hmmm," Rulfo said, looking around like he was sightseeing.

Bill took that as a yes, reached down around his belly and came up with a flesh-colored plastic plate from the stack under the counter. He turned to the stove shaking water off the plate, stepping over pieces of the Coke dispenser which the Polish guy had taken apart even though Bill told him not to do it. "NOT NOW! NOT DURING DINNER!" Bill couldn't speak Polish and the Polish guy couldn't speak English, so they yelled real loud at each other in their own languages. Dave leaned over the counter, looked at the Coke tank, and laughed. It was the type of thing Dave would have fixed before we began working in wardrobe. The tank was wrecked. No Coke tonight. Everyone wanted Coke. Bill looked grim and was sweating into the giant pot of spaghetti.

Next to the four-burner gas stove was a grill, two deep fryers, and one of the first microwave ovens. There was an eight-slice toaster, a forty-cup coffee machine, a twenty-five-plate saucer stacker, a stainless-steel refrigerator with a separate freezer, and down at the end by the sliding door two deep sinks with black rubber hoses attached to the water faucets. The most used item was a large beat-up Rubbermaid trashbarrel lined with a heavy-duty plastic bag. No cover. It stayed in the aisle next to Bill, blocking the path to the eating area because there was no other place for it and because it had to be handy since cooking produces lots of eggshells, coffee grounds, burnt toast, rank grits, greasy paper towels, flipped-to-the-floor burgers, bacon bits, old hot dogs, wrong orders, the flotsam of short-order chaos necessary to feed a trainful of people, and also because Bill needed to kick something when he was mad.

"That it, Rulfo?" Bill held a plate of steaming spaghetti in the great plain of his palm, his elbow on the counter, a stainless-steel fork stuck into the heap of spaghetti, his no-neck cranked so he could see Rulfo's face. "Three twenty-five," Bill said.

"Hmmm," Rulfo said. "Lemme get a Coke."

"Can't get a Coke," Bill said. "Pump's busted."

"Hmmm."

"Orange?" Bill said. "Grape? Dr. Pepper?"

"Yeah. All right."

"All right what?"

"Gimme a Dr. Pepper. No ice."

Bill set the plate of spaghetti down, leaned to the drink dispenser, and pushed a waxy paper cup against the Dr. Pepper lever. "Three seventy-five," Bill said, setting the Dr. Pepper down on the counter. Rulfo dropped a fistful of change and a crumpled one-dollar bill on the counter. Bill poked through the money with his finger but didn't pick it up. "Two eighty-five," he said.

"Hmmm." Rulfo turned his head, scanning the crowd. I was at his elbow. His forearm looked like the upper leg of a Hereford steer stripped of hide. Rulfo and Buzzi were part of an extremely aggressive act, a basketball game played on unicycles with a lot of loud music and yelling. But outside of the show, as if storing energy for the act, they were very slow. They smoked boxcars of pot, wore sunglasses at night, bed-dazzled showgirls, constantly lost their stuff in wardrobe. Rulfo looked down at me. "Yo, Gary man, lemme hole a dollar." I raised my dukie book so he could see it. Dukie tickets, the equivalent of food stamps, came out of your pay and were generally an embarrassment but could be an asset when performers wanted to borrow money. Performers could not use dukies; they were for workingmen only, part of an old show caste system. Rulfo looked past me to his cousin, Buzzi, who was much smaller than Rulfo, and was ignoring him. Rulfo didn't even ask. He looked over our heads at Dave and the line of hungry faces behind him. "Hmmm," Rulfo said.

"What's it going to be, Rulfo?" This was an old game for Bill. I'd seen him let the workingmen slide if they were short, because we didn't earn much, and Bill knew what it was like to be down. But the performers were paid well; some of them, like Rulfo, had never had any other job. Their attitude, I think, affected Bill the wrong way. He gave nothing to performers. He picked up the plate of spaghetti, like he was taking it back, and said, "You got it or not?"

Rulfo put a look of real concern on his face. "Bill," he said, "how much is a cheeseburger?"

Bill rumbled out a groan from deep in his chest. "Two seventy-five."

Rulfo nodded. He had his forehead knotted up like he was working on high finance or a tricky basketball shot. "Hmmm," he said. "How much is tuna?"

"Two-fifty." Bill was still, staring down at the counter, his eyes glazed over.

"Soup?"

"Buck and a quarter." When I saw Bill lock up, his fuse lit, his water boiling, his steam rising, having to name the price of every damn thing on the menu, holding a plate of hot spaghetti with about a hundred really hungry people waiting in line, I eased back from Rulfo's elbow. I turned to look at Buzzi and raised my eyebrows. Buzzi, who could go days without moving the smallest muscle in his face, thought about shaking his head.

"And Bill," Rulfo said, "how much is a grilled cheese?"

Bill smiled. "A grilled cheese?" Rulfo nodded. Bill nodded. They looked at each other nodding and grinning. I saw a dark line of sweat roll off Bill's forehead and pave a road south; catching a crease near his mouth it rode to one side of his chin where it gathered, quivered, then dropped onto the counter where it sat like a bead of hot shining wax. "A grilled cheese is a dollar eighty-five." Bill could be very articulate. He was talking to Rulfo as if he were a five-year-old. "You have two eighty-five. You might purchase the grilled cheese, the Dr. Pepper, and still have fifty cents for breakfast."

These calculations puzzled Rulfo. Was his behavior calculated to bug Bill? Was Rulfo bored? Did he hate homos? Big guys? White people? He broke off communication until Bill dropped the phony smile, thrust his head across the counter, and said, in Rulfo's slooow, spaced-out style, "What's it going to be?"

Rulfo said, "How much is an order of toast?"

I squished back into Buzzi. He was squishing back into Dave. We had nowhere to go. The aisle behind us was packed with people extending out the door, across the vestibule, down the steel steps onto the stones of the cinderbed. Rulfo blocked the way forward into the eating area. If Bill let Rulfo have that hot plate of spaghetti square in the chest, there'd be a backlash, with us likely to remain hungry. Rulfo had both fists resting on the counter. I watched a muscle in his biceps pulse under a prison tattoo, a small cross done with a straight pin and India ink.

"How much is toast, Bill?"

Bill's big square jaw hung loose. He looked at me. Bill never tried to be funny, but he was. I know he did this hanging jaw thing to football coaches, to referees when he couldn't believe their calls, to his superiors in the army. I put my hand over my mouth so he wouldn't see me grinning.

"Toast?" he said. Like he was trying to remember what it was. "Toast?" Then he smiled. What else could he do? He looked up at Rulfo and spoke as if he was explaining to a child at the zoo the nature of a ferocious gorilla: *Your gorilla is naturally a calm, well mannered* . . . "Your toast is fifty cents," he said.

"Hmmm," Rulfo said.

They stared at each other.

Finally, Rulfo took a deep breath and said, "Gimme an order of toast."

Bill looked at me again. "Toast," he said sweetly. Bill was nodding and smiling, and I went along with it because I couldn't stop grinning anyway, and I pretended everything was normal, hoping Bill would go with it and give this asshole his toast so I could get some food. I was the next person in line, for God's sake. But then Bill went not normal. He reared back with the plate of spaghetti, which was doomed from the start, and I heard Buzzi moan behind me, and Bill roared, "FUCKING TOAST!" and hurled the plate of spaghetti the length of the pie car. I couldn't see the sliding door where it hit, but the Polish guy ducked and I heard the plastic plate clatter to the floor. "HE'D LIKE AN ORDER OF TOAST!" Bill was yelling loud enough to be heard outside in the trainyard. He grabbed a full loaf of Bunny Bread and repeatedly slammed it down on top of the eight-slice toaster until the bag burst and pieces of bread crumbled over the counter and fell to the floor. He was yelling, "TOAST! TOAST! TOAST!" and bashing the toaster lever down again and again with his fist, until it caught, and the chrome box began to heat up and melt the plastic bag.

Rulfo turned to me and shrugged. He looked genuinely perplexed. I raised my eyebrows and Buzzi shook his head for real. People behind us couldn't see and were grumbling. We ignored them. People in the eating area could see plainly. They didn't care. They had their food. Then I heard the swoosh of the sliding door that Bill pied with the spaghetti plate. It was the drunken Polish guy reporting loudly for work. He sounded completely wasted so I leaned over the counter for a look. He took two steps onto the spaghetti-slicked steel deckplate and went down flat on his back. The sober Polish guy was trying to save the toaster and didn't know which way to turn. He was yelling in Polish at Bill who turned his back on the kitchen. It was a certain type of back-turning that another backturner would recognize. There was a finality about it, an inevitability that was expected if not hoped for by people who have a history of fast retreat, of running away just when things came up tough and they were needed most.

The sober Polish guy helped the drunken one to his feet and gave Rulfo an order of toast. Rulfo moved on. I came face to face with the drunken guy. He was redfaced and sweating and had squished noodles and red clam sauce stuck to the back of his head. He held a pad and pencil ready, but I'd lost my appetite.

Bill kicked the trashcan out of his path and walked through the eating area. He was not mad anymore. He moved slow and stooped, like he'd been sent to the showers late in the game. People at the bolted-down tables held their food in midair. Huffy pressed his face against the bars of his pay window and yelled, "Bill, where the hell are you going? You got people to feed." But Bill didn't answer, not even his buddy Huffy, who'd been on the show for thirty-five years.

Trainman

In a Texas town in winter, a southern railroad yard, an old man and old dog stand in the shade of a concrete block wall. The old trainman, his scruffy terrier dog, and the building wall weathered to the same cracked paint-chipped and pockmarked gray. The shade comes on like dusk, envelops the old man and dog. They blend, absorb, turn to face the dark closing over them. You can smell them if you come close, an old man and old dog smell.

The mutt squats on a wormy haunch and claws at the flea-flecked pink skin behind his ears; his tail is a stiff hairless stub. The old man grinds his toothless gums. They lack the basic amenities of body: teeth and hair. Like everyone, the old man has lost things. He works the underbelly of traincars, filling water tanks, emptying human waste. It's a hellish place. Once he saw his hand clamped fast between wheel and brakepad, trapped, his head thrown back, until the brakeman released the air. His hand came away with only a thumb and forefinger. Three fingers stuck to the wheel five days until they dried to black skin and bleached white bone. When the train moved down the line they were gone.

The old man's train is special, a white train, home to people and animals from many places. From the shade of the wall he watches the boys set ramps to flatcars. The old man loves trains. You see that if you look. He watches the other trains: the dirty colored boxcars he rode when he was young, the sootblack engines, coalblack caboose. As he watches, his skin turns a lighter shade of gray, his loose eyeslits close tight and grit seeps out through the lashless cracks. He slumps slowly, scrapes down the gray wall onto the crushed-stone trainyard as dry as that field of burnt wheat he ran through when he was a boy. He sees the house he ran from, the father shouting and the mother weeping. If they were ever happy he doesn't see that. They're dead now too. Where was it he lived? Where was that field he ran crunching down the dried stalks, crumbling to dust what leaves were left? He ran aimless until he heard the low murmur of a freight train miles off across the sky.

The trainyard is hot. His body is washed out in sweat, the ground beneath his cheek is cracked white, caked, wafered. His wet skin sticks to the dry stones. He feels the grit that was pushed into his face when he was a boy on his stomach on a boxcar floor, the men teaching him his place among them as he later taught others.

The light is so bright it's as if smoke were stinging his eyes, he's blinded to everything but light, he can't reach his dog. He feels burning in his head, cold in his body, then nothing. The only movement is the wiry-haired dog, licking nervously, whimpering.

The old man's back arches at the end, his head goes back showing his hairy nostril holes. His mouth wide open. A seventy-five-year-old mouth. Go ahead, go on in. Two black molars in the back, the hard dried gums, the brown stub of a tongue. In the tent days he'd answered back railroad bulls who called him Gypsy and one sat on his head and another knocked his teeth down his throat with a pair of boltcutters. Then they took the boltcutters to his tongue. He'd made only sounds since.

There is nobody to talk to anyway. The bums today are not the same. Kids who smoke that shit, that smelly shit, in the caravan cars. They care nothing for trains. Dopers, runaways, he'd been too old to deal with them. He unrolled the firehose from the possum belly, he found the water, he pulled out the waste. Until now. Now there is only the slight mewling, not quite crying, from the dog, and the clattering of the ramps and rails being rolled over by a traveling show, which will leave him behind.

Waste

I walked into the pie car and saw Bill sitting in a booth with his head down on the tabletop. One side of his face was flattened against the Formica like a deflated tire. He said he was blowing the show. I went to the counter and bought a coffee from the Polish guy. He pointed at Bill, held his arms out around his head. "Vodka," he said.

I carried my coffee to the booth and sat across from Bill. A few guys were eating breakfast. Bill said he couldn't take it, the pie car had driven him mad. He talked with his face down on the tabletop, his eyes closed. This was the famous Bill Doyle? High-school football star? Decorated Vietnam vet?

"You're blowing the show in Texas?"

"I told Huffy you should have the job."

The old trainman came in, trailed by his small terrier. Both were filthy and carried a stench stronger than Bill's hangover smell. Bill welcomed them to the booth. He scratched the wiry hairs on the dog's head. The dog wagged his hairless stub. The old man wore a brand new cap reading: *Waste, by Laser Man*. It was the speedy modern graphic of a sewage disposal company, cartoonish, completely out of sync with the soot-pitted face of the old man, the crushed bulbous nose, the damp rims around his eyes mascaraed in black cinders.

When Bill said he was quitting, people looked up from their plates. Bob Furr was eating scrambled eggs with Radar and Rollo. There were a few sleepy workingmen, mostly animal people, no performers this early. "I told Huffy you were the one I'd trust with the job."

"Shit," I said. "No way he'll give me the pie car."

The Polish guy signaled Bill. A delivery man. Bill struggled free of the booth, and I was left alone with the old man and dog. I'd bunked across from them in the workingmen's car since I'd been in wardrobe but we'd never exchanged a word. I heard Bill's gravelly laughter. He had a coffee in his hand, probably had a shot in it. The delivery man was laughing. Bill recited the same jokes he'd told the last twenty-five delivery men in the last twenty-five towns. It made their week, coming to a circus train, talking to a guy like Bill. They'd repeat the jokes to their friends, tell their kids about it when they got home, they'd look forward to next year. Bill signed for a dozen loaves of Bunny Bread, fifty boxes of pasta noodles, ten cases of canned tomatoes, some honeydew melons. He was stocking up for the run.

Huffy walked in, trailed by a few workingmen. "To the flats!" he screamed. "Everyone to the flats!" He needed people to set the ramps. It was teardown, which meant two shows, loadout, and run to the next town. Extra work for the old man. He was one of the few on the train who knew how to hook and unhook railcars; he knew what the signal lights meant, how to switch lines manually when the electricity failed. Huffy told Bill the old man was nothing but a yard bum, a hobo in the tent days, but Bill liked the old man and slipped him food for his dog. The old man knew which iron plates in the trainyard covered the city water. On setup he'd unroll the firehose from the possum belly of the pie car and hook onto the city line using a wrench as long as his leg.

He filled the watertanks on each car so we'd have water on the runs, and in the afternoons he moved slowly down the line of cars, dragging a thick black hose connected to a disposal truck, pumping the crap out of the tanks while the rest of us were at the show. Only Bill, Huffy, and the train porters saw him work. The show was everything to most of us and nobody wanted to be stuck at the train.

"To the flats!" Huffy stood in the aisle pointing his finger at my face. "To the flats, Mr. Performer. Now!" He hated me since I practiced wirewalking. I didn't do it to bug him. There was no particular reason for that. It's what workingmen did; we dreamt of performing. But Huffy had been a performer, and he hated anyone who stepped beyond his control. I got to my feet, heard a low buzzing behind me. The dog bared his teeth at Huffy who was pointing his finger at the old man. "Hey Laser Man!" Huffy hollered. "Get your sorry ass to the flats." The old man just laughed at Huffy who was in a vicious mood because Bill was quitting. Huffy didn't want to lose Bill, not only because they were poker buddies, but because Huffy controlled the cash flow for the pie car. He took the cash to the bank and gave Bill the ornate checks that came from the home office. They were pie car partners, sharing skimmed money, and maybe more. Huffy's wife, former flyer, was in a wheelchair in Florida, and Bill spent a lot of time in Huffy's car. There were rumors, but there were rumors about everyone. Huffy moved up the aisle, arms out like he might punch someone in the gut.

The old man followed us to the flats parked where the tracks crossed an access road. He was too old to help, but ramp-setting was a train job, and he was the trainman. He knew the routine, where the ramps were, where the crew would move next; he could have directed the job if he were younger. Eight of us carried a five-hundred-pound ramp pallbearer style, four guys to a side. The sharp-edged steel cut into our hands, the footing on the cinderbed was dry and loose, small stones rolled away from our feet. Huffy drove by in a unimug raising a cloud of dust and yelling, "Step it up! Move your butts!" He watched closely, making note of the missing, and of those who slacked on the heavy lifting. I tried to look lively that morning, tried to show off, in case he was considering me for the pie car job. We attached one end of a ramp to the edge of a flatcar, set the other end on two small A-frame supports, then set another ramp from the supports to the ground. Up those ramps unimugs would bulldog wagons of rigging, ringcurbs, rubber floormats, wardrobe and lighting boxes, tigers in cages, Louis Morgan's gold Rolls Royce, the exploding clown car, the white school bus that took us to the buildings, everything rolled up those ramps except the people and certain large animals.

Setting the ramps was such a miserable job you looked anywhere for distraction. I saw the old man and the old dog standing in the shade of a cement block wall. They were blending into the concrete, old man, old dog, old wall gray-weathered to the same decrepit degree of decay, the color of oldness. The only thing not blending was the logo on the Laser Man hat. The old man disappearing into the wall, only the word *Waste* remaining.

After the ramps were set I walked back to the pie car to look for Bill. Huffy was in his office down at the end where we collected our ninety bucks each Friday. "Seen Bill?" I asked.

He stared with his head cocked, aiming his good eyeball through the bars of the window. "I've got news for you, Mister." He pointed his finger out through the bars. "You're in for a surprise." He nodded his head up and down like he knew something. "I've got a treat for you." I didn't know what he meant and I didn't think he did either. I took his words as a general threat, his way of saying he had it in for me. Two things were certain: Huffy didn't want Bill to go, and Bill was crazy to think Huffy would give me anything good.

Bill wasn't in his room so I headed to the building, which was within walking distance. I checked the nearest bar. A few workingmen, Dave with Cuts of the unicycle act, a couple of ringstock guys. Nobody had seen Bill.

I practiced on my wire behind the horse stable. If I practiced each day, if I made progress, I didn't mind wasting my time in wardrobe. After practice I showered in the men's showers, put on clean coveralls, and went to sleep in a wardrobe box. When the performers came in for Opening they'd heard Bill was leaving and weren't happy about it. Prince Paul said he saw Bill packing his old army duffel bag. Prince called me "kid" and said the pie car was a gold mine but dangerous with Huffy in there. He stepped into the tiny purple pants of his Mad Hatter suit and thumbed the suspenders over his shoulders. I held his coat open by the padded shoulders and he stuffed his sausage arms into the sleeves. He said he'd heard Huffy's daughter might return to run the pie car.

"The stockbroker's wife?" I said.

"I heard she quit him." I handed him his mad top hat and cleared a path to the curtain.

A Bulgarian bareback rider screamed, "Vadrobe! Vadrobe!" He'd lost his shoes and was frantic over the fine. They were fined for being out of costume. Had to have the shoes, the gloves, everything, otherwise a fine. Dave went over and found them for him.

Two shows passed without incident. The acts cut time because it was teardown. I took down the curtains while Dave packed the costume boxes and helped roll them to the wagons. Transportation guys hooked the wagons to unimugs and pulled them through the dark city streets to the flats. Everything rolled: the boxes to the wagons, the wagons to the train, the train to the next town.

I caught a ride on the back of a unimug. We passed the horses walking with camels to keep them calm. In front of the Loan Star Bank piles of elephant shit were squashed in the road by rubber wagon tires. I jumped off in the trainyard and dodged unimugs and rolling boxcars. I passed the little terrier dog scampering about. He'd obviously lost the old man, but I didn't think anything of it. They knew their way around trainyards. When I got to the pie car, Bill was gone. The Polish guy stood behind the counter looking miserable; Huffy was back there bossing him around. Everything was battened down for the run, salt shakers, napkin holders, the toaster; everything clamped in cupboards, latched in closets, wedged into cubbyholes, everything in its place. Everything except Pie Car Bill who was loose somewhere on the Texas panhandle.

Huffy looked low and mean. Looked like he'd been drinking. He glared at me, daring me to mention Bill. I ordered a grilled ham and cheese. No dinner specials on the runs, no French fries, only sandwiches. I sat in a booth and ate while the train was pounded from both ends. Yard engines slammed the cars one direction, then the other, rolling them back and forth over the switches to change lines. Little by little, piece by piece, with the animal cars hooked up first and the flatcars hooked up last, the train became a single mile-long entity, poised and alive, inhaling and exhaling, rocking slightly with its own movement and the movement of the people inside.

Taken off the weedy, collapsed, holding tracks where we spent the show days, the clotheslines taken down, the barbecue grills and plastic furniture packed away, lights in the windows, the steps folded up and the halfdoor bottoms clamped shut, the train was at its best. Its power to move me hadn't diminished since the first time I'd seen it. The train made me proud and happy to live on it, and made painful the idea of leaving, of packing my bags and turning my back on it. Yet that is what Pie Car Bill did. I can only imagine that when he did it, however he did it, drunk or hungover, crying or dazed, by walking away, or calling a taxi, or hooking a ride with his thumb, that he must have done it not as Pie Car Bill but as William Doyle, some other guy who lived some other life. Or thought he did.

Near midnight the pounding and rolling stopped. The train was hooked up ready to go, so I went to my bunk. Couple of guys were snoring, stray arms and feet stuck out through curtains. Dave was passed out in the bunk above mine. The old man's bunk was empty. He always stayed outside until the signals turned in our favor and we rolled onto the main line for the run to the next town, and he was first up and about when we got in. We stopped on the runs to let other trains pass or to wait for switches, but he always knew when we were in for sure, and he'd get up with the dog and go hook up the water. I fell asleep that night before the train started moving.

Some hours later, daylight, we were at a standstill. Through my curtain I saw the old man's bunk empty so I figured we were in. I dropped out into my sneakers and squeezed quietly into the pisser. When I stepped on the flush peddle there was no noise, nothing, no swoosh of blue water. That meant the tank was empty and that was impossible: the old man would never forget to water his own car. But there it was, no water. I went out onto the vestibule. There was a bright field of grass the size of an ocean. Miles off, black rocking-horse contraptions seesawed up and down. Just over a barbed-wire fence wild longhorn steers stood staring at the train. When they saw me they snorted, wagged their heads, and jumped clean off the ground. I figured we weren't in and returned to bed.

I slept hard. Dreamt of the old man out in a cattlefield that was dried to wasteland. I followed him around in the crunchy grass yelling, "Water! Water!" I woke up so thirsty I couldn't swallow, yard engines were slamming the train, Huffy stood at my bunk with his stubby finger in my face. He had pulled back my curtain and his unsynchronized eyeballs roamed over me. "To the flats!" he screamed. He went up and down the row of bunks yelling at everyone and punching what curtains he could reach. "To the flats! Get to the flats!"

We fell from our bunks and filed into the pie car, took a coffee from the Polish guy, and carried it over the cinderbed to the flats. We were in the yard but the train wasn't broken up so it was a long walk over the rocks with the coffee sloshing about and burning our hands and lips.

Huffy was down there taking names of the absent. Bob Furr

paced and watched his watch. Up on the flats the transportation guys sat in unimugs already running and hooked to wagons. As soon as we set the ramps they rolled off with the layout stuff: the hundred-foot tapes, the redheads, the beckets, and mainfalls. Then the school bus for the workingmen, the floor rubber, secondary rigging, ringcurbs and bulltubs. Then the delicate stuff from the tunnel cars: cats in their cages, spotlights the size of cannons, Spec floats, the clown car, the gold Rolls Royce.

The routine was the night before reversed. Everything rolled off the train and through the city streets to the building. Down at the animal cars the bulls with their handlers, the horses with their camels, walked down low-angled wooden ramps and stood yawning and shaking dust from their bodies. They lowered their snouts and trunks into water buckets while men with brooms swept dust and bits of straw from their backs. There would be a parade to the building. Clowns would ride in the clown car, one playing a tuba, another banging a drum. The ringmaster would ride in the gold Rolls Royce with Louis Morgan himself at the wheel. Animals led by ringstock boys would shit and piss in the streets while office workers, free for the moment, would laugh and point from windows that did not open.

We walked from the flats to the pie car to wait for the bus. Huffy wanted everyone on the bus, riggers, prop boys, no stragglers. Performers were not up at that hour. They would sleep late then take a taxi to the building for the night show. I sat outside on a rail when Huffy appeared. "You," he said. "Hey you. You don't go to the building." He fingerwagged me after him. I couldn't believe it. I figured I was going to get the goddamned pie car. But when we went inside I saw Huffy's tiny daughter standing behind the counter with a big woman. They had white aprons tied high around their waists. I'd heard from Bill that Huffy's daughter was a real piece of work. He said she'd quit the show in New York to marry a stockbroker. I guessed it hadn't worked out because there she was as predicted by Prince Paul.

"I hear you're looking for a new job," Huffy said. He leaned on the counter talking with an unlit Chesterfield between his teeth. He had his head back, looking down his nose at me, which wasn't easy him being so short. I knew he was pulling something, so I stared until he said, "Well I got one for you." He had a Zippo in his hand, which he'd already struck twice without result. "You're the new trainman."

"Trainman?"

"You don't go to the building no more. No more bullshit practice." He watched my face, so I was careful to give him nothing. He knew the show meant a lot to me, that I had notions, dreams even. "You put the water in, pull the crap out. Any questions?" I played dumb, frowning, scratching my head. That, I realized later, had always been my mistake with Huffy. Playing dumb was his game too. He'd been at it longer than me and was hard to fool at his own game.

"Trainman?" I said. "With the old man?"

He concentrated on his Zippo, his thumb set, and struck a small blue flame. Cupping the flame he held it to the tip of the cigarette, careful not to suck the fire out, then dropped his hands from his face, shoved the lighter into his pants pocket and exhaled a cloud of smoke.

"Old man's dead," he said.

"Dead!"

"Dead in the last town." He squinted at me through the smoke, picked a piece of tobacco off his tongue and thumbed it off onto his pants. "Found him in the yard."

"Near the flats? Did they find him near where the flats were parked?"

"How the shit should I know where they found him? They found him that's all. You don't go to the building. Water in, crap out. Got it?"

"What about the dog?"

"What about him?"

Just the four of us were in the pie car. Huffy's daughter was babbling nonstop and smiling whenever I glanced at her. She had big tits for a midget. I considered moving behind the counter, casually choosing a cast-iron skillet, and pounding on Huffy's head until it was even with his shoulders. I considered running away, maybe catch up to Bill. But I didn't. I shrugged my shoulders and nodded as if it didn't matter. I wouldn't let Huffy see me upset. I moved to the counter where I could get an eyeful of Alberta. That was her name, Alberta. Her friend's name was Marge. They'd run off from their husbands and now would work the pie car. "We're fugitives," Marge said.

"You'll feel right at home," I said.

"I hope not," she said. This Marge was huge, but she seemed smart and had a cheerful face that was a lot more pleasant to look at than Bill's gorilla mug. Alberta was something else. If she wore tight shirts like that every day with the apron tied up high over her waist, well, I figured the pie car line to be moving a lot slower from then on.

Huffy had me fill the water tanks left empty by the old man. It wasn't a hard job once you found the city hookup. Out in the yard I spotted a yardman, walked up to him with the giant wrench and said, "Old man's dead. Where's the water?"

The pie car possum belly held the tools and hoses, the main water valves, which served as the junction point for the other cars. When I had the hoses connected, the tanks filling, I set up shop at the counter and listened to Alberta talk about her marriage and how she ran off. Once she started talking you couldn't stop her, you couldn't get a word in. She wanted to get the full story off her chest, which I was very interested in. I wanted to check out a piece of her work, Bill's words, before some performer did. But ol' Huffy had different plans. He watched me most of the day listening to Alberta, every so often yelling for me to get off my elbow and do something. Couple hours before the show, he collared me behind the counter helping Alberta lift a box of honeydew melons. He grabbed me by the neck as if I were a little kid and pulled me outside. "This ain't gonna work," he said. "Get your butt back to the building."

"I was just starting to like this job."

"Yeah." He shook his finger in my face. "I know what you like. I know! You get over to the goddamned building before I send your ass down the road. I'll move your butt to ringcurb, that's what I'll do. Next town, you're on ringcurb."

I knew better than to push him. Ringcurb was shoveling shit out of the ring during the show. When elephants and horses crapped during the act you had to run after them and scoop it up with the people laughing and pointing. It was the one job on the show I knew I couldn't do.

I had no idea Bill had gone back to New England until weeks later when Dave received a letter from his mom. Show mail came to the buildings, relayed from the home office. It felt odd to see mail from the outside, maybe the way soldiers or prisoners feel when they get mail about things they are removed from. Enclosed was a newspaper story, a police report: *Man Stabbed in Bar Fight*. The clipping was about William Doyle, local war hero and football star, killed outside a bar in Providence. I knew Bill would have been drunk. My first thought as I stared at the newspaper clipping was, Bill didn't feel it, he was wasted.

Dave's mom wrote about Bill's poor parents. She wrote what a disappointment Bill had been to them since he came out of the army. She told Dave to call home, said we should send something to Bill's parents. But why? They didn't know us. Hell, they didn't even know Bill. The newspaper failed to even mention that Bill was a legendary circus cook. William Doyle might be dead but Pie Car Bill lived here with us.

The letter made me more mad than sad, at least at first. And I knew what I'd do about it. I'd go to the train and find Huffy, that little bastard. I'd go to his private car with the newspaper clipping and pound on his door. I'd point my finger in his cross-eyed face and say, "You! Hey you!" This time I'd be the one breaking the news.

Alberta Huffstetler

Show dreams sack my sleep. Startle me awake. Start another day sick, tired, wanting to go back. I'm sick and tired of wanting things that make me sick and tired—in that way I'm no different than regular folks. Just the things I want are different. Short people are different. My parents said it. They were sad when I married a big person. A stockbroker, a bigshot nine-to-fiver. Five feet ten, 160 pounds. So what?

Whattaya, in the circus? People say that. Regular people, in convenience stores, the supermarket, in the neighborhood where I live with John, the stockbroker. They gawk then look away. They measure with their hand to see if I come up to their bellybuttons. They want something from me.

Yeah, that's it, I say. I'm a circus midget. What do you want to know?

They say they've been to the circus once, like there's only one. They want to know how much an elephant weighs. They want free passes. They want magic. How do all those clowns fit into such a small car? Have you seen anyone fall off the tightrope? I want to ridicule them but it's not their fault. They are curious. I tell them things they want to hear. I tell the lady across the street, fat Marge Johnson, that midgets are grown in jars, that highwire walkers have magnets sewn into their feet, that all clowns are faggots.

Marge wants to lose weight. Your body is perfect, she says. How'd you get so small? Her husband's name is Frank. They have no children. Marge tried to kill herself last Christmas. She went to a fat farm in Scarsdale to steam fat off in a sweatbox. When you were in the circus, she says, did they pay you? Did you get money or what?

Peanuts, Marge. We get paid in popcorn and peanuts.

Through the window I see Marge in her monstrous housecoat sweeping her driveway.

I dress, go outside, get the paper.

The headlines startle me again: Wire Walking Wallenda Falls at Shrine Circus. I know Ricky Wallenda. He's from a long line of dead wirewalkers. He works for himself now. Wants to top his grandfather, a famous wirewalker, walking until at age seventy-three he fell 150 feet onto the trunk of a yellow cab. Grandson Ricky, age twenty-five, fell forty feet to the cement floor of the local civic center. A burlap sack of water balloons, that's the sound a human body makes hitting cement from forty feet up, that's the sound my mom made when she hit. It's an unnatural smack.

I drive to the hospital and walk freely into intensive care. Ricky is conscious but in no-joke pain, no good humor, even with the morphine drip. It's been a while but he's not surprised to see me. Alberta, he mumbles, Alberta Huffstetler.

Nice head, I say. It's the size of a medicine ball with odd bulges and dents, both eyes black, three teeth knocked out. He has multiple skull fractures, a broken cheekbone, broken jaw, collarbone, elbow, arm broken in three places, hand crushed, some broken ribs, hip not broken because the thighbone snapped above the knee—had to give somewhere—the lower leg fractured, the ankle, the foot. All this damage is on the left side of his body.

Right side's perfect, he says. He wants to talk but can't move his mouth. He wants to be famous, but he's kissed concrete in front of a building full of Marge Johnsons, people who sweep driveways. Life is hard, I tell him. No more leapfrog, he says. That's the trick that got him, the leapfrog. One person bends at the waist, second person leaps over straddle-legged. Ricky did the leaping but missed the landing.

No more leapfrog?

No more leapfrog.

Implied by no more leapfrog is the fact that everything else will go on. He is hurt, his family has moved to the next town, but in two weeks he'd rejoin them, in eight weeks he'll start back on the wire. Even this hurt, he knows he's lucky. I know he's lucky. I tell him he'll be back at the show. He wants to smile, I see it in his eyes, and that makes me ill, makes me homesick. I want what's in Ricky's head, not the pain, but what stops it. I want to go back.

I drive home mad. I want to drive to Toledo, to Albuquerque, to Spokane, but I drive to the damned neighborhood. Marge is in her driveway waving the newspaper. I want to drive over her body. Tell the police my foot slipped off the wooden brake block. I'm a freak, they'll believe me. Freaks are accidents, I'll say. Never pat a midget on the head. I am the freak at my husband's office parties. The men in suits, the wives strapped, buckled, and sprayed. They stare and flatter me. Why, Alberta, how that dress becomes you, they say. I get drunk and tell them about the guy who lived across the aisle from me on the train, who performed fellatio on himself. The wives want to know more. He let you watch?

The husbands wrinkle their foreheads. A regular human pretzel, they say.

Not regular, I say.

The stockbroker brings home children's clothes. A cherub suit, a brownie scout, a cheerleader. How old are you, little girl? He says things like that. Only thirteen? Makes me sick. But I do it. I bend. I squat. I stare out the window. I want to drive away. I want him off me. I want to sleep without dreams. I want something special on waking. I want to wake without being startled. I cannot not be *startled. I see a man in soft shoes leaping. I hear an unnatural smack. Look, Mom! A midget! I hear laughter. I suffer stockbrokers. I want to know who will bury me when I die—not regular people. I will outlast the bastards, belie their short-person myths. I will die on the tracks, next to a ravine, on some wide river. Some workingman will stumble over my body. Someone special, not regular, will pick my pockets clean, set foot to my hip and roll me into the river. Maybe light me on fire, make a spectacle of it, charge admission: A burning dwarf cast on an open waterway free of want, regular people chained to the shore, pointing and shouting questions.*

Yoo hoo! Alberta. Marge walks into the house without knocking. She wants to know have I seen the paper. Is he a friend of yours? Did you know him? Is he dead? Why are you packing?

To get away from you, I want to say. But no. Marge doesn't deserve that. Have patience with regular people, my mom told me. Yes, I saw the paper, Marge. Yes, he is a friend of mine. But she has forgotten him.

A suitcase! A cardboard box! Where are you going?

I want to calm her. My head almost reaches to her gigantic breasts pressed flat by the pink housecoat. I'll let her lug my stuff out to the car. Marge, I'm going back to the show.

My goodness! My God! My word! She walks around the house wringing her hands, not knowing what she wants. What about—? I mean—when did this—?

I haven't told him, Marge. Nobody knows. Only you.

Only me! But how can you—?

I want to see my family. I want to go home.

Home?

Home, Marge. I slam the suitcase. I've played suburbia. I'm loading out. She looks horrified. That's circus lingo, Marge. We don't say big top or roustabout or ballet slippers. Elephants are called bulls, trapeze artists are flyers, vendors are butchers. Get it?

Marge shakes her head sideways, then up and down. I make her lug the suitcase and box while I walk through the house I've lived in for eighteen months. It is a beautiful rambling colonial house with stairs in it. John's house. A stockbroker's house. I want to kick in the TV. I want Marge to throw a headlock on me and drag me across the carpet. A clue for him to find. He'll call the police. That's for sure. He calls me his child, his baby lover, his show doll. I should have left earlier. Months earlier.

Outside, Marge is teary eyed. She figures we're friends. She flutters like a giant pink bird blocking my way to the driver's seat. Move, Marge. I have to go.

Take me with you, she says, and I burst out laughing.

Marge, you wouldn't even fit into a room on the train.

Train!

Train, Marge. I'm driving to meet a train in Texas.

Texas!

Marge, Marge, Marge. Everything I say makes it worse. She says she hates her life, wants a new one, will kill herself if I don't take her. You'll miss Frank, I say. He'll come after you. She bursts out laughing. She says she's old, she's fat, she cannot conceive a child. Frank will break out cigars, she says, he'll drink champagne, he'll jump on the bed singing the witch is dead.

An unusual logic develops in Marge's favor. She is the only one who knows I'm leaving. If I take her with me, no one will know. But she'll be a bathroom goer, I know it, a restaurant stopper, a scenic overlook looker, a sucker for unbelievable billboards. She'll want to see Rock City, walk underground caverns, investigate the upside-down town, see the spot where water flows uphill. She'll want to stop in Memphis. Home of Elvis.

We're not stopping, Marge. Not in Memphis, not in Mississippi.

The mighty Mississippi!

It's a mud trench, Marge. A mile of mud with a trickle of liquid. Marge is aghast.

I won't stop. I'll be mean. I'll make her piss in a widemouth bottle. I'll leave her squatting in the woods at night in Appalachia. But no. She won't go in the woods, she'll hang onto the doorhandle. I should have run her over with the car when I had the chance.

I back my hatchback into Marge's driveway. She loads a toaster oven, a portable TV, a table lamp. Things I insist are ridiculous to carry to a train. I could never leave Petey, she says, carrying a parakeet in a cage.

Petey?

My punishment for attempting escape. I shut my eyes and see my dad standing on the steel steps of the train vestibule. He's not a real dwarf. None of us are genetic mutations, none lacking pituitary secretions. We're just very short people. Because he was so small my dad became a rodeo clown. He'd hop in a special barrel and a bull would knock it holy hell around the ring. Later Dad became a circus acrobat and met Mom. After she fell he couldn't take aerial work and became a strawboss. Dad, I'll say, meet Marge and her bird. They need a job. He won't be set back for a second, nothing surprises my dad. He'll just welcome me home and say where to put Marge and her bird.

You won't be living with me, you know that Marge? You're on your own when we get there. I wonder if I've ever seen a bigger person on the train. Marge will not fit into a roomette, which is what she'll qualify for as a butcher or train porter. She might work in ladies' wardrobe or on props, but she still won't rate a stateroom.

I walk around her house and marvel at the ways it's different from mine. In the refrigerator the vegetables are washed in their bins, the freezer packages neatly labeled and dated. I go upstairs, open closets, drawers, the medicine cabinet. I stand in a walk-in closet and yell for Marge. She carries an electric toothbrush from the bathroom exclaiming the virtues of clean teeth. I was a dental hygienist once, you know.

I didn't know that, Marge. You see this closet?

That's how I met Frank.

Can you live in a room smaller than this closet?

With all my stuff?

You married a man whose teeth you cleaned?

He had very clean teeth.

Don't bring so many plug-in items, Marge.

Actually I dated Frank for some time.

I've never dated.

Never dated?

I never had a town to date in.

I pick up a battery-powered radio. Bring this, I say. Bring canned goods. Bring cans of corn you can eat in the car, bring apricots in heavy syrup because we can't stop, bring a can opener, not a plug-in, and some crushed pineapple, and tuna in oil or water, and a loaf of bread in a box so it won't get squashed, and bring cans of Bergamo's baked beans.

I love Bergamo's baked beans.

Brings cans of Sterno, with stick matches.

We'll cook while we drive.

We'll skip truckstops.

We'll be fugitives, Marge says. We go downstairs to the kitchen and put food into a box. Marge is laughing and sweating. She thinks we're on TV. She pulls, I push the heavy box across her linoleum floor, down the steps, and across the driveway to the car.

All this stuff is not going to fit, Marge.

Maybe we can tie the spare tire on the roof.

We go inside. I search the basement for rope. Find a box of photo albums and peel back a cover with my thumbnail. I see small black-and-white glossies stuck down with corner tabs on flat-black pages. There are dozens of them. Photographs with someone's faded fine-line script across the bottom. I see Marge when she was little. Marge when she was thin and had a corsage and a beehive hairdo. Our family has photos like any other, more than others probably, but ours are in show programs or hanging in the circus museum in Florida. To have pictures buried in books in a damp basement gives me the creeps, so I go upstairs and call the building in Texas.

I leave a message for my dad with a ticket guy. Ticket guys are phone-room types. They live on the train but are not really show-folks. This guy doesn't know me but he knows my dad. Everyone

knows Huffy. Arriving Abilene with fat woman and bird, I say.
Ticket guy doesn't know building location. Abilene's a new town on
the route, he says, nobody's been there but the Twenty-four-hour
Man. Get to Fort Worth and follow the arrows.

He's telling me! This chump, this PR man, this first-of-
May ticketpusher is telling me to follow the arrows when I've been
following twenty-four-hour men since I was born. Before mom
got hurt we always drove overland and I was her arrow spotter. I
sat up front with her while she drove, and I never missed the
red arrows stapled to the telephone poles. All at once I can't say
any more to the guy, my throat feels like I've swallowed a water-
melon and I hang up the phone. Marge comes downstairs carrying
a plug-in plastic globe. We don't need a globe, Marge.

It's not for navigation, she says. Frank gave it to me for an
anniversary.

But it's a plug-in, Marge, a plug-in.

I wanted an engagement ring, never had a ring, Frank gave me
a globe. Said I deserved the world.

Was it a joke?

I've never been able to figure that out.

It's a reminder of why you're leaving, Marge. I need something
like that.

I'll remind you, she says. More of Marge's unusual logic. With
her along I wasn't likely to forget what I wanted. Her company
would boost my waning resolve to return to the show and face my
dad, and people who'd told me not to go.

If we only had a motorhome. I can't see sharing a stateroom
with Marge, too small, but a motorhome, that I can see, Marge driving and me up front watching for the arrows.

Marge has more stuff but the car is full. The spare tire is under
the floor of the hatchback. We take everything out: the two suitcases, the table lamp, the toaster oven, the birdcage, the TV, the
cooler of food, a portable sewing machine, some blankets, and a
pillow. Marge pulls open the compartment and hauls out the
spare. I couldn't find any rope, I say. Then one thing becomes

perfectly clear. Marge, I say, do you know how to change a flat?

No, she says.

Me neither.

Marge holds the tire with both hands. She turns the tread toward me and I set my foot against it, and together we send it rolling down her driveway. It rolls across the road into John's front yard. We cackle like witches and throw everything back into the car. Pulling out of the driveway I ask Marge once more if she is sure this is what she wants.

It's all I ever wanted, she says.

Corn Palace

In Des Moines, Iowa, I stood in line to get paid. Backdoor Jack sprawled in a booth next to the pay window with a box of new route cards, his bum leg in the aisle so everyone had to step over it. The pie car was packed with workingmen studying the card, pointing out new towns, arguing over old. The card told our future: the places we would play, dates of the stay, names of the buildings, and how many miles it was to the next town. In days of constant drift, the card was our calendar and map, the card anchored us. Towns played were crossed off and considered past yet they stayed with us. Forthcoming towns were anticipated but also remembered from previous visits. Sometimes the past showed up in a future town. That happened to me when I got to the pay window, collected my ninety bucks from Huffy, and told Jack to give me a card.

"Ten cents," Jack said, holding the card to his chest like a poker hand.

Huffy set Jack up in the card racket to give him something to do. There was little money involved; it was more a power trip for

Jack. He held the cards as long as possible before handing them out so there would be no time for the men to quit if they didn't like an upcoming town. There were often problems in a town: old debts, a warrant, an ex-wife. Estranged from my family, I dreaded going anywhere near New England. I gave Jack a dime for the card, and I stopped in the aisle staring at the first town. "Mitchell, South Dakota!"

"New town," Jack said. "Move out of the way."

"That's where my grandparents live," I said.

"Good for you. Move!"

My grandparents didn't live in Mitchell proper but in a farm town a few miles away where my dad grew up before heading east to college. Two weeks every July when we were kids he would pack the Rambler wagon for all five of us—I had two younger brothers—and he and Mom would take turns driving so we'd have time with the grandparents. They wouldn't know I was in Mitchell, they weren't circusgoers, even if they were they wouldn't see me in wardrobe.

"Kick that motherfucker in the ass," Jack said to the guy behind me.

I moved down the aisle and out onto the vestibule. I hadn't seen my grandparents since my mother died. My father remarried and the stepmother was not a South Dakota fan. The family excursions were replaced by two-week stints with a babysitter while Dad and his wife jetted off to Bermuda and places like that. The Rambler was replaced, along with everything else. *Wouldn't a brand new house be nice? One nobody's ever lived in?* Even the dog we'd grown up with. *Miserable. He wants to die.* She lodged herself into our lives and ordered things the way she could, swept away connections to the past, packed our memories off to the dump. Within a year I began running away from her new house, a house nobody would ever truly live in.

Sunday night we loaded out of Des Moines and Monday rolled into Mitchell on a day so hot the railspikes loosened in their holes. The hard rhythmic jolts at the railends became mushy thuds, the trainride spongy, the engineer taking the turns slow to avoid derailment on the decrepit third-string line.

The Corn Palace was too small for the show, a bad building. I remembered the place the way a kid remembers a castle, a source of wonder, a monument to corn. The front façade was decorated with thousands of colored corncobs: sunburnt yellow, rockhard red, Indian blue corn, black corn, green corn. Even the husks and stalks were used to make the elaborate designs that told Indian creation stories, the planting, the sun dances, and the harvest. These were portrayed on large panels bordered by corn-silk-covered columns that ran to the roof, on which sat onion-shaped domes and huge banner-topped ears of corn that looked like cartoon rocketships. My dad explained the stories to me every July. Kids don't see the old brick building behind the façade. In fact the Corn Palace is nothing but a cramped auditorium on a downtown corner.

Across the street from the Corn Palace was a Morrison's Cafeteria with a phone booth. I found my grandparents, Leo and May Ruden, in the book. I knew they were living three years ago when I last spoke to my dad. I loved my father and my grandparents, yet I couldn't bring to mind a single instance in the last three years that I'd considered contacting them. This made me feel like a bad person. I walked around all day during setup with the number on a scrap of paper in my pocket. The building had no air conditioning. We had to take a section from each ringcurb to fit three rings on the floor. The horse people howled. Their horses couldn't work in anything but a forty-foot ring. The center ring rigging was left out to make room for the flying rigs over rings one and three. Flyer Lalo Cadonna stood in center ring complaining about the low ceiling to Louis Morgan who was all over the building, measuring with his hundred-foot line, laying down bench-marks in silver duct tape, scrawling rigging notes in ballpoint pen. Everyone was miserable because of the bad building. I fingered the paper in my pocket and was distracted by how effectively I'd blocked thoughts of the past. Everything was bad, bad, bad.

Wardrobe was in a tight spot under the seats. I helped Dave wrestle the boxes between steel bleacher braces. They were folding bleachers of polished wood, basketball seats, with a sealed floor so nobody could fall through. Still, if someone got down on their hands and knees and put their eye to a crack they could peek into wardrobe. If someone spilled a Coke it would come dripping through. The place had only two dressing rooms: Home and Visitors. Clown alley was out back in a tent. The clowns were disgusted by the heat that melted their greasepaint.

I was too tired after setup to call my grandparents. I stalled. I showered in Visitors, put on clean coveralls, and slept in a wardrobe box until the show. The opening show was bad, everyone's timing off because of the building. Lalo Cadonna swung too high on his first trick and broke his hand on a ceiling beam. I didn't want to call my grandparents at night so I waited until the next day, silently rehearsing what I would say, what they would say, what I'd say if they didn't say anything. What if one of them had died? What if they'd both died? I meant to call after breakfast, but the train wasn't parked near any phones so I put it off till I got to the building. Then I had to set up my low wire so I decided to call between shows, but once the show started I couldn't stand any more stalling and moved it up to after Spec, then chickened out and put it off again. Finally I walked out of wardrobe right after the elephant number.

When I got to the back door Jack growled, "The hell you going?" I didn't answer him. Jack had no authority over me, or anything else, except the route cards and back door. Jack's job was simply rear guard. He studied the backlot grimly, viciously abusing hapless gawkers or people trying to find their way into the building. I walked by him, across the backlot, around the block to the phone, and dialed my grandparents' number.

They had an old black pyramid-shaped dial phone so heavy that as a child I thought it was permanently anchored to its corner of the wooden desk. An identical phone sat on Grampa's desk "uptown" at his butcher shop, Ruden's Meat Market, but there'd been no listing for the shop so I figured it was gone. He picked up the phone and I heard his strange South Dakota twang. "Hallo."

"Grampa, it's Gary." I said it fast so he'd know and it would be done.

"Gary. Well, I'll b'darned."

"I'm in Mitchell."

"The hell!" He sounded genuinely pleased, which made me smile. But it was sad too, to hear him using the same old expressions, hurt me to think he'd been using them for the last ten years without me being around, scared me to think that somewhere my dad was talking the same way he always talked, saying things I'd never hear, doing things I'd never see.

"Yes, I'm fine," I answered.

"Sure you're all right? A circus? You don't say? Well, I'll b'darned." Gramma's having a nap, he said, said she wasn't well. "Getting old," he said, "all getting old. Talked to your dad?"

"Not for awhile."

"Pretty bad back there, was it?"

"Bad."

"We visited back there a couple years ago, your Gramma and me took an airliner out that way, and I want to tell you it was hell. I couldn't stay in the house with that woman, and I told your dad so. Told him it's no wonder you run off."

Grampa was a tough old chopper. German ancestors that farmed Pennsylvania before spreading westward: Wisconsin, Iowa, and South Dakota. Grampa was the first to break away from farming by opening the butcher shop. The shop faced a gravel main street, wooden storefronts, cars parked nose-to-the-curb. Our vacations were spent in that shop—Gramma worked there too—being shown off to the customers who banged through the screen door. Many were relatives, but Grampa was the center of our attention. He'd fill us with ice cream, soda, candy, whatever we wanted, and he gave us flat-folding paper butcher hats like he wore, and white aprons, and coats when we went into the deep freezer.

Grampa was likely to untie his apron any time during the day, pull it over his head and say, "Kids, let's go for a ride." We would pile into his giant Chrysler Imperial and take the paved highway to the lake or to the Indian reservation. We loved watching the red speedometer needle creep upward: Seventy! Eighty! Ninety! We'd scream out the numbers and laugh like hell and say *shit* and *damn* like he did, and later when we got back to the shop he'd catch hell from Gramma when we blabbed that he drove ninety miles per hour. Grampa would whisper to me, "I guess it's butterknife time." That meant we had to be humble and smooth things over with Gramma. Grampa had reduced all of life's problems to which knife to use. There was a time to chop, a time to slice, dice, pare, carve, and butter. When he got riled, watch out, it was chopping time. I recall him hollering about different things and it always involved "carvin" someone up bloody or grinding them to mincemeat. He'd "hit the grinder switch," which was his term for having shit hit the fan. When we'd done something to make Gramma real mad, he'd say, "Well, she's hit the grinder switch, Gary, better get out the ol' butterknife."

Grampa was nothing like Dad who never drove his Rambler over sixty and had trouble carving the Thanksgiving turkey with a power knife. Dad was the first one in his family to go to college, and I'm not sure what Grampa thought of that. They looked nothing alike. Grampa was six feet two inches tall and lean as lizard skin with a grim downturned mouth and heavy overhanging brow, eyes deepset and dark. It was a gothic face like you see in old black-and-white photos, usually on a man in overalls with large hands weighing down his stretched-out arms, standing in a plowed field next to a draft horse. Dad was short like Gramma, smiled easily, and had grown pearshaped from days spent in a padded accountant's chair. It occurred to me during the twenty minutes we spent on the phone that my dad must have had a tough time growing up with Grampa.

Grampa asked me twice to come see my grandmother, said she wasn't well, said, "I'm not sure you'll have another chance."

Mitchell was a three-day stand so there was little time. "Tomorrow is teardown," I told him. "We open in Rapid City on Thursday night." He said they frequented Morrison's for lunch, so I agreed to meet them there at noon the following day. As for the show, it was Grampa's idea, and it was just like him to want to go. "Do your grandmother good," he said. "Been years since she's set foot in the Corn Palace. If it's no trouble?"

"No. No trouble," I said.

Walking back I remembered Backdoor Jack. I'd rather buy tickets than have to walk my grandparents past that old bastard. He was leaning against the doorframe watching me walk across the backlot. I gave him my best butterknife smile.

The Corn Palace was a bad place to sneak people in. There was one stagedoor half blocked with Jack's folding chair, which, in spite of his affliction, he rarely sat in. Jack was a former aerialist hurt years ago just before the show went to buildings. He worked with his wife in a cradle high up near the roof of the tent. Jack hung from his legs while his wife shifted smoothly through his arms to his neck to his teeth. Then she'd juggle and spin and hang from one foot. Nobody knew what went wrong but one night they both came down. His wife hit first and Jack landed on top of her and killed her. His back was broken and according to Huffy, who was a performer at that time, they had to take pieces of bone from his hip to relieve pressure on his crushed spinal column. As a result Backdoor Jack had one leg about four inches longer than the other and a spine permanently arched like a strung bow. Being too stubborn or poor to wear one of those special thick-soled shoes, Jack chose to drag his log-limb around like a ball on a chain, a private burden to bear for whatever happened that night in the tent when the only family he had died under the weight of his own body.

"The hell you been?" He never looked at you when he spoke but roamed the backlot with his eyes as if at any moment a herd of gatecrashers might jump from behind the cat tent and storm the door. I squeezed past him. No way I wanted to walk my grandparents past that grizzled old fart, at least not without paperwork.

That night in the pie car I asked Huffy for two ticket vouchers. Employees couldn't have actual tickets, only backstage passes. To get them you had to secure ticket vouchers from your boss, take them to the boxoffice where the PR people exchanged them for passes, which had to be turned in to Backdoor Jack at the time of use. This rigmarole was the reason friends and relatives were often snuck in. Jack could be a terrible embarrassment to clowns and showgirls bringing family and friends to the show when we played their hometowns. Jack would spot them out on the backlot: Mom and Pop, grandparents and cousins, *Look, there's an elephant!* Old boyfriends and school chums, *Don't get near the cats, they shoot peepee ten feet.* Regular people who went to college or worked at town jobs, excited, proud of knowing someone making a bold venture into showbusiness. They came like insiders to a mysterious world, ready for hard answers about how those stunts were pulled off, ready to grasp some secret stuff. Then they came face to face with Backdoor Jack blocking the door with his deformed leg slung off on its own, his gut arched out in front of him, the side of his shoe worn through where he dragged it around. And the weird thing was that Backdoor Jack was who they came to see, they just didn't know it.

Jack would wait until they were too close to turn back, until they were hooked, then he'd yell, "The hell you want?" There was activity in the backlot before the show, people and animals lined up for Opening, and Jack yelled loud enough for everyone to hear and turn to stare at the poor townies. They'd begin to sweat under the stares of the old-timers and the scowl of this gray-haired, stump-bodied ogre wearing a guard hat and the old-style show uniform: blue workshirt untucked with buttons missing, grease-stained pants with a wide red stripe down each pantleg. "Round the front folks," he'd bellow, waving them off. "Round the front. Now! Let's go!"

There was something disheartening about having to take that

kind of crap from a crumpled old man whose only function was to sit at an open space and make sure anyone who crossed it suffered his grief. I wondered if I should tell him I had the passes or spring them on him when my grandparents arrived. I didn't want him sitting around thinking up insults particular for me. On the other hand, I'd seen him take offense at passes for no good reason and ignore people for five minutes or more. "I'll get to you when I'm good and ready," he'd say.

Next morning I woke early, rolled from my bunk, clamped my mouth over the crusty water spigot. Hard South Dakota water. Dad knew why it was hard, used to tell me the names of the minerals, why they were there, and what the water needed to be softer and better tasting. I got into my sneakers, walked through the generator car into the pie car. Huffy and Backdoor Jack were sitting in a booth sucking on cigarettes. I ordered coffee and a fried-egg sandwich and took a booth next to Huffy and Jack. They'd been murmuring but quit when I came within earshot. When I was done eating I carried my plate up to the counter, and on the way back I pulled the passes from my pocket and thanked Huffy. I ignored Jack, and Huffy just stared. With my building bag over my shoulder, shower stuff, clean jumpsuit, wire shoes, and a book to read in wardrobe, I went out to catch the 10 A.M. bus.

The building was quiet; the gift shop had just opened, the same gift shop that was there when I was a kid, selling the same wooden Indians, cardboard warbonnets, made-in-Japan peace pipes, the same damn stuff my dad bought me years ago. I wanted to buy a postcard and send it to him. *Dear Dad: Remember that compass inside a rubber tire you bought me at the Corn Palace? I found my way back.*

In the center ring Diana Sabastian drove a pony in circles on a long line, a pony so small I couldn't hear the soft padding of its hooves on the thick rubber. In front of the backcurtain a rigger called Highrise juggled more rubber balls than he could hold in two hands. He could juggle nine balls once he got them airborne, but when he tried to stop, his hands weren't big enough to catch them. Highrise had been practicing six years and was better than the jugglers in the show, but nobody would hire him because he had no personality. I went to the backlot and tried to practice on my wire but was distracted. I worried I'd end up like Highrise. The show wasn't until one, so the backlot was deserted. It was hot. I kept falling, getting back up, falling. No Backdoor Jack yet. The animal people, having completed their morning work, slept on feed bags and baled hay inside the animal tents with the sidewalls pulled up for air. A tough stand so far. Two people had sustained minor injuries. Circus people being inherently superstitious, everyone was quietly dreading the last two shows, hoping that when the third accident came it would also be minor. After a few minutes I gave up on practice, showered in Visitors, and dressed in street clothes.

At noon I sat at Morrison's Cafeteria on a bench in the foyer surrounded by potted plants in copper spittoons, a milkcan umbrella holder, a gold-framed mirror, old washboards hanging on the wallpaper with old firearms, an iron pumphead, tintypes of white men in suits with Indians in top hats and animal skins. Grampa had a barnful of this stuff and Dad liked to drag it home to New England. The wagon always went east heavier than it went west. When my stepmother came on the scene she said it was all junk and made him throw it out. I remember one minor argument he put up about a pig-bladder flask that he said "Nigger Pete," a farmhand they'd had when he was a kid, made and carried when they went to work the fields. The bladder was dried hard as wood, had a worn mouthpiece, but the top plug was missing. "Who?" she said.

"We'd be miles from the house with only a cart and plowhorse. We had to have water and the pigskin kept it cool."

"You drank from that thing?"

"Well, sure."

"With a Negro?"

"Well, we didn't think of him like that."

"Throw it out."

Looking through the plate-glass doors, old folks shuffling in and out, I saw the front panels of the Corn Palace. Two corncob Indians offered homage to the sun. I saw myself age six, seven maybe, standing on the sidewalk with my dad and him explaining to me the story behind each decorated panel. That was before my mother died and he became the quiet man married to someone who said of him: "He knows everything, but everything he knows isn't worth knowing." This she said within earshot of his children. And being children, what could we say? We could not answer her back. Even when the words from her mouth said things I knew to be untrue I could only answer her by running away. I knew my father knew a great deal that was worth knowing and did the things he did out of necessity, and so did I.

When they came through the glass doors they looked like the other old folks. Grampa was how I remembered him, tall with a summer straw hat like men wore in the 1920s, thick wrists and large hands hanging from gray suit sleeves, a brilliant white shirt and a thin black tie. But Gramma struggled with an aluminum walker. She had trouble maneuvering it over the rubber weather strip. Grampa held the door open with his foot, reached around her, and jiggled one leg of the walker, then the other, over the bump. I met them just inside the door, awkward, with them trying to get out of the way. It seemed like Grampa wanted to shake my hand but held back sensing I was too stunned to touch Gramma. I couldn't get near her anyway with the walker.

Grampa did all the talking: "The hell. Gary, you're all grown up." We shuffled by the chalkboard: meatloaf, creamed corn and stringbeans, custard—$3.25, and down the narrow aisle to the foodline. Gramma made whimpering birdlike sounds that Grampa understood and acted on. They managed well as a team, down the foodline, her whimpered choices picked up and set down on the tray he pushed along. They moved ahead of me, and we took our separate tickets from the cashier and found a seat by the window.

Gramma had had two strokes and though she couldn't talk and was partially paralyzed she could still smile and follow a conversation. We spent a lot of time staring at each other, and I spent a lot of time blinking, having to turn away, remembering that dark-haired woman with a white butcher-shop apron tied around her narrow waist, wagging her finger when we pounded through the screen door of the shop screaming, "Grampa let us drive the car!"

When we finished eating Gramma had to go to the bathroom, so we all stood up and Grampa got her on her way shuffling across the carpeted dining room with the walker. "The second stroke took her voice," he said after we sat down. "Was after we come back from out east." Grampa had always referred to New England as "out east." I always thought South Dakota was in the middle of nowhere. But to Grampa his home was the center of things with odd places like New York and California slung off to the outer perimeter of the universe.

"So you didn't like it out east?" I said.

He made a dismissive sweep with his hand as if to wipe away any doubt that New England was beyond help. "Can't see why anyone lives there," he said. "All the houses have stairs in 'em." I thought of how much fun his house was for us kids, nine rooms all on one level. We could leave the kitchen in one of four directions and by twisting and turning through a bedroom, a bathroom, a laundry room, a dining room, a living room, a hallway, we'd return to the kitchen. "And the weather," he said. "Wasn't a day I didn't ache from dampness. I don't know what happened to your dad out there," he said. A waitress offered coffee. "None for her," he said, putting his hand over Gramma's cup. He glanced back toward the restrooms. "She don't take coffee." When the waitress was gone he said, "You planning on calling them?"

"Well, I'd talk to Dad."

"Spoke to your brothers?"

"Don't know where they are. You?"

"No. They were gone when we were there. Nobody could live

with that woman. She ruined your dad and I told him so." He shook his head and in his tight-lipped way chewed his dentures, pulled them loose with his lower lip, pushed them back in place with his tongue.

"I told him not to marry her," I said, "but I was eleven years old. He was alone with three kids. Had to do something, I guess."

"I had no idea." Grampa tapped his temple with his index finger. "I think she's—" Then we saw Gramma shuffling across the room and we both took a drink of water as if to wash the conversation from our mouths and rose to go so she wouldn't have to get settled again.

We stood outside getting used to the glare, heat rising from the sidewalk through our shoes. Gramma was white-knuckling the walker and staring at the Corn Palace. She said something to Grampa. "That was years ago," he answered her. "She gets confused sometimes," he said to me. "She says your dad worked on these panels. He used to do that when he was in high school. Some club or another he was in. Anything to get off the farm," he said grimly. "When he received a scholarship to that school out east he had his bag packed a month in advance."

We crossed the street and headed down the sidewalk to the backside of the Corn Palace. Grampa questioned me again about whether I was all right, as if maybe I was shanghaied and in need of assistance. I told him I'd made a home at the show and everything was fine. "We thought maybe you'd enlisted."

"No. That's not the place for me."

"I guess things have changed since we went to war."

"I guess." We shuffled along for half a block without saying anything, then stopped to let Gramma rest in the strip of shade offered by the building. I asked him when he closed the shop.

"In '69."

"Sell it?"

"Had to. Hospital bills. No one to leave it to anyway."

We took one step every three or four seconds. Gramma's white sneakers struck me as odd when I first saw them with the long blue dress, but when I saw how much trouble her feet gave her I understood. It was as if her legs were hanging onto her thin body by threads, so that when she picked a foot up off the ground to take a step it swung free and haphazard, as if the wind took it and she had to use all her effort to rein it in and have the foot find the ground.

At the end of the building we turned into the backlot shimmering with heat waves and moved between the animal tents reeking from cat urine. The elephant muck pile smoldered in the sun. A half-dozen unimugs were lined up next to wagons that had curtains across the doorways. People came and went in shorts and T-shirts. Crisscrossing the lot were black electrical cables and water hoses. We had to help Gramma with the walker each time we came to a cable or hose. Where bunches of them ran together they were covered by steel crossover plates so they wouldn't be wrecked by unimugs and elephants. The crossover bridges proved difficult for Gramma, and when I saw how many there were I knew it was a mistake to come this way. "We have to go through that back door," I said, pointing about fifty yards away where Backdoor Jack leaned against the doorframe watching us. "The backdoor man can be a bit gruff," I said.

"We landing you in trouble?" Grampa said.

"No trouble. Jack can be grumpy, that's all. Old performers live in pain." Grampa nodded as if he understood, and we went on slowly, sweating heavily, across the cables and hoses and crossovers. I watched Gramma and whenever she hit a stumbling block I'd grab hold and lift the legs of the walker over the obstruction. I kept my eyes down, determined to ignore Jack, until I heard some racket and looked up. He was pushing a Corn Palace wheelchair toward us. He dragged his dead leg along behind him and slammed the wheelchair over the crossovers with powerful arms. We stopped to watch and I felt my heart pounding from the whole thing: Jack, the heat, my poor practice, Gramma and that damn walker. I wished I'd never called them, and the wave of guilt that came with that made me hate myself.

I heard my stepmother's voice: *Go ahead, run away*. I felt low enough to tear into Jack if he unleashed any bullshit on us. He came up dripping sweat from his jaw onto the front of his shirt. The underarms were wide dark rings. Jack rarely left his shady doorway; it was too difficult for him to get around.

I held the passes up in front of my face like a crucifix. Jack ignored me. He went directly to Gramma and said, "Ma'am, this will make things easier." He spoke in the sweetest voice I'd ever heard from his mouth. He didn't even sound like Backdoor Jack. I had the odd thought that this must be how he spoke to his mother, or maybe his wife. Grampa was about to answer for her, but Gramma understood and said something. Jack took her arm and settled her into the wheelchair.

"Thank you very much," Grampa said.

Jack ignored him, scooped up the aluminum walker, and shouldered it. "Set this by the back door," he said, and turned to go. I still held the passes out stupidly when Jack looked back and scowled at me. "Push the chair for your grandmother, idiot." He clumped and dragged off across the tarmac lugging the leg, carrying the walker.

When we made it to the building Jack was blocking the door looking out over the lot like we weren't there. "Got some passes here for you," I said.

He moved over and dropped into his folding chair leaving just enough room to get past. I pushed Gramma in and she murmured to Jack and he said, "You're entirely welcome, Ma'am."

Inside the air was cooler and the chair rolled easily over the cement floor. I wanted to unload the passes on him, so I went over to his chair. He'd lifted and shoved his bum leg across the doorway. He watched Grampa who stood behind the wheelchair patting Gramma on the shoulders. I followed his gaze and saw Grampa bent over Gramma, hands on her shoulders, speaking quietly in her ear. I'd seen my dad in exactly that position with my mom before she'd died. Every evening when he came in from work, after fifteen years of marriage, he bent over her in just that way and told her she was the most wonderful woman in the world. I heard him say it every night. Jack and I watched Grampa and Gramma. I shuddered feeling somehow akin to him. Things vanish and you cannot get them back. Like the changing images on the Corn Palace walls, like time that does not change the sound of a long lost voice, like love killed by your own mistakes. I set the passes down gently on Jack's bum leg.

We were late. I'd made us late. I'd cut the luncheon time too close, figuring to give my family an hour and go back to hiding in wardrobe. Now I regretted it. I needed to make up for lost time. I didn't want to lose Gramma and Grampa now. I wanted a knife to cut bitterness from my heart. They were waiting. The show was about to begin.

The only quick way into the arena for wheelchairs was through the backcurtain, so I took the back of the chair from Grampa and pushed it through the crowd of performers waiting for Opening. The curtainman cracked the curtain to let us pass. Heinemann had his whistle in his mouth. The band members were in their places. Just as we got through the curtain the house lights went out, the spotlights came on the ringmaster, and he launched into his spiel. We rolled down the backtrack in the dark to the wheelchair section, Grampa took a folding chair, and I squatted down between him and Gramma. I wanted to sit with them, like the families around us, sit and laugh together and applaud everything and remember it years later. But that couldn't be. I'd made my choice. The performers pounded down the track wearing the wardrobe I had to take care of. In the backlot my wire sat waiting. "I'll come for you after the show," I shouted at my grandparents. "I'll come and get you. We'll drive to your house. We'll talk and watch TV and eat snacks and go to bed." I was shouting as loud as I could. But in the dark, with the music blaring, they couldn't see me or hear me. Hell, I couldn't even hear myself. The show had taken over everything.

Marge Johnson

If Frank could see this tiny room they've given me. (I'm here Frank, you poor bastard.) Why not swear? He'll never know. I love my room! Alberta says it belonged to someone named Pie Car Bill who was also big. He covered the walls and ceiling with mirror tiles. My goal is to shed some weight, create some space, since everything is small on a train. The window shade slides up into the wall, the door slides sideways, the sink and bed fold down. There is a strip of floor space with a blue shag carpet, a closet and some drawers, cubbyholes in odd places, toilet down the hall. Is that ever a tight fit. I find the flush pedal on the floor, and there is a rush of blue that smells like ammonia. One of my neighbors, John the Porter, meets me in the hall and backs down to let me pass. (Alberta says he's gay.) He gives me sheets and blankets and says we'll rig Petey's cage for the run. Says to leave my trash outside the vestibule daily, and my linen outside my room on the first day of each town. Setup day. Alberta didn't let me bring much, drove like a madwoman, thought my bladder would burst. On arrival her dad (Huffy) sold me a route card for a dime and asked me if I cook! Of course I cook, cooked every day of my life. Never got paid to cook. Paid! My own money! A Polish gentleman shows us the pie car. His name I can't say, Yanush, or something. Alberta knows it all, spends all day yakking to a young man named Gary.

I'm sitting on my bed using the fold-down table in front of my window. Loadout makes Petey nervous, and he flutters about sending feathers onto the carpet. John the Porter has drilled a hole in the ceiling between mirror tiles and hung the cage with a brick in the bottom to keep it stable. Still, with the pounding and jerking of hookup, the cage jumps around. Twice now I've left the country. We walked in a group across a bridge into Mexico. I'd have been frightened to death if not for Rulfo the unicycle rider who guided me through the pushy vendors. I broke my diet to try a burrito though everyone warned me not to. (I'm in Mexico, Frank! You son of a bitch.) I love writing bastard and son of a bitch. I feel like I'm writing this to Frank, but he'll never see it. I wouldn't care if he did. Poor Frank. I wore my long calico print skirt and peasant blouse and Rulfo took my arm (a black man, Frank), and I guess we looked like a couple or something (a very large black man), because a man with a camera jumped into our path, snapped a Polaroid of us, and demanded money. We'd ordered no photo but he began yelling in Spanish and then there was a policeman at his side. Rulfo is well over six feet, with a body that stands out even on a show full of people who look like body builders, and he had no intention of paying for the photo. There would have been trouble but flyer Lalo Cadonna stepped up to the policeman and began arguing in Spanish. I have no idea what was said but the policeman and the photographer backed off. We walked back across the bridge with Lalo and a blond showgirl named Kitty. The train starts rolling so slowly I don't notice. A fire moves across the river and I know it's us. More fires move faster on the black window and someone runs by on the cinderbed below. People here hold a remarkably casual attitude about the train. Often I see them stum-

bling over the sharp rocks and swinging on board just as the train picks up speed.

Clattering across the desert for twenty-four hours, the clicking of steel wheels over railends puts me to sleep. When I wake the clicking goes on. My world is spinning. Alberta was wrong about that: a plug-in globe is perfect for a train. I've glued the base of it to my writing table in front of the window. When we roll, the train sways top-heavy side-to-side, and the globe spins as if the rails actually crisscross the tiny sphere, as if the moving train drives the globe in circles. When the train speeds up, the globe spins like mad, when we slow down, its revolutions slow accordingly. (Thanks for the world, Frank.) I keep it plugged in and the light dances about my mirrors. With the shade up I watch the globe's reflection spinning in the glass, spinning in the black space outside my window. When I sleep it spins on. When we stop and I leave my room to walk in the trainyard, I see it glowing from way off, calling out to me, a yellow beacon steering me home.

There are 150 vestibules on this train, each with its own distinctive atmosphere. A vestibule is merely a crossroad of fold-down steel steps when we park, but on the runs with the steps folded up and the bottom half of the Dutch doors closed, the vestibules become our front porches. On a vestibule you might meet anyone. People cruise the vestibules to see who is doing what. Rulfo has begun frequenting my vestibule. We lean our elbows out the door, our hair struck back by the wind, watching the night country blow by. He's not a great conversationalist, so the noisy vestibule is perfect for us. Out in the wind, side by side, our shoulders press together. Rulfo pulls his head inside and lights what he calls "a bone," which is a marijuana cigarette. He offers it a few times before I take it. We do this quickly because my car is next to the pie car where Huffy has his office. Huffy doesn't like to see any pot smoking. Highrise the rigger lives on the one side of me. Program Lenny, a bigshot butcher in romantic liaison with John the Porter, lives on the other side, then Donna and Doo Doo a couple of girl clowns, then Rollo and Radar, and Shorty the ringcurb boss, and a guy who wears a tie and works in the ticket office. And me: Pie Car Marge Johnson. I'm one of them.

I take the bus each morning to shower in the building. Sometimes I accept a ride with Rulfo in his troupe van but I don't like to. I want to stay independent. At a supermarket I weigh myself and I've lost eight pounds. I'm stunned because the diet was just a vague notion. I think it's the work. The grills and ovens are hot, and when everyone comes in from the show to eat I do some heavy sweating. Everyone says don't miss the opening in Los Angeles. They have movie stars as guest ringmasters, so I go and watch Burt Reynolds and Cher ride an elephant. I stand next to the bandstand until after Rulfo's act then take a taxi back to the train. It's such a relief to come back. The building seems like another world. My world is a neighborhood of small rooms and vestibules instead of houses with driveways. I still put my trash out, and could get mail if anyone knew where I was. On long runs I sit for hours in the pie car writing in this diary and reading excerpts to the workingmen. I'm a mother to three hundred children. The only fly in the ointment is that Alberta is unhappy in the pie car. She is supposed to be in charge but I've been planning the menus, and Huffy has been telling me when to expect deliveries. Tonight the special is Hungarian Goulash, which everyone raves about, except Rulfo. He complains that the pie car never serves "soul food." What is soul food, anyway? Around 2 A.M. Alberta and I leave Yanush to mop up under the pallets. The pallets are my idea (yes, Frank, I thought of something); after hours of bacon and hamburger splatter the steel floor becomes slick as a greasy spoon. Alberta cries and says she feels stupid living with her dad and working in the pie car while her sister and friends work in the show. She feels like a failure, leaving to marry a townie and then having the marriage fall apart. You're not thinking of going back to him, I say. Relieved to hear her say no. She may go stay in Florida with her mom. I wish I could help her but my own situation is so different. Thanks to her, I've never been happier. For the first time in my life I'm faced with endless possibilities. When Rulfo comes knocking on my door I tell him to go away.

I'm going overland in the van with Rulfo on a run from Anaheim to Fresno. First time I've been off the train and I feel nervous leaving the pie car to Alberta and Yanush, but Huffy says go, have a good time. Rulfo drives the coastal road onto route 101, stopping at every wine tasting room, then tries crossing the mountains. I tell him we are going wrong but he refuses to consult the map. We end up lost at a twenty-four-hour horseback-riding stable. Rulfo is insane. I've never ridden a horse in my life. He says that doesn't matter, he can't ride either. Near midnight the man in charge leads two sleepy horses from a pen, holds them while we climb on using a wooden step. The man acts as if it is perfectly normal for two greenhorns from New York to go riding in the middle of the night. I'm thinking that any second something normal will happen, like the man will lead us twice around the parking lot and that will be it. But once we are up he walks away and the horses stroll off into the darkness. We go up and down hills for hours and there is no moon or stars and we can do no more than hear the creaking of our saddles and hang onto the horses' manes and trust them. There is no steering, they go where they go. At times there is a path, other times they push through low bushes, and once we end up on a dirt road so close together I reach over and hold Rulfo's hand. I know I'll never look at a map again. We sleep in the van somewhere in the San Joaquin Valley, with the windows open, and the dew comes in and nestles in our hair. I wake while Rulfo sleeps. The sun clears the top of the hills to the east, mist hangs low in the valley, steam rises from the places where there is water. I pull the blankets around my bare shoulders and rest my chin on the door so my face touches the cool morning. It comes to me that either this is normal or nothing will ever be normal again.

Huffy says don't go outside the train alone in Oakland, the holding line where we're parked is in a notorious area. This is a burden because I've been sleeping down in Rulfo's car. I don't like walking through the train after the pie car closes. I've lost another four pounds but crossing all the vestibules with the heavy sliders is still a chore. Suffering the foul-breathed drunks who won't get out of the way is no fun, and the showgirls are bitches, muttering "coalburner" when I pass through their sweet-and-sour-smelling car. When Rulfo comes to my room it's no better. Program Lenny and John the Porter stand in the hall when Rulfo's with me and talk loud: Don't knock on Marge's door, she's burning coal tonight. How Rulfo finds this funny I have no idea. Y'all jealous, he yells out, even while we're doing it. (We never really did it, Frank.) Not of you, they yell back, and laugh like hell.

Rulfo is teaching me to ride a unicycle. I practice on the cement platform next to the train. He holds my hand and we go up and down, but he gets frustrated easily so I've learned to do it without him by keeping one hand on the flatcars that overhang the platform. I practice during the day when everyone is at the show. The men who work in the trainyards get a charge out of seeing a fat lady riding a unicycle. I've broken the two-hundred-pound barrier. I've dropped a total of twenty-five pounds. (Without even trying, Frank!) It seems odd now for me to write the name Frank. I forget completely about my old life for weeks at a time. I've figured out that living on this show is about looking forward. People are always talking about the next town, or their favorite town, or a great time we had that can be looked forward to next year. If you don't happen to like the place we're at, you have only to wait and it goes away. The fundamental requirement of unicycle riding is to look and lean forward. Always forward, never back, Rulfo says. And that's what I'm doing. The first thing I see in the morning is my route card taped to a mirror next to Petey's cage with the crossed off towns, and more importantly, the towns yet to arrive.

Setup day in Seattle Alberta says there's an opening in the show. One of the seven dwarfs broke his ankle and she fit the costume. Hey, nobody said it would be all glamour. The pie car is mine if I want it. Pay raise to $125, and Huffy says I'll be getting another Polish guy. You're not a first-of-May anymore, Marge, he says, I'll show you how to make some money on the side. He says I'll be ordering food and keeping the books. In big cities we stock up, buy cheap from warehouses and carry all we can across Canada where everything is expensive. Places like Winnipeg you can't buy anything. Seattle you buy seafood, Texas beef and beans, Colorado chili peppers, Idaho potatoes, and so on. Rulfo is excited, suggesting a soul food night. But I tell him I'm in charge. We'll do what I say. He makes a big show of saying, Yes, ma'am!

At Moosejaw, Saskatchewan, we stop to take on water. It takes about half an hour. Everyone climbs down onto the platform and walks up and down, relishing the feel of solid earth under their feet after two days on the train. The workingmen run for the nearest bar. In the tiny station I post an envelope to my old address in New York. It is a spur of the moment thing, to postmark something to anyone from a place like Moosejaw. In the envelope is a Polaroid picture Alberta has taken of me. I don't have time to write anything, have nothing to say anyway. (Sorry, Frank.) Maybe I should say that I do feel sorry if I hurt him, but not that I left. The picture is of me riding my unicycle in a pink leotard that I bought with my own money. I'd gotten free of the flatcar and was peddling down the platform on my own. Rulfo is running along beside me wearing a pair of green nylon shorts. He leaped into the air, grinning and clapping his hands, just as Alberta snapped the photo. My car is in the background and my globe is lighting up the window of my room. (The world you gave me, Frank.) It's not a high quality picture or anything, it's an average picture, entirely what you would expect to see on a station platform in Moosejaw, Saskatchewan, next to a white circus train. My head is up, my mouth and arms are wide open, I am looking forward.

Things Vanish and Reappear

I remember the children's faces best, **Bob Dylan wrote. But I don't.** Maybe the clowns remember the children's faces best, but children's faces were far from the wardrobe, far from my practice wire, and far from the bars I spent my time in. I remember the towns, the bars in the towns, the sidewalks of the towns, how we walked the sidewalks, Dave and me staggering, sloppy hands-and-knees drunk, or desperately sober, demanding directions to the nearest bar. We always said "nearest bar" because we didn't care what kind of bar it was as long as we could walk to it from the building and as long as the proprietor and patrons put up with us, which they did, the proprietor happy for the business—we drank a lot—and the patrons recognizing us as people not likely to be around for long and possibly of exotic interest. We knew, for instance, that an erect elephant penis drags on the ground, that chimps are more dangerous than lions. We were the people to ask about those blond girls who tied themselves in knots. Yes, they are very stretchy. Yes, they shave their armpits, and then some. Of course, we didn't always tell the truth.

In Minneapolis I remember the parking lot best because that's where we saw Bob Dylan. Dave had had his ups and downs but was pretty sick by then. Doubled over in wardrobe, washed out in sweat, holding his stomach. And I was worried because I was the only one who knew he was sick. He denied it was getting worse, tried to stifle the pain with a steady intake of alcohol. The nearest bar was a Holiday Inn lounge, a terrible place across the empty parking lot, which was huge because the building was next to a football stadium. Twin Cities Stadium, home of the Vikings. I'd practiced early that day and walked over to the bar between shows. It was a hot day, late summer. I found Dave there with Cuts of the New York Wheels, both of them dead drunk.

Dave wore his blue coveralls, and Cuts had his unicycle hooked over the padded edge of the bar. They were socked and that soured my taste for a beer. I left fast to avoid walking back with them. As I was going out I tried to tell Cuts he was in trouble. "You won't be able to ride," I said. "Go to the train and pretend you're sick." They howled with laughter, too drunk to be offended, their eyeballs lit with the white flame that comes with early-in-the-day drinking.

Earlier that year Dave and me hitched to see Dylan playing at the Redrock Amphitheater outside of Denver. I still have the ticket stub. We were supposed to be in wardrobe and Cuts covered for us. We had to give Cuts pot. He always hit us up for pot, which got us in trouble with TC who, as boss of the Wheels, was supposed to keep Cuts in line. Cuts had problems with drugs and alcohol. We'd been warned by TC not to give Cuts any dope and not to drink with him. Cuts traveled with the show by permission from his parole officer. I didn't know why Cuts had been in prison. He liked to say manslaughter, as if in a rage over something righteous he'd crushed someone's head. But Cuts was a small man and that probably wasn't true. He had a sky-blue pimping outfit: wide-brimmed hat, blue suede boots, which he'd don in big cities and go to the hangout strips to look for women who would put out for money. He got one for Dave once. A young black girl. Dave paid him fifteen dollars and took her in his bunk on the caravan car with a few of us sitting around, smoking dope, and listening to them screw. I wished I had the nerve to do such things. After twenty minutes Cuts reached up and wiggled the curtain and the girl climbed down and waved goodbye. Dave lounged in his bunk smoking a cigarette and flicking ashes out onto the floor. He said the girl was very nice. I said I didn't have fifteen dollars, which was not true.

The day in Minneapolis, when Cuts fell on his face in front of a packed house, Bob Dylan sat on the backtrack about halfway up the section in front of center ring. We didn't know it at first. I was back in wardrobe when Dave came tipping in from the Holiday Inn grinning like a fool while everyone dressed for the show. "Cuts is drunk out of his mind," he said, as I guided him to a folding chair. After Opening I left Dave nodding and went down the hall, slipped through the backcurtain, and stood in the dark under the bandstand vibrating from the music. The unicycle riders rolled down the spotlighted track in two neat lines. They entered center ring from the back and scattered. The house lights came up, and about half of them were speeding around the ring with the basketball bopping between them when Cuts peddled in and fell flat on his face. He was on his bike, then sprawled on the rubber, arms and legs askew as if he'd fallen from a high place. And the bad part: he stayed there. He lay in center ring face down like a dead man while his partners whirled around him. Maybe he wished he were dead. When he struggled up and remounted his bike he floundered. He couldn't catch the flow and they wouldn't slow down. Their mouths slashed at him, their faces furious. They'd send the poor bugger back to New York. He stayed on his bike for the rest of the act, going slow, trying to keep out of the way.

Dave was closer to Cuts than I. Cuts said I was too serious. Dave was more "slapstick." That's the word he used; I don't understand why it hurt me, especially since Dave had to bear the brunt of TC's wrath when he came around. Who knows what happened in the Wheels' dressing room after Cuts fell on his face, but we never saw Cuts again. TC came into wardrobe after Finale and without a word punched Dave in the chest so hard I was afraid he'd cracked Dave's breastbone. Dave's not a small man and there was daylight between the floor and his bootheels. He landed flat on his back and lay there trying to breathe until Dean the clown charged in and swore to God he'd seen Bob Dylan in the audience. Dean was recently in love with a tiny Polish acrobat who hadn't been in America long enough to learn English. They were lavishly in love, going everywhere together, hanging on, pawing, sharing food in public. Dean threw off his Finale stuff, and ran to get his tiny Polish girl, who had never even heard of Bob Dylan.

We ran to the backcurtain, Dave with one arm across his chest and a hand on his head. Out on the track we scanned the seats. People herded out shoulder to shoulder, bumper to back, making it difficult to distinguish between them, but when we spotted him, there was no doubt: it was Bob Dylan. He shuffled along on one of the middle tiers, not even wearing sunglasses, surrounded by regular people. He had two kids with him, another guy, and a teen-age boy.

We swung over the hockey boards and hopped the seats upward but couldn't get through the crowd as they passed into the corridor that circled the arena. Butchers screamed their final pitches for programs and blow-up toys. There were many exits off the corridor. Outside we watched people disperse across the grass to the parking lot. "Lost 'em," I said to Dave. But then he spotted two workingmen running, and when we plotted their course we saw the Dylan party moving across the backlot. They had parked among the animal tents and prop wagons.

We caught them just short of their car, a regular car, parked in the open shade of the stadium that dwarfed things generally considered huge. The wagons and trailers viewed from the top of the stadium would look like bugs, the elephant and horse tents like frail campers. Dylan seemed frailest of all, pale and squinting, surrounded by a group of misfits. He held hands with two little kids, a boy and a girl. The other guy unlocked the car while we smiled and nodded at Dylan, and it dawned on me that this must happen to him all the time. Wherever he went people came charging up in great urgency only to stop short, stand dumb, and stare. I wanted to say we'd stood like this before. To say I'd seen him a decade earlier in Newport, Rhode Island. It was after my mother died, all sorts of big-brother type people appeared to do things with me. One of them, a friend of some new friend of my dad, took Dave and me to the Newport Folk Festival of 1964. That was the first time we saw Bob Dylan. He looked like a kid on our street who went to the high school. He had a hollow guitar that covered half his body and a chrome harmonica gizmo hanging in front of his face. The big-brother fellow said he knew a guy whose roommate had had a date with a former girlfriend of Bob Dylan and that was reason enough for us to go backstage. Not really backstage. In those days everything was wide open; they played on plywood platforms three feet high. The big-brother fellow said this man in bluejeans, work shirt, and a pair of polished but worn boots would change everything. Dylan mumbled a few things, sang some songs. I couldn't understand a word he said.

In 1965 I saw Dylan again in Newport. Things had changed. The big-brother fellow had been drafted. Some new friend of my dad became my stepmother, and I ran away for the first time. Not farther than Dave's garage the first night, hid in the rafters and Dave brought me food. That summer I found nobody sees a twelve-year-old. People spot smaller kids on their own, adults are subject to scrutiny, but I could slip in and out of places without notice. I shifted with the wind, invisible, alone, and I found in loneliness a kind of identity. I'd go days without saying a word. When I heard myself speak to a service station attendant, or a clerk in a store, I'd be startled. Whose voice was that? Sometimes I was scared, but in that too I found something indicative and unchangeable. I slept in woods, on beaches, stole food from supermarkets, got caught by the police. Dylan, who had been on the radio a lot between '64 and '65, had switched his big hollow guitar for a solid body electric. He wore sunglasses, a silk polka-dotted dueling shirt, striped bellbottom trousers, and had some friends with him from New York, one of them had a set of drums. That time I understood exactly what he was saying.

I wanted to say thanks for the information. But I was struck dumb. I knew I was struck dumb but couldn't do anything about it. We stood in an awkward circle—a few hippie workingmen, couple of butchers in candycane smocks, the Dylan party—not saying anything, when Dean saved the day. Running across the parking lot yelling, "Wait! Wait!" Everyone, Dylan too, turned to look. Dean, clutching his ninety-pound Polish girl to his chest like you'd carry a child from a burning building, was running as fast as possible in a pair of red leather clown shoes. He wore boxer shorts and a T-shirt, kneesocks crumpled around his ankles, and somewhere his wig had fallen off exposing his curly brown hair. The girl wore a pink bathrobe, tan fishnet pantyhose with seams up the back of both legs, and show makeup. She was pretty, but fair, so she had created a face with black lines and brushstrokes. Her arms were locked around Dean's neck. He was sweating and gasping and explaining to both her and Dylan, explaining for all us stricken dummies, everything we wanted to tell Bob Dylan, and he did it while giving the Polish girl, in about thirty seconds, the history of America for the previous ten years. "She's never heard of you," he said to Dylan, "but I've been telling her, telling her everything." The girl looked embarrassed, clutching her bathrobe; her tiny netted feet stuck out into the circle of people. And Dylan, it's hard to say what he thought because he didn't say a word, but he didn't try to get away either. Maybe he stood there so his kids—both had his wide pointed face—could get a close look at a clown. He looked curious, a bit amused maybe, not tense and not relaxed. He eyed us up and down. I saw him study the tiny feet of the

Polish girl, the feet of someone who'd never heard of him. He examined the dark trails of sweat ruining Dean's powdered-on whiteface, blurring the red and black greasepainted lines. Who knows what he thought? We probably weren't the strangest people he'd run into, but you never know. He'd written about us only in conventional ways: about traveling 'round with carnival trains, about clowns crying in alleys, and remembering children's faces best; romantic nonsense. I suspect we were the first real circus people Dylan had met because he seemed to study us as much as we studied him. Dean blabbed nonstop about everything from how he made his parents buy him a guitar when he was ten after he'd seen a girl sing "Blowin' in the Wind" on the Ted Mack Amateur Hour, to how he convinced his film-studies class in college that Fellini's *Satyricon* was a step-by-step visual manifestation of the Dylan song "Visions of Johanna." Dylan nodded his head once or twice but mostly the squinty look on his face gave no indication that he recognized anything in Dean's monologue. Soon Dean had talked, carried, and run himself breathless. We stood there looking at each other, all of us looking at Dylan, sort of handing him the situation, hoping he'd take it. He was born 150 miles from Minneapolis, yet I never read in the papers about him going back there. I know he came from a big family. Presumably he had old friends like anyone, relatives to visit, people you'd go to the circus with. Finally Dylan shrugged his shoulders, straightened up, and said softly, "Well. Gotta go."

They got into the car and drove toward the Holiday Inn. We waved and he actually raised his hand and gave a salute from behind the glass in the backseat where he sat with the kids.

Dave was down on his knees on the tarmac, his arms wrapped around his stomach. It was the end for Dave. The real pain, and the need to do something about it, began in Minneapolis. I remember that moment as an ending for me too. As I waited with him out on the parking lot, grit blowing into my face, an old restless enemy came back to me. I felt pressure building with Dave being sick and Huffy attacking me every town. I felt trapped, unsettled. Inside me the decade of running clawed. If things didn't suit me, if I was simply bored, I ran away. I wondered for the first time if I'd make it to the end of the season. The thought was sudden and scary because I had no intention of leaving the show. I wanted to practice and build a highwire act and look down onto baldheaded Huffy, and watch him hear the people scream and stomp for me. Out on that barren parking lot, old friend bad off, I became aware that what I wanted wasn't going to happen easily. *Too many things working against you.*

When Dave was ready I helped him back to wardrobe. I helped him through that summer. Some days you'd never know anything was wrong, but on bad days he couldn't move from his bunk on the train, or he'd make it to the building only to crash in a wardrobe box. I suspect that is why Huffy left me in wardrobe; he hadn't forgotten his threat to stick me on ringcurb, but Huffy was not dumb, he knew something was wrong with Dave. I pictured Dave dying in a wardrobe box, or laid out stiff in his bunk when we came in from the show.

Sometime that summer Dave's family came to the show, the sisters and brother, the mom with her second husband. I urged Dave to tell them. He wouldn't. I felt guilty for not telling them that a doctor in Florida had diagnosed intestinal cancer. I never heard the details, though Dave may have told me. I didn't want to know. I don't think Dave did either. He needed to have surgery, chemotherapy, the whole routine. And he might have gone for it but for that night in Venice when I'd hooked up with the show, because there was nothing else, and got Dave a job too and we were living on this white train having the time of our lives. We didn't want to think about doctors and hospitals and dying. Dave wanted to live. He wanted to drink and smoke and travel the country and screw girls.

On traveling shows things vanish and reappear. Passing hundreds of towns, you'd sometimes want to stop and stay someplace. People walked off. Often they were never missed. And when they reappeared, having gained nothing by the experience, your memory of them, which you didn't know you had, was restored in a way that made you wonder if anyone would notice when it was your turn to go down the road.

Raymond and Bertha

Raymond wakes up on the wrong side of the cage, maybe. Maybe he thinks he is playing, he's bored, whatever the reason, he reaches through the bars while waiting for Finale and idly hooks a single protracted claw into the heavily sequined drapery of a showgirl named Bertha. Stiltman sees it and cries out. But he's twenty feet in the air. Then the whistle blows and the band cranks up and the curtainman pushes back the curtain, and the crowd of painted faces surges forward smiling and waving into the spotlights.

Raymond has a special cage with black decorative bars four inches apart so the people can see him. He's been raised by the children of the trainer, he's been inside their trailer, slept on their beds. Raymond is the special Opening and Finale cat because he can be trusted to not do bad things. Bertha screams hard and loud, and strong performers try to pull her back but Raymond is stronger and reels her in, both arms through the bars now, clawing and pulling and shredding the dress until Bertha is pinned with her back against his cage.

Curtainman pulls a knife and tries to cut Bertha free of the dress but Raymond, intrigued now, drives his right foreleg up between her legs and sinks all five claws into the softness just above her pelvic bone and pulls, pulls until he feels her crack. That is the turning point. The point when Raymond marries Bertha. The point that makes this day, and this place, permanent and neverending.

Sigfried Heinemann runs from the track, sees black spotlit blood filling Bertha's shoes, and he yells at the curtainman to shut the damn curtain. He yells, someone call an ambulance. A selfish picture crosses his mind; he is on the phone to the show owner, and he yells gottdammit at the catman who is stabbing Raymond in the eye with a sharp stick. Hilmer runs up with a fire extinguisher and fires it into Raymond's face, the nozzle in his mouth, his ears. Raymond presses his face to the cage floor and screams with Bertha. But he will not let her go.

Probably didn't even know he had her at that point, Hilmer said later. Finally Hilmer shoots Raymond in the head with a gun. The first three chambers of his revolver are loaded with blanks. These are usually enough. Blanks fired into a cat's face will drive the cat back, but not Raymond, not this day. He takes the final three 158-grain wadcutter .38-special slugs into his brain before he relaxes his grip on Bertha.

Raymond rests on his face, his mouth open wide, his four long incisors embedded into the plywood floor of the cage, eyes pinched shut and dusted over. There is no explaining or forgetting some things, so people go on talking about them, until neither the story nor its place can be thought of independently. Raymond and Bertha are buried under fire-extinguisher snow, the whole scene dusted white, except Bertha's womb on the floor between her legs.

Wardrobe

Midway through a grim two-week stand in Chicago's stockyard arena Jimmy King locked himself in a wardrobe box and would not come out. This on a Saturday morning late enough in the season that I had to muster a survival mentality merely to roll from my bunk, get a coffee from the pie car, and trudge across the muddy stockyard to the wardrobe.

Hungover, I skipped practice and wanted to skip the first show, but the pain in Dave's gut was worse since summer. I carried his share of the load. I resented it, but it wasn't his fault. The work was nothing: round up stray shoes, set out hats and gloves, help midgets get dressed. People came in to change, a marching soldier for Opening, a groveling troll for Spec, a charming Prince in the end. For me wardrobe was the place things stayed the same, a slacker's paradise, refuge from the frantic pace of the show. I'd grown comfortable there in the last ten months. But now Huffy had put his size-four foot down. "Ringcurb," he said, "starting tomorrow."

I slipped between the curtains, elbows out, protecting my

coffee cup. The rule was no food or drink in wardrobe, but it was too late in the season to care about rules. I sat on a folding chair sipping my coffee. Dave was speaking to a closed-up wardrobe box. He smirked at me, wiry brown hair ponytailed back, scraggly chin whiskers. He seemed to be having a good day.

"Got any aspirin?"

He jutted his jaw toward the box. "Jimmy King," he said.

"Jimmy's got aspirin?"

"Jimmy's in the box."

So Jimmy was sleeping in a box on Saturday morning. This was not odd. The oddity was the box being locked. Wardrobe boxes, tight canvas over steel frames, were locked only for loadout. They were vaults on wheels, six feet high, four feet wide. A heavy zipper ran down the middle with a suitcase-type hasp at the bottom.

"How'd the box get locked?" I asked. The canvas skin fit tight over the frame and snapped to it along the bottom; if Jimmy popped the snaps he could have pulled the zipper down from inside and slipped the stem into the latch. "Where's the keys?"

Dave pointed to the box. "Jimmy's got 'em."

Tino the Rumanian, from the teeterboard act, came in and laid out his Opening stuff. Dave went over and continued a conversation they'd carried on for months about how Dave would visit Tino in Rumania and they'd go fishing together and Tino would show Dave everything about Rumania. They had every detail planned, where Dave would sleep, what they would eat, where they would fish, what sort of hooks they would use, the fish they would catch, how they would cook the fish, how the fish would taste. Total bullshit.

Boris, a teen-ager from the Bulgarian riding act, came in carrying his lunge whip, spread his bathrobe on the table and stretched out on his back. He wore red nylon underpants and white soft-soled riding boots. He couldn't keep his hands away from his crotch. Said a town girl did him all night long. He talked like that, using expressions he heard on American TV: "She do me all night long, man." More bullshit.

Sure, we had it easy in wardrobe, but sometimes the bullshit made me feel like beating someone over the head with a shoe.

Old Swede shuffled in, baggy undershirt, boxer shorts slung to his knees, no clown shoes. Everyone said, "Morning, Swede." Swede never said anything. He went to his spot and stood scowling in scant whiteface powdered over greased wrinkles with barely visible black laugh lines stemming from each eye. His unpowdered baldhead gleamed green under fluorescent lights hung between steel I-beams overhead. He had a Pall Mall wedged behind one ear. My grandmother had smoked Pall Malls, the long unfiltered ones that came in a red pack, and that's why I liked Swede. His hands reminded me of hers: thin leather skin, old yellow index fingernail thick as a bird beak. His red wig was built into his hat, which he put on after I helped him into his Humpty Dumpty suit. The costume had a number of flexible plastic hoops sewn into the fabric to make Swede, who was a stick figure, appear to be the shape of an egg. Swede walked over to the mirror, pressed a red rubber nose to the center of his face, pulled the cigarette from behind his ear, stuck it unlit between his white lips, and shuffled out.

"Sixty years on the road," I said to Dave. He shrugged his shoulders, gave me his hey-what-can-you-do look. That's what worried me. What could we do?

My head ached. I went over to the locked wardrobe box and slapped the side. "Jimmy King," I said, "you've got twenty minutes."

Oaks and Rulfo walked in. Oaks carried a copy of *The Lord of the Rings*. Rulfo yelled "Yo!" and fired a red, white, and blue basketball at Dave who caught the ball, beat it once on the floor, and hooked it into the plastic trashbarrel. They went one on one, pounding around the table, slamming the ball into the trashbarrel. Dave looked like he did when he played basketball in high school, before we turned to dope and rotgut.

Oaks held up the Tolkien book that I'd loaned him. He grinned and shook it in my face. "This book, man! This book!" Oaks and me were into books then: Herman Wouk, Taylor

Caldwell. We read anyone who wrote fat books. We spent days sitting in wardrobe on folding chairs lost in other worlds. When we weren't reading we were talking about reading. Dave never read anything. The horse guys read Louis L'Amour. Jimmy King was a periodical reader. *People, RollingStone, Playboy.* Jimmy's girlfriend Shelly, farm girl from Kansas who I was secretly attracted to, carried around *The Prophet* and books by Hermann Hesse. The eastern Europeans read newspapers sent from their homelands. Clowns and showgirls read *Circus Report, Variety, Amusement Business.* They dreamt of moving up: circus clown— movie star. When Oaks said he hadn't read the trilogy I gave him my copy. He was immersed that morning not in basketball but in the world of Bilbo and Frodo; he took no interest in the Jimmy King barricade.

"Got aspirin, Oaks?"

He headwagged me over to his reading corner, slipped a half-pint of Christian Brothers from his shirt. "Starting fluid" he called it. I unscrewed the cap, took a gulp, handed it back while Dave relayed the King situation to Rulfo, and he began jabbering at Jimmy in the box. The Wheels were on early in the show so they wore their spangled basketball stuff for Opening.

Outside the wardrobe, Siegfried Heinemann stalked the halls calling, "Ten minutes! Ten minutes!" Six clowns clomped in smelling of baby powder. They wore boxer shorts, T-shirts, and giant leather shoes that they called "beavertails."

A clatter of female voices came over the top of the boxes from ladies' wardrobe. Boris got up from the table and began cracking his whip. He knew the voices came from girls in various stages of undress. Five minutes before the whistle a half-dozen unicycle guys came in, hooked up with Rulfo, and yelled at Jimmy to get out of the box. Dave beat the basketball against the floor. Oaks held the book to his face. Someone said TC was coming down the hall.

TC acted as spokesman for the Wheels; he dealt with Heinemann, levied fines for being late, and reprimanded those who were deficient in the act. But he had problems with Jimmy King because it was Jimmy's father who had started the troupe of basketball-playing unicyclists on the streets of Harlem. Jimmy secretly wanted to quit the act and become a radio disc jockey. He had the voice for it and entertained us with impersonations of radio personalities. He did Murray-the-K, Wolfman Jack, the Greaseman. He did an ace copy of Heinemann's heavy German accent, and a cruel parody of show manager Louis Morgan's condescending voice. But Jimmy refused to play the role of boss so the job fell to TC. When he walked in, everyone backed away from the box. TC was taller and blacker than the other guys and when upset would talk lower and lower, each word the click of a spring cranking down. TC figured all workingmen for bad news and we were wary of him. He squatted by the box and spoke to Jimmy.

Exactly eleven o'clock Heinemann blasted his whistle, the band cranked up, and Opening began without Jimmy King. TC got up scowling and everyone followed him out. Dave went for a smoke so I pulled a chair to Jimmy's box. I heard him rustling around, shifting his weight. "Jimmy," I said. "Hey, Jimmy. You doing your act?" I don't know why I thought he would talk to me. He hadn't said a word to TC. But what did it matter if he talked to me? I was nobody. A wardrobe guy who wanted to be a wire-walker who was sort of a friend of his girlfriend.

"You know how many times I've done that act?" he said. "Straddled that damn bike?"

"No idea."

"I get paid for ten shows a week, fifty weeks a year. That's five hundred shows a year. Know how long I've been on this show?"

"No."

"Twelve years. That's six thousand shows. You know what it's like? I circle the ring twenty times every show. That's a hundred twenty thousand circles. I'm worn out. I'm a dizzy rat. For what?"

"Money, I guess."

"I'm twenty-seven. Been here since I was fifteen. What's that worth?"

"Beats hanging around New York."

"Shit. I got no home in New York. Those people think I'm a freak. They say, 'Jimmy King got hisself some fine circus pussy.' They don't know me and I don't know them."

On the floor next to the box were Jimmy's famous python boots. The boots reminded me of when Jimmy and Shelly and I went overland with Dean the clown. That was after Shelly dumped her boyfriend, a horse worker from Kansas, and before she hooked up with Jimmy. At the time, I saw myself as one of her possibilities, which was probably never the case. I'm not sure where we were, maybe California, but we stopped at night to walk in the woods. We'd smoked a boatload of pot and the moon was covered with clouds. I recall Jimmy among the trees, glowing in his metallic-silver leather jacket, a pair of double-knit bellbottom trousers, and the python boots—wooden platforms four inches high. Dean was from upper Michigan so he wore woods clothes. Shelly and I wore the uniform of the day: army field jackets, patched bluejeans, beat-up sneakers. Jimmy was having a hell of a time walking over the rough ground in his platforms. He tripped over roots, fell into us, knocked his head on limbs, and all the time he kept calling the woods "nature." Said how "connected" he felt to "nature." How he'd like to stop and take up residence. "Like, really get into it, you know what I mean?" We knew. But we didn't laugh at Jimmy King, in fact, that may have been the moment Shelly fell for Jimmy, or just the moment I noticed the smile on her face when she looked at him.

"You and Shelly get into a fight, Jimmy?" I asked. He didn't answer, which made me think I was on to something, something that started my foot tapping, that got me up and moving. They may have broken up altogether.

The music switched to the Cossacks. I stood back as people swarmed in from Opening, dropping coats and hats onto the table, grabbing hangers, kicking off shoes, jabbering in a dozen languages. Prince Paul pushed through to me; I took his Mad Hatter hat, his tiny coat and pink trousers with elastic suspenders. He turned to go but Heinemann and the Wheels stormed through the curtains with TC and Heinemann shouting a head above everyone else. I was afraid for Prince so I pushed through the horde with my arms over Prince's head. "Let Prince out, let Prince out." Down at knee-high Prince slapped his way through a forest of thighs and shinbones.

Heinemann yelled "Vadrobe!" Grabbed the front of my jumpsuit. He'd been a bear trainer for years and had come to resemble one. "Gottdamn you guys." Whatever went wrong in wardrobe was our fault. "Going to be down the gottdamn road," he bellowed.

Strictly speaking, Heinemann was in charge of the performance and had no authority over workingmen even though it took about fifty of them to run the performance. What enraged him was that we'd lost control of the box keys. His problem was not that Jimmy missed Opening, that's a fifty-dollar fine and no big deal, but Jimmy was in danger of missing his own act which is a five-hundred-dollar fine and screws up the show. Not that Jimmy couldn't afford the five hundred bucks, performers were well paid, it was the idea of it. There was no excuse for missing your act. People did it; they got sick, hurt, thrown in jail. But when it happened the doer was always subject to ridicule and scorn. TC produced a jackknife and stabbed a hole in the top of the box. He was attempting to cut Jimmy King out. Heinemann let me go and started arguing with TC about the box.

"Fuck the box!" TC yelled. "How we going to do our act?" They had ten minutes to plan the act without Jimmy King. They pushed out through the curtains.

Heinemann shook his fist at Dave and me. "One more thing, you guys are down the gottdamn road."

Oaks rose grinning from his reading corner, took a hit off the Christian Brothers, bounded across the wardrobe shouting, "The

King's in exile, Frodo! Storm the castle!" He sent the curtains flying as he ran out.

"Who's Frodo?" Dave said. We heard Heinemann down at clown alley blowing his whistle and shouting for the clowns to get a walkaround together to give the Wheels more time. The music switched from the raucous Cossacks to the melodious handbalancers. Dave was showing signs that his good day was crashing. He slowly gathered coat hangers, kicked shoes to one side, set out costumes for the next number, then collapsed onto one of the folding chairs. "Who the hell is Frodo?" he said again.

My head pounded. I went over to Oaks's reading corner and rifled for the bottle under the book. I took a sip, eyeballed Dave bent over, holding his stomach. I stuck the bottle back. "I'm going to find Shelly," I told Dave and went through the curtains.

Shelly was a beautiful butcher; seller of plastic rayguns and astrolites, blond girl from Kansas, and lover to black man from Harlem Jimmy King. She ran the seats in a candycane smock for Pierre who was envied by his fellow joint operators because he had a girl who could move souvenirs. Pierre had already heard about King in the box. "Where is she?" I said. "Did they get in a fight?" He stood counting crinkled currency behind a table surrounded by inflated Dumbos, balloons on sticks, programs, and coloring books. "Got any aspirin?" Pierre kept counting.

I went through the doors to the arena and scanned the seats from the third tier. The old cow smell wafted up from the acres of pens below the building. Down on the floor Tino and his teeterboard family pounded through their routine in full house lights. The band blasted cannonball music as small men and women rocketed head over heels from heavy seesaws into space above the ring landing on the shoulders of their compatriots. The Saturday morning house was mostly giveaway seats: state hospitals, homes for the physically or emotionally impaired. They were lined up in wheelchairs on the cement among the thick cables and light boxes in front of the first row of seats, close to the rubber track where the clowns could get at them. In the shadows of longmounted elephants they lolled at the ceiling with their tongues out, their eyes wilder than the horses', their handlers propping them up and wiping drool from their mouths.

I spotted Shelly on the second tier, one section over, straw-colored hair covering the back of her smock, smiling sweetly—innocence was her gimmick—passing astrolites and rayguns to the kids, the mother shaking her head *no*. The mother's mouth moving, *no*, her head sawing side to side, *no*, her palm out in front of her purse. *No!* But the toys were already in the sticky hands of her kids, and they pulled the strings and triggers and pointed the guns at their mother's head daring her to take them. Shelly had her victory sign fingers in the woman's face: "Two dollars, ma'am, just two dollars each." The woman shook her head *no* even as she unsnapped her purse. Who could resist that cream and corn look?

Shelly slipped the money into her smock and moved up the concrete steps. I intercepted her at the top of the section. We stood on the landing and shouted over the music. "Jimmy," I said. She touched my lips with her index finger. The music switched to walkaround as the clowns appeared. Heinemann stood at the backcurtain, arms crossed, whistle in mouth. He blew it after the clowns circled the track, then the curtain was drawn back, and the spotlights picked up the New York Wheels on their unicycles. We stood close enough that I felt the heat of her arm against my elbow. The ringmaster was screaming, ". . . from New York City!" as the riders burst into center ring and into their rigmarole with the red, white, and blue basketball bobbing among them. There were two hoops with glass backboards on poles, and the riders flew in liquid patterns around the ring, juggling the ball to one another and periodically sinking it through the hoops. Then a pass hit Oaks in the chest and dropped to the floor and the flow sputtered while the ball was retrieved and set back in motion. We saw their mouths moving, yelling at one another, pumping around the ring as fast as regular people might go on a two-wheeled bike. I watched Shelly's pale profile in the dusky arena light. I felt the spot where she'd touched my lips with her finger. They finished, standing on the ringcurb, an empty space in front where Jimmy usually stood. The whistle blew, the lights went out, and Shelly took my arm. We went into the hallway where we could hear. "Got any aspirin?"

She shook her head, as if in despair. "Shouldn't eat aspirin. Terrible for your stomach."

"Drank in the pie car till 4 A.M."

She gave me a scornful look and recited, "I wake at dawn and give thanks for another day of living."

"I wake at noon and clamp my mouth to the crusty water spigot," I said. She studied me with pity, not fooled by my cockiness. "Need to get Jimmy out of the box," I said. The look of despair again, the shrugging of shoulders, shaking of head. "Did something happen between you two?" I tried to sound concerned, not hopeful. We strolled in front of Pierre's stand.

"Did Jimmy talk to you?" Shelly asked.

"He's having some kind of identity crisis. Must have a calculator in the box with him. Was whining about how many shows he had to do."

Pierre knew how I felt about Shelly and interrupted us. "How many you sell, Shelly?" he yelled. "How many lights? How many guns?" She ignored him.

"I thought you might know something," I said to her.

"I found this great restaurant and took Jimmy there."

"Name?" Pierre said.

"Earth's Garden," she said, and Pierre rolled his eyes.

"Healthy food," she said. "Cool people."

"Rabbit food," Pierre said.

"Jimmy just sat there," she said. "It was embarrassing. Wouldn't eat anything. Kept saying he wanted to go to Arthur Treacher's Fish and Chips."

"So," Pierre said, "what's wrong with that?"

"He eats there every day! Like he's hooked on Arthur Treacher's Fish and Chips."

"You had a fight about food?" I said.

"Hey, I'm trying to clean up his system. The man is full of mucus, that's why he's upset, he's not well balanced."

"I'm just asking," I said. "What happened after that?"

"I wouldn't go to Arthur Treacher's. We argued in the cab and by the time we got back to the building we were screaming and he got out and ran."

"Man has a right to eat what he wants to eat," Pierre said.

Shelly shook her head, her gray eyes staring, like she wanted to give up and go back to Kansas. That scared me. I didn't mind the notion that she might dump Jimmy, but I didn't want her to blow the show. "The important thing is to get him out of the box," I said.

Shelly agreed to come down after intermission and talk to Jimmy. I knew she wouldn't go back to Kansas, to her old boyfriend the horse guy. She might dump Jimmy, but she'd move on, and it wouldn't be to me. She'd passed me on her way to Jimmy.

My head throbbed as I walked back to wardrobe. Nothing had changed. The box was shut tight. Oaks read in his corner. Dave curled up on the table. Old shoeguy rummaged around for heels to replace. Hats and gloves lay everywhere. I picked up a hanger and the tiny pants of Prince Paul's Mad Hatter outfit and hung them on the outside of a box to dry. Prince had very short legs and sweated a lot. I was having one of those desperate hangover moments when quiet and loneliness converge upon you with increasing gravity until you feel yourself pressed so firmly down you cannot move one foot in front of the other. What the hell was I doing in this hiding place, this changing place? The truth was heavier than hangover: I had no place to go.

Oaks jumped three feet in the air with the book in his hand. "Frodo!" He was grinning like a fool. "You're it, Frodo." He came over and wrapped his arm around my neck. "The more I think about it the more you remind me of Frodo. That's got to be your name."

"Who's Frodo?" Dave said, struggling upright.

"Him!" Oaks said, pointing at me. "He's Frodo."

I shrugged Oaks off and moved away. For some reason it disturbed me to be identified with Frodo, who was basically a bungler, tripping through life from one accident to the next. Nobody wanted to be at the mercy of his or her own life. Everyone wanted to be Gandalf: powerful, in control. For a moment I saw myself as I was, caught and named, hanging up the smelly clothes of a midget.

People drifted in to get dressed for Spec. Everyone was in Spec. Flyer Lalo Cadonna had a brief appearance as the beast that turned into a prince. He wore a fantastic silver and turquoise costume with a hideous beasthead that fit over his entire head. The mask was made of lightweight fiber-mesh, brown and gray, the face misshapen like a large clump of clay beaten with a baseball bat, yellow fangs protruding from the yawning mouth, a furious brow above the eyeslits, the top and back hung with snakes. Lalo came in all smiles and spoke to the room at large in perfect English with only a slight Mexican accent. He talked to Jimmy in the box: "Jimmy. My Man. What are you doing in there, Jimmy? That's no way to get a raise, Jimmy." He flashed his teeth at everyone and winked.

Old Swede shuffled in scowling. Dave sat on the table looking clammy. Prince Paul was one of the seven dwarfs along with midget Larry who had achieved notoriety by getting himself pictured on the cover of a rock album. There was also Minno, billed as the smallest man in the world, who, by that elite designation, was not reduced to playing dwarfs. He had his own smallest man in the world suit. Minno was Hungarian and hung out with his countrymen who happened to be unusually large people. They came in together, two seven-foot guys and Minno at thirty-two inches. One of them carried Minno since he had trouble with crowds. They were good-humored people, big wine drinkers, very loud, and they hated Boris. Called him "gypsy motherfucker" in English. One of the Hungarians, an ex-boxer named

Nasho, yelled that we should give Jimmy King the "pizza treat-ment." Everyone roared with laughter. "We stick a hose up Dave's ass, put it under the box." Dave had the foul habit when wardrobe was packed of cutting huge farts and yelling, "Pizza!" People would scatter half dressed through the curtains.

When they were gone, Spec music playing, Dave crashed on the table. I sat with my ear to the zipper listening to Jimmy. "People have no life beyond this show. Undress dress, go out, do tricks, undress dress. We're maze rats. Windup toys. Heinemann blowing that fucking whistle, pushing people around. What kind of life is that? What motivates that man?"

Because Jimmy seemed to be talking to himself, or because he was invisible, or because it seemed anything good was impos-sible, I said, "You know what, Jimmy? I figured to be going out with Shelly by now." It was risky. Jimmy could be dangerous. I'd seen him almost kill show manager Louis Morgan who didn't even speak to workingmen and who, after twelve years, had not accepted the idea of black circus performers. Morgan said some-thing Jimmy didn't like and he exploded onto Morgan's body and would have throttled the man to death if half the Wheels hadn't pulled him off. But Jimmy had a druglike, tongue-loosening effect on me. One time I said to him, "Good thing about being black must be that nobody can tell when your hands are dirty." He smiled sadly at that, said someday he'd show me when his hands were dirty.

"Shelly's a good person," Jimmy said. "We wouldn't be together anywhere but here."

I wasn't sure what he meant so I said, "It's not bad here."

"You like making ninety bucks a week? Living in the caravan car? Having assholes scream at you? It's a trap. I came here when I was a kid, now I can't leave."

"You make good money. You work an hour a day. What do you want?"

"I want a place where nobody knows me. I want a house, mailbox, regular trash pickup."

"You're just burned out. End of the season bullshit."

"We keep on here, they won't know where to bury us when we die."

I looked at Dave stretched out on the table. The Spec music heightened to a climax. I saw Shelly's blond head between the curtains. No telling how long she'd been there. I waved her in. She looked embarrassed to be in men's wardrobe. "Not working intermission?"

She shrugged, whispered to the box. "Jimmy?" Looked at me. "Can you open it?"

"He's got the keys."

She pressed her cheek to the canvas. "Jimmy?" The keys dropped through the crack at the bottom just as Spec ended and the ringmaster announced a fifteen-minute intermission.

We heard them coming down the hall as I unlocked the box and pulled up the zipper. Shelly looked like she was about to run but voices were just outside the curtain so I grabbed her arm and pushed her into the box, downed the zipper, and pocketed the keys. The curtains flew open and a herd of men elbowed in. Lalo strolled with his beasthead, tossed it to me, slipped off his costume, and threw it on the table where Dave slept through the racket.

It was quiet backstage during intermission. The musicians climbed down off the bandstand and smoked pot in the bathroom or grabbed a bite to eat. In wardrobe Oaks sat with the book in front of his face. Dave slept on the table. Jimmy and Shelly were talking in the box. I walked around picking up things and putting them down, bent up a couple of coat hangers, peeked through the crack between the curtains. I saw Heinemann push his way to the front of the food line at the pie car junior. Then I heard the zipper and turned to see Shelly looking at me. "He wants out," she said.

"Don't we all."

"What?"

"Go now, the coast is clear, vamoose, beat it, don't come back."

I raised the zipper and handed her Jimmy's python boots. His feet came up one at a time, brown socks, dark hands pulling on the boots, zipping them up the back. He leaned from the box and spotted Lalo's beasthead on the table. "Give me that."

"What?"

"That head," he said, "give me the head."

"Like no one will know you in those boots."

"Just give it."

To keep him moving I handed over the head. "It's not going to change you into anything," I said.

He gave me a look and slipped it on. "You never know," he said, then added, "Frodo."

I saw his eyes through the eyeslits of the beast. He was smiling. He emerged platforms first, wrinkled clothes, a leather totebag on the shoulder of his silver jacket. Oaks glanced over the top of the book. "The King! From his rampart of canvas." Jimmy moved toward the curtain.

"Can't leave with the head," I said.

"I'll bring it back."

"Let's go," Shelly said, pulling his arm. They moved through the curtains and down the hall with me at their heels afraid to lose sight of the beasthead. We passed a couple of Bulgarian girls, a herd of showbrats, a building man. At the freight elevator, which went down to the stockpens, Jimmy pushed the button and the doors banged apart.

I held my foot against the door so it wouldn't close. "Come on, Jimmy, I have a headache, give up the damn head."

"You want aspirin, Frodo? I've got aspirin." He opened his bag and rummaged around but couldn't find any. "Just get in," he said. So I did. The doors rolled together and the elevator lurched down and we got off in the pens where it was dusty and quiet and the smell of old cow much stronger than above. Jimmy set his bag on the dirt floor and hunted for the aspirin. Shelly smiled her milky smile and shrugged her sloping shoulders. We both looked at Jimmy and I reached out and took hold of the beasthead and he slid from under it holding an aspirin bottle. "How many?" he said. He was talking to me but looking at Shelly.

"Six." He dumped them into my hand. I held the beasthead under my arm and downed two aspirins, swallowed them dry, as we walked up a cement ramp into the stockyard. The day was overcast white and the wind jolted us like waves. They hung onto each other as they turned to cross the yard, headed toward the train. I had no reason to go that way. Their squabble of the night before would provide, I imagined, an opportunity for special making-up sex. The kind that might go on all afternoon. The kind that made you believe in permanent changes. Jimmy would shake his end-of-season blues. He might even try tofu.

"Later, Frodo," Jimmy said. He had his arm around Shelly, and she had both arms around his waist. They were smiling like everything was fine and that's the last I saw of them.

I had four aspirin in my hand and a beasthead under my arm and not a thing in the world to do. I entered a red brick building adjoining the arena, a shortcut to the street. In the lobby stood giant stuffed bulls. Bulls of all types: Longhorn, Angus, whatever types there are. Testicles hanging to the floor. On the walls were long black-and-white photographs of the stockyard in days past when it was mobbed with cows and rail-cars and cattlemen with old black trucks and dusty Negro farm help. Another world gone.

I walked out the front door and across the street to a bar. There were two workingmen down the end of the bar, arrogant grizzled bullhands. I ordered a draft. The bartender eyed the beasthead. I swallowed two more aspirin with the beer, stashed the remaining two in my pocket, ordered two hard-boiled eggs that I ate doused with hot sauce. My headache was buzzed over by beer so I imagined I felt better. I imagined I wasn't in a puke-stinking, old cow dirt, stale-beer-cigarette-butt-smelling dive with nowhere to go. The bullhands looked at me and looked away when I looked at them. Those two had been around since the tent days, part of a clique of old-timers, nothing but winos who looked down on everyone. They were bums who had outlived the hobo age, and they irritated me the way they walked around as if they belonged someplace. Was I afraid of seeing myself in twenty years? A ringcurb man, shoveling shit for the masses, old Huffy waving a cane and yelling *Move yer butt!* The next time the old bums looked over to see if I was looking at them, I said, "You guys got your burial plots picked out yet?" They looked away.

I finished the beer, scooped up the beasthead, and walked out onto the sidewalk. A bus lumbered by belching blue smoke, grinding off toward downtown. Chicago was the last big town before winterquarters. I'd hoped to make it to collect my season's-end bonus. "Survivor's pay," they called it, but it was really sucker's pay because there were no shows for eight weeks and they put you to work at half wages scraping props, painting wagons, steelwooling elephant tubs. No time for wire practice, no reading, plenty of shit shoveling. Actual labor of the type I didn't want and doubted Dave would survive.

I put on the beasthead and stood at the curb. Hidden inside the beasthead my head felt better than it had all day. Maybe I could change into something. I stuck my thumb out at a car, a family: Mom and Dad, two kids in the backseat. They slowed, gawked, zoomed off. I had most of my pay in my pocket. Stuff in my bunk was all crap, a few fat books, some ratty clothes. Only thing I wanted was my wire and I couldn't carry that with me. I walked away from the building toward downtown which was across the south side. Not a safe place. But I wasn't afraid of places. I was afraid for Dave, but not afraid to walk away. Without me Dave would go home and get the help he needed. I was afraid to be on ringcurb. I was afraid of Huffy. I was afraid of big things. But if I could walk a highwire I could walk through the south side of Chicago. I'd learned from Jimmy King once when we were playing New York how to walk in Harlem without being mugged. "Act nuts," he said. "Rant and rave, stagger and shout, wave your arms around." But I didn't have to act nuts that day in Chicago. I was torn crazy leaving the only place I'd ever loved, a place I had to leave to come back to. And besides, nobody messes with someone walking the streets in a beasthead.

In a Weird Head

Outside at night on Lake Michigan, sliding over the frozen deck, beating back the ice with baseball bats and sledgehammers while the ship climbs and falls, the tyrannical skipper shouting from the wheelhouse—blazing away with a pickax at a stuck-fast boom-house door, rubber raingear neck to toe, a curious misshapen mass as head protection from the razor-edged icechips and sheets of black sleet searing sideways across the deck—raging ice that molds half-inch steel cables into the milky thickness of telephone poles. The cables snap under their own weight. Loose-cannon booms swing out of control, sweeping men from the deck, threatening to drive the ship, listing, tipping, swaying, rocking to the bottom of the freezing lake.

Flung together for work on deck, sleeping in rolling bunks, eating meals in the cold galley; veterans are guys who survive two weeks. A French Canadian is screaming that he will kill anyone who beats him at arm wrestling. Two are new, sitting side by side in the galley. One in a weird head does not arm wrestle. A big Iowa farmboy says he'll take the challenge. He wins and the French

Canadian pulls a .44-caliber revolver from beneath the table and shoots him in the center of his forehead. I warned 'em, the Frenchman says.

The bloodgray grit of the kid's head is splattered among the fjords and gullies of the mask's fake gore. Carried at arms' length outside on deck, overboard it goes. The ship is a place you prove yourself by violence or other means. Back in the galley ready to kill anyone who can walk the boomline from the winch on deck to the top of the boom. There are no takers. Crazy new guy, no one can do it.

The night is calm, too cold for snow, the galley-stove-warmed boots are soft, pliable, almost sticky. Bets are made. Skipper holds the money. The inclined cable tightened down with a ten-ton Sealand container is a mild angle, thirty-five degrees maybe. They don't know anything about circus. They don't know anything. The boom sways slightly with the ship, but it's an easy regular roll. The stars reach from the blackness. The top of the boom is tricky, the boom pole slick, but the feat is done. They all watch from the deck below, and sliding down the boom like a fireman is fun. The backslapping skipper hands over the money, hands over a new job, boss of the night crew. Pay raised and sitting out the winter in the boomhouse running the winch, moving the containers around, telling the men what to do on deck. The game goes down well, beating the elements, and the work, not dying at the hands of chance, or madmen.

When the ship puts into port for refitting, places like Sheboygan, Escanaba, Muskegon, the men vanish. Some will return, some not. Some have proved to no one who matters, save themselves, that cold hardens, that hard work, high wind, rough water, and rougher people temper resolve. And one, who has straightened out his head, still won't take lunatic challenges like betting his life on arm wrestling, but by the time he walks away, lunatics do not challenge him.

Lot

Twenty-eight hours out of Mackinaw City I drove down U.S. 41 in Sarasota in a 1966 Chevy pickup, sky blue, slide-in camper. I was warm, my face out the window, my mouth open. I wanted to eat the sun. A one-ring tent show sat behind a supermarket. I pulled in. They call these mudshows, dog-and-pony shows, ragtops, but it was the first show I'd seen in months. I ran for the tent, slipped under the sidewall, my face on the canvas. I wanted to eat that too.

The first person I saw was Tino the Rumanian. He sat with a towngirl in the bleachers. A skinny guy was in the cage with three old lions, all asleep. The audience slept too. There was no band. A tape recorder on an upended bucket by the backcurtain made the noise and it sounded like it came from under water. The lion guy walked out of the cage, no bow, no styling, just walked out switched off the tape and that was the end.

"Hey, wardrobe man!" Tino pointed at me and shouted. He had one arm around the towngirl. "I know that guy," he told her. "Hey, man, shit! It's Gary, right? I know you, man." I walked over and we shook hands. "Shit, man, what you doing here?"

"Saw the tent, pulled in. You?"

"Shit, man, been here two months. Got my green card, man."

"Green card."

"Shit, yeah. I'm a waiter, man."

We went to the nearest bar. Towngirl drove Tino in her hatch-back. Tino ordered pitchers of beer and chainsmoked.

We'd been acquaintances at the show, but here, on neutral ground, we were two guys who missed the show. We'd both quit in Chicago. "I was stupid, man. This Betty I met, she say she love me, say we be married." Tino called all girls Betty. He wanted to stay in America, and with the season nearly over he tried to marry so he could become a citizen. Didn't work. The Betty was thrilled with Tino as a performer but less so after he quit. "Shit, man, I am now without protection in this country." After she dumped him he went to Mexico with Rodrigo the butcher to practice a highwire act. "Shit, it was bad, man, you can't believe the way they live."

"So you came to Sarasota."

"Where else?"

I said I was driving to Venice to see if I could track Dave, maybe get a job at winterquarters. Tino said the show had already pulled out, said Dave lived in a house on Third Street, they'd planned to go fishing. I left Tino with the girl. He didn't know I'd been practicing the wire. Something told me not to mention it. That night I parked my camper under the Longboat Key Bridge, a fishing spot where the cops wouldn't bother me, and the next morning I drove downtown. There were two rooming houses on Third Street. Dave was on the first floor of a house run by the ancient May-Lee sisters. It was a two-story white stucco place. In a sitting room at the front I saw two old ladies watching TV. I drove around back where the tenants parked and entered a rubber-tile hallway. It was quiet as I moved toward the front of the house. I passed closed dark-stained doors with glass handles. A door on the right hung open, the bathroom. I stuck my head in, big clean porcelain sink on a pedestal. A door opened behind me and Dave walked out in his socks and undershorts. "Figured you'd turn up sooner or later," he said.

"Hey!" I said. "What the fucking hey?"

We stood in the dim hall light grinning. I felt like throwing my arms around him just because he was still breathing. But we didn't do stuff like that; a pat on the shoulder, a variety of handshakes, that was it. The other was understood. He knew that I knew there was something tentative about him even standing there. I was glad to see what was left of him wasn't that bad. Dave had always been long and thin, but now he was bones with pale film draped over them, his head covered with peach-colored fuzz. "Completely bald a month ago," he said. "Better now." Dave had made it to the end of the season and collected his bonus. Dave was a survivor.

We went out to look at my truck and I told him about Lake Michigan. Something happened there, wasn't sure what, something to clarify things. I'd carried the show with me through the winter, wanted to be back on the show, but not like before, not a wardrobe boy. I was just playing then, hiding in wardrobe, playing at work, playing at practice. On the lake I came to understand what Rudy meant by *If you're serious go to Sarasota, put in a year*. I knew I must find within myself how much work had to be done. So here I was, not quite admitting to being *serious*, but not quite Frodo the Wardrobe Boy either. I knew instinctively what I couldn't explain to Dave. I told him about the money I'd made, showed him the gun I'd taken off a French Canadian. He said he just started working at a salvage yard. "I go to the doctor a lot," he said.

I took to parking my camper on the crushed-shell parking lot behind the house and using the shower. The May-Lee gals were too old to argue about it. They liked Dave because he was a handyman, fixed their toaster or TV antenna. Whatever broke Dave rigged it, and the old ladies gave him a break on rent. I went to the unemployment office and began collecting seventy-seven dollars each Friday.

Against the back of the house hummed a big green refrigerator used by an old carp catcher who lived upstairs. An orange
extension cord ran up the side of the house to his window. The
man lived on carp. Walked off with his rod and tackle each
morning. Every evening fried carp, baked carp, smoked carp on
a barbecue grill. Dave and me ate ham and cheese, flat packages
we swiped from the supermarket. The carp catcher let us have a
spot on the door of the refrigerator, but the ham and cheese took
on a carpy taste. "Garbage fish," Dave said. We kept our beer in
a cooler, and when we couldn't afford ice we'd use frozen carp to
keep the beer cool.

I kept track of Tino, met him as he left work around midnight. He had a good job as a waiter. The boss, a middle-aged
matron who loved his dark European looks and his accent, told
everyone he was French. Tino talked a lot about making a wire
act but had dubious wirewalking skills, big plans, and nothing
more. I said nothing to him about practicing the wire. It was
dangerous to give away too much, better to wait for a clear picture to present itself, then jump in. I let him run on. He had little rigging, no vehicle, not even a place to live. He sponged off
different "Bettys" he picked up in bars. Said he practiced in a
girl's front yard. "What time do you practice?" I said.

"Early, man, around ten."

"Every day?"

"Shit, yeah, man. Got to. Every day early. The only way."

I had nothing to lose by showing up.

The quiet early-morning neighborhood: pastel ranch houses
with carports, shade trees and palms, small sandy yards. In one,
a short rusty half-inch cable stretched over two cinderblocks,
tightened with a turnbuckle. I sat for a while in the truck, no cars
came by, then went and knocked on the door. No answer. I got
my walking shoes from a canvas sack they'd been rolled up in for
months. They were stiff and crusty. There were two plastic lawn
chairs facing the wire, a piece of a cardboard box on the ground
at one end of the cable, white smear of crushed rock rosin, a

short piece of rope hung over the cable. I ground the ball of my foot into the sticky grit on the cardboard, then the heel, and stepped onto the wire. I lurched to one side, overcorrected, went the other way. Then it came back: *arms up, knees bent*. I settled in, going back and forth, smiling as if I were on drugs. The soles of my feet were screaming.

Around noon Tino came out clutching a coffee, a red box of Marlboros, and a lighter. He was barefoot, no shirt, obviously just out of bed but was trying to act like it never happened before. "Whoa," he said. "What happened?" He sat in a lawn chair smoking a cigarette as I worked on my turns, to the right, to the left. The wire was dead, no spring, so I didn't try jumping. "Shit, man, I didn't know you walk the wire," he said.

"Started back at the show," I said. He got up went into the house, came back with his wireshoes, sat down and scraped the soles with a short-bristled steel brush. When he had his shoes on we switched places. Tino did a cartwheel on the wire and maybe ten or fifteen jumpropes. That's the way he said it; not "I skipped rope ten times," which is what he meant. If his foot slipped to one side of the wire he'd say he missed his foot, instead of his foot missed. Every time he fell he grabbed the cable with both hands even though he was only a foot off the ground.

Tino said practice anytime, so I bought a jumprope and showed up each morning around seven. This upset Tino's girlfriend. She went to work at eight and did not want to see a stranger walking a wire in her yard. She scowled at my truck parked in front of her house and complained to Tino. After a week he told me he was moving. "I was sick of her anyway," he said.

Tino was a lucky break for me, he knew a slew of showfolks in town, always had the word on where there was a party or a show to go to. But he could not find anyplace to practice. When he was a kid in Rumania his parents put him in a government-run gymnastics program, then a circus troupe took possession of him for his acrobatic skill, which was how he ended up on the train show. He'd always had caretakers, but now, set free in America, he had no idea how to get anything done. He expected people to give him things. Still, he had worked the wire in Mexico, he knew the popular tricks and how to do them. I figured the way to get Tino to practice with me was to scrounge up a wire and a place to set it up. Dave came through for me. We swiped some cable from the salvage yard, and Dave said a guy he knew had a farm east of town.

The lot was a corner of a field on a no-name dirt road. Barbed wire on listing posts, some docile cows chewing, an old mare that looked like Bullwinkle the moose. There were a dozen loblolly pines, a bunch of white cowbirds, an overgrown sinkhole, and some grapefruit trees. The guy who owned the lot wore a straw hat and rode around on a red tractor and called his place "The Ranch." He thought I was insane to string his trees with cables and spend my days walking between them while he was out working.

I worked ten hours a day in the lot trying to jumprope. I figured if I could get a dozen I'd ask Tino to practice, but jumproping came slowly, the weather grew warm and rainy. Tiny green pinecones replaced the hard burly ones that had fallen from the trees in the winter.

When I had ten jumpropes I met Tino at the hotel and invited him to the lot. I told him I'd been practicing. He asked me if I was trying to make a solo act. He said solo acts were out. What was hot were two-man freestyle acts. "It's like two guys working solo together," he said. "What about rigging?" he asked. I had no idea what was needed. "Shit, man, rigging is expensive, but I know this guy," Tino said, "he say there are rich Bettys who stay at the hotel. You treat them right, man"—here he made a fist movement as if he were plugging something into a wall socket—"they give you money."

"That sounds nice," I said, "but in the meantime, if you want to practice I'm at the lot every morning."

He didn't come right away. By the time he came I was up to

fifteen jumpropes. He said he'd worked years to get to fifteen jumpropes. I did the best jumproping of my life the day he came out. Ten, twelve, then eighteen in a row. "Shit, man," he said. "I might come out here regular, if I can get a ride."

Tino's idea of practice was different than mine. I practiced all day; he practiced at a certain time. "What time tomorrow?" he'd say. I'd have to come up with an exact time like 9:45 or 10:30. By then the grass would be dry and I'd have completed warmup and jumproping. Tino said we needed a wire high enough to practice *catching on*. So I scrounged four ten-foot pipes from the salvage yard, borrowed a drill from Dave, bolted them together to make A-frames. Over these I stretched half-inch crane cable cleaned with engine degreaser. I practiced catching on, practiced swinging around on one arm like a monkey, practiced catching with my legs only, I hung from my toes, stood on my head, my hands, walked on stilts, rode a bike. I practiced everything, practiced all day at the lot, ate grapefruit off the trees, slept in my camper with the door open in the afternoon heat and the flies buzzing in, woke and practiced until dark.

Tino always arrived at the agreed upon time. Sometimes the same girl drove him for a week or two, then a different one. We never declared ourselves partners, or made commitments, but we began working on tricks that Tino had done in Mexico. "We practice one hour," he'd say, pointing to his fat chrome wristwatch. "We do the two-high." He drew a line in the dirt with a stick. That was the wire. I stood on the line holding a long piece of waterpipe. Tino showed me the position, how to stand with my back leg bent into a step, my upper body cocked forward from the waist so he could climb up my back to the shoulders. I was weak and often dropped one shoulder and dumped him into the dirt. His elkhide shoes tore the skin on the back of my neck. "Shit, man," he said, "we got a big job to turn a wardrobe guy into a wirewalker."

One night I picked him up at the hotel. I had Dave with me. "I know where there are some poles," I told Tino. We drove to

Venice, to the winterquarters. Just after the inland waterway I cut the lights and turned onto a dirt road, then into the palmettos. There was no light from the sky, and the bushes lashed the underside of the truck.

When I saw the dark shape I stopped, and we climbed out into waist-high palmettos. "You boys wearing your snakeboots?" I said. We stood in front of a rusted trailer with the wheels sunk into the ground. Dave had a pair of boltcutters but there was no lock. I swung back one of the doors and the hinges screamed and snapped and the door fell into the weeds. I shined a flashlight into the trailer. It was full of six-inch aluminum poles covered with palmetto bugs and spiders. They were thick-walled poles, twenty feet long. We pulled out four poles and tied them onto the roof. We took two sleeves that connected them and two mud-block bases for the bottoms, and drove back to the main road.

"How'd you know about the poles?" Tino said.

"Back on the show I heard Huffy telling Pie Car Bill that there was twenty thousand dollars worth of aluminum sitting here since 1960. Said it was his retirement money. I didn't think about them until you told me what we needed. You know what those poles held up, don't you?" I said.

"Shit, man, the world's biggest tent. There's no way we won't be good on those poles."

I scavenged stuff all over town. Tino had no notion of scrounging. "No one will give us anything," I told him. "If you want something in America, you have to take it." I found old car axles made great stakes, cranes in junkyards had miles of cable on them, and after three months, just about the time we moved the two-high from the line in the driveway to the two-foot wire, we managed to get a makeshift forty-foot highwire set up between the two largest pine trees.

The highwire transformed the lot. People stopped to watch us walk the inclined tailends, which was the one thing we had to practice on the high rigging. Two guys named Zeke and Messina who did a comedy wire act liked the lot and came to practice when they were in town. They brought other people, towngirls to show off for, showgirls to practice with. On Sundays Dave sat drinking beer with the farmer, laughing at the crazy things he saw us doing. Zeke did pratfalls on the ten-foot wire; Messina was the straight guy. Tino did somersaults over cow pies for the girls. I became the king of jumproping, doing more each week, with double jumps and arm crosses. For a while Tino stayed with me—he'd do twenty, I'd do twenty-five—but once I hit fifty he never tried to catch up.

After practice Tino would want me to drive him to the beach or someplace. "I know some Bettys, man, we take them to Busch Gardens, drink free beer." But I wasn't drinking much and wouldn't do anything that interfered with practice. I lived for practice. Who can say why? *You find something and you work on it.* I missed the show and practice was my way back. But I loved the lot too. When I left the lot my legs ached, the tricks rolled over in my mind, I couldn't stand to be anywhere else.

The exceptions, the contradictions, involved Dave. He wasn't drinking much either, the medicine made him sick, but we managed to see Bob Dylan three times when he was into his Rolling Thunder thing. Big band, a dozen players, makeup, disguises, an electric violin. There was a short segment when he took the stage alone, acoustic guitar, single white spotlight, and that old harmonica gizmo, and he looked and sounded so much like he had a dozen years earlier it made me uncomfortable. Because it wasn't a dozen years earlier, because when he sang *times they are a changin'* it seemed obvious and yet not true, it seemed he might be making fun of us, playacting the ghost of something gone. The times weren't changing, they had changed, and there was no going back.

Elaine

When the hot weather came the snowbirds swept up I-75 and the showfolks went with them. Sarasota, the old circus town, became small and sleepy again. If there were parties, or wind of parties, those of us left went sniffing after them.

"Parker Brothers' winterquarters on 41," Tino said, "you know it?" We were in the lot after practice, the high grass clumped around dried cow pies. Tino sat on an empty wooden cable spool near the barbed-wire fence and pulled off his wireshoes sweatsoaked from the hour we'd spent going back and forth. A towngirl waited to drive him away. I knew Parkers'.

"Couple hours jumproping," I said, "I'll be along."

Tino always had the word on parties: A double kegger in Fruitville, open bar at Showfolks in Venice, free food on Siesta Key. That afternoon's bash was in a tractor-trailer truck. Just the trailer part dumped in an open field. The Parkers were on the road in the Midwest but had sent their man back to gut the trailer and turn it into living quarters for workingmen. The showhand, named Dwight, had wired the trailer, slapped plywood on the walls and ceiling, cut some ventilation holes, and fixed a brace of makeshift steps so we could climb inside. There was a boombox on the floor, extension cords running everywhere, heavy sawdust smell, and on a long wooden table some pretzels and chips among the hammers and nails. There were folding chairs and some five-gallon paint buckets to sit on. Against the front wall was a keg in a tub of ice. People stood drinking beer on the steps in the sun, the trailer's double doors swung back and latched. I saw Tino in the doorway talking to a blond girl. He waved me over, and I stepped around the people on the steps and into the trailer. That's where I first saw Elaine Bonnet.

She sat close to the edge of the trailer on a folding chair. Tino introduced me as his partner. It was warm in the trailer. The girls wore bathing suits tops and cutoffs. The guys wore shorts, tanktops, and flipflops. Elaine had on a loose white blouse, short skirt, and a pair of handtooled leather sandals. Her hair was long and sunbleached almost white at the tips. She was very tanned. A hot breeze blew across the field into the trailer and she kept her face turned to it, sipped from a Pepsi can, and listened patiently to Tino's spiel about his highwire act.

"Been practicing long?" she asked. "Do you have an agent?" Elaine was smart, not Tino's type, he soon left us alone. I could tell she didn't think much of Tino, especially his ability to make a highwire act.

"I ran into the guy," I said, "at a mudshow." No response. I tried out my Michigan story on her: *". . . and then this lunatic pulls out a .44 magnum . . ."* She nodded politely, glanced at me like she might be listening. Elaine had grown up on the road. Her father was Sidney Bonnet, famous slackwire comedian. Circus Bonnet was a dynasty in France. Elaine had worked as a rider, a juggler, an aerialist. Her older brother was a well known illusionist and her younger sister did a Hula-Hoop act. Elaine was in town practicing a handbalancing contortion routine on swinging rings.

"My grandparents had a wire act," she said.

"Your family has done everything."

"They've always been showfolks," she said.

She wasn't easy to stand in front of beerless and babbling, so I said I had to get a drink and moved toward the keg and began shoveling down beers. I don't remember how or when the party crashed, but around dusk I remember seeing Elaine's small red car roll slowly across the grass. I knew she was going to practice. She'd told me she worked on the ring act in the evenings. "At a gymnastic school," she'd said, "run by a family friend. A good place to get in shape," she said, "if you're serious." That's what I remembered the next day . . . *if you're serious*.

I wanted to be serious, I thought I was serious, but I didn't really know what serious was. I thought I was serious about practice back at the show when, it turned out, I was just playing. Getting serious was learning to walk again, one step and you think you've got it, but no, there is another step, and one after that. There is walking and then there is walking.

I was vastly taken with Elaine. She was a beautiful girl, cool, but I liked that. And I felt badly out of shape next to Tino who was very fit. So one evening I drove to the gym. It was north of the airport on 301 in an aluminum warehouse. I was nervous walking in there, serious people in action, and started sweating when I saw how little room Elaine had for getting into better shape.

She was on her hands in a pair of wooden rings eight feet off a blue ten-inch mat. She wore a black leotard cut to the hips, a pair of flesh-colored tights, and wristbands. She did not have one of those gymnastic bodies divided fifty-fifty between legs and torso. A half-dozen tiny girls eyeballed Elaine's long bronze legs pushing toward the ceiling. She was at home in the air, like a sleek bronze bird, casually swaying hair tied off to one side of her head. She saw me and let her arms ride out slightly from the shoulders and her body fell belly first toward the floor. Then she piked into the momentum and whipped her body up into the handstand again. That was the first time I saw a giant swing. She swung around twice more then came gliding feet first onto the mat. "So," she said, smiling, patting her face with a towel. "I'm glad you came."

We stretched on the padded floor while the gym girls tumbled around us. We played on the trampoline, worked on handstands on the parallel bars, and swung on the high bar. "That's your place," Elaine said when she saw me swing. "Everyone has a specialty, something their body is built for; you're wiry, whiplike, born to swing." She was right. Since I'd started practicing on the ten-footer I'd fallen in love with the feeling of falling and flying, that rush of dropgut adrenaline that came with losing your balance, grabbing the wire in midair and using the momentum to swing under the cable. "Can you teach me that swinging trick?" I asked.

"Take it slow," Elaine said, "or you won't be walking tomorrow."

I took it slow. A few days, a few weeks. I went to the gym most nights, worked on giant swings, gradually got stronger, more confident. The giants did not come fast, but working out in the gym helped my balance as Elaine said it would. "Center-body fitness," she said, "that's what wirewalkers need." She dug her fingers into my belly. "This needs to be like stone," she said. We'd lie on the floor and do one thousand situps. Ten sets of one hundred in thirty minutes. Elaine could do five hundred without stopping, but I had to stop every hundred to walk around, catch my breath, hold off abdominal cramps.

Elaine had the gym guy give me a pair of leather handgrips. She talked about giant swings as if they could be done on the highwire. When I mentioned that to Tino he said, "Suicide." But Elaine made me think that anything was possible. Soon we began sharing rides to the gym, and soon, we began sharing other things.

I never stayed with Elaine overnight. She lived on a houseboat docked at her parents' property on an inland waterway. Weeknights I'd park my truck at her place, and we'd take her small red convertible to the gym then go back to the houseboat to shower and rock the boat for a few hours. We abused every part of that boat: the floor, the tables, the bathroom, the shower stall, the toilet, the sink, the walls, the furniture. Out on the deck in the dark on no-moon nights we'd crawl naked onto the roof and do it with her parents' house lit up across the yard and the blackwater slapping the sides of the aluminum boat. Her parents were in the house every night watching TV until eleven while we screwed to rock and roll, making as much noise as we wanted, drinking ice water and sweating like greased pigs, and taking showers and doing it over again. We fell together so well in that houseboat, our bodies swollen and battered from the gym, we knew we would be together for a long time.

But I couldn't stay overnight. Elaine was firm about that. "My dad likes to fish while the sun comes up," she said. "Can't have your truck out there." It amazed me that she did that for her father. She was twenty-three years old, it was her houseboat, but she thought enough of her dad to consider the things he saw. I was in love with that idea, never disputing it, wishing in fact that I could show my own father such consideration.

Each night after a half-dozen showers I drove back to the old ladies' house where I parked and slept until dawn, then got up still smelling her and drove to Oberlyns' Diner for breakfast. I'd be out at the lot before the sun had dried the Bahia grass, while the cow pies were steaming, the morning doves coo-cooing. Only then would my head clear of her, and I'd begin concentrating on practice. The warmup sweat tickling as it arrived new and sticky under my chin and down the small of my back while Elaine got up in the houseboat and went about her own practice and old Sid Bonnet fished undisturbed.

Elaine had worked through her childhood at a variety of acts and could perform most circus skills well, and consequently had a difficult time deciding what to do, and a harder time pleasing herself when she did decide on something. This was common among Sarasota showbrats. They'd think of a new act, run it by the old folks, spend a bunch of money on rigging, practice for a year or two, take it on the road only to become dissatisfied almost immediately and return to work on something else. They seemed to be addicted to practice. The accomplishment didn't make them happy, only the challenge of accomplishment. It was building an act that rewarded them. Once built, they abandoned it.

Elaine planned in minute detail the improvement of physical skills, she mapped progression, how many months, the stumbling blocks, how to work around injuries, how best to present the material. Presentation was everything. She made me conscious of my physical presence.

"It's not enough to simply do tricks," she said. "A dog can do tricks. You must project your personality to the people. If they cannot feel you, as a person, anything you do will be second rate."

We watched films of her family working in Europe on shows where the people were close enough to shake her dad's hand, where he held them in his hands every minute of his routine. The aged fisherman, a stout quiet man, balancing on a slackwire on one arm, the people close enough to see the sweat roll off his face. It was nothing like what I'd seen on the train show. That was one kind of circus family, this was another. American audiences stomped and hollered for a motorcycle in a globe because they were used to big loud spectacles. But Elaine showed me there was another level, an older place where the traditional circus family lived.

We didn't practice together. Elaine had her spot down by the water and I had the lot. We came together at night like a couple home from our jobs. We spoke of how practice had gone, celebrating if there was some leap forward, consoling on bad days, and making up for it in the gym where we worked to the point of pain and exhaustion. We were very aware of each other. The scant clothes. The friction of our bodies. Pushing and pulling, stress and release, and the satisfaction that came later in the houseboat. What we took from each other was more than physical. We wanted each other, sex, yes, but also I wanted her life.

I wanted her history and understanding and experiences. I wanted to belong to the circus the way she did. And she must have needed the one thing I had: hunger. I was starved for what she'd had all her life, what was old to her now. She must have seen too many performers like Tino, who worked, performed, but never found the passion for practice. Elaine and I were alike in our approach to practice. And there was the danger. The comfort of practice, the constant repetition, the minute improvements, and a strict routine all had a lulling effect. I was hooked, addicted, to the lot, to the place I knew best. Practice was a safe place like wardrobe had been. A place like home yet not home because practice is not performing, and performing is the reason for practice.

I couldn't have become the person I did in the lot without Elaine. She pushed me into giant swings. Tino said forget about them. "Too hard," he said, "we don't need them." He said the same about Elaine. "We don't need some Betty hanging around on the road, man." Tino knew I'd gone past him on the wire, but that was not something he cared about. He only wanted to be good enough to work; he didn't have the desire to be the best. I would have stayed in the lot many years, maybe forever, if it wasn't for him, because in spite of the fact that Tino couldn't organize two shoes, he talked nonstop to everyone he met about the "big act" we were making.

Lot II

We'd been practicing a year when one morning we sat on the rickety highwire platforms, Tino on one side, me on the other, doing nothing, watching the cows below with their white birds. Across the dirt road in a field the farmer drove up and down on his tractor plowing under dried cornstalks. We watched a cream-colored Lincoln with a tinted sunroof turn off the main road and roll like a ship at sea down the bumpy lane and park next to my pickup. A short barrel-chested man climbed out, hesitated at the barbed wire, pushed down with two fingers on the top strand and stepped over. He came bowlegged and stiff-backed, an old rider, around the cow pies and clumps of grass, pausing to judge where we were, and where he would position himself.

"Hello," he yelled. He stood under the wire not sure whom he should be facing. "Guy Aaronson," he shouted, shielding his eyes from the sun with a business card. "Aaronson Entertainment," he said. "I don't believe I know you guys." He had on a sportcoat, no tie, beige slacks, and two-tone patent-leather shoes, one of which was planted squarely in a mound of fireants. "I'd like to see what you can do," he said.

We climbed down, shook hands, then showed him our act on the ten-footer. We did the opening, sit-down jump, roll jump, headstand with the pole, jumprope, leapfrog, and finished with the two-high and the jump from the shoulders. We had over ten minutes. "You don't need the headstand," Guy said. "It's the jumping that's hot, the leap from the shoulders, that's what all the shows want." He leaned against the grill of his car picking fireants off his socks. We stood on the other side of the fence. He was a new agent from an old show family with connections throughout the business. "I heard you guys have a highwire, some tricks, and that's it."

He was right. We had nothing to go on the road with, no wardrobe, no music, no publicity photos, no connections. All we had was the thrown-together rigging and one old pickup. "Come to my house," he said. "We can talk about work."

Two days later we drove to Guy's house and met his wife. She showed us a closet full of ugly riding outfits like they wore in Europe. "You can have them," Guy said. There was never any doubt in his mind about selling the act. "You guys are too good to not work."

"We're not ready," I said. "The rigging is a mess."

"I can fix that. You know Zerbini the human cannonball? He's my brother-in-law. He'll make anything you need in his machine shop."

Tino nodded his head like mad, saying, "Shit yeah, man." He had no practical solutions to anything, but he'd been ready to go for months. For me there was more at stake. More than just Elaine, who wouldn't go on the road with me. I liked practicing, liked the lot, liked the person I had turned into in that lot. I was building something that worked, something stable, and the idea of leaving it scared me.

"What about one show?" Guy said. He was talking to me now, Tino was sold. "Orlando, on New Year's Day. The Sunshine Bowl, they want a few acts. Just to see how you'll do."

"Shit, man, we do it," Tino said.

"It's too soon," I said.

"We'll drive down the morning of the first," Guy said. "Get a couple of guys to help set up."

I argued but there was no way to win. We'd worked for this, our own sweat had brought us to this point, brought Guy to us. Besides, we needed the money. Guy called the Cannonball and without a penny up front he took an order. A week later we had two aluminum platforms with Plexiglas floors, new stainless steel cables, guy wires, a six-ton chain ratchet, and a new balancing pole. We kept our famous tent poles, cleaning them up with one of Dave's car buffers.

"No trees in a football stadium," I told Tino. "We'll have to drive deadmen."

"Shit, man, I know how to drive a deadman. We used them in Mexico."

"You didn't work in Mexico long enough to become an expert deadman driver."

I bought a twenty-pound sledge and some stakes. Elaine's dad showed me how to pound in the stakes until twelve inches remained above the ground, four stakes in the front as straight as soldiers, two behind with backward slant, then one at the back. A steel bar lay behind the front row, a place to attach the tailend, then all the stakes were half-hitched together with nylon rope so that a solid triangle of earth became an anchor to crank against. Sixty-year-old Sid Bonnet threw this together in his front yard in about ten minutes. Took me two hours to drive one at the lot, but when it was done the farmer was amazed that I could crank six tons against Florida sand.

Tino wasn't interested in deadmen. Since we'd secured the Orlando date he'd missed a few days of practice. A week before the show I met him as he got off work, and we had our first standoff. I told him I wouldn't go unless we did the whole routine at least once on the highwire.

"Shit, man, you sign the paper, you gotta go."

"No," I said, "I don't." It was midnight and we sat in the truck in the parking lot of the hotel. I'd always compromised with him, but at some point, maybe about the time he couldn't keep up with me at jumproping, maybe because of Elaine, I'd gained an advantage. I never said I would do this act no matter what. I said we would practice and see what happened, but I would not wait until the show. I needed to know that what we made could be carried away from the lot.

"Shit, man, it's stupid," he said. "Nobody practices up high. The audience pushes you through." But I didn't trust him, or I didn't trust myself. He backed down and on Christmas Day we were in the lot running through the routine on the highwire.

The day was overcast, cold, cows lying on the wet ground. On the platforms at forty feet a slight breeze felt like a hurricane. The pines swayed and large dried cones thumped to the ground. The problem with performing without an audience is that there is no reason to do it, and your brain never lets you forget that. We scowled at each other across the wire and began walking. We abbreviated the tricks, the jumps short, low, and because it was not the way we practiced them, dangerous. But we did it. I was satisfied, but scared, shivering in the cold. Tino was mad. "We could be killed for what!" He climbed down the ladder instead of walking down the incline, then sat sulking in the truck until I was ready to drive him away.

Before dawn on New Year's Day we drove to Orlando with Zeke and Messina and two pickups full of rigging. Elaine took the day off from practice and drove her car with some girlfriend of Tino's. Guy would be along later.

I asked Dave to come too, because this was a big thing, and because the things that separated us were also the things that brought us together. I worked on the highwire act to get out of town, to get back on the road, to get away. Dave knew that. He and his doctors had their own vocations. Dave was trying very hard to live, and that was a big thing too, and neither of us had any way of knowing if we were winning or losing. Neither of us knew what would happen, but we sensed we were on the brink of changes that would send us on different roads, and that brought us closer than we'd been since we were kids.

We set up along one sideline behind the bench. Tino and I pounded the deadmen while Zeke and Messina put the poles together and attached the cables and guywires. Two of the guy-wires hung from railings in the stands. "We use the Bettys to watch," Tino said, "so the people don't mess with them." The field guywires would hook to a portable stage that would be driven onto the field for halftime.

The rigging was up by noon just as people began coming into the stadium. Guy came to the dressing room and gave us a grand, minus ten percent. He was robbing us but we didn't care. We had other worries. "You guys pull off this show and there will be plenty of money," he said. The dressing room had wooden benches bolted to the floor and gray lockers for football players. Tino and I sat on the benches while Guy hovered around talking about work. "Good money dates," he said, "a week in Saint Louis, two days in Newfoundland, three days in Montreal." He said he would provide unlimited work if we signed with him exclusively. Such a contract meant we were his act. Other agents who booked us would have to split the commission with Aaronson Entertainment. Tino was nodding his head up and down. "We'll think about it," I said.

There were three acts in the Sunshine Bowl, all supplied by Guy, all set to work at once during the halftime show. A girl with an eighty-foot sway pole was on the other sideline, and a troupe of tumblers would pass down the middle of the field between marching bands. Tino worried that it was too much for a first gig: sixty thousand people filled the stadium above us. "Shit, man, you must block everything out, don't look around, stay on focus," Tino said.

I couldn't say much. I took a shower and lay on my back on a bench and waited. Zeke and Messina laughed at us for being in costume two hours before the show. "Don't want to be late," Zeke said. They were good to have around, kept us distracted, kept Guy away from us. He ran around jabbering and sweating.

We waited through the first half of the game. There was a TV in the room, I didn't know who was playing. We warmed up too soon, cooled out, warmed up again. We waited in the damp cement tunnel on the ramp to the field. Elaine waited with me. She did handstand pushups against the wall, looked beautiful in faded blue jeans, white sleeveless blouse, and one of my black warmup jackets. She yawned a lot. "You're bored," I said.

"No," she said.

"My stomach is jumping."

"You'll be fine," she said. "Don't think," she said, "put one foot in front of the other." I walked to the end of the ramp, looked at the stadium full of people, walked back to the bathroom.

"Another two-high," Tino said when I came out. He climbed up and I walked down the ramp, did a couple deep kneebends, then he leaped to a crack in the cement. "When we get up there," I said, "remind me to breathe."

We waited at opposite tailends, kicking the deadmen stakes, jumping up and down. We waited while Zeke and Messina hooked the field guywires to the portable stage. One of the football teams had a longhorn steer for a mascot and he was on his feet. Dave gave our name to the announcer. We rosined our shoes and waited while some guy sang a song with a band, waited until someone said go, then we started up. Two steps, then three, pretty shaky, not breathing well, mouth like sandpaper. I paused, took my eyes off the wire, looked over at Tino. He had stopped to look over at me. We were fine after that. Committed, grinning, I didn't think about where I was going, I just put one foot in front of the other and ended up on top of our famous poles.

I expected a blur. I expected to rush. But that's not what happened. When I got to the top I turned 360 degrees. The stadium was a bowl of paint-dabbed people in red, white, and blue seats, green grass with football lines, and blue sky over all. I felt finally arrived, relieved, comfortable. I wanted to study this place I'd waited so long for, this place oddly familiar. I sucked huge gulps of air, waved to Elaine standing by the guywires, to Dave on the field drinking stadium beer from a paper cup. I looked down into the upturned faces of Zeke and Messina. They looked serious, knowing what would happen if one of us fell. The spotter, if he did his job, was always hurt worse than the faller. Finally I looked across the wire at Tino. He was waiting, and I realized everyone was waiting. If I controlled anything in my life it was the next ten minutes. I could make time go fast, slow, even stop if I simply chose to stand still. The wire stretched thirty feet between us. Marching bands pounded away down on the field. In the seats people clamored for Cokes, hot dogs, a clean trip to the bathroom, yet Tino and I could hear each other clearly. We seemed very close. "Is it too late to back out?" I said to him.

"Shit, man."

We walked toward each other, slowly, so the people would think it was difficult. There was suspense because it was obvious we would meet in the middle and the people couldn't imagine the jump. Tino sat sideways on the wire in front of me, like you might sit on the top rail of a fence, hunched over, legs hanging beneath. I waited, to give the people time to think. I stood there until Tino said, "Ready." Then I leaped, knees pulled to my chest, cleared him by a foot and landed. The wire barely moved. The jump was nothing like the short nervous jumps we'd practiced the week before. I collapsed on my back before the people had time to recover, put my head back so I could see Tino's feet when he stood up. I reached over my head and grabbed the wire with both fists, balanced with my legs. "Ready."

"Ready," he said, and jumped. At the same time I rolled, pulling with my hands, the wire riding over the trapezius muscle behind my collarbone, legs wide allowing space for Tino to jump through. Another trick so easy it seemed unreal, as if we were not on a highwire at all but in a protected bubble, a world not connected to the world below. I knew that was a dangerous feeling so I took extra time sitting up. Tino bounced to the platform. I looked out at the people, they were not pounding or screaming, but I saw some heads watching us, some hands clapping. Tino was wrong about the date being too big. It was so big it was as if we were anonymous. We were a tiny part of a huge event. A small intimate show would have been more difficult.

I started slow with the jumprope, as if a couple of passes were all I could do, tripped up a few times, settled into a tempo, did fifty, a hundred, lost count, speeded up until I heard the people and knew it was for me. Guy was below yelling, "Okay, great, go on in." After a series of doubles I let the rope ride around to the side instead of passing under my feet and I fired it toward the ground. The rope hit a foot from where Guy stood and I hopped to the platform.

"Leapfrog, two-high, and we're out of here," I told Tino.

Technically the leapfrog is the most dangerous trick simply because of where the feet have to travel. On most jumps the feet and body maintain a straight line over the wire. On the leapfrog the feet go out and around the bottom guy. The wire is only five-eighths of an inch in diameter. Once the feet go wandering it's hard to get them back home. The trick looks like play to the audience, but more guys have been hurt or killed doing the leapfrog than any other trick. I felt the slightest breeze just before Tino went for it. He should wait, I thought, but we'd already said "ready" and I felt his steps coming. I knew as soon as his hands hit my back that he was crooked and would land sideways. He cleared me and the balancing pole but turned his feet to one side for the landing and went backwards off the wire. He grabbed it easily as he was falling and swung under. "All right," I said. "Don't worry about it."

He climbed up and walked onto the platform and I followed him in. Guy was shouting, "Good enough. You did it. Come on down."

"Don't listen to him," I said, "the man's a maniac." Tino was shaken by the blown leapfrog. "You'll be fine," I said. I took up the pole and walked out onto the wire. "Don't forget to breathe," I said. He came along behind me and climbed without hesitation and I took the four steps we'd practiced so many times and Tino made the leap to the wire without a problem. He went forward while I backed up and tied the pole to the platform and we walked down the inclines to the ground, which was never the same from then on.

That night we got as drunk as we'd ever been. We got so drunk we had to take a hotel room. Just one room, all of us passed out on the double beds and the floor. Even Elaine had a drink or two and didn't go back to Sarasota until the next day. Tino skipped a couple of days, but I went right back to practice. The farmer was dumbfounded when I handed him a hundred bucks. He'd never asked for money, but he'd endured a lot of traffic on his dirt road. We'd also caused some minor damage to his trees.

Guy bugged us about the contract. We knew he wouldn't want a contract if the act was not good, and being good we might book ourselves. Still, we had nothing but a highwire, which we now owed money on, some lousy costumes, and one dilapidated truck. "Don't worry," Guy said, "I can help with that." I had mixed feelings. The show had convinced me that I was about to embrace something which would change my life, maybe end it, but I wanted more time in the lot. After a week of arguing we went to Guy's house and signed a contract for a year. Elaine urged me to do it. She was being pressured by her family to help her brother who needed a girl to saw in half for the summer. It was the showfolk way when it came to work: lovers often split up, but families stuck together.

True to his word Guy booked us a dozen dates around North America. Three days before we were to leave for the first town Guy drove to the lot in a new one-ton pickup with an overhead rigging rack. "Give me a ride home," he said. When we got there his wife was mad. "Don't worry," Guy kept saying to her, "they won't fall." He co-signed a loan for the truck. If we fell he'd be responsible. As it happened we wrecked that truck driving drunk in Canada. Then Guy showed up with a motorhome under the same arrangement. We burnt it to the ground in Milwaukee. Then he was fed up, and we lived in orange pup tents we bought at K-Mart for twenty bucks. Our fellow performers had Winnebagos, Holiday Ramblers, Airstream buses, while we slept in tents that leaked like hell. It rained everywhere we went. I took to erecting my tent on a slope so the water would drain to one end. In the morning I'd wring out my sleeping bag, hang it somewhere, put on my costume and go walk on the wire. We paid our dues. We made some bucks. And we did not fall.

However many gray hairs we gave Guy that year, we did the most innovative tricks around, his phone rang nonstop and we all made money. He'd call us in building dressing rooms, and I'd tell him we got mugged and they stole his commission. I'd hold the phone up so Tino could hear him yelling, his wife screaming in the background. We missed important dates, got into drunken fiascoes. One long-term contract was ruined when we dropped our rigging into the audience on opening night. It was one of those rainy towns where the ground was saturated. The deadman pulled out and the whole shebang toppled onto an old lady who survived to sue the show. We acquired a reputation as much for our ground exploits as for our wire act. Guy told me show owners would call him up and ask, "How much do you get for those wild men?"

In California Tino was thrown in jail for working with an expired green card. Guy came to fix it. He arrived in time for a big Shrine opening in the L.A. Forum. Much had changed since that day in Orlando when he was yelling for us to come down halfway through. From the platform I saw him standing against a wall wearing a suit and tie and shiny black wingtips. He watched with a parental look, a look of satisfaction. The people were pounding and screaming. When we came down he was smiling, slapping us on the back, beaming. "You guys are a royal pain in my ass most of the time," he said, "but when I watch you work, I forget all about it."

We worked steady that year and near Christmas returned to Sarasota, our contract with Guy about up, and though he tried to hold us, to re-sign us, he knew we'd moved past him. We had offers from many places, and since the best money and working conditions were overseas that's where we were headed.

The day Tino and I got back to Sarasota we drove to the lot. We each had a new truck and trailer by then. I'd given my old blue Chevy to the farmer. We planned to offer the farmer money to let us park and set up on the lot. When we arrived I thought we were in the wrong place. There were a dozen trailers parked there and rigging of various types strung among the pines. The cows were gone. The barbed-wire had been replaced by a white rail fence. The grass was neatly mowed and the dirt road had been graded. Over the entrance to the lot a sign with screw-in lightblubs said Circus City Trailerpark.

We pulled in. A Mexican guy came over and said he was "the manager." Said he owned the highwire that ran between the two biggest pines. He knew who we were, knew the tricks we did, where we'd been working. He said we could use his wire, or if we preferred, he'd move it.

"Not necessary," I said.

I found the farmer sitting in an air-conditioned trailer watching TV in the middle of the day. "They came after you left," he said. "At first I turned them away. But they wanted to pay to practice here. Called it the Tino Brothers lot. Offered money to park their trailers." He shrugged his shoulders. "Lot of changes," he said. "Had to have the zoning people out here." He smiled. "Hey, I was getting too old for farming anyway."

We took a spot down by what used to be the sinkhole. The farmer had employed Dave to clear the weeds, scrape the edges clean, and fill it with water. Everyone called it "the lake." I set up the ten-footer near my trailer and tried to recapture the momentum I'd known previously in the lot. It had been hard to practice on the road; often dates were short and there was no time to set up a low wire. I'd lost ground, lost that comfort in routine I'd enjoyed at the lot.

Elaine survived getting sawed in half all year and came to stay with me. We went back to the gym at night and, reluctantly, gave up the houseboat to Elaine's sister. In spite of distraction I regained my old form and began again to work on the swinging trick Elaine had showed me.

Before we left for Europe in March Elaine gave me a small black puppy that had been born on the lot. I didn't know I wanted a dog. Didn't know I needed one. It's the things you don't know about yourself that become most valuable once revealed.

A long time passed before I saw the lot again, and it was never the same; I was never the same. We had an easy time in Europe, working one show a night for big money. Elaine became a bored trailerwife, hanging around with nothing to do, not practicing anything, looking to me to provide a life for her. Again, it was hard to practice on the road. I often regretted not hanging onto the lot, often wished I had told Guy we needed more time. But we did go, and the lot went too. People I didn't know living there, talking about the Tino Brothers, which was okay I guess. But I never stopped missing the lot the way I'd first come to know it; sweating all day alone under the pines with the morning doves coo-cooing and the cow pies steaming in the clumps of dew-wet grass, and the animals chewing and watching me on the two-foot wire getting one, two, three jumprope passes, before tripping over the rope, and going at it again.

The Guilty Flee

Below the clouds, in a small private hospital, the rooms airy and car-peted, Dave smokes pot. A fat bag of marijuana on the sideboard next to his bed. The doctor brought it. A good doctor. Taking on a destitute youth as a project because it's rare to find such cancer in one so young.

Propped up on the bed, rolling a wastefully huge joint, using four doublewide papers, Dave fires it up, staring at a TV mounted on the wall. A game show, the volume turned down all the way. Overhead a ceiling fan spins. If the surgery goes well he'll have half a stomach and virtually no small intestines. He'll never have kids.

On TV a lady in a housedress goes nuts on Monty Hall. Jumping on his head, screaming in his face, messing up his hair. She's won her dream house, a new car, a Lazyboy recliner.

Dave's mom comes to visit him, tries to give him money.

What would he do with money?

He says he'll take the money for a coffin. He's only kidding, but not really.

Half a joint down, big-time cottonmouth. He pushes a button on a squawk box and tells the nurse that he needs a case of cold ones. He's kidding again, but not really. The doctor won't let him drink alcohol or smoke tobacco.

The lady on TV finds a motorboat behind door number one and falls over in a swoon. Monty Hall tries to catch her, but he's holding the microphone. Her head bounces off the floor. Luckily it's a phony TV floor. They break for a commercial.

After a while Dave nods out. His mom slips two one-hundred-dollar bills under the clock radio and leaves. A nurse walks in and clicks off the TV. There is the room bright and airy, the color TV, the white ceiling fan spinning, the bag of pot on the sideboard, the gleaming corridor with the elevator crying down to the street.

There are things that cannot be left behind, things you cannot run from, flying away feeling guilty as they roll him into surgery, sure he is a dead man at twenty-three.

Exile

We went to Charlie Chaplin's house long after he was dead. Few in the group had known him: the show owners, the director, couple of clowns who stayed on this show year after year. The rest of us were new, working for a season, ten months driving around Switzerland, and this was part of it, going to Charlie's house so that the owners could show off, show us they had friends in high places, show us our place.

About twenty of us were ushered into the "drawing room," whatever that means in a house like that. A fancy house, but lived in, not like Graceland or the Hearst Castle. A house with hardwood walls, oriental rugs, twenty-foot-high windows of beveled glass. Not what I'd call a mansion, but probably as expensive as a mansion, sitting where it did on a mountainside overlooking Vevey on Lake Geneva.

Charlie's wife was there, and some of his kids. I guess they were his kids, they were our age, and I thought *finally, people to hang out with*. But they didn't say a lot. Shrugged their shoulders, said:

"Not much."

"Don't know."

"Well, maybe."

to our narrow, churlish questions:

"What do you do around here?"

"Any good bars in town?"

"Want to get high?"

They didn't want to get high, not with us anyway. I'd driven up there with Elaine and Tino. Elaine didn't want to get high either; she didn't even want to speak to me because we'd quarreled about going to Charlie's house. I wanted to go downtown to a jazz club, but she said everyone was going to Charlie's house and we had to go for "appearances." Elaine had worked in Europe before and understood these things. I knew she was right about the appearances thing—in Europe they called us "artiste" and expected us to act a certain way—but still I wanted a medal for going along with her.

We settled into the drawing room, and I told Tino I was going to make an appearance in the bathroom. Elaine stood with a group of performers who were smiling like mad and making fawning sounds over Charlie's wife. There were gilt-framed paintings on the walls, old cracked oil paint as thick as roofing tar. The bathroom was a marble affair down a black-lacquered hallway. Tino sat on the toiletseat cover. I sat on a spindly chrome chair. We shared hits off a tiny stone hash pipe and tried not to cough. "So this is where the big guy took a shit," I squeaked out above a lungful. Tino didn't say anything. Actually this must have been a guest bathroom. Charlie probably had a major throne upstairs. Tino grimaced and held his breath. I don't know what was upstairs because we weren't allowed to go roaming around. We had the drawing room and the narrow hallway off which were the bathroom and a small trophy room.

We came out of the bathroom to find Elaine and a half-dozen others cramming into the trophy room. Charlie's wife was herding them in. She was thin and handsome for a grandmother-age woman, knew exactly how far to stretch her cheeks when she smiled. She looked serene in a neck-to-floor outfit of—*what?* Brocade silk, some drapery material—*what color was that?* Deep blue or dark crimson. "Good God, don't touch it!" Elaine had taken hold of my arm just as I was about to fondle the old lady's sleeve while she held her arm out, palm up, inviting us into the trophy room.

"Whooee, look at the Oscars," someone said.

"Shee . . ." Tino was trying not to say "shit" in mixed company, so he said, "Shee, is that real gold?" The other performers gave him pitying looks even though they didn't know if it was real gold or not. The big guy's wife probably knew, but she wasn't saying. The Oscars sat faceless and forlorn on a shelf, a myriad fine scratches all over them. "Looks like the maid went nuts with a Brillo pad," I whispered to Elaine.

She kept a tight-lipped smile on her face, a firm lock on my arm so I wouldn't touch anything. There were bunches of awards and shrinelike mementos in the room, the walls covered with photos of Charlie shaking hands with formally dressed people, people with really white teeth, people we were supposed to recognize but didn't. I didn't anyway. Hell, I didn't know anything about Charlie Chaplin.

I didn't even know what we were doing there.

The director said Charlie's wife invited the cast for a reception after the opening performance because Charlie did it when he was alive. *He started on a circus ya know!* The clowns never let you forget that. The big guy had been fond of the show and tried hard to be on time for it, they said, but in fact was never on time. I suspected Charlie's annual late arrival made the show the only event in Switzerland that did not commence at exactly the designated second. If Charlie was not in his box on opening night, the show did not go on. The people didn't mind waiting, Charlie not being Swiss after all, and never more than two or three minutes late. He was old at the end, rolled down the aisle in a wheelchair covered with a wool blanket while everyone in the tent stood and applauded. The clowns behind the curtain trembled with apprehension.

Elaine said I had to stop calling Charlie "the big guy." There was a life-size statue of him outside in the front yard. "He was a rather small man," she said.

We were in close quarters and couldn't talk loud. To get her riled up I whispered, "What! The big guy was a midget?"

"Shut up," she hissed through her teeth.

"How can that be?" I said. "I heard he was a giant, a comic genius, very rich."

"I'm never going anywhere with you again," she said, and moved off. She'd been saying that since we left Florida. Bored, that's all. Tino and I were a big part of the show. Elaine was the number girl. A job they'd made up for her because she was Elaine Bonnet. Number girl like in boxing. She sashayed around the ring looking good with a flashy number signaling the acts. The first few weeks it was great to be in another country, but then we got bored. We did mostly two-night stands, driving a truck and trailer, squinting at strange signs, trying to remember where we were going and why.

Brooding on jazz I wanted a drink and shouldered my way to the door. Performers who'd seen enough of the big guy's prizes filed out. In the hallway Elaine was chatting up Mrs. Charlie. The woman must have been a knockout when she was young, but Elaine in her light summer dress, cream-satin jacket, blond hair tumbling over her shoulders made the woman look old.

I leaned against a grand piano and tried to engage one of Charlie's kids in conversation. "So," I said, munching on snacks that were brought around. This wasn't a beer-and-chips operation like I'd been to in the States where piles of cheese squares and crustless coldcut sandwiches in geometric shapes were laid out on tables for the houseflies to walk on, everyone leaning over the stuff without protective barriers to catch nose hairs and whatnot, everyone thinking *free food* and jamming brownies into their pockets. This gig had special women in black and white outfits, tiny aprons around their waists, lacy pillbox hats like maids wear on TV. They strolled with small food on trays, tasteful offerings, mushy shit on weird crackers, not Ritz or Saltines, and fishy things to dip into sauces. Were we supposed to talk to these folks? Say thanks? Or merely nod our heads without looking at them as if we were used to this? "So," I said, "I'd like to get a serious drink." The kid, with shoulder-length hair and a mustache, raised his eyebrows slightly, and a man appeared with two different kinds of wine.

Hell, I didn't know what to think.

We hadn't been in Europe long enough to dissolve the clinging nimbus of America, pushing outward, creating awkward space, keeping whatever I reached for just out of my range. "So," I said, "been to a joint called the One Note?" No answer. What was wrong with these kids? They were my fellows Americans, for crying out loud. They should show us the town, treat us to some fun, but whenever I spoke to them they froze, stared, shrugged, mumbled. Was it snobbery? They spoke freely with the Swiss director, the Hungarian tumblers, the Spanish riding couple. Maybe they'd been so long in Europe they'd forgotten how to converse in American. Maybe they didn't want to remember.

About two in the morning—I'd been watching the clock since I hadn't given up on the jazz club—the old lady with her grace and the stoic kids began herding us out. I went through the front door while Elaine lingered with the others smiling and gushing. Tino went off to take a piss. I walked across the wet grass in the dark to talk to bronze Charlie. Elaine was right, he wasn't a big man. I was on eye-level with him but he was standing on a pedestal. Cars were parked in the driveway and out in the road, and people started getting into them and driving away. "No goodbyes," I said to Charlie. "That's gratitude for you, big guy. Come up here, eat your food, drink your wine, blow off without a word."

Charlie's statue was not faceless like his Oscars. It looked like the man himself standing there in his Little Tramp outfit—his skinny cane hooked over his forearm—covered with hot liquid bronze, real dark bronze, almost black under spotlights hidden in the grass. Every line on his face, every nuance of expression in his eyes said he was really in there, heartless maybe like the Tin Man but ready to grind to life if only I had a spot of oil or if I said the right words. "People are ogling your stuff," I said, "smoking dope in your bathroom." I tapped on his chest. Solid as stone.

"How does it feel, Charlie?" You have to wonder how he felt about making a buck playing a bum after his mother dumped him on a doorstep. I was about to say something else but Elaine and Tino overtook us. Elaine said he was wealthy by the time he'd donned the tramp outfit, wildly successful, tramping a path he could not change if he wanted to. They threw their arms around Charlie and had their photos taken. I took one of Elaine with the camera she pulled from her purse. She took photos everywhere and spent time between shows pasting them into display books. Charlie was plenty lit up, but I flashed him anyway to eliminate shadows.

"You know they stole his body after he died," Elaine said.

"Who did?"

"Someone," she said. "Someone stole it."

"You mean someone dug up his dead ass and carried it off?"

"That's what I heard," she said, "all very hush-hush."

Elaine was no longer mad. She'd had a couple of cold white wines, which was all she ever drank, and they made her tired and silly. Driving down the mountain she was only mildly disgusted with the behavior of Tino and myself. "You're both socially unattractive," she said. Tino said he didn't know what that meant. I said it meant we shouldn't have smoked hash in the big guy's bathroom. "I can't believe you said 'where's the beer,'" Elaine said to me. "Don't you know that woman's father was one of America's greatest playwrights?"

"I knew that."

"Who was it then?"

"You know who he was, Tino?"

"Shit . . ."

Elaine had a familiar bemused look on her face, waiting to see how I'd get out of this.

"Well?" she said.

I named the only playwright I knew: "Tennessee Williams."

"Ha," Elaine said. "I'm not even going to tell you."

"Well, I don't care. I'm going to see Big Miller."

That cracked Elaine up for some reason. "Big Miller," she said. "Nobody's name is Big Miller."

"Ha," I said, "you never heard of him."

"Nobody ever heard of him."

"You heard of Big Miller, Tino?"

"Shit . . ."

Elaine kept repeating "Big Miller" and shaking her head and laughed us down the mountain into town. I tried to talk them into going to the club, but they were done for the night. Tino never had any staying power when he drank, and Elaine disliked jazz intensely. "Four guys playing four different songs. No thanks," she said.

I dropped them at the lot. "Thanks for tonight," Elaine said. "I'll civilize you yet." She blew me a smooch from the other side of the truck. I waited while she unlocked our trailer, spoke to the dog—*Ben!*—beating the air with his tail. *Could she ever do more than give me that dog?* Ben was born under a trailer in the lot, the runt and ultimately the only survivor of his litter. Eight weeks into his life we flew to Switzerland. I had a big canine kennel but he charmed the flight attendants. "You can't put that poor puppy in the luggage bay," they said. He slept at my feet on the floor of the plane, and they fed him cheese and crackers across the ocean. Ben was a backlot dog who knew how close to get to the cats, how to move around elephants, horses, camels, trucks, forklifts, he knew to avoid live electrical cables. Once he got away from Elaine, who loved to walk him, in a park in down-town Geneva. She returned in tears without him. We hurried down the sidewalks, across major boulevards, streetcar tracks, speeding cars, two miles to the park. We screamed his name for hours, then, resigned to the fact that he was gone, returned to the circus lot. He was sleeping in his box under the awning of my trailer. He'd navigated his way through downtown Geneva to a lot we'd been on less than a week. He was six months old.

She paused in the doorway to let Ben in. Watching her from the back, swinging open the door, wild hair on the satin jacket, legs outlined all the way up by the backlight from the trailer, I almost shut the truck off and followed her in. We'd been together two years. Seemed like no time. Seemed like a lifetime. She'd put on one of those Pink Floyd tapes real low and look at a book for about one minute before sailing off to sleep. I almost went with her. But the door banged and she was gone. I dropped my foot from the brake pedal and the truck rolled, as if on its own, a few blocks to the club.

It wasn't far. I could have walked. Along the lake the clubs buzzed until 5 A.M., and people, foreigners mostly, strangers all, walked the promenade along the waterfront. Jazz music was not new to me, I'd been to Newport after all, but in America I'd had no access to it live. I'd had no access to anything in America, but now, here, across an ocean where I was an alien, a complete unknown, I had a job, a partner, a girl, a dog, my own rolling home, nobody telling me what to do, and bebop till dawn. What else could there be?

The One Note wasn't crowded and Big Miller was on break. At a tiny round table close to the stage I sat drinking Remy Martin on the rocks. I had to fight like hell to get them to dump the stuff over ice.

Big Miller came out and the man was a giant. Really big. Maybe six-foot-five, three hundred pounds. Like most of the musicians there, an American black man, jazz players who came out of Harlem during the age of Charlie Parker, who left America when they were still called Negroes. They were forgotten in their homeland. Their music once embraced was now forsaken. So they lived here, among strangers, and nightly in small clubs expelled in notes whatever pain that caused them.

Big Miller played three saxophones, a nose flute, and a con-
trabass clarinet that rested on the floor—it had a skinny mouthpiece sticking out of the side, and a whole world of big silver
flapping and clapping pitch-hole covers. The notes blurped out
the top like the sound of a ship leaving port. He performed with
a drummer, guitar player, and a guy on cello. Very clean, original
tunes with amazing contrast. He had great big feet, God, I don't
know, size eighteen if there is such a size, and he wore giant
shoes the color of pancake batter. They were grungy leather with
a strap across and a little buckle on the side. Big Miller pounded
out the night with those giant flapjack feet shaking his plywood
platform and the floor all around my table. I had to hang onto
my drink.

Because we were Americans I felt free to speak with him
between sets. But he said he hadn't been to the States in years.
Said he traveled all the time, France, Germany, Switzerland,
took a room wherever he happened to be if things got slow. I told
him I was with the circus, said I'd been up to Charlie Chaplin's
house. "I thought he was dead," Big said.

"He is," I said. "But there's a statue of him up there."

"So people hang out with the statue, that it?"

"Not exactly," I said.

"I gotta get some cigarettes," he said and walked off.

At 4:30 the band put down their instruments and the bright
lights came on. There were about six people in the club, all sitting at different tables. I paid and went outside. The cognac had
settled heavily and safely in my gut, in my heart it seemed, some
new love, but I didn't feel drunk and wasn't a bit sleepy. I drove
two blocks to the lake, the streets black and deserted, parked
close to the water and sat on the stone wall in the early chill and
watched the lights from the town smeared all over the dark
water rocking and rolling like water does. I sat still, comfortable,
safe as stone, as solidly ingrained in that place as any I'd ever sat
waiting for an unknown day. I could live here, same as anywhere,
there was no doubt.

There were specks of light up on the black mountain, like mica, marking the places people had homes. And above the places people lived eternal waves of constellations swept over the lake, over the town, swept everything over time and again: Big Miller in Vevey, the lot in Sarasota, New England the day I was born. And beyond: Saint Helena when Napoleon died, San Salvador when Columbus came, Arthur in Avalon, the arrival of the Magi—okay, maybe the heavens paused for a moment that night. Maybe time stops for a moment every time something changes for good. *Whose Oscars are those now, Charlie?* That's what I meant to say to him. *Where do you live now that your body is gone?*

Tonight I'd be here, and tomorrow night, and then I'd move to the next town and the next, and maybe I'd be changed after all, after the music, under the mountain, above the town, with the stars busy burning out, and Charlie out there tramping in his front yard, being pawed over by strangers, forever watching his dark road for familiar faces.

Kiel

We came out of the old town, a dense quarter of Zurich by the River Limmat, walked along the lake to the lot. Two blocks of clipped grass, stone paths, flat-topped hedges under looming elms, maples, and oaks in full leaf. Emerging from the trees, as if billowing up out of the greenery, a great blue ocean swelled over the center of the lot. The tent. A great wavy top dressed in fine morning mist with a wide, flagtopped, vertical façade like a shining blue-vinyl wall. On both sides of the entranceway under a gold canopy trimmed with fringe, painted clowns juggled the block letters K I E L. We walked on the grass under the canopy past a barred ticket window, a shuttered souvenir stand, through the façade into the foyer. The director sat at a glass table with a reporter for the Swiss daily *Neue Zürcher Zeitung*. He wore a tweed jacket and a Tyrolean hat, and had a tape recorder on the table.

"Coffee?" Elaine asked.

"Hmm," I said.

"Tino?" she said.

"I'll get it," Tino said.

Behind the stainless bar two teen-age girls took up bottles of rum and cognac and polished them with cloths. The bartender, a rotund man in a short white jacket over white shirt, a thin red bowtie, ground beans for espresso. The director and the reporter stood until we sat. The ground was covered with artificial turf. A Moroccan man in uniform, *Kiel* stitched across his back, swept a brace of stairs which led upward from the foyer to the tent. I did not speak German so someone had to translate the reporter's questions—questions that were always the same, always personal: "Do you think about falling?"

And translate my answers that were also personal and brought other questions: "What does he mean?" I said. Tino spoke five languages, none German. Elaine spoke High German but the reporter spoke Swiss German.

"How many hours a day do you practice?"

I said come to practice if you want to understand. The director said that was not a good idea. He said he would translate, but the director could not be trusted. He told the man lies about us. Someone would read to us what he said in the newspaper. About how we learned to walk the wire, about why we did it, about practice.

"Do you practice falling?"

The director, incredulous, "These boys can jump from a ten-story building."

I sipped espresso and sulked. "Come to practice," I told the man in English. "You sit and watch. You figure it out. Maybe you can tell me what it is."

You walk across the bridge over the outflow along the tail end of the lake full of boats, past the landing-stage Bahnhofstrasse. Walk to the central station for bratwurst—ahh, that mustard—but hurry, practice is at a certain time. Walk to Belvoir Park, a green place on the lake lined with willows, and there you will see the trail-

ers. *There are perhaps twenty-five of them, neatly spaced with awnings and outdoor furniture, close to the lake, and the gentle lapping of water against the bank. From a long fifth-wheel trailer, the type Americans call "gooseneck," with two pullout rooms, two air conditioners, a diesel generator, a striped awning with a black dog tied to it, you see the wirewalker step from the screen door followed by a weeping woman. She is blond and slim in halter top and shorts, and she does not appear hysterical; she is not weeping from sudden sadness, from sadness maybe, but a sadness she's lived with and does not expect to be without. Despair, you might say: she's crying in despair. Maybe she's sick, has known for some time that she will die, though she is no older than twenty-five. Look at the man and you know it's not sickness, at least not the physical kind. He keeps his back to her wherever she turns. His expression not accepting or sympathetic but dismayed and persecuted. It's not a scowl but almost, a look grimly determined to look away. I'm only asking for some consideration, she says.*

The man stares at the steel apparatus erected on the grass alongside the trailer. Are you going to let me practice?

Your practice! she says. All you care about.

It's what you taught me, he says.

The wire over his head is low enough to jump to. He buckles leather handgrips around the wrists like you've seen gymnasts do on TV. Thin strips of rawhide to protect the palms. Two inches by six inches with holes for the middle and ring fingers and straps to pull the leather tight across the palm. Under the leather straps terrycloth wristbands keep the sweat from his hands. He wears white kneesocks and shorts over a pair of black tights. On his feet are white leather pull-ons similar to ballet shoes; he has them stuck inside an oversized pair of clogs. Clinging to the top half of his body, more decoration than shirt, a white tanktop. He stands under the wire and flexes his shoulders, rotates his head, arches his back, bends over and places his palms flat on the ground in front of him. There is the sound of breathing and the cracking and popping of joints over the sound of the water lapping at the black roots of willows.

He takes time loosening up, one by one, each muscle in no particular order. He works his neck, his ankles, calves, hamstrings, thighs, rotates his hips, windmills each shoulder joint, back to the neck, back to the ankles, the calves, the thighs. All the time the weeping woman is watching, waiting, dabbing her eyes with a tissue. Then she goes back inside, slams the screen door.

The dog, part husky, lies on his belly, head resting flat on the ground like a snake. For a home he has a large airline kennel. Also under the awning a round-covered barbecue grill, a pink cooler, a croquet set on a wheeled stand, two Mopeds, a lineup of shoes, two dog bowls, and a welcome mat on a small wooden pallet.

The man pulls a plastic bag from his waistband, digs out a piece of rock rosin and, lifting each foot in turn, crushes it into the leather soles of his wireshoes. He takes a white block of chalk and covers his hands and handgrips, places the bag back in his waistband, then leaps up and clamps his hands onto the wire. He hangs twisting one way then the other, stretching his shoulders, craning his neck, lifting his legs till his toes touch the wire then lowering them slowly. You hear creaks and pops, grunts of breath. The wire, steel cable the diameter of a broom handle, dips slightly where he hangs in the middle. It's about as long as the trailer, is tightened over two A-frames of steel tubing, and staked into the ground at each end. You wonder will he do anything but hang when he drops onto his clogs, pulls his fingers from one of the handgrips and studies his palm. He pokes at the hand with his opposite index finger then goes into the trailer. He leaves the door open and is back in a moment sitting on the step with a single-edge razor blade. Holding his palm close to his face he slices off thin curls of rubbery skin. The dog sniffs the peels as they fall to the ground. After each slice he runs a finger over the spot. When he's shaved both hands he sets the blade down and picks up a piece of fine sandpaper and rubs it over both palms and his fingertips. Finally, he drops the sandpaper, rechalks his hands and grips, walks back to the wire, steps out of his clogs, and jumps.

Hanging by his hands he lifts one leg and hooks it over the wire, pulls himself to a sitting position, then plants one foot under his body and stands up. What was dead geometric form comes alive; the wire bounces under his weight, the A-frames flex as if breathing. When he walks his feet make a dry squeaking sound on the steel cable. There is none of that signal-arm stuff. He has no pole or umbrella. He walks as you would walk on the ground, not swinging his arms but not waving them over his head either, more like an ape would trudge along a tree branch. In the middle of the wire he stops, his body cocked at an angle, his back foot perpendicular to his front. He raises his arms over his head and goes still. His hands move slightly from the wrists, fingers flickering like the tip of a cat's tail. When the fingers stop fidgeting you see him reach upward and tip forward onto his hands like a wagon wheel starting to roll. But he only rolls halfway, half a cartwheel, and stands on his hands with his feet pointed skyward. He teeters, arches his back, pikes from the hips, pushes away from the wire, and falls bellyfirst toward the ground. He does not let go. He swings, flies, 360 degrees around the wire connected only where his fists grip the cable. The wire descends like a bow and springs up with each rotation. The A-frames bulging out on the downdrop almost jump off the ground on the upswing. His body rides smooth circles around the wire, arms stretched above his head, legs stiff and pointed, as if he were a spoke to an axle with only air for a rim.

Each time over the top he slows his body, watches the wire intently. After a half-dozen rotations he stalls in a handstand, jackknifes his body, and without bending his knees spreads his legs and plants his feet firmly on the cable. One foot on each side of his hands. Elbows and knees remain locked. He is attached to the wire by hands and feet. With his body length bent in half the four-point straddle rotation is viciously fast. For an instant you feel him flying, you think he's been whipped off because just past the halfway point on the upswing he lets go with his hands and rides the momentum to a standing position. But he fails to stop precisely over the center of the cable. With arms chopping the air for balance he flies over the top and off his feet. He's sideways in the air, heading into space.

Twisting 180 degrees he grabs the wire with both hands. Hanging under. He looks down at the ground and spits. He looks up at the wire, hooks his leg over, pulls himself to a loose hunched sitting position, elbows resting on his thighs, feet crossed and still. He slips his fingers from the handgrips and studies his palms.

The screen door bangs. The blond woman comes out composed and dressed for town. Going shopping, she says, watching him for any reaction. He pulls the rosinbag from his waistband, rechalks his hands and handgrips. Need anything?

No.

Sure? I'm taking the car.

More tissues, he says.

Tissues? He stares at her. Okay then. She turns to the dog lying under the awning. Bye, Ben, she says, and walks off down the row of trailers. She looks back. He is studying his palm. His dog hasn't moved.

He stands, walks back and forth, bounces on the wire, settles in the middle, and raises his arms. Same cocked position with the back foot sideways to push with. He puts his arms down, breathes, shakes his arms loose, raises them again. Then he tips over onto his hands. Again he stays in the handstand just long enough to get the position, then falls bellyfirst and whips his feet around into the handstand again. This time he's got the speed right and goes around twice before planting his feet for the fast short circle and the attempt at coming out of it standing. This time he falls short. Instead of flying over the wire he doesn't make it to the top and he falls away backwards. Again he is airborne. He grabs the cable. Hangs under. Again he hooks the leg, pulls to sitting, removes the handgrip, studies the palm, pokes with his finger, pulls out the chalk bag. He stands and does the whole thing again.

He repeats the pattern for thirty minutes and not once manages to come out of the giant swings standing up. He flies over, falls back, sometimes seems to come out perfectly only to lose his balance at the last second and collapse onto the wire. You find yourself rooting for him, spreading open your fingers as he does when he's trying to catch his balance. As the attempts continue you consider the harnessed violence of traveling at that speed upside-down on your hands while trying to toe a line at a dead stop in perfect balance. On one attempt his foot fails to plant, causing his body to twist wildly out of control. He is forced to let go or dislocate a shoulder. He does a crablike 360 in midair before thudding onto the grass ten feet from the wire on his hands and knees. He crawls over and slips on his clogs. Picks up the sandpaper and begins scraping the grass stains off the handgrips. He gets up, paces under the wire studies his palms, talks to the dog. I don't know, Ben. What do you think? The dog lifts his head, looks at his owner, puts his head back down.

He is back on the wire when his partner arrives and sits in the grass. How's it going? he asks. Make any?

No. He's in his ready position, slightly cocked, flicking his fingers. He goes still and wheels into the handstand.

Push! He flies toward the ground. Ends up on top with his arms windmilling wildly. Knees! Knees! His feet go out from under him and he catches the wire with one hand and one leg. Shit, you have to bend the knees, man.

He pulls up, studies his palm. Can't bend 'em. Too fast.

Slow down.

Don't make it around.

How the hands?

Bad.

Ripouts?

Cracks. He shakes his head in disgust.

Shit, when Mendoza did this he wore gloves.

Mendoza ended up eighty feet from the wire with a crushed skull. He tries the trick again.

Shit, man, gotta go. Try to bend the knees, keep the head up.

An hour goes by. You wonder how long he can do this. He goes into the trailer, comes out with a clump of paper towels. After each attempt he removes the handgrips, dabs blood off his palms, rechalks, replaces the handgrips. There is no change in his demeanor. He moves primatelike, does only the one trick, paces the ground, talks to the dog, or sits on the wire reading his palms, as if seeking the design flaw of the human hand, or some insight into whether this trick can be done.

Finally, on tipping into a handstand one hand misses the wire entirely. Maybe he's grown tired, or the wire jerked in an unexpected way. The hand goes down grabbing air and he takes the cable in the face. Anyone would come out of it with some broken teeth, at least a bloodied nose, but he turns his head fast, the cable catches him on the ear and scrapes down his neck to the collarbone. Looks like a collarbone cracker but he hunches his shoulder like a boxer and takes the brunt on the muscle. He hangs by one arm and one leg, looks up at the wire, then drops onto his clogs and slips his feet in. He shows no sign of pain but you see something in his face has changed, a scrape puffing up on his neck, but also resignation, sadness. He tugs at the handgrips with his teeth. Sits on the step of the trailer. With the tips of his fingers he pulls off the handgrips, the sweatsoaked wristbands, the wireshoes, the kneesocks, and places his feet into the clogs. He holds both hands in front of his face, flexes his fingers, closes them, opens them to study the center of his palms.

I don't know about this, Ben. The dog, whose attention has not wandered from his owner the entire practice, watches as he walks over to the croquet set. He closes his swollen hand around the handle of a mallet and stares at the hammerhead. He tips the top of the stand with his knee and the balls roll onto the ground. He pushes two balls together with his foot, steps down hard on one ball with his thick-soled clog, and takes a full backswing like a golfer. He slams the mallet against the ball sending the other ball out into the lake. He backswings again and cracks the remaining ball. The dog sits up to get a better view of where the balls are going. All the balls one after another he slams into the lake. When the balls are gone he smashes the mallet down on the score pegs, the wickets, the stand. When one mallethead breaks off he flings the useless stem into the water and picks up another. The man raises the last mallet over the soft rounded cover of the barbecue grill, thinks better of

it, and whips the mallet end over end like a hatchet against a wil-
low tree. When the croquet set is demolished, all the pieces floating
in the lake, he slumps his shoulders and lets out a long breath. He
pats the dog on the head. Good boy, Ben. Then he picks up his
handgrips, wristbands, wireshoes, socks, rosinbag, sandpaper,
razorblade, and clump of bloody paper towels, and peels back the
screen door with his fingertips.

After supper we took a taxi to the show. Over the bridge, past
the landing-stage where a ferryboat had docked. We had to be
there early on opening night for meet and greet. People in the
foyer were having drinks under lights that bounced around their
faces and eyeglasses and transformed the tent, electrified guywires, brought life to blue plastic. "Mingle with the people," the
director said. "Special guests," he called them. "Talk with them,
smile, it won't kill you."

"Do you expect to die on the highwire?"

"What do they mean, Elaine?"

"Nothing," she said. "They don't mean anything."

The reporter with the Tyrolean hat was standing at the bar.
Elaine went to practice her Swiss German on him. She'd begun
to like him. We'd argued all day about nothing in particular. She
wanted to know if I would make an act with her, if I slept with
the bargirls, why the dog wouldn't listen to her, was I ever going
to speak. Ongoing discussions.

The men were dressed for dinner, the women heavily made
up with large jewelry glittering. I pushed Tino ahead of me, trying to avoid questions. "Tell them we have to go," I said. "Tell
them we have to go warm up." I hid behind a big Moroccan guy
but got cornered by an English-speaking couple. Pretty little wife
in a black dress with thin straps, smart looking man with wire-
rimmed glasses. Said he was with the Office of Municipal
Direction. I nodded my head. What could he possibly mean? A
city worker of some kind. He held out a picture of me jumping

over Tino. "Am I to understand that this takes place at ten meters?" The wife held out a pen and I took it and scribbled my name across the photo. I stared at her face, innocent face under makeup and lights, handed her the pen. Elaine watched from over by the bar. People aimed their eyes at me. I should learn to call up nausea when needed. A little throwing up act, that would get them moving in different directions. I thought of Dave, European style: *Pardon me, Sir and Madame, I feel the presence of a bowel in movement. Defecation is imminent. I really must, pardon my American, go take a good shit for myself.*

"Don't worry," I told the man, "you'll understand everything when you see the show." The director moved through the crowd touching shoulders, taking elbows in hand, saying it was time to go in. "You go on," I said to the couple, "go on in. You'll see. That's why they call it a show."

A uniformed man takes your ticket at the top of the stairs. You duck through the inverted-V-shaped entrance, tent flaps tied back by white cords. You are at the back row, looking down over twenty-five hundred seats surrounding the ring that is filled with white smoke, fog maybe, some kind of machine-made mist. Blue lights low on the ringcurb give the fog a cold, seething look. You stop and stare, but there are people waiting, so you walk down the wooden ramp covered with thick red carpeting. There are two such ramps, one on each side of the main section of seats. Two side sections sweep around the ring to the bandstand set up on an elevated platform over the backcurtain. The heavy crimson curtain is closed and white fog billows from beneath it.

You come to your row, shuffle down to your seat, which is in the middle just behind the boxed seats enclosed by brass railings hung with velvet curtains. You see the cushioned chairs with armrests and drinkholders and the carpeting on the floor, each box with a wool blanket for chilly nights. The name Kiel emblazoned across everything. There is not a speck of dust. Even the less expensive

seats are covered with white cloth. The boxes are filled with men
dressed in suits, ladies in long coats.

At 9:30 the tent goes dim, only the blue moonglow covers the
audience, conversation ceases. Bandmembers slip into their places,
take up their instruments, the brassmen wipe down their horns,
the wind players twist and lick their mouthpieces, the drummer
careful with his sticks and feet. The fog has begun to move, rise,
grow thicker. The anticipation increases until there is not a sound.
People look discreetly at their watches. It's 9:31. An unseen hand
pulls back the curtain under the bandstand and out strolls a perfectly white horse. It's a round-in-the-belly, wide-hipped horse. A
mare. She ignores the audience, glances back the way she has
come. Soon her baby totters out after her. A foal no more than a
month old. There is from the audience the affected sigh, the sim-
pering smiles. The mare seems to float into the ring on her belly, the
baby just a pale head and neck hugging her side. The mare moves
to the front of the ring and lies down. The baby stands over her.
Another white horse wanders out, and another, then in pairs and
small groups they move around the ring and lie down.
Occasionally one noses another, one snorts, one shakes its shaggy
head. There are a dozen of them, all white and free of halter or bri-
dle, lying in the fog and blue light with only the baby standing and
not a sound in the tent. One by one the horses put their heads
down and disappear into the mist.

There is a man in white tails bejeweled with tiny stones.
He appears not from the backcurtain but from the audience. He
moves down the aisle with his finger to his lips, turning to each
section of people, soliciting their silence. A warm light emanates
from the man, and you realize dim white spotlights have been
turned on him. With his finger to his lips he moves to the boxes
and selects a young woman. It is the wife of the municipal clerk.
She is reluctant to leave her husband, but the man takes her by
the hand and helps her over the ringcurb. He is Gustav Kiel, tall,
dignified, the sixty-year-old patriarch of the Kiel family. They walk
slowly to the foal and he puts his arm around its neck and runs

his hands over the back, and he talks to the mare now with her head up. He invites the woman to take hold of the foal. She hesitates. The foal, wide-eyed and shivering, doesn't move. Gustav speaks to the mare, and as she rises carefully from the mist he backs off, leaving the woman with her arms around the baby's neck. He moves away toward the backcurtain and casually waves the trio after him. Come, come, he encourages. As they follow him, the mare first with the baby and woman picking their way through the prone horses, it is difficult to tell who is leading whom. At one point the woman looks back at her husband, a wild look, as if it might be the last exchange they ever have. At the curtain where the fog dissolves into the blackness Gustav takes her hand just before she disappears. The crowd begins to clap. The mare and foal melt away into the dark. Gustav leads the woman back across the ring to her husband and joins the round of applause. In this brief adventure Gustav has successfully bridged the gulf between himself and the crowd of strangers. There isn't a person in the tent who didn't cross the ring with the young woman, and she has returned safely. They are his now.

Gustav produces a cordless microphone and quietly thanks everyone for coming and tells what will be seen, and how it all came together. He mentions the American highwire act, pointing to the rigging over the ring. He refers to years past, family members that are familiar to the audience, some of whom are the same age as Gustav and have been coming to the show since they were children, and Gustav's father, and before that his grandfather, stood on the ringcurb where he stands now. He talks unhurried in the low light while his horses lie invisible in the fog. Not one of them has moved since Gustav tiptoed down the aisle.

Now he picks up a white lunge whip from the ringcurb, steps into the ring and addresses his horses. Excuse me, please. One of the horses raises its head and looks at him. If you don't mind . . . Gustav turns his palm outward to the audience. These good people have come to see a show. The beast moans and struggles to its feet, and the others look up. One by one they get to their feet, shake their manes, snort loudly, and flick woodchips from their tails. Gustav nudges the stragglers and thanks each one personally. Thank you, Baron. Thank you, Troy. When they are all up and milling about he raises his arm, cracks the whip over his head, and the band comes down hard on the first note. The lights come up brilliant white and the horses rear and buck in an explosive gallop around the ring as the fog dissipates.

One act blends into the next without a lot of fanfare. The Kiel family taking care to provide great contrast while not intruding upon the flow of acts. There is a delicate handbalancer followed by fast unicycle riders followed by chimps followed by acrobats. The clowns are not slapstick but comics in the Chaplin mode. And between acts you see the blond woman, stunning in a high cut costume and brilliant smile, subtly moving over the ringcurb, a much appreciated accent to the acts.

Near midnight men in uniform stretch two wires from the highwire platforms across the ring to the ground and crank them tight. With a slight introduction the wirewalkers emerge from behind the curtain, acknowledge applause, and step out of their clogs onto the wires. They stand on their toes on the wire sharply inclined, shifting their arms, switching quickly from one foot to the other. Gradually they settle both feet onto the wire and begin to creep upward. They move the back foot to the front so fast you miss it, but there is a pause after each step to adjust to the new position, each step requires a rebalance, windmilling arms, subtle pelvic shifts. Near the top they move slower, tighter, as if the air has thickened and they must push and chop their way through with their hands. They reach the platforms and you do not go with them.

They seem unfamiliar, like aliens, as you watch the reckless way they work. But it mustn't be reckless. It must only appear reckless. They must make it look that way to scare you. Obviously they are experts, but also there is an element of uncertainty, and you cannot tell when they are close to that point. There must be a line that if crossed results in failure, in this case falling. They move about the cable freestyle, no balancing aids, and they are very smooth, the air around them not thick like on the inclines. They flow and float and swish into position: one sitting, the other leaping. The leaper in the air, hands high over his head, feet out in front in the position they will hit the wire. You realize when you see him free of the wire that there cannot be a distinct shape to the edge he pushes toward. The line between success and fail-ure, life and death, cannot be clearly defined. He lands solidly and takes up the bounce with his legs. His arms stir motes of dust in the hazy spotlight. At times they disappear in the backlight, they become silhouettes, with only an occasional glint or flash from the rhinestones and mirrors on their tights and chainmail tops to assure you that they haven't slipped through some gap between here and hereafter.

The act defies the laws of human ability. It is puzzling how they can do these things. A skipping rope segment seems frivolous and playful, mocks the ten meters between playground and ground, then he trips, falls flat onto the wire. It is a moment that stops band and breath. He catches the wire with both hands. Swings under. The rope falls and the shocking thing, even if you suspect the trip was contrived, the thing that makes you jump in your seat, is the thud the rope makes hitting the ground. You're pretty sure he did not mean to drop that rope, and you feel it hit from across the ring, and feel the hairs rise on the back of your neck. If a rope hits with such force . . .

He climbs to his feet and you see he favors one hand, pushes off the wire with only the heel, keeping the palm off the wire. There is no change in his demeanor. It is as if he lives only for these ten minutes a day, and this brief time gives him what he needs to with-stand all that is not these ten minutes.

On the ground just inside the backcurtain the number girl has picked up the jumprope and coils it under a thick terrycloth bathrobe she holds over her arm. She watches the ground. When there is a gasp or sigh of relief her eyes sweep over the audience, her barometer to what is happening above. Only when the boys are on the ground does she raise her eyes. The applause continues as they back out. The spotlights cut away and Finale begins. You watch the jumproper hang his head as she wraps him in the robe and hands him the coiled rope. She takes his face in her hands and raises it to her own and speaks to him as you would a small child. He nods his head up and down and then stops and kisses her mouth. With both her arms around his shoulders they move into the dark, and the curtain closes over them.

Never Going There Again

We were at the Italian border again, me and Joe from Southern California in a silver Lancia, a very bad car for money smuggling, playing an old game: move lira into Switzerland without getting caught by border cops whose job it was to catch foreigners who came to their country to make money and take it away. There was a law against exporting lira, though everyone did it to avoid the high Italian income tax and a very bad exchange rate.

We'd done this before and never were asked to step from the car. I've always felt it was the car that caused the trouble. That damned Lancia. I didn't know what it was—it looked like an average car—when I rented it in Rome, which was another problem: we had started too far from the border to make a money run in the time we had. But there was no choice, we were loaded with cash and wanted to get rid of it before we began the winter tour to the south.

"We'll make good time in that thing," Joe said when he saw the car. We'd parked our trucks and trailers at the lot in Rome. I had no time to hook up the water and electric. I

214

collected fifteen million lira from Tino to help him out because he was loaded too, told Elaine to look after Ben, and we were on the road by midnight. We had to be back for setup the next afternoon.

Another thing that screwed us up was Joe wanting to cross at Domodossola, a strange place. We always crossed at Saint Bernard or Como and went to the bank in either Martigny or Lugano. But all the way up the country with me at the wheel pushing the Lancia to two hundred kilometers per hour, only trucks on the dark highway, Joe talked about crossing at Domodossola and going to the bank in Brig. I couldn't figure out why he wanted to do that, until finally when it came to a logistical choice—I could go left to Aosta or right to Como or straight to Domodossola—he told me about the girl.

"Hungarian girl," he said, "horniest girl on seven continents. Trust me. She'll take care of us." Maybe because it was straight ahead, or because it was late and I was too tired to argue, I went toward Domodossola. Sure, there would be some girl—who cared? Joe was ten years older than me and his idea of a suitable girl and mine were different things.

When I saw the border crossing I knew I'd made a mistake. We'd been climbing steadily since Milano. The road deserted, curving. Then blocking the way were low cement buildings with the road narrowing to a single lane between them. There wasn't another vehicle in sight. We'd been driving in the dark for hours and drinking from a bottle of China Martini, and we came into the light too fast. A dozen overhead vaporlamp suns glared through the windows and sunroof. There were four border guards with machine guns standing there with absolutely nothing to do. We rolled into the slot between them squinting like cavedwellers on Mars.

The routine was to roll down the windows, slow to a crawl, hold up our American passports and grin like we needed directions to the Matterhorn. The borders between European countries were casual. The guards didn't usually make us stop, but simply glanced at the passports and waved us through. This time we faced black-gloved hands, palms pushed flat toward our windshield, there was no doubt we were to stop.

Joe's Italian was better than mine so he did the talking, which was another thing that got us in trouble. It might have been better if I'd spoken my broken Italian and pretended we were new visitors. Joe had been in Italy many years and his Italian was too good. Besides, we were wearing about a thousand dollars worth of Italian clothes and shoes and driving that damned Lancia which I had no idea was such an expensive car. We were asked to step from the car.

The border guards were no different than other cops in Italy. In front of banks, at train stations, they carried Uzis with their fingers on the triggers. They were jumpy in those days: Red Army paranoia. A carload of uniformed cops in a Fiat would stop at a red light in Rome or Verona, the barrels of their rifles sticking up between their legs, and someone on a dirtbike would toss a grenade in the window. Very jumpy.

I shut the car off and we got out. We moved slowly, both of us jabbering to cover the crackling of the bills we had stuck to our bodies under our clothes. A rule among money smugglers: never try to move more than you can carry on your body. Cops freely poked into your car and belongings but didn't search anyone they were not arresting.

My whole body was covered with bills. I put them under stacks of books in my trailer to pack them flat, then bound them with masking tape. I stood before a mirror taping the packets to my legs, stomach, under my arms. Sure, you lost a little hair pulling them off, but it was the safest way. I tried a body suit of nylon tights once, like the flyers wore. I didn't tape the packets and they shifted around and I about itched to death inside the tights. Grimy bills and sweat sliding all over my body. I tried taping the packets to the tights but the masking tape wouldn't stick, maybe duct tape would have stuck, but that's heavy and would have wrecked the bills. You had to be able to unstick the whole thing in Switzerland. The bills were often wet and stank, but Swiss bankers were fazed by nothing.

We moved into the small cement building with two of the cops while the other two tore apart the Lancia. "Bello auto" one of them said. Inside, more cops. Joe wasn't bending his knees, so I knew he had bills down both pantlegs. I didn't know how much money he had on him, but I was severely regretting taking Tino's fifteen million. The problem with lira was that it came in large denominations that did not add up to much. One thousand lira equaled about sixty-five cents. Tino and I were paid the equivalent of twenty-five hundred dollars a week. That came to nearly four million lira. They paid in cash, no taxes, and were not real strict about keeping to the weekly part of the deal. Sometimes they'd go a month without paying, and then we'd need a good size box to carry off our pay. Joe had an aerial spaceship act worth about two grand a week but didn't have to split it since he worked with his wife. Joe wore a knee-length black leather Gestapo coat buttoned up tight, the whole thing lined with bills. He must have been sweltering. He held a Sam Spade hat tightly against his stomach. I wore brown leather pants—leather clothes were big then—and a puffy yellow suede jacket. I was carrying about sixty-five million lira, or thirty thousand dollars. Joe probably had about the same. Not a fortune between us, but still three months of our lives and labor, and certainly more than you'd want to have taken from you by people who would throw you in jail and demand more money to let you out.

They separated us. I heard Joe one cubical over jabbering like a madman, too friendly, trying to impress them with the truth. We were American circus artists with the Italian National Circus. We tried to get them to take the free circus passes we carried. They weren't interested. I couldn't understand what they were interested in. Maybe terrorists. If we'd had Joe's wife with us we'd have been screwed. She carried a German passport, and Germans in Italy at that time were not popular. We were polite, Joe overly confident, which kept us there longer than we would have been if he'd shut up. But Joe was a big talker. He told them we were going to Circus Altoff in Brig to visit friends. We had a day off and had to be back to work in Rome that night. I guess that made sense because after about two hours, which I spent in a hard plastic chair sitting on packets of bills, they brought Joe in and gave us back our passports.

We stood at a desk side by side holding our passports and were told we could go. I saw Joe raise the hat slowly up his body and lower his head into a pile of hundred-thousand lira notes. We walked out like stick men. If this were a movie a little corner of a note would be poking from under Joe's hat to give us away. It was close. If so much as a coin had dropped from a pocket, we'd have been strip searched.

Back in the car we drove off slowly, smiling and nodding our heads at the cops. "Nice place you picked to cross, Joe," I said through my teeth.

"Never going there again," he said, grinning and waving. As soon as we got clear of the border I stomped the gas and headed up the Simplon Pass.

"A horny Hungarian," I said. "We end up in the slammer because you want to see a horny Hungarian girl."

He wouldn't be drawn in. Besides, it wasn't his fault. That could have happened anywhere, but it hadn't happened at Como or Saint Bernard, and we never did pass through Domodossola again. If we had even a minor problem at a town, a restaurant, a border crossing, or truckstop, we never went there again. We had that luxury, we were travelers. We went where we wanted and we didn't stay long. When we told someone we'd never see them again, we meant it.

The north side of the mountain on Simplon Pass Road was steep and we were going too fast. Joe was rummaging under the seat for the Martini bottle that we knew was gone. "Those bastards," Joe said. We were mad. Driving near dawn with nothing to drink. That first gray tinge of illuminated fog that nobody who stays up all night wants to see was just appearing below us in the valley. Brig was about thirty minutes away and I held the gas peddle down, driving reckless, and saw the big yellow and black arrows that looked like > > >, which in Switzerland means you need to take a ninety-degree swerve to the right. Soon.

I applied the brakes and tried to turn the wheel, and I found out that damned Lancia had front wheel drive. That bello auto simply wasn't going to turn at that speed. Luckily there was a good solid guardrail which we slammed into broadside. It was a ninety-kilometers-per-hour jolt. I cracked my head on the side window but it didn't break. It was remarkable how well that car took the hit. We got out and stood in the road in the fog with the land around us going straight up on one side, straight down on the other; we heard our shoes on the wet asphalt. It was as quiet there as heaven, quieter than heaven. We spoke in whispers saying nothing. The driver's side of the Lancia had a new design: the inverted shape of a guardrail down the door and both fenders. The front fender just touched the tire. We took hold of it together and pulled it back an inch.

We drove in silence after that and the beautiful car which had only six thousand kilometers on it vibrated a bit. Luckily I'd checked the full-coverage box at the rental place. We'd been sufficiently humbled by the road, and not for the first time. Joe had been on the road since the fifties. Too long to quit, he said.

It was daylight, overcast white sky, when we rolled into Brig and followed the arrows to Circus Altoff, a small round tent on a corner lot of wet grass. Everyone was asleep. I parked back among the trailers, caravans shaped like frogs, made in Poland or someplace. Joe identified one belonging to the Hungarian girl. I couldn't move or listen to him. "Go, Joe," I said. "Do what you're going to do."

"Come on."

"Forget it." I lowered the seatback all the way and shut my eyes. "When the banks open we're out of here."

His door clicked. I tried to get out to take a piss but my door was guardrailed shut. I climbed over the stick shift and across the passenger seat and stood pissing behind the door. I'd been in Brig on Circus Kiel but had no memory of it. It appeared much like any medium-size Swiss town. I saw a middle-aged woman in a bathrobe slip down a gap between trailers. I got back in the car. My window wouldn't go down.

It seemed like I was asleep about a minute when Joe jerked open the door. He was in midsentence. I thought he was talking to me but then there was this other guy talking over Joe. They were talking loud and fast, almost shouting in some kind of Italian-German-English mix, with the guy, who had one of those droopy-dog Hungarian mustaches, talking a bit louder than Joe and holding a claw hammer in his hand. He wasn't threatening anyone with it: just had it hanging in his hand like he was doing some early-morning carpentry. Joe got into the car waving at the guy like he should go away because he was not worth listening to. The guy was acting quite serious, frowning, and bringing the hammer up for emphasis. I could tell they knew each other, and I recognized in Joe that look he had when he knew he was wrong about something but was pretending it was trivial. Something told me to turn the key. Joe slammed the door on the guy while he was still talking, and BLAM, the guy brought the hammer down hard on the roof of the Lancia, and I put it in gear and drove away.

I looked at Joe. He stared straight ahead out the windshield until I said, "Well?"

"Fuck this place," he said. "Never coming here again."

We drove to the main street and stopped in front of the first bank we saw and sat there until nine when it should have opened. Only then did we notice there wasn't a soul downtown. Joe checked his watch. "It's not Sunday," he said. "Monday, 9:10 in the morning. So why the shit is the bank closed?"

"Maybe they open at ten." We got out and walked up to the bank doors and there was the sign, and Joe, a hard man to beat down, sat on the stone steps, rested his elbows on his knees and put his face in his hands. I was not good with German but I knew the word *Geschlossen*, and the word *Feiertag*, which I took to mean holiday. "What?" I said. "What holiday?"

"Local," Joe said through his hands. "Some fucking Swiss thing."

"What holiday?" It was important to know precisely which patron saint or petty politician had caused us to drive this far, to risk our lives and livelihood, for nothing. It was a form of denial, trying to lay blame, to escape the sense of our own stupidity.

Joe stood. "Who gives a shit what holiday! It's the fucking Swiss Fourth of July! Saint Bumfuck of Egypt Day! It's a fucking holiday, that's all. They're closed and they won't be open until this fucked day is over."

"What are we going to do?"

"Let's get this money off us for one thing," he said. As he got back into the car he gave the side of the Lancia a good kick square in the center of his door. On the roof was a half-moon ding about the size of a silver dollar. "Son of a bitch Hungarian bastard," Joe said. "Are you getting hungry?"

We drove around until we spotted the Bahnhof. We weren't strangers to Switzerland and knew that even with the holiday the situation was not as dire as it would be in Italy. Nothing could really go wrong for long in a country as efficient as Switzerland. Joe and I had agreed long ago that it was our favorite place on the planet. Bahnhof stations in each town always had certain things: a restaurant, a currency exchange, and a communications center where you could call or telegram anywhere in the world. You could also wire money.

In the restaurant, we ordered breakfast and went one at a time into the bathroom to organize our money. Joe had a leather shoulder pack and I had a gym bag. Ten o'clock the money exchange opened and we cleaned them out of Swiss francs. The guy there, who took about half our lira, said the holiday was in honor of a Dr. Ernest Guglielmetti of Brig, known locally as "Dr. Tar," who in 1910 invented the asphalt-surfaced road. That was too much for Joe who went around exclaiming, "Fucking tar! A tar inventor has fucked us up!" The man at the money exchange didn't understand English and thought Joe was a Dr. Tar fan and directed us to his monument that stood in the Marktplatz.

We didn't have much time. The show was at 9 P.M. and Joe was the first act. We had a five-hour drive back and Joe had rigging to do. Tino would set up without me once it got late. The highwire was the last act. We started up the wire at ten of twelve each night and finished two minutes till midnight. I told Joe we could wire the money to someone through the telegraph office, the Swiss equivalent of Western Union, or go back to Circus Altoff and try to get them to exchange lira for francs. Joe knew there would be plenty of francs on the Altoff lot. The owner traveled with the show and Joe knew him. He'd have enough francs in the office wagon to buy our lira. But Joe had already said he wasn't going back there. "Shit," he said, "nobody wants to give up francs for lira." But we both knew Joe could talk the owner into it. The next day he had only to go to the bank and switch them back. He could make money on the deal. We argued about this for awhile and finally went out to the car and drove over there. I parked in front hoping to avoid the hammer guy, hoping the owner would be in the office. Show people were late risers but owners had worries that prevented them from sleeping. There was a tiny bar wagon inside the entrance. I ordered an espresso and sat down to wait for Joe who went to check out the situation.

Before long I saw him waving me over to the office wagon. I shook hands with Franz Altoff, a tall man with a browbeaten forehead, crushed nose, and a tattoo of an old-time bare-knuckles boxer on his chest. He wore an unbuttoned white shirt and the tattoo was about a foot long. "Wirewalker, eh?" was all he said to me. He had thousand franc notes piled on his desk, and behind the desk the door of a safe hung open. So we got francs, a strong currency that took up considerably less room, and packed it away in our bags and thanked him and left. We took a beating on the exchange but not as bad as we would have at a bank in Rome. Still Joe complained all the way out of town and, as always, swore to God he'd never go there again.

There was no question about the route back. We headed southwest, skirting Zermatt, to the Saint Bernard tunnel that crossed into Aosta, my favorite part of Italy. Joe said that was because it didn't resemble Italy at all but was much like Switzerland. This route meant more driving in Switzerland. The roads were better and there was little traffic. The Swiss liked everything perfect, and they were so used to perfection that it worked against chaotic souls like us trapped in an Italian world where the only things approaching perfection were certain pasta dishes and handmade shoes. In Switzerland, even five kilometers from the border, things were very regular. I can only guess at how irregular Joe and I looked that morning passing the police car in that damned Lancia. We passed them on a two-lane road that went only to the Saint Bernard tunnel. We were in an unmistakably Italian car. They could have let us go. But no. When I saw them U-turn in the rearview mirror I wanted to open my door and step out onto Dr. Guglielmetti's asphalt going 150 kilometers per hour.

"Damn, damn, damn," Joe said, and a minute later in front of the cops, "Good morning!" Perfect Swiss German with a professional smile. "Nice day, isn't it?" The fog was so thick our passports were dripping when we handed them over along with the car papers, our reasons for traveling in Switzerland, and eventually two hundred francs for driving a dented vehicle. That was their gripe, no lie: it was against the law to drive a vehicle in Switzerland with a dent in it. They also mentioned we were speeding and possibly left of center. They were absolutely amazed at the wrecked Lancia and that someone would keep driving it. We told them it was nothing, how in America people drove dented cars all the time. They walked around the car, mumbling to each other and looking at us as if we had the plague.

Their main concern, besides getting the two hundred francs, was determining without a doubt that the damage to the Lancia had not occurred in Switzerland. We swore up and down that it happened in Italy. But that meant we smashed the car and kept on to our destination. They couldn't comprehend that. Any Swiss person would have had the car towed to a garage and called off the trip. Since we were not Swiss, and obviously heading over the border, and maybe dangerous lunatics, we had to pay the fine right then. Another Swiss rule. Aliens, as they called us, must pay out of pocket. In Italy you paid out of pocket too, but the money only made it into the cop's pocket. These Swiss cops would really turn in the fine.

It struck me then that in all my time in Switzerland I'd never seen a dented vehicle or a rusted one, or one with a cracked window, or a bumper missing, or a headlight out. It just didn't happen. And when you didn't see those things you forgot they ever existed. After the tunnel, between Milano and Rome—and I'll tell you right here, we got back without further incident—I said, "Joe, how long since you've been in the States?"

"Hell, I don't know. Six, seven years maybe. Why?"

"I'm forgetting what it's like."

"Nah," he said. "There's no place like home, believe me."

"Couple years ago I flew into New York and fat people were yelling everywhere, pickpockets, muggers, drug addicts. And that was in baggage claim."

"Well, New York, L.A., Miami, those places all suck. You get yourself a nice hometown in someplace like Ohiowa, or ah, someplace like that—"

"You mean Iowa?"

"Well, whatever—"

"Or Ohio?"

"Whatever the shit they call it—you know what I mean, a nice place you can stay without any fucking assholes in it."

Two subjects were common between us: where we would

work next and when we would retire and settle down. Joe was nearly forty and reputed to have a huge nest egg. He'd been on the road twenty years and always talked about a time when he would settle somewhere, pick a nice hometown off the map, in a state he could remember the name of, and buy an apartment house. I still had time. But sometimes I thought I'd hang myself with a water hose before I faced one more nightly tromp through mud looking for the water and electric hookup.

We got back to the lot and Joe went to set up his rigging. Tino had ours up and was settled down to dinner. I went to my trailer where it was parked in a good spot. It was important in a big city like Rome to get a spot away from the edge of the lot. The show put up a fence for long stays, but if you were near the fence townspeople looked in your windows. Ben came out of his house under the awning, and I saw the food and water Elaine had given him. She'd hooked up the electricity and the trailer was warm inside, and I read the note that said she'd gone shopping. I ate, took a shower, and went to bed. There was no need to tell Tino I was back; he knew.

Six o'clock was my naptime and I always woke when the show started at nine. The music wasn't that loud and my trailer was well insulated with curtains and shades, but an internal alarm woke me just before Joe blasted off. That's how the show opened: the Arrival of Aliens. *It could happen in your town.* There was space music and sound effects and Joe's spaceship, spinning in smoke and colored lights, descended from high in the tent. When the audience was sufficiently blinded by light and noise Joe and his wife, scantily clad invaders, popped out and went through their routine.

I dressed and began warmup in the trailer. Elaine came back and I told her about the trip. At twenty to twelve Tino knocked on the door and we walked to the tent and he said everything was fine—he'd been up on the rigging and it felt good and tight—and I told him about the money and Dr. Tar and how I'd exchanged his lira for francs. I felt so relieved to be back that I didn't even bring up that damned Lancia and forgot completely about the border police.

At ten of twelve our music began. It was a switch thrown inside us igniting a routine we knew so well it could only be a comfort. Like a suburbanite pressing his garage-door opener and getting out of his car after work and stepping into his warm kitchen to the happy squeals of his kids and the smell of dinner prepared by his wife. Maybe like that. I don't know.

Alone in the dark, on separate sides of the tent, we began our ascent up the inclined wires to our platforms. For the first ten steps or so no one could see me because I was back in the shadowy gap between bleacher sections where the spotlights didn't reach. The music was suspenseful, the audience stirring, looking around, because they felt something was starting, but they couldn't see me for those first steps in the dark. Those were my own steps. Sometimes I'd stop walking and look up at the platform gleaming in the lights near the top of the tent, a familiar place. A place you take big loose breaths, like you might take when it's late and your day is done and you have no intentions except to eat and lounge in your easy chair, the kind of breath that makes you relish breath. Yes, we were working, this was what we did for money. But not really.

I balanced in the dark, stood on air where no one could see me, let the music play and waited until I saw Tino across the tent emerge into the light. I watched the audience turn as they saw him and ooed and aahd thinking he was the only one. I'd wait, maybe two, three steps, then walk again toward the place up the line where the spotlight man had the beam fixed on the cable, waiting for me, wondering: *where the hell is that bastard?* I'd walk on before Tino looked up and not seeing me became nervous, thinking I wasn't coming, thinking maybe I'd come to that point he too must have considered—the point where another step was not possible.

Sure, I could have demanded a light back there, hung over my head so I didn't have to walk ten steps in the dark. But it wasn't like I didn't know where I was. It wasn't like the wire moved around. The wire wasn't going anyplace. I knew exactly where it was all the time and how it would react to each of my steps. It wasn't a big thing really, but it was straight, and solid, and reliable. And it was always there, the only place it could be, the place I needed it to be.

Ben

A tin knock in a piston shaft, a ping of escaping gas with each
explosion, a high-pitched squeak in the left rear brake heard by
no human ear, a dry bark from the transmission when the truckdriver downshifts onto the lot: these particular sounds pull the
black dog out of sleep, onto his feet, out of his house. He lets loose
a low whine, then one sharp yelp before turning to face the line that
holds him, and pulling straight back until the collar slips over his
head he's off across the lot like blackwater through rocks.

He zigzags over wet pavement under mist between trailers,
lowdown nose, ears forward, nostrils open to one smell only. Sleek
as a black snake leading with pointed face too fast for the cluttered
terrain, except this is a place he knows, this is his home. He avoids
puddles, leaps low dips, skids around electrical boxes, hops water-
hoses, waste drains, extension cords—shortstop—skirts the doorstep
pallets, a kid's bicycle, a rival chomping a bowl of nuggets, a lost
kitten—can't bother now. Legs churning a hard lope and hitting his
stride in the open area behind the tent he sees the truck where he
knew it would be.

And the idle truckdriver with his smoking mouth. And the dangerous cat man with his long-handled, doubledged hacking blade with which he'd lop off a set of backlegs in a single sweep. The black dog has seen him do it. An old white poodle came too close once. The backlegs sweep, the howling head, two fast whacks and into a tiger belly. The hacker pocketed the rhinestone collar.

The truck comes each day in the vicinity of horse killing. Not malicious killing. Horses simply unwanted by humans so knocked in the head, but wanted by other animals so worth a few bucks. Dogs wanted them, but horses were for the cats. Always in the morning the horses came, as if they'd spent the night getting killed and chopped up. The truckdriver pulls the canvas back and the hacker jumps into a shimmering black cloud of golden, green-backed flies. He claws out the parts with his hands. Horse heads on necks, hocks and hearts, lank flanks, shoulder blades and ribcages. The fly eggs, hatched and burrowing into the meat, stick to the hackers hands and the edges of the black raincoat trailing over his rubber boots.

The black dog watches from behind a wagon wheel. Unseen. Unhackable. He studies the hacker and listens to the cats going mad inside their cages. He never looks directly at the cats. They slam and scream, rock their cages nearly over, jam their claws through the bars and slash up the air. He knows better than to look at them. Even their eyeballs can cut you. In the elephant tent the swaying beasts give each other knowing looks, one sounds a mighty trunk blast, mocking the cats' rage. In the horse tent the confused horses snort and stomp. Their men rise from the hay to comfort them.

The hacker jumps from the truck onto the pile of parts and the truck grinds away. He takes up his blade and hacks off meal-size pieces, spears them with a wooden stick, and moves within clawing range of the cats. Most of the cats snatch the meat cleanly and bury their faces. But the hacker has his enemies. Those cats who watch him with purposeful, sidelong glances, the clever ones who hold back, waiting, pretending they can't reach. Then moving fast they pass the meat and hook his stick with one claw, pull him off balance and with the other claw reach for his coat. The hacker knows these tricks. He's been with the cats a long time. He too holds back, pushing the meat within reach then pulling it back when he senses the claw coming. He laughs at their rage. He curses them in his Gypsy tongue and they scream and reach to snatch off his arm while he pushes out the meat and pulls it back. In the middle of this game, the black dog makes his move.

Like ink spilled across a page, a black line to the pile of parts, pulling free a legbone the hoof still attached, he is spotted too late by the hacker. The hacker drops his stick and grabs the blade, but the dog is gone around the cat cages and under the tent flap. It is not lost on the dog that the cats are unwitting allies. If he could communicate with them he might time his move to distract the hacker at exactly the moment they could reach his flapping coat and pull him to the bars. But the dog has never found a way to talk sense to cats. Elephants can be dealt with, but the dog finds horses and cats hopeless.

He stays under the seats not moving, in the dark, until the cats are quiet. Then he picks up his prize and cautiously, balancing the big bone in his mouth, takes a longer, safe way home.

We Could Have Been
in Pictures

We went down forever in the bootheel, the butthole Elaine called it, dried out towns like Taranto, Brindisi, Lecci. Towns that buried us, made us think we'd never get out. Bari was the capital butthole of the bootheel, the place Elaine said for the last time, "I'm going." I didn't say, "You've been saying that," which she had—we were beyond saying mean things to each other. I'd been saying that too, saying she had to go, but we were having trouble with the actual bag packing, the divvying up of photographs, the saying goodbye to the dog.

She packed the things I knew about her, things that were hers but part of me too, things I wouldn't have known without her. Twenty bottles of vitamin pills, a battery powered television, a pearl-handled revolver I'd given her, a black string bikini I would miss very much. She packed her books and postcards and her pile of programs from shows we'd visited, shows worked at, shows heard about. Elaine had relatives at various French shows and, since she wasn't working, she'd go visiting. She'd bring back programs and pictures and tell me about the acts. Showfolks don't have houses to display their material possessions; they value programs, photos, posters, and newspaper clips and gossip to prove their past and the things they know.

She packed the antique clothes she shopped for in bazaars. Shoes, gloves, scarfs, glasses, hats. I'd never even heard of antique clothes. Elaine said she wanted to open a shop in New York City. That was her favorite place, New York City. "I'll retire," she said, "when I'm forty, and never leave the city." Total crap. Like Joe with his apartment house. Twenty years down the road she'd be saying the same thing to the kids she'd have with someone else, kids molded to her image, acrobat kids working to support her closing years.

"We could've done it together," she said, "if only you'd worked with me." I refused to be drawn into that. We were composed, cold, out of necessity. I didn't say a word when she packed all my Pink Floyd tapes. But when she stepped through the door with her shoulder bag and light jacket, after I'd lifted her trunk and suitcases into the truck, and she reached out for the dog— there was no question about the dog—pulling him to her and pressing her face to the fur behind his ear and whispering, "Bye, Ben," I had to turn away.

I couldn't look at her or say a word all the way to the airport. It was a long drive. Rome would have been convenient, anywhere would have been better than the bootheel with its winding broken roads, mixed up signs, withered grape arbors. But we couldn't wait any longer. Time had shuffled us along. We were like a wornout pair of shoes that refused to come completely apart so had to be resigned to the closet based on shabby appearance alone; still useful but too lined and cracked, too sad and tired, from too many steps over rough terrain of our own design, to be happy any longer.

I cannot remember her walking away from me at the airport. Maybe I looked away. Maybe I blocked it out. I remember her at the trailer with Ben in her arms, I remember the silent drive, and

I remember having to pull the truck off the road leaving the airport. It was not the truck breaking down.

On the way back to the lot black olive trees twisted in the dry wind, gray roots pinched in the rocky earth, like spindly witches screaming at me. I stopped to photograph them. Didn't get too close. Later, after Elaine arrived in the States I mailed her a picture that looked like *your bullfighter's enraged wife*. I wrote that along the bottom white border in blue ink. I couldn't remember his name, Octavio or something, she'd know who I meant.

At the show that night Tino offered his condolences. "If there's anything I can do . . ."

"We'll go for a drink after," I said, "if you can." Tino had had girlfriends come and go, but unexpectedly the year before he'd married an American showgirl. She was very strict with him, knowing his reputation, and he seemed embarrassed by being genuinely happy with her.

Tino and I hadn't been close for some time. We saw each other on the wire each night but otherwise led separate lives. But after Elaine left we began taking photographs together, for something to do. I'd been hiding behind the camera for a while, which irritated Elaine. *Must that box always be between us?* Now that Tino was married he needed something to do. About noon each day I'd hear him under my awning wrestling with Ben, I'd grab my camera and a dozen rolls of film and head out.

"So where we going?" he'd say. We'd walk to the nearest coffee bar. "Got film?" He knew I had film. After Elaine left I threw out all the food and filled the refrigerator with blocks of Ektachrome and Plus-X Pan. "Let's go look at hats," he'd say. Tino was a big hat wearer and Italy was a big hat place. Stores filled with nothing but hats. He'd try on every hat in a place. I'd flash some black-and-whites, driving the salesman nuts, then we'd leave without buying anything.

We often took Ben with us. Ben didn't care in any case. He'd been with us enough to know the things we did were not that interesting. It was winter but warm in the southern towns along the ragged sole to the tip of the toe. From the burntover look of everything, the bleached-white stone on the south side of the buildings, the orange dust as fine as talcum, we knew the area was a blast furnace in the summer. Ben didn't like tramping around in the sun while we stopped to shoot buildings and people. He liked going out to eat after the show and was welcome in restaurants. He loved waiters, and if the chef appeared dressed in his puffy white hat Ben treated him like God, and on occasion, because Ben had manners, he'd be invited into the kitchen.

On the beach in Carrazio I shot Ben sitting in the shade of a lifeguard station crowded with lean bronze men with slick blue-black hair and magazine-cover faces. They bent over the dog flashing their white teeth. I sent one to Elaine. *Meeting friends*, I wrote along the bottom white border. When Ben was a puppy, both of us new to Switzerland, Elaine said I used him to meet girls. Said I encouraged him to fawn up to the prettiest girls on the streets. Maybe this happened once. But on the Adriatic beaches last summer, at Rimini, Pesaro, Ancona, she did the same thing with the lifeguards. We laughed about it then, saying "We won't always be young in these places." But I wondered now what we'd done by our habit of "sampling the natives," as Elaine put it. "When in Rome do the Romans," was my cruder version.

On the southern coast I shot pastel towns piled on rocks above the sea, the buildings connected and stacked like blocks, sunburnt orange blending into faded pinks and waning yellows. Rickety blue and red shutters hung on rusted hinges and brick chimneys poked through the tile roofs. Towns within stone walls that had faced the sea since Troy's exiles floated up and slept on the shore, the same stones slightly worn, the water deep steel gray, and of course the sky azure like you read about. I put a polarizer on my lens and made it more azure. I made it blue till it hurt. I sent them to Elaine. At the bottom in ballpoint: *The box between us*.

There was always something between us. Good sex, bad self-ishness, and some malady going back before our time. We shared other people, together and separately, that was never a problem. The problem was we could not share work. Circus families work together. Mom works with Dad, the kids have their own acts, when Mom and Dad are old the kids work for them. Elaine's great grandfather owned his own show. Her grandparents, her parents, aunts and uncles, brothers and sisters, all show people. She wanted me to be with her that way, to make show kids, to build a show family that would be us when we were old. She didn't care what we did: an aerial act, an adagio routine, handbalance. "Other couples do it," she begged. And I said I would do it. I wanted to do it. I had cradle rigging built the way she wanted it, I hung it low to practice, and hung in it by my knees to display her twists and tricks in the best possible light. But I hated the monotony of it, and the swinging—the giants—kept my hands too torn up to hold her. I promised I'd work with her. I wanted to do it. But I never did.

She doesn't know that I'm sorry for that. Or understand that I had no control over not being able to do it. Even in my partnership with Tino I worked alone. Tino knew that. While he taught me the two-man act, he saw much sooner than I that my life remained only with the cable. I worked daily, alone, swinging on a makeshift highbar more out of habit than reason. Often he'd ask: What will you do when you finally have that trick? Dreading that day because he knew then we would be near an end. Tino accepted that, which is why we worked so well together. Elaine wanted something more, something I couldn't give her, even if I wanted the same thing myself.

On narrow convex roads with gullies along the sides, running circular to the center of town where there was always a church with arrowslits high up, I shot thick low portals, stone alleyways built by slaves for chariots, hand-pounded-in bricks covered with dust. In photos the towns looked like someone had sprayed adhesive over the whole place before a Sahara sandstorm swept across the Mediterranean covering everything. There was not a tree, not a blade of grass—I shot that, the absence of life—and there hadn't been for so long it was as if never. I shot that too, the absence of time passing, which is one way photos do lie. Life goes on, remembered or not.

Tino shot whole buildings while I was more interested in joinery, in cornerstones, in the way things were constructed. I shot the shadow of window bars on dirt. I shot a bricked-up doorway. I shot pasted-over cracks in a church wall where Elaine would have posed for a picture. I wrote along the border *Places you were* and mailed them to wherever she was.

In the trailer at night I slopped developer and fixer onto the bathroom floor. We found an old enlarger in an inland town and I took the towels and washcloths from the bathroom closet, the extra sheets, whatever Elaine had in there. I unscrewed the doors, knocked the centerpost free, beat the shelves out with a hammer, pried the mirror off the medicine chest and filled it with packages of granulated developer, fixer, bottles of stop bath, and rinsing agent. I tore down the curtains and covered the window with black plastic and tin foil and used the shelf over the sink for my three trays. I rolled up the shower curtain and washed prints in the tub.

Stooped in the darkroom all night, printing pictures a dozen times over until the blacks were infinite and the highlights ripe with detail and the decision to shoot, to record, to make memories, borne out in prints and waste water, blackened developer, exhausted fixer, everything except the images on paper and the solace they brought me, flushed down the drain through the plastic pipe to the ground. Proofs and prints hung on strings crisscrossing the trailer. Every picture I made I imagined Elaine's reaction to. I didn't send her many, she'd never asked for photos, but somehow they all turned out for her. The way you make something to be rid of it, the way you leave to go back. None of them were circus pictures and all of them said goodbye.

I'd print until I heard pounding on the door, Tino's frantic shouting, "Time! Let's go!" I ran, pulling on my costume, smelling of photo chemicals, to the tent to do my lackluster performance, dangerous without warmup, without care. It wasn't that I despised my work. I was grateful for that eight minutes a day. It was such a small thing. I'd be in the tent at 11:40 and back at my trailer about midnight including Finale, yet the whole day revolved around those minutes. It wasn't as if we could ever forget about them. We grew tired, Tino too, of the routine which we couldn't take further, of the trucks and trailers, the flatbeds and forklifts, the living route of towns, the highway riding, the road relentless, the people who came to the show and sat in the seats and clicked their snapshots and stuffed their faces and clapped their hands for the acts—my act. I did my job, I tried to stay alive. With Elaine gone the life of performing went out of me. I was fined each night for working without makeup, for failing to shave, for failing.

The show owners didn't speak to me after Elaine left. As if her leaving verified what they'd already decided: that I was not truly one of them. I watched them climb from their vehicles each morning. Eighty years old, living in trucks. But they were not alone. Their families parked all around them. Beautiful great-granddaughters called them to breakfast. I thought of Elaine's dad. Could I be like that? Unsure now. I was among these people but never at home. There would be no one to take care of me. There would be no great-granddaughter to call me to breakfast. I'd die in the cab of a truck and decay into the seat springs.

Business was not good in the south, the tent half full each night, and sometimes I thought they kept us down there so many months simply because they knew we would blow the show as soon as it went north. We wanted a break, a rest, maybe a month in the States, or somewhere north, someplace high up, with thin coolblue air. Somewhere everything didn't seem old.

In Palermo we shot a pit full of men fighting dogs for money. We threw down bets so we could shoot. A large Mongoloid handled the dogs. I shot him until he held up his hands. "No photos," he said. "Photos are dangerous." He looked like Elaine's Mr. Tazooka. Or whatever his name was. I wrote that in ballpoint

blue on the bottom white border. He'd been a Hong Kong entre-
preneur she'd met in Switzerland. An overly endearing man,
impossible to hate, even when he would not go away. He wrote
to her constantly, sending gifts and plane tickets, and arrived
packages in hand from places across the globe to spend two
nights with her. "How can you maintain a relationship with
someone named Mr. Tazooka?" I asked her.

"He has a first name," she said, "I just can't pronounce it."

I made her send him away once for no reason other than jealousy, after I said that couldn't happen to me, after he'd flown from
Hong Kong to Geneva just to see her. And he left gracefully, that
was the infuriating thing, giving her a watch to give to me. Later I
let her down badly with a married woman, refusing to give her up
when Elaine asked me to for no reason other than jealousy. I
claimed it was out of my hands, fate, an act of God, or Cupid that
bastard child with the weapon no one can control. It's the unexpected things that linger to hurt you after someone goes, the look
of threatening olive trees, a free watch, two words spoken to a dog.

Tino and I worked up the Tyrrhenian Sea to Cosenza,
Portolone, Salerno. In Napoli we shot people living outside on
foot-pounded earth. No indication that they had evolved a day
since the caves except for their scavenged miscellaneous clothing
and their fire in a steel barrel. Whole families sleeping on flattened cardboard using newspaper for blankets. We shot them at
a distance, three hundred millimeter, in black and white. There
were roaming dogs, makeshift clotheslines slung low with wet
clothes, sewage ditches of black waste, herds of naked urchins, a
single pubescent womanchild bending low in a loose shift without underclothes. Gray baby faces cradled in the arms of little
girls. Old women stirring steaming pots over fires. Men lounging
in the dirt smoking brown cigarettes. The sepia-toned prints
were unusually warm and well balanced. I sent one to Elaine, to
some address I'd gotten from her mom. Along the bottom white
border I printed the word *homeless*, which wasn't at all true of
those people.

One Saturday afternoon dressed for the act, warmup jacket over my costume, I stopped by the office wagon to check the mail. Giuseppe the office guy handed me a manila envelope from the States. I knew it was from her because I didn't get mail from the States. I walked toward the tent and saw Tino dressed exactly like me making his way around to the other side. The chimps were on, I heard them screaming over the music, which meant we had about ten minutes.

I sat down on the ropes of my deadman and opened the envelope. There was an eight-by-ten-inch color glossy, a publicity photo of Elaine, the kind shows print hundreds of to give away. It was a glamour-girl-held-aloft-by-muscle-man shot. Your classic muscle man. Huge guy with a head like Mr. Clean, a gold earring, leopard-skin over one shoulder, a Genghis Khan mustache. With one arm he held Elaine clad in a few rhinestones high over his gleaming head as if she weighed as much as a piece of paper. *Holding up well*, she'd scribbled along the bottom.

I studied the photo with the sun glaring on the shiny paper. Was her comment supposed to be funny? The chimps ended and the clown walkaround music began. I was on in one minute. I took off my warmup jacket and folded it around the picture and stuck it between the deadman ropes then ducked under the sidewall and pulled myself up onto the wire and stood there in the dark. I'd heard that Elaine was working in some kind of jungle act. The music switched and I started up and Tino went up the other side and we ran through our tricks without incident. I was distracted and didn't notice the house.

Back on the ground, retrieving the photo from the deadman, I heard some giggling and looked up. There were some damn people. A whole family right on top of me. Mom and Dad and two teen-age girls. We were face to face, no way to escape. Dad held up a program and pen and Mom clicked my picture with some shitbox Italian point-and-shoot. I paused, smiled, and tried to beat it around them. But Mom was quick. She wanted my picture with the girls and pushed them at me. Dad still held up the program and pen. I took the wide-eyed girls around the shoulders and pulled them to me, wiping sweat on their clothes. The flash didn't go off. Dad jabbered at Mom to hold down a certain button. Finally she fired successfully and I released the girls and took the program and pen from Dad. Goddamn people will take my picture home, perfect fucking strangers, stick it under plastic in a book, show it to relatives once a year, saying that's when we saw a circus guy, that's when we saw a circus guy, that's when we saw a circus guy. There I'll be living in some foreign household year after year until I grow old and the picture turns gray and flat and nobody who comes after will remember whose picture it is or why it's in the book. I pressed Elaine's glossy down on top of the program, held the pen above it. How white were the perfect rows of her teeth. How smooth that flat rippled stomach. I punched the button on the top of the pen, laid my name boldly across her pale body, and handed it to Dad. Let her grow old too.

Mail

Italians steal mail; it's not sacred to them the way it is to Americans. To the showowners mail is information. They want to see invitations to arrive, words of farewell, gossip from other shows. They want this place, the place they own, to remain home and citadel.

The months roll on, the road relentless, the boneworn weariness of days in days out, costume on costume off, up the incline, down the wire, black dog on a line, and waiting for the mail every morning. They won't deliver it, there is no mailman, a stroll to the office wagon is required. Mornings are chilly so a cheap electric heater sits on the Formica counter, air pushed over glowing coils, warming the trailer. Going out to get the mail—big deal of the day—maybe knowing the heater is on and figuring it will be okay, or forgetting about it because monotony is distracting, banging the screen door, tripping over the dog, trying to find a way out of Italy, the whole business of coming and going sounding discouraging chords, like the wailing of time; like maybe it doesn't matter if the goddamn heater is on or not.

And that's when they get you. When you lack attention, or pretend not to give a shit, when you act like a victim, a spoiled brat, a martyred soul, that's when some god takes notice, raises his big-head, and casts a narrow eye your way. Not the kind of attention one hopes for. THERE'S ONE STEWING IN HIS JUICES. HAND ME MY LIGHTNING BOLTS. *Not the kind of firing-up one needs.*

The office wagon is about a hundred paces across the lot in plain view of the trailer. The dog takes off on his rounds that bring him in pissing contact with every other dog on the show. The old office guy, Giuseppe, sits at a desk piled with boxes and envelopes from many countries. A stamp collector's paradise. Giuseppe is a collector of mail. He scours each envelope for the return addresses of rival shows, agents, variety artist guilds, anything the owners might not like, anything to indicate someone is trying to escape. Giuseppe locks the suspicious mail in a filing cabinet and pockets the key. That's why everyone asks him, Did I get any good mail? Giuseppe plays dumb. Points to the pile on the desk. Postcards, periodicals, fanmail, notes from old friends.

About the time the dog makes it around to the office wagon it's time to walk back. Reading the mail, flipping through a copy of Circus Report as a way to keep up on other acts, read where they've been, where they're going, catch wind of change, who has died and who's been born—and accident, who has fallen and who has arrived to take their place. Fifty paces away the trailer takes on a sinister look. Check it out. God! Yeah, you with the lightning bolt. Why do the windows look so dark? Walk faster. Those windows are fucking black. Run! The dog thinks it's a game and runs interference. Twenty paces away grayblack smoke comes seeping upward in thin sheets from the seams between walls, the roof erupts in flame, and the useless mail goes sailing on the wind.

The Big Letdown

I tracked Dave—still living—to a car wash in Sarasota. Since I had more money than I knew what to do with, I sent Dave a plane ticket. The trip was as much for me as it was for him. I needed to see an old friend. He arrived with a full head of hair at a tiny airport in Bologna. He seemed healthy, but was unhappy with the weather. "It's not like the poster in the travel agency," he said, pulling a crumpled brochure from his back pocket. Pictures of white villas gleaming on the Mediterranean. "Sunny Italy!" the brochure proclaimed. Not Bologna.

Not Milano. It was a weeknight show, not a great house. Dave's face floated in the dark down in the gap between bleacher sections where he stood watching as I carried Tino on my shoulders for the final trick. Tino stood solid and straight, his feet firm pads pressing my trapezius muscles flat. Parallel shinbones pushed against the back of my head. I pressed back with equal resistance. After I crossed the middle of the wire and stopped five steps from the platform, he didn't pause for effect, to make the people wait, he was anxious to get the damn thing done and get down. As soon as I stopped he said "ready" and anticipated my answer even as I repeated it back to him. He leaned into the jump. If I hadn't been ready it would have been too late for him not to jump. But I was always ready and he knew that, and he was in a rush, so he leaned to go as he asked permission and I said "ready" and felt his shins press forward, my head giving, my body tilting from the waist. He slid by, taking my ears for a flick, then bingo, he hit the wire.

And he bounced.

That was the beginning of the screwup. He bounced crooked, one foot about two inches higher than the other, his body weight unequally distributed between them. In itself bouncing isn't cause for alarm, in fact, I remember smirking because it was his own casualness that had messed him up. He had anticipated the jump too much, doing it in his mind before doing it with his body. If you go with your mind alone, dismissing the trick before finishing it physically, you will mess up. Tino jumped in a hurry, hit the wire hard without absorbing the shock with his legs, so he bounced. Being careless wasn't typical of Tino. He was good at jumping from the shoulders, could do it stifflegged and blindfolded if he wanted to, if he thought about it and acknowledged what he was doing. But before the act he said he was starved, said his wife had been cooking all afternoon. They were going to have a candlelight dinner, etc. His stomach or his wife or both occupied his mind more than jumping and landing a highwire trick. So he bounced. And if he had bounced straight up—no problem. And if he had conceded to the crooked bounce—no problem. If he had simply been humble and bowed to the blown trick, bent to the wire and grabbed with his hands—no problem. But he didn't do those things. Instead he committed the ultimate highwire no-no. Something any novice wirewalker knew not to do. Tino got it into his head that he could make it to the platform whacked way out of balance. He was in a hurry. He did not want to take the time to lose balance, catch onto the wire, swing under, climb back up, and walk calmly onto the platform. Instead Tino made the mad dash. The wild leap. The fuck-you-God-you-can't-stop-me-I-push-through-outta-my-way *lunge*. Bad idea. He tried to make it the easy way but the highwire is very unforgiving of cheaters, of being taken for granted, of those gone stale. The highwire is a selfish beast. Wants one hundred percent of your time. Your eyes wander, you lack attention, you slip callously to one side, the wire like a bitter lover will let you down hard.

If you are five steps from the platform, or three steps, or even two steps, and you have lost balance, or attention, you drop to your hands, that's the rule. If you've lost balance throw in the towel, forget it, dump the monkey, cash it in, fuck it—just drop, grab, swing, climb back up, walk to the platform, and you will live to walk another day. Never, ever, lunge for the platform railing because if you miss it you're air swimming. That is what Tino did, the dumb ass. Out of sheer hunger and laziness he dove crooked for the platform. After the bad bounce I saw him hop once on the right foot and I thought, *Don't do it.* He made a stab with his left foot, which caught the wire with the big toe, that was enough for him to push off with, and he lunged with both hands going for the right side of the railing. Both hands grabbed air and that was it. There was no wire under his feet, no way to alter the direction he was moving, and nothing except blackness below to drop into.

Before I had learned to walk the wire I saw a wirewalker fall. A German kid working with his "brother" who wasn't, and his "uncle" who was a notorious pedophile. He fell straight down, as if standing in the air perpendicular to the floor, only dropping, fast. Too fast for his spotters. They saw him slip—blink—he stood on the cement floor of the building ten feet from me where he had not been a fraction of a second before. If he made a sound arriving I didn't hear it. I was holding a rack of floss. He looked down at his legs, his feet in gold leather shoes flattened out on the gray concrete. A shiver ran from my head down my spine and out my heels when I looked at his feet. For a second I denied that he'd fallen at all. He turned his head up to his partners who were crumbled all over the cable and staring down at him. The audience didn't know if it was a stunt or what. The kid looked at the palms of his hands, probably tingling as blood rushed to his legs and feet. The band, seeing the act was shot, launched into walkaround music. The director hauled ass down the track toward us. The kid looked at me, shrugged his shoulders, and muttered something. Then, as if this happened every day, he walked off. He walked down the backtrack past the director and the band and through the curtain. The kid didn't even limp. Walking on air.

They said he was in shock, which is why he appeared to walk normally. He had a broken thighbone and some damage to the heels of his feet. He didn't wear shoes for a while. There is no way in the world to walk with a broken thighbone. But I saw him stroll down the track all the way to the curtain without acknowledging in any way he'd just fallen from the highwire.

Months later when he got the cast off he became a vendor and moved into the butcher car with his "brother" who had left the "uncle" who had been using and abusing both boys for years. The boys were fed up and the fall had set them free.

Tino didn't do any strolling after he fell. He was out cold and had to be carried off on a stretcher. I have a picture in my mind of him swimming in the air just to one side of the platform. He's parallel to the floor, arms and legs rowing frantically; there is a guywire glowing in the spotlight about a foot in front of him, everything black beneath. Some quiet roar in my head. Dave's face down in the gap opening up a bit while Tino swam. The picture doesn't last, then *whump*, the vacuum-thump noise of the audience intaking air at once with Tino's body hitting the sawdust. Dave would be the first to reach him. We were at thirty feet in the tent. Tino nose-dived, swam, bellyflopped down, and would have landed on his hands and knees if we hadn't had spotters.

We had spotters.

I was a spotter once on the train show; filling in when they were shorthanded. Shorty the prop boss curled his finger at me. "Com'ere," he said. I followed him to ring three. In the five-second dark while the band took a breath and the lighting guys held their fingers on the switches, ringcurb men scooped monkey shit into barrels, prop guys unrolled a strip of red carpet, a Bulgarian wearing a black tuxedo under a bathrobe loosed a tieback rope allowing a trapeze to swing free overhead. The whistle blasted and the band kicked in and the lights came up catching everyone jumping out of the ring. Everyone except Shorty and me and the Bulgarian.

"Stay put," Shorty said, positioning me just off the strip of red carpet under the trap. He stood facing me across the carpet as a Bulgarian girl fresh from having a baby came strutting into the ring pulling a half-dozen spotlight beams with her. She wore a white leotard with rhinestones sewn onto it and a sheer veillike cape that she shed as she came to a stop between us. She flipped the cape from her shoulders and her husband, sans bathrobe, caught it. The act was all his doing. I'd seen him pushing her to get into shape, making her practice while the newborn slept in a stroller. Sitting on the ringcurb the woman nursed the baby between rounds of situps and pushups. A young woman, maybe twenty, maybe three feet from me, the spotlights glaring off her face, a black pencil line around her lips.

She reached out to the people and there was some clapping, but I couldn't see anything outside our burning circle of light. She was sweating through her makeup and I saw a white bra strap peek across her shoulder. She had great shoulders, but her belly was still soft, pushing out against the sheer Spandex above where it vanished between her legs. She looked to the chrome bar hanging thirty feet above us. I'd forgotten it for a moment, forgotten what we were doing there, and it startled me when she slipped out of her silver spray-painted shoes and took the webbed climbing rope from her husband and pulled herself hand over hand into the air. The spotlights went with her, leaving

Shorty and me in the dark. She withered and posed, hung from her knees, her feet. Her face pointing straight down. I saw the dark crevice between her breasts. Beads of sweat flew from her body and made tiny dark spots on my coveralls.

Her husband moved around us with the web in his hand. Shorty didn't like the guy. "Know-it-all," he said. The husband spoke to his wife in Bulgarian. When it was time for her to swing—the finale of these acts always involved swinging—he moved the web between her legs so she could hook her foot and be pulled into the air to get started. She attached a thin leather mechanic belt around her waist, and once the husband had her swinging he tied back the web and took hold of the rope that ran up through a pulley wheel then down to the thin wire attached to her belt. The husband stood behind us in the dark taking up slack when his wife swung his way, letting it out when she swung away from him.

She had only two swinging tricks, the first a standard where you sit on the bar until the peak of the backswing then let go of the ropes and fly off the bar backwards only to catch the ropes with your feet. Done correctly, with a great airborne show before the feet hit the ropes, it looks dramatic but is really easy since you are looking forward the entire time at your feet and the ropes. The girl performed it in a subdued and undramatic fashion. Still, she did it. Then came her big trick, the one she'd been working on hardest, the one she'd lost sleep over, the one her husband browbeat her about. It's a difficult and respectable trick, which again required catching the ropes with the feet. Only this time you lie on your belly across the bar until the apex of the forward swing. On letting go the body sails forward away from the trap. The trick is to do a half twist before you get too far away and catch the ropes with your feet. It's known to be a nerveracking trick and I saw that the girl was tired and washed out. *Forget it*, I thought, *throw in the towel, skip it, come on down*. The band was silent except for the drummer doing a low roll and the girl kept waiting, swinging back and forth, not to build suspense but because she didn't want to do it. The trick is easier with a big swing but she let the swing die way down because she was scared shitless. The husband babbled at her in Bulgarian. "Fucking do it," Shorty said. My eyes followed her dying swing. She had the mechanic after all . . . She went for it early, before the apex of her pitiful swing. I watched her push off, fall limply away from the trap, turn sideways a bit, and drop plumb like a lead fishing weight to the end of the mechanic line. The husband was on the rope, he had her and her weight pulled him up off the ground for a moment, but then he was back down and holding her firm. He had her. And as I let out a breath she dropped again all the way to the floor. Faster than anyone could move, faster than blinking your eye, she hit the cement floor on her face.

"Christ," Shorty muttered. The husband flew by us. We knew it was bad; the sound of it said it was bad. A thick slab of raw fillet slapped down hard on a butcher's block. A wet fish knocked senseless on a wooden deck. The woman was meat. She was a dead mother.

It was the husband's fault, Shorty said. The guy had crimped his own mechanic wire instead of letting the riggers do it and he'd crimped it wrong. The cable hadn't been properly pinched and had pulled out of the sleeve. His wife left a wet stain on the floor. It looked black under the spotlights. Shorty came sprinkling sawdust from a coffee can. Told me to get a broom. I swept up her fluids and dumped them into the muck barrel with the monkey shit.

No one expects a spotter to do anything when someone falls. There's no time. A thirty-foot fall is too fast for reasoning and action. By the time you understand something is wrong, it's over. On the other hand spotters are not merely for show. Spotters exist because in a handful of instances they happen to be in the right place at the right time to save a life.

Tino was lucky. After bungling the shoulders jump, he dropped almost straight onto his spotter. We thought of them as his spotter and my spotter because one always followed my steps and the other followed Tino. We didn't look at them and had no idea what their names were. We were adversaries in a way. If I fell my job was to land directly on my guy. His job was to break my fall without killing himself. But there must be two kinds of spotters: those who work inside your body and those who just stand there looking up. The latter group knows they aren't going to kill themselves trying to save someone nutty enough to dance on a highwire. Tino's spotter must have been in the first group. He stood directly under Tino when he made the shoulders jump, took exactly the same steps Tino took to the platform. In my peripheral vision I caught Tino's sudden lunging motion mirrored below us. It wasn't so much that the spotter took a step, there was no time for that, more like he threw a hip, made a shift of body weight, a tucking of the elbows, a ducking of the head. He saw Tino lunge for the platform railing, and knew as he did it himself that they were going to meet at last.

He was an Italian boy, joined the show in a southern town and was using it to see the country. He saw Tino miss the railing and he hunched his shoulders, tucked his arms and head, bent at the waist and showed his back to Tino in a standing fetal position. It looked, I suppose, as if he were cringing, trying to protect his head. But he was doing exactly the right thing. Tino came down kneeling in the air with his arms stretched out in front of him as if he were crawling through space. He hit the kid's back high up near the shoulder blades. The kid hit the ground instantly and didn't move. He's dead, I thought. Tino fired off the kid's body at an angle and smashed through the railing in front of the first row of seats. He didn't move either. Everyone else moved. I ran onto the platform, tied off the pole, and started down the rope ladder. The people in the front row looked horrified and tried to pull back from the bodies, but the people behind them wanted a closer look and were pressing forward. Workingmen ran over and tried to push the crowd back, the band blasted walkaround music, and the clowns ran in trying to distract the people. Dave knelt by Tino who was out cold. The director ran to the office to call an ambulance. Some of the workingmen formed a human stretcher with their arms, lifted Tino and carried him into the back. There was no talk of not moving him. They had to get him out of there and with everyone yelling no one could hear anything. The scariest thing was that he had pissed his costume. I thought that meant he was dead, and I started screaming for a blanket because I knew his wife bolted from the trailer as soon as our music broke into the walkaround, and I didn't want her to see the wet pants. I had the odd thought that she should be sure to shut the stove off because Tino was going to miss dinner.

The ambulance came fast and the paramedics knew what to do. Dave wrestled with Tino's wife who was wailing and throwing her hair and hands all over the place. Her name was Anna. They strapped Tino to a stretcher and loaded him, and Dave handed Anna off to me and with two attendants we climbed in and the huge door slammed shut. We were plunged into quiet. I couldn't look at Anna as the vehicle pulled out of the tent without the siren on. I held my hands over my eyes, trying to block out the white lights in the back of the ambulance, and I saw Tino swimming in the dark.

When we arrived at the hospital there was another ambulance pulling in and I remembered the spotter. They yanked both stretchers, lowered the accordion legs with the big black wheels and rolled through giant swinging emergency doors. The spotter was alone and as he rolled by I saw his eyes wide open. He was awake, alive, looking right at me. I tried to block Anna's view because I didn't want her to see him awake while Tino still looked dead. It scared me that this kid was awake. If he was going to live then who would die? Someone had to die in this mess and if it weren't him it would be Tino. But that's not what happened.

That's just the way I was thinking, confused and scared at the hospital with everyone rushing around jabbering in Italian and whisking Tino and his spotter out of sight, leaving Anna and myself in a waiting room. People were eyeballing me shivering in my costume. Asking questions with their eyes. One of the nurses gave me a white hospital gown. I needed something to drink bad but didn't have money and Anna wouldn't respond to any questions. Dave soon arrived with money and clothes for me. He got Anna to drink a hot chocolate from a machine. She wasn't from a circus family, but she'd been around shows a long time and knew this situation was inevitable. Given time, wirewalkers fall. She knew that. She just wasn't ready for it. They'd been married less than a year and she had Tino's favorite dish on the stove.

If I shut my eyes I saw Tino swimming over the black hole, the spotter hunched below him. I saw the impact, heard the whump and smash of the seating rail. That kid lived. That kid who looked at me from the stretcher. It was an honest look, but I felt accused: aerialist walking around on the ground perfectly fine, regular kid laid out flat. I found out his name was Marco. He made the equivalent of eighty bucks a week. Room and board. No health insurance.

News came first about Tino: hairline skull fracture, broken collarbone, broken arm, dislocated shoulder, four broken ribs, and a punctured lung. The doctor delivered this news with the deepest gravity and was surprised that we were elated. If you fall from the wire and end up alive and still walking it is cause for celebration. Tino, from our point of view, was virtually unhurt. The spotter was a different story; they wouldn't talk about him yet. We went in to see Tino but he was doped up and not in a good mood. Anna would spend the night.

The sky was light when Dave drove me back to the lot, and that's one time I remember missing America. Dawn after a rough night. You're out of the hospital, it could be jail, or maybe you just woke up in a ditch. What do you do? You go to Denny's or Waffle House or IHOP to have some big fat sunny round eggs on toast with home fries and bacon and buckets of scalding stomach-cauterizing coffee to burn your brains out. There was nothing like that in the world. Nothing like that in Italy. They never even *heard* of breakfast. I was too tired to be actively pissed off about it, but it was discouraging and made me long for the States.

It was dark again when we went back to the hospital and heard that the spotter kid had a broken back high up between his shoulder blades and might not walk again. I wondered if the kid knew that he'd saved Tino's life by the one simple movement, the only correct thing, he could have done. You cannot catch a 150-pound person falling from thirty feet. One hundred fifty pounds of anything, a sandbag, a haybale, makes a beeline for ground zero. And when it hits, forget it, splat, it's all over the floor, split and messy. But if the angle of the fall can be changed even the slightest degree, the velocity is dramatically reduced. That is what the kid did when he offered his back as shield between Tino and the ground. He deflected the fall a mere three or four feet from the floor, changing the angle from ninety degrees to who knows what. Whatever it was it stopped Tino from plummeting straight down and sent him skirting off into the seats. That saved his life. How the kid knew to do that no one knows. Maybe he understood geometry, maybe someone told him to do it, maybe it was instinct. I never had the chance to ask him. Only time I saw him in the hospital he was sedated. They said he didn't speak English anyway.

I sat in the room with Tino over the next few days while he regained his senses. He wanted to do something for the spotter. We had nothing but money, a poor reward for a life, but it was all we had so I packed a shoebox full of lira, wrapped it up in brown paper, tied it with string and left it at the nurses' station in the kid's name.

Permanent changes dropped from the sky. Tino said he felt fine during the act, "very ordinary," he said. That struck me as wrong somehow. We walked the highwire, for God's sake. How did it get ordinary? The day highwire becomes ordinary is a day bound to end in the dust, sawdust in Tino's case. It wasn't a bad fall in the sense that it didn't kill him, but all falls are bad, all falls kill some part of the person. The moment you hit the ground something dark and unwieldy slams down on top of you, sticks fast, and you're lugging it around for the rest of your life. I don't know if this is true of bridge painters who fall into safety nets, or construction workers who fall from roofs onto bricks and paint-cans, or the rich falling into poverty, or politicians falling into scandal, the powerful falling helpless, it is probably true of inno-cence falling Humpty-Dumptylike onto experience. Falling from a high place is no fun for anyone. But for aerialists, even if they can be put back together again, falling tears down to the ground years of practiced confidence, skewers time spent developing a working relationship with fear, kills in sudden flight long-honed skills. This may be because the fundamental job of the aerialist is to stay up; failing that pretty much shoots the idea of enter-taining anyone. For the aerialist, falling is the big letdown.

Tino and I had been burned out for some time. We'd talked about taking a break. Tried to book ourselves out of Italy with lit-tle success. We did have a short holiday festival booked in Munich. We said we'd stop when we came north to relax before Christmas. But we came north and stalled, saying next town, saying after Milano. Milano was a big town for the owners. Highwire was a big part of the show and the owners took it personally when we wanted to leave. You don't quit an Italian circus, you sneak away. But now the fall had narrowed, and broadened, our options. The owners sent the director to try and talk me into working alone. "Another partner," he said, "is not out of the question."

The question wasn't one of abandonment; I could work alone, or recruit another partner. That was common. People got hurt, people died, and were replaced by the living. But I had not been living for some time. Not since Elaine left. Not because she left, but because of the reason she left. I'd traveled all my adult life, slept in woods, on beaches, lived in cars, trucks, trailers, trains. I used up three Chevy pickups, one Dodge, a Minnie Winnie, a Royal Coachman trailer, a Holiday Rambler, a few bicycles, and what seemed like a thousand hotel rooms, and now—one partner. Yet I was never at home on the road. I thought I was, I wanted to be, but I wasn't. So the question became: why continue at all? For Tino there was no question. He was like Elaine; he would recover and go back to work. I went along with it, telling him he'd be back on his feet in no time, telling the owners I'd work alone for a while, but not until the next town.

Milano was an eight-week stand and every damn day was shrouded in mist and drizzling rain. Dave would rise from my couch bed at noon, look out the cracked windows of the trailer and say, "Another gray day." Not having to work, I took to hanging out at the bar drinking hot tea and rum in front of the tent. Sayid, the barkeep from Cairo, received small shipments from his homeland. Supposedly cocaine. Should have known better. Cocaine from Egypt! Gray pebbly stuff so weak we had to ingest huge amounts. Cement we called it. Early one morning Sayid banged on the trailer door gasping for breath. Back to the hospital we went, his lungs and nasal passages impacted with fine Cairoan cement. Solid black X-rays. The doctor shook his head, disgusted with us. Dave, familiar with doctors, told him to shut up.

Tino wanted to recover back in America. We sold his truck and trailer to gypsy butchers, and when they released him from the hospital he and Anna flew to Sarasota.

Dave helped me tear down and load the rigging onto the truck. We told everyone we'd see them in the next town, but when we pulled off the lot in Milano, Dave drove the three thousand pounds of rigging straight to the train station where I had it shipped into Switzerland. We left the truck in long-term parking, and it was time for Dave to use his return ticket home. He wasn't sorry to leave. It had been good to see him, we had a good time, but Dave had a home to go to in Sarasota. He had a job managing a car wash, and I saw he looked forward to going back.

So it came down to just Ben and me barricaded in a hotel room near the station. Everything I owned packed into crates and boxes and trunks. Ben, getting old at my feet, watched me closely, nervous that I didn't know what I was doing. I had lira stuffed into socks and underwear, into books, down the tips of shoes, inside the lining of suitcases. I was starved but too paranoid to leave the room. In the sleepless night there was scratching in the walls, something with hard nails patrolled the unseen side of the ceiling. I writhed fitfully on the narrow bed, dreaming of splintered doorframes, men in uniforms, circus police in boots and chains, the owner with a contract and a whip, screaming, *Back! Back to the tent!*

The Story

In Zurich in the dead of winter, the snow outside six feet deep with a glistening surface crust thick enough to walk on, the young reporter is upset. He can't get a story out of these people. Circus people harboring out the winter in an underground parking garage. It's not really a garage, but a building like a garage, multilevel with high ceilings for trucks and giraffes. Performers have wintered here for years at the Kiel winterquarters. They're like groundhogs, rolling trailers together like nests, making places to practice out of ringcurb and sawdust, bedding down horses and elephants in makeshift stalls on straw and woodshavings. They come from all over Europe to this winter community, relaxed and easy without the pressure of shows. Neue Zürcher Zeitung finds them interesting so they send a kid over. We run a story on them every year, his boss tells him. Go over there and find something.

But the kid can't find anything to write about. He wanders around the trailers and wagons, the people and dogs friendly, and he finds an odd blue truck with a bunch of people sitting behind it. How can a truck be homemade? And a homemade trailer goes with it, detached now, moved a bit to make a sitting space between, a patio covered with a patch of Astroturf, and over the patch a roof tarp which makes no sense since they are inside.

Why the tarp? Uncle Lee's idea, they say. The proprietor of this gathering being Uncle Lee. Why do they call him Uncle Lee? That's his name, they say. Even his wife, Mary, calls him Uncle Lee. Mary stopped performing no one can recall how many years ago at a sensible age, but Uncle Lee still works as catcher in a flying act as he has since no one can remember when. Lee is the oldest performer anyone has ever heard of. He looks about seventy with four-hundred-year-old hands. He's tall and straight-backed for his age except for his legs, which are like strung bows, and those remarkable claws that hang at the ends of his stretched-out arms. Well, he's a catcher, which explains that. Explains what, the kid asks. He doesn't get it. This is how catchers look, Lee says. Lee is hospitable and tells the kid what he can, never says his age, says he was born in Texas when they still rode horses. He checks facts with Mary. Lee has never kept records but Mary says he has fifty years of Circus Report in the trailer. That tells you how long we've been in Europe, she says. The kid keeps asking the wrong questions and is not getting anything he can use. Performers wander in and out, sit on lawnchairs or on the Astroturf. What do you know about Uncle Lee, the kid asks them. There he is, they say. Mary offers anyone who shows up a beer or a coffee. You boys sit down and eat, Mary says. After practice, they say, and wander off. A shiny black dog pads silently into the patch and Uncle Lee jumps up. Ben! he yells. We've got something for you.

The reporter looks confounded. How much longer will you work, Uncle Lee? Mary laughs. Until he goes to heaven, she says. Lee scoffs at her. Not true, he says, I only work because they need me.

They sit there talking while Uncle Lee feeds Ben dogbones from a box. The reporter says things like, Well . . . hmm. Then a middle-aged man rounds the corner of a trailer and enters the circle of people. Lee, he says, what's up? Lee looks up from where he's sitting with Ben. Hey, what's going on? The man is clearly a circus person but dressed a bit less casually in a jacket and cowboy boots than the tennis shoes, shorts, and T-shirts pervading the group. No one seems to know him and after chatting amiably with Lee for about thirty seconds he says, See you later. Lee says, Bye, and off the guy goes and nobody pays any mind. After he's gone Mary says to Lee, Boy, ol' Harvey looks pretty good. Yeah, he does, Lee says. He still married to that footjuggler? I haven't heard different, Mary says. About then the reporter chimes in with, Who was that guy? That was Lee's baby brother, Mary says. He sure has lost weight, hunh Lee? Sure the hell has, Lee says, he must be forty pounds lighter. Well, when was the last time you saw him? the reporter asks. When was the last time you saw your brother, Lee? Lord, I don't know. What do you think, Mary? Gotta be, hmmm, twenty years.

Flight

I flew with Ben to Munich on a frozen day in December after a layoff in Switzerland. The circus-festival committee, stuffy Germans who did not like Americans, sent a truck to Zurich for the rigging and provided room at the Kaiser Hotel. I had to pay extra for Ben. Each morning I hooked him to a leash and trudged across the icy sidewalk to the building. I told the director I had something to work on so he cleared an area, roped off a space, back by the cats. It was the old swinging trick I'd begun back in the gym with Elaine, worked on sporadically in Switzerland and Italy, picked up again during the off time in Zurich. I needed it now that I worked alone. The practice wire was a ten-footer cranked between steel I-beams. It had a crisp, sharp feel to it that was absent when it was staked to the ground or attached to trees. I swung early when the tigers clamoured for their breakfast. There was a rhinoceros back there behind a ring of thick black bars. One morning I saw him eat nine heads of lettuce and a dozen cans of dog food.

I worked on the gymnastic skill known as the giant swing,

which everyone said was nuts to do on the highwire. I'd
performed it twice before during long stands in big cities. Giants
were trouble because rigging lives, rigging moves when moved
upon, is affected by what it's attached to. The amount of tension
put upon it, the length of it, and the environment where it's
set up affects those who interact with it. Swinging was never
consistent on a wire that moved every few days. For a time
giants had been performed by Gino Mendoza who flew off in the
fifties. I wanted to do it because nobody else did, because it
made me feel like I was flying, because it was as close as I could
get to freedom.

There were no teachers of this skill. Other wirewalkers said,
Highwire giants? No way. Tino had always said forget it, too hard,
we don't need it. I knew *we* didn't need it, meaning the act
already commanded all the money anyone was going to pay for
it. We'd already won two televised circus competitions. We didn't
need it, but I did. I needed it to finish what I'd started back when
this whole thing began. It was something I needed to push
through. I needed to drive with the points of my toes, the small
of my back, and what must be the part of my brain that lived
closest to the skull and rushed with heat when I approached
what I could and could not do and live. I needed to swing then,
in Munich, because the last few years had worn me down, had
made me want to quit and become a plumber, a mailman, clerk
in a shop, anyone but someone with something to push through.

The Munich show was an elimination competition, meaning
highwires worked against highwires, flying acts worked against
flying acts, jugglers against jugglers, etc. The best in each category would be given a phony gold statue and prize money. They
would receive prestige. Performers less accomplished would
talk about the winners, say they were the best, and aspire to
rise. The judges were members of the Munich Festival
Committee, an old-school bunch who rarely invited American
acts to their show. They invited us because we'd been working
in Europe too long to ignore, and Tino being hurt did not void

the contract. We could back out based on his injury, but they could not cancel us. Tino said it was up to me. I wanted to do it, to do my giants and win with them. Then I'd have a big homecoming in Sarasota, sit out the winter on the beach, maybe go back to the lot to make a completely different act. The lot again, the long hot days sweating out a new routine, starting from scratch with money this time.

I was in Munich a week before my competition arrived. British wirewalker Henry Stratford came at me smiling with arms outstretched in the hotel lobby. "I've heard so much about you." Then went to the building and threw a fit when he saw I'd been given practice space. Stratford had survived twenty years of wirewalking. He was in the history books, a good wirewalker, always a loner. In the old days there were many solo acts, guys tough as bootheel nails, wearing plain tights and no shirt or shoes. Stratford still worked that way. It was rumored that he was worried about us, that he'd developed a new trick for this competition. Of course, that was before Tino got hurt. Still, I wasn't worried about Stratford. He was over the hill, legendary at forty-six. He'd fallen twice, both times lucky. I patronized him and waited for the show when I'd make him feel his age.

Other acts arrived. Tumblers from Russia, horse people from France, aerialists from South America crowded into the building with their rigging and their animals. The morning after Stratford's arrival two members of the festival committee and the show director interrupted my practice. I was swinging without handgrips, adapting to the wire barehanded. They were tall mustached Germans wearing great wool coats, black leather gloves, and shiny leather shoes. I wondered how they got around the icy sidewalks with shoes like that. I took my time, finished a round of giants, and swung down onto the cement. The director was a Hungarian, a nice guy just doing his job. "Mr. Ruden," he said, "we have a problem. There's not enough room for two wire acts to practice so we were hoping, maybe, well—"

"You will share this space with Mr. Stratford," one of the

Germans said. "Any dispute and practice will be discontinued."

Then Stratford himself stepped from behind a cat cage as if he'd happened by. Phony smile, overgracious. "Not a problem, not a problem in the world," he said to me.

"You're welcome to use my wire," I said, knowing he would refuse. He laughed, knowing that I knew he would refuse, both of us knowing he had no intention of practicing anything. The acts in Munich didn't need practice; they were perfected, that's why they were there. I wouldn't have been practicing myself except that the giant swing is not a trick, the giant swing lives, it's something you live with the way the tiger trainer lives with his cats. One doesn't do giants, as you might do a somersault, or do a handstand. Giants were engaged in with the benevolent hope that whatever forces controlled gravity and other universal laws would smile on you. Giants were never the same twice.

"No, I couldn't possibly. It's perfectly alright," he said, holding up his hands in front of the Germans. "Let the kid practice," he said.

"It's no trouble to drop it," I said, pointing to the rigging, "then you can set up yours."

He paused for a moment, checking my eyes to see if I meant it. "No, no," he said, "I don't need to, really." He waved the Germans off and began walking away with them, then he repeated, "I don't need to practice."

"It's up to you," I said.

"When I was younger, yes. A show like this would be a big thing to me. Not now. I do not need to practice."

He glanced back, flashing his phony teeth at me. "Do your best," he said.

I let him walk away. "Count on it," I said to myself.

The day before the show opened a flying act from Las Vegas arrived. The only other American act, flyer Don Love, a former gymnast, unquestionably the best flyer anyone had ever seen, would share a dressing room with me. He was a cantankerous little man, maybe a year or two older than myself, crew cut, old broken nose. We'd worked with him in Monte Carlo this past Christmas, and in London the year before. We took the top honors in London, but in Monte Carlo the judges split the award between us, the Flying Loves, and a Russian bear act. Don was aggressive about the giants, about everything. "Eat it up," was one of his favorite expressions. I told him to check out the rhino. Mornings he unfolded his tumbling mats between the wire and the cat cages and did his stretching and tumbling. "Forty-foot-in-the-air giants is about the craziest thing I've heard of," he said. Successful craziness was the most admirable thing in the world to Don Love.

The opening show was a long dress rehearsal with all the acts working so the festival committee could see what they had. It was in the afternoon and took nearly four hours. After that the program alternated with only one act in each category working each night. After a week the judges would post the award-winning final program which would run into the New Year.

I worked six shows the first week without platforms. The cables hung from the ceiling, common in some buildings, but a bad habit. No place to go home up there without platforms. Just the geometric configuration of cable with the artiste-rigger like a spider on a web, arms and legs churning askew, hands and feet coated with sticky stuff, but without the strong safety line the spider has trailing him. The building was designed expressly for circus, everything exactly where it was needed. Steel rings embedded into the floor for tailends, eyebolts in the walls for guywires, small defused spotlights recessed into the ceiling, cushioned theater seats on sloped carpeted floors surrounding the ring. When I'd previously tried giants in shows the spotlights had been troublesome. Revolving around the wire on your hands in a huge open space is disorienting enough without being blinded by spotlights. That was not a problem in Munich. On the downswing I saw the wire, then the floor coming at me behind two spotters, then the backwall with three lights, the middle light quickly blocked by my rising legs, then wire again in my hands and the mishmash color of blurred audience with a line of white spotlights over them, and the floor coming again. I flew fast, hands squeaking on the dry rock-rosined and powdered cable, free for five seconds, six, breaths in blasts, then piking the legs, planting the feet for the short circle. If I saw the middle backwall light flash between my legs, if it drew a bead deadcenter across my body I knew I was going to come up straight and catch my balance. Twice I saw it off to the side, creasing across my thigh instead of straight up my gut, and those I missed, balance lost, off feet into the air to look for the wire and grab.

Free for those seconds I never wanted to quit knowing the feeling. Even knowing it was temporary, knowing it could not last, I wanted it. I wanted it long and smooth, a drawn out post-orgasmic sigh. How fleeting the feeling was made me want it all the more.

But the audience reaction to the giants was disappointing. They clapped, they wagged their heads, but it wasn't the type of thing that made them jump. The giant swing lived well above the average person's head. They saw it but could not feel it. Some tricks were visual, meaning the audience had some sense of them—walking, jumping, riding a bike are all things people did on the ground. Other tricks were more illusive: people saw, but said, *What does it mean?* My fellow performers knew what they were seeing. They studied me when I came down, gave me plenty of room in the hallway.

One night I came off the wire into the back. Stratford pretended to read the bulletin board. "How's the house?" he said, as if he hadn't been watching through the curtain. The giants were no surprise to him. He knew I did them. I shrugged off his question. He smiled and said, "You do a nice job." I turned toward my dressing room. "Do you know Diana Mendoza?" he said.

"Rudy's wife?"

"Ah, yes, Rudy Sabastian. They're divorced now."

"What about her?"

He walked over to the curtain and cracked it with his open

palm. "She is there," he said, "in the center box." I saw the woman I once knew as Diana Sabastian. She seemed padded, heavier. "I knew her husband," Stratford said.

"Me too," I said.

"I mean Mendoza."

"Were you here when he was killed?"

"No. I saw him the year before in Berlin." He dropped his hand and the curtain fell together. I turned to go. "I think you may swing better than him," Stratford said. I looked back. He was not grinning. "Better form," he said. I went down the hallway to the dressing room, and I knew I had him. No matter how this competition came out Stratford knew I had him. I was the only person on the planet performing giants and he knew it.

Don Love was on his back with a towel over his face. I showered and changed into street clothes. "How'd they look?" I said.

"Fantastic, man. How'd they feel?"

"Felt all right. The people—"

"Fuck the people, man. They don't—"

"I know, but—"

"You're not doing it for the people."

"Well, I'm suppose—"

"You're supposed to do what you do, get the fucking prize, and forget about the people."

I went out down the hall around to the side door where I could get into the boxes without attracting attention. Performers weren't allowed in the seats during the show. I waited by the door until the end of intermission, then moved to her box. When the lights came up I was sitting behind Diana. She had a guy with her about my age, performer of some type, rider probably. She introduced us. "Fantastic act," he said. Spanish or Italian, I couldn't tell. "You are best I've seen," he said. I thanked him. Diana was staying in Germany now, her parents had died and she was running their small show. We didn't mention Rudy. I knew he'd dumped her a while back for a nineteen-year-old showgirl who'd subsequently dumped Rudy after he was injured and couldn't walk.

She politely kept one eye on the cat act as we spoke. By the time they brought the rhino out her companion was ignoring us, and she turned around in her chair and looked at me. "You've come some distance from the wardrobe," she said.

I nodded, shrugged. "Some," I said.

"You look good." She jerked her head in the direction of the wire.

"I've done some work," I said. The cat guy was trying to get the rhino to jog around the ring so one of the tigers could leap onto his back—he wore a thick pad to protect him from the cat. The trainer cracked his whip and stabbed the beast in the rump with a stick but the rhino just stood there looking out at the people. The Latin boy thought that was a riot. Diana looked at him, then at the rhino. She had the same slight smile, same eyes like sea jewels. She wore her hair up, drawn back, the lines on her face lifted out, tucked away. She was heavy but retained much of her seductive coolness. I guess she was matronly, yet if she got up and moved down the aisle it wouldn't be the stuttering, ungainly step of an overweight woman.

The rhino was moving now and in spite of his remarkable bulk he seemed to float over the floor as if he were swimming slowly through water. He bounced along at a jog, and the cat ran at him from behind so he wouldn't see her and spook and spin, and he kept running after she hopped up on his back. The Latin laughed and pointed at the workingman running around the outside of the ring pulling a pan of dogfood just ahead of the rhino. Diana looked at him and rolled her eyes over the audience. They were clapping and pointing at the dogfood puller.

"I heard about your partner."

"He's going to be alright."

"How long have you done that trick?" she asked me.

"Long time," I said. She didn't ask why I wanted to do it; she just nodded her head. The slight smile was gone. "I might scrap it. I don't know." She turned back to the cat act.

I sat with them until the flying act came out. Don Love and

his girlfriend. An unusual act because it was just the two of them and a catcher. Most flying acts had at least three flyers. The Mexican family Don worked against had a double rig with six flyers and two catchers. The Flying Loves was all Don Love. He did every trick, every trick anyone had ever heard of, and then some. "I haven't seen him before," Diana said.

"Remarkable, isn't he?"

"He's too good, the people cannot appreciate him." I'd heard that before about Don. He threw into the air such complicated maneuvers and came out of them with such ease that there was no sense of danger or excitement. After he threw his first trick with gymnastic perfection the audience knew he wasn't going to screw up, so they sat back, watched ho-hum calmly and clapped politely every time he settled easily into the hands of the catcher. Each trick Don did, like my giants, lived well above the audience's head. "At some point," Diana said, turning to look at me, "you have to ask yourself who you are working for." I knew she was speaking about me, but we were in no situation to talk about it. "If it's not for them," she said, waving her hand over the audience, "then it's just a lie."

When the band stopped for the ringmaster to announce Don's big trick, the blindfolded three-and-a-half somersault, I stood up. "Got to go," I said. "Finale." She nodded her head solemnly, as if I was dismissed.

"Take care," she said, and that was the last I saw of her.

When we came out for Finale she and the boy had left the box. Her question stayed with me throughout the week. Who was I working for? Don said we were working for the judges so that's what I tried to do. I enjoyed myself, did perfect giants, and never doubted that the judges would reward me even though their faces stared blankly at me each show and they never clapped. Of course they didn't clap for Stratford either. But once I saw him dressed for dinner, walking through the hotel lobby with two members of the festival committee.

Stratford had a bunch of visual tricks: he walked on stilts, carried a big pole, rode a unicycle, stood on his head, hung by his heels, grinning like a hyena the whole time, and he had his trademark chair which he balanced on the wire then stood on with his pole held high.

He didn't unveil his new trick until the final night of open competition, and when he did I burst out laughing. I stood behind the curtain peeking through the crack, something we were not supposed to do. A number of performers were gathered behind me because we knew if Stratford was going to show his trick he'd do it that night. I knew it had something to do with the chair. All week he'd been sliding the chair out onto the wire instead of carrying it out which was common. I couldn't be seen near his rigging, but I figured the chair was attached to the wire by two tiny steel brackets. "He's got that chair hooked to the wire," I said to nobody in particular. He ran through his normal routine then quickly tied on a pair of leather boots he had stashed on the chair. Evidently the boots had some kind of locking devices sewn into the soles. The chairseat must have had corresponding keyholes. When he stood on the chair he twisted his feet in a locking motion. It was obvious to us that he had locked his feet onto the seat of the chair. Then he raised the balancing pole over his head, got all wobbly and shaky, which was when I began laughing, then pretended to lose his balance. He threw the pole to one side, and the chair, with him attached, took off toward the ground. Because it was hooked to the wire it came back around to the top again. And again, and again, and every time it did I laughed harder. "This is a comedy routine," I said. He went around three or four times as if he and the chair were caught in a whirlpool. Then a workingman on the ground pulled a comedown rope over so Stratford could grab on and stop himself. He unlocked his feet from the chair, slid down the rope leaving the chair hanging upside down from the wire. A gimmick trick if there ever was one. A trick anyone in the world could do. It was absurd, the audience loved it, and the festival committee promptly declared Stratford the winner of the high-wire competition.

Later I heard the judges were appalled by my giant swings because Mendoza had been killed doing them. He was the only one ever killed in eighty-five years of Munich circus festivals, and the committee never got over that. Someone told me they never would have invited me had they known about the giants. After that I got pissed. Now whom was I working for?

Don Love was pissed too. His act had been beaten out by the family of Mexicans. They had these little kid flyers that weighed about sixty pounds each. Their mother or someone would hold them up on the pedestal board so they could reach the flybar, then push them off as if they were on a swing and the kids would fly a mile high because they were so light. They had no form whatsoever, but however badly they turned the tricks, their fathers, who were the catchers, could always grab them out of the air, straighten them out, and fling them back to the flybar. They sent two of these spidery brats out at once to loud trumpeting music and lots of shouting. It was chaos, it was absurd, the audience ate it up, and the Flying Munchkinos, or whatever their name was, won the award.

"What are we, the ugly Americans?" Don Love said.

We were downstairs in the Kaiser Hotel. It was very early in the morning. Ben was asleep on the floor. We'd stayed up all night drinking, sitting in a room off the lobby that was full of luggage after the bar closed. The room had long fluorescent lights on the ceiling and stiff plastic seats and bright white tiles on the floor. Suitcases and trunks were piled all over the place. We were slouching back on the seats with our feet on the suitcases drinking from bottles of whiskey and waiting to go to the airport. It was five or six hours until our planes left for America so we decided to sit up and drink rather than pass out and miss our flights. Don was going to Vegas by way of London, New York, L.A. Ben and I were going to Sarasota by way of Zurich, Miami. A group of Irishmen came in. They didn't say where they were going or what they were doing there. They had their own booze and drank with us for a while but got mad when we wouldn't sing. "Jump in mates! Everyone sing!" They were wailing away at some song.

"Americans don't sing," we told them. They all got red in the face and started calling us names we couldn't understand and walked out. "Fuck 'em," we said. We didn't care. We didn't care about anything. We were the losers. Outdone by an old fart on a wire and about a hundred Mexican kids screaming *olé*.

"The fuck does *olay* mean anyway?" Don said.

"Must mean, *we win*," I said.

"Hey, I don't give a shit. Those kids will grow up fast and that act will be history."

I agreed with him.

"You know what I mean? In five years you'll never hear of them."

"You're right," I said.

"I don't give a shit. I'm going to be here. I'm in for the long haul."

I nodded. Across the hotel lobby some guy with an electric floor polisher was humming over the tiles which were beginning to glow with daylight.

"I'm the type of guy who doesn't give a flying fuck, you know what I mean?"

"You are the kind of guy who doesn't give a flying fuck. Absolutely," I said. "Me too. I don't give a flying fuck either." We each took another gulp of whiskey. Ben was out cold on the floor. Everything in the room was green. I put my arm over my eyes to block out the glaring lights, and I saw old Henry Stratford shuffling through the backcurtain after his award winning performance. He grinned sheepishly at me, not bold at all, almost guilty looking. I shook my head at him, and he shrugged. We understood each other perfectly then. There was no hiding the reality that time takes its toll and there is no way to hide from it. I knew that he knew that somewhere inside me, even as I shook his hand and said congratulations, was the satisfaction of knowing that I would not end up like him.

It wasn't until I got back to America and spent three days recovering from my hangover that I realized I'd never worked for anyone but myself. Selfish, sure, but it caused conflict and grief to pretend otherwise. So I stopped lying about it. I stopped pretending I worked for the people. And that's when I knew what it was for me to be a wirewalker, not for anyone to be a wirewalker, just me in particular. And once I knew what it was, and realized I already possessed what it was, I didn't need it anymore.

Of course, I didn't tell anyone that. I told Tino we'd start working again soon. I told Don Love I'd see him back in Munich next year, or in two years, or five. I told him I'd visit him in Vegas, we'd kick ass out there together, drink some whiskey, do some tricks. I told him we were the kind of guys who didn't quit, who ate it up, who didn't give a shit.

Neighbors

The company van halts where the asphalt ends. Two men get out with tripods and toolboxes and go afoot into the woods. After school the neighborhood children find the stakes and the plastic tape around the trees. Then dumptrucks arrive and yellow steel-necked dinosaurs that mouth pine trees and wrench them from the ground. Palmetto bushes are bulldozed into piles and burned. Snakes and rodents scoot down the tire ruts into the adjoining neighborhood south of Sarasota.

When the workers go home the kids ravage the site, finding tiger skulls, elephant tusks, bear claws, then argue with their parents who claim no prehistoric land carnivores lived in Florida. Seawater, the parents say, sharks and crustaceans. But one day construction stops. Police rope off the site. The coroner arrives, then a university specialist, and media people hear something is happening and send a news team.

There are bones in a box, not unusual nowadays, but these are huge bones, and the box is an old traincar, the whole thing buried thirty years or more. The bones of a woman, they say, a huge woman, legs like treetrunks, fingers like baseball bats, a ribcage the size of a room. No way, the neighbors say, they don't believe it, they want answers, but the police won't let them see. The neighborhood men talk night raid: they'll go with flashlights down the street to climb the fence with the NO TRESPASSING sign—it's their neighborhood dammit, they have a right to know. But they don't dare. Their wives say, no, say stay home where you belong.

Rumor of the giantess travels around to Circus City Trailerpark and down to Showfolks Lounge in Venice. Calls are made to the newspaper. They say her name is Mildred. Nobody remembers her last name or how she came to be on the old Hubert Faughpaw show. Someone thinks she came from Arkansas. She traveled the country in the boxcar following World War II and on up into the fifties. She couldn't get out of the boxcar, couldn't move at all. Workingmen built her a huge bed—haybales set into a wood frame. They lugged in masses of food, and carted off the tubs of her waste. People paid a nickel or a dime to stand at the boxcar door and watch her eat and sleep and read serial romances.

They say she had trouble with summer heat, so the boxcar was packed with ice blocks. One night on a mountainous run in West Virginia, the train rocking hard through tunnels and around tight turns, a wall of ice blocks broke loose, pinned Mildred to the bed, and she froze to death. It was the heart of the season and the show had towns to play and no way to get her out of there. When an elephant or horse died they hacked it apart where it lay and fed the meat to the cats. But Mildred was well liked on the show and nobody was willing to hack her up. They simply packed more ice on top of her and closed up her boxcar. Every town workingmen added ice until they returned to winterquarters in November.

The show owner didn't want word getting out that he had a fat lady on ice. Something had to be done. They could expand the boxcar doorway with a cutting torch and the elephants could pull her out. But then what? What mortuary could handle such a thing? What cemetery would take her? Who'd be willing to buy a dozen adjoining burial plots?

The story is that they decided to bury the whole car. Winter-quarters was a private place then. No neighbors. Over eighteen hundred acres owned by the Faughpaws since the turn of the century. It's circus ground after all, a fitting place, and who will ever know where the fat lady is buried.

They separated Mildred's car from the train and pushed it to the end of the spur where the carstop had been removed and the ties pulled from under the rails. Using a crude diesel powered earth-mover they dug a hole big enough and the elephants, harnessed and chained, pulled her car into the hole and they covered it over with dirt and built a toolshed on top of it.

That's the story according to the newspaper.

The contractor says, Bulldoze her out of there. The coroner says, That's not possible, it's a human body. Some women show up and say, It's not an it—she's a woman. The university guy says she's an archeological find. The curator of the Ringling Museum offers to take Mildred as an exhibit, but only if the city pays. The mayor of Sarasota, who wants to attract people to the new neighborhood, is overheard muttering, Goddamn circus freaks.

One morning, after the right people are paid off, two cement trucks roll up and one fills the boxcar with concrete and the other covers it over, and when the cement is dry the hole is filled with dirt and the police tape taken down. The adjoining neighborhood goes back to normal. Sort of. Nursery palms are stabbed in along curv-ing streets, lots are filled, new homes built, and new people come to buy them, and nobody can say for sure exactly where Mildred is.

It's a place where new neighbors meet old. The yards roll and buckle in unexpected ways. Potholes drop out of brand new streets, houses settle badly, cracks appear in walls overnight. There are things under the surface, things manmade and not, things grown over and remembered by none that live on macadam drives with cracked swimming pools and Jacuzzi tubs listing on their sinking decks. Go ahead; take a walk among the insects and ghosts. Follow the waves underfoot, the ground softer than it should be here, hard beyond reason there. Grass growing in clumps, unexplained baldspots, circular depressions like ancient astrological signposts that might be seen from the heavens. At the end of one street broken rails reach from the ground like the tentacles of some great steel octopus. The rails and the ties that held them broken and running nowhere, old timbers notched and tied with cable, steel wagon hubs, wooden stakes, coils of rope cocooned in spider webbing and the sucked dry shells of the fed upon, the remains of a galvanized roof with the miniature petrified forest which collapsed it, all preserved underground in the dark as if some unnatural disaster had come down on this place rendering all life frozen in a moment.

But that is not what happened. The folks who lived here in the winter were driven out in the early 1960s by a horde descending from the north like a tidalwave of time and urgency; they moved south to an old airport nobody wanted. They didn't forget Mildred, but they couldn't very well take her along, so Mildred lives with the new people now. Grinning from her boxcar—she is the gawker now—a bloodless skull with teeth the size of flagstones, coarse hair a mile long, and a bile system that could hold the whole world. Who is to say she does not have friends down there? Maybe the Lobster Boy with scales for skin and snappers for limbs, the Inside-Out Man with his gut-sacked organs gurgling and farting outside his body, the Siamese twins, the androgynous dwarf. Carry a flashlight when you walk after dinner—forget about Halloween—watch where you dig.

One Show, Goodbye

Tino recovered in Sarasota with his wife and infant son. In three months since the fall he'd purchased a massive Holiday Rambler with two pullout rooms, sliding glass doors, and a deck, and he found this kid Mikey to stand in for me so he could get back into shape. Tino said they'd been practicing. But when I flew in from Munich I saw that only the kid Mikey had been practicing. He was young, sixteen, seventeen, and good on the wire. Good enough to push me when I had no reason to go on. He wanted nothing in the world more than to be what I was—a wirewalker. I rented a trailer in the park and practiced with him just because he was always one step behind me, doing the next day what I'd done the day before. I had to constantly revise the old tricks: the short rope with a half-twist; and after Mikey got the half, the full-twist, the twist-and-a-half. There was no end to it. Yet I knew there had to be.

The trailerpark was packed with families practicing acts and plannng their routes for next season. Everyone except us. We'd been in Europe so long we didn't have an American agent. Tino took that role since he liked to talk on the phone. He got us a week with Tommy Parker. A show the Shriners put on every year in Detroit. The show was in March, cold and icy, one of the first big dates of the season. That was all we had, just one date. We figured more would follow. Tino didn't want to take his new trailer, or his family, north in the winter for a week, so when the time came we rented a truck for the rigging and got Mikey to drive it while Tino, Ben, and I drove up in a Cadillac I bought.

We took turns driving straight through—eighteen hours. When Tino drove I slept, when I drove Tino slept. Ben slept all the way. There was nothing to say.

Detroit was a popular date because Tommy Parker, sixty years old and still working, was known to be trustworthy and would pay a good price for a quality act. He claimed to have been born in the ring when his mother delivered prematurely during a show in Topeka, Kansas, 1922. "The first sound I heard on earth was applause," he said. "What an Opening." Tommy and his brother Carl ran the Parker Brothers Circus. They were reputed to have toured America without a break since that day in Topeka. They knew everyone in the business in North America.

The show was in the arena at the fairgrounds on Woodward Avenue. The arena had a huge indoor parking arrangement, a heated garage as big as the arena itself and connected to it. The elephants, horses, camels, even the cats were set up inside along with tractor-trailer trucks and buses, tag-along travel trailers, pickups with slide-in campers, and trampolines, and dog kennels, and practice rigging hung all over the place. After the night shows someone would fire up a gas grill outside Tommy's trailer, and one of his people would arrive with a stack of steaks a foot high. Someone would dump bags of ice over cases of beer, and when Tommy came out in his bathrobe and sat on the Astroturf under the awning of his trailer, one person, then another, would drift over and take a seat on a folding chair or a rigging box or a turned-over bucket, and someone would bring a guitar and someone else a boombox. Elaine Bonnet's younger sister was there, the Hula-Hoop girl, grown even more beautiful than Elaine. I didn't dare look at her. Teen-agers hung around the backside of trucks, little kids bolted in and out of trailers slamming the screen doors, all the performers on the show would be there eating Tommy's food and drinking beer and soft drinks and talking tricks and road trips and telling of places to work both good and bad, both now and then. Nobody had been on the road longer than Tommy, so you couldn't out-bullshit him; not that anyone wanted to, him being the owner of the show. But Tino and I didn't have trailers so we weren't there. We were forced to take a basement motel room on Six Mile Road, the closest place to the fairgrounds, one-fifty for the week. Two beds, lightbulb hung from a cord, small rectangular window high up near the ceiling. I stood on the Naugahyde chair and saw a parking lot at pavement level, car tires touching those cement slabs people parked cars against to go next door to the mudwrestling joint.

In the building we set up a low practice wire but rarely walked on it. We hadn't performed together in six months but the act went smoothly. The two-high moved around a bit, and we cut the leapfrog altogether. My jumproping was strong but I was careful, conservative, Tino too, the fall moving with him now. After a few shows, when I felt good, I experimented with some fancy footwork Mikey and I had developed and that amused me for a short time. Tommy stood at the edge of the ring watching us; he watched all the acts, but ours was the one he hadn't seen. The rest of the acts were like family to him. We were lackluster compared to what we'd been. We were a regular act. Not many of the performers had seen us, unless it was on television, but there was one guy I knew from the days spent in the gym before we went to Europe. He had a tape of me performing in Munich and he knew what giant swings were and wanted to see them. "Can't do it," I said. "I've lost them."

The loss was not so much physical, it hadn't been quite ninety days since Munich, I could have grunted out a turn or two. Tino spoke to Tommy about the possibility of us going on his show permanently. Tino, who'd always been against the giants, said, "You should do it. For Tommy, man, he knows what they are. He'll take us for the whole season."

I stared at him. That was what he wanted. To begin again. To start over. To buy a new truck and trailer and continue down the endless American interstate system, the dreary truckstops, the fastfood, the black ribbon of asphalt disappearing over a rise only to reappear around the next curve, the delusion that if you kept driving you'd get someplace.

"I'm not in shape," I said.

I barely had the heart for the regular parts of our act. Tommy wasn't fooled. He knew something was missing in our act and he knew it wasn't giant swings. The act wasn't short on time or tricks—other than the leapfrog we had all the popular stuff. What was missing was the guy who used to do them. The sense of accomplishment the act used to bring me was glaringly absent. I danced, I smiled, I styled; yet it was nothing but an act, and if an act is only an act it's only a job, and old-timer Tommy Parker knew better than anyone that performing is no job. If it's not a religion it's an exercise in faithlessness, and a wirewalker without faith is a dead man.

Tino kept on me about the giants, appealing to my ego, and telling me how much money we'd get from Tommy if I did them, so I decided to go for it on the last day. There was no way to practice them or even warm up effectively. I knew I'd ripout my hands right away so I'd only be able to do them one show. It was a Sunday night early show, 7 P.M., so the people could get home to bed and we could tear down and be on the road. I warmed up my shoulders on the flyer's practice trap and did handstands for about an hour before the act. "I'll do them tonight," I told Tino. "But if he gives us the contract I can't guarantee them every show."

When we came through the curtain Tommy was standing by the bandstand telling the ringmaster what to do as if the guy had never seen a show before. The house was good for Sunday night, not packed, but the building was large with steep high-tier seating. Detroit had always been a good circus town. We were set up along the front track adjacent to center ring. We went up the inclines faster than we used to—neither of us could stand that fake suspenseful stutterstep anymore. We galloped up the inclines in time to the new jazzy music we'd found in Europe. The people clapped along with the music. On the platform I turned from them and looked down at Tommy and nodded to him, then we went through the opening and the first series of jumps, first mine then Tino's. That part of the act had never changed. Me over Tino, Tino over me, Tino onto the platform, me left sitting on the wire taking the people's applause.

That was where the giants came in if I was going to do them. It was the logical place since I was already out there alone on the wire. I stared out across the arena. The applause trailed off and I sat there. "Come on, man," Tino said. "What are you doing?" He was waiting for me to get into position. I threw one leg over the wire then the other and supported my weight on my hands. This was the hardest part. The casting up position put me perpendicular to the wire. There was no other way to do it. You had to turn and face the people directly, and you had to put your head up or there was no way to cast into the initial handstand. And there they were, staring straight at me, questioning, what would I do in such a position? Not afoot like a wirewalker should be, not moving but suspended on the hands, braced, ready to go. Tino said, "Go man, do it." But I couldn't move. I was unable to stop looking down into the faces of those people. They were close. But I wanted them closer. I wanted to understand the distance between us. I wanted to follow them home to see what comfort they took from where they lived. I wanted to sleep in their beds, watch their evening news, eat their family dinner. My home was not a place to relax. My home demanded attention. Tino knew, he found out the hard way, the wire would not forgive looking to those people. Life depends on movement. You can stand on one foot, you can hang by your hands, but success means moving constantly forward, waving your arms, hopping from one foot to the other, swinging around in circles, and moving over roads, over time, always looking forward to the next trick, the next town, with big men in suits handing out money, saying, "Great, come back next year." And I did, happily. For years I took their money and their praise and danced the phone lines, spun through towns and people and time without looking back or up or down or forward, and I never tried to describe for myself the home I'd found. It was a home. And more life than I ever imagined living.

But there were problems with that life.

Moving constantly is an unstable means of stability. I couldn't escape the world by walking above it. I became confused by strangers and strange places that were my home that were not my home. The wire, high above the people sitting with their faces in their hands, their mouths agape, waiting for me to move, was a remote place to make a stand. I felt the people pulling me down. "Man, are you going to go?" Tino said.

"Yeah, I'm going to go," I said. I threw my leg over the wire. I saw Tommy down below scowling. I pulled myself up onto my feet, and walked to the platform, and brushed by Tino.

"Shit, man, what the hell are you doing?"

I didn't know what I was doing, but whatever it was it felt done.

Back in Sarasota I shared the rental trailer with Mikey. At night too Mikey stayed with me. Whatever I smoked, swallowed, snorted, inhaled, ingested—he did. Tino always fell apart early, his last meal half digested on his shirt by midnight. We'd carry him back to his trailer, Mikey and me, to his wife who wouldn't speak to us, and we'd press on. We did the same bars, the same towngirls, and in the morning ridden with hangovers we did the same tricks. Hangovers didn't matter to Mikey and me. They were something to relish, a measure of how well practice was going. The speed with which the beer-tainted sweat flushed our hazy heads indicated how hard we were working. Two feet off the ground between the loblolly pines in the trailer park, the old lot transformed, Ben sleeping in the shade, just Mikey and me going back and forth for ourselves alone, hitting the ground and not even trying to catch on, developing footwork no one would ever see on a highwire.

Tino never practiced. He sat in a lawnchair smoking cigarettes and scraping his wireshoes with a steel-bristled brush. Every so often he'd stand up, have a coughing fit, sit back down, smoke a cigarette, scrape his shoes, and moan about his hangover. He bragged to whoever came around about Mikey and me. Saying how we were the best, how they were seeing stuff nobody had ever done. I saw one girl who was not impressed and went after her.

We were supposed to be getting ready to move that summer, to go back to work. Tino studied *Circus Report* for possible dates. He called and sent out letters and photos, trying to find a decent place to work. He'd blown all his money on the fancy trailer. I still had most of mine, and I had this girl now, a person both regular and not, someone to take me—incredibly—places I'd never been. And I had Mikey, fresh young Mikey, still trusting fate, trusting me. He wasn't afraid to push every step, every jump, every new thing to the limit simply because I did. I had. Maybe that is why I stayed behind when Tino got the Vegas contract. Maybe I was afraid Mikey would kill one of us. He was young, it was his time. Tino took him to Vegas while I stayed behind and married the towngirl.

Calling in the
Holiday Season

After my daughter is asleep my wife and I wrap presents on the living room floor. When the phone rings Ben lifts his head off the carpet. We know it's one of them. One of those long gone callers who hasn't called since some other late night of some other holiday season. I let my wife answer. Not that I'm afraid to talk to them. I just want them to remember there is someone between us.

My wife finds them odd, these callers from the past that she doesn't know, that she has trouble understanding. She holds the phone out from her body, eyebrows crowded together. "It's one of those guys," she says, "one of your old circus friends."

It's Mikey. Well juiced in the holiday spirit. He's left Las Vegas for Canada, can't say why, something about agents' fees and a fight with Tino. "Turned into a hectic scene," is all he will say. He stays now with strippers in Canada. Claims to be an agent for strippers. Gets them work in clubs, collects commission, drives them around in his Corvette. "It's a yellow convertible," he says, "like that Caddy you had, same color, rag top."

"Same high-heel shoe hole in the top?"

"It's too small for that. I put the top down."

"That must be chilly in Canada." He lets loose his high-pitched lunatic giggle. He asks what I drive now. I don't tell him about our old van with the roof rack and the faded paint, a "Mom's Taxi" type of vehicle. My wife stops wrapping and digs at her fingernails with a pair of scissors. Mikey asks about Ben. "Still with us," I say. Ben watches, ears perked, listening to Mikey chatter from one subject to the next, the words rolling together into a snaky knot, rolling back the clock to that time we spent in the trailerpark in Sarasota.

My wife sits on the carpet cutting and folding the red wrapping paper precisely for a Barbie doll box so that Santa and the reindeers come together correctly at the seam. She scowls at me, points to a pile of tricycle I have to master by dawn. I hold the phone away from my ear. Mikey is babbling nonstop. Talking too fast. Talking as if his life depends on it. I try to break in, to shut him up. But he is in the middle of the Longboat Key Bridge driving drunk in my yellow Cadillac after bar hours, driving seventy miles per hour dead on the centerline. There are stockinged legs across my shoulders, Ben hogging the backseat. Shortly after is when the high-heeled shoe went through the canvas top. "Mike!" I yell, "Mike!" But he will not stop. He runs on about what went on, spinning through tales, words I've heard, words I've spoken, about living for eight minutes a day bejeweled and blinded by spotlights, but making it somehow, by some small margin, same as we made it across that bridge to that girl's house, the girl with the really sharp shoes.

When he finally hangs up, my wife hands me the presents, and I nudge Ben over and slide them under the tree. Her eyebrows go back to normal. "I hope we have enough stuff," I say.

"Mother will bring stuff too," she says. "And my sister and brother will be here."

I have the tricycle half together when the phone rings again. It is after midnight. My wife stares, her eyebrows crowding each other. No one she knows makes phone calls after midnight.

"Who in the world?" She picks up the phone, then covering the receiver with her palm, says, "It's the one that talks funny."

Tino asks how I'm doing. I make things sound better than they are. He makes sure I haven't resumed drinking. My wife smiles when I say, "No. No drinking for three years."

Tino says he's quit everything too, even cigarettes. His wife is fine and pregnant again. But there is a problem. There's always a problem when Tino calls. "That damn Mikey," Tino says, "he screw me over. I need you out here." He lists all the bad things Mikey has done. He misses shows, drinks nonstop, disappears for days nobody knows where. "I can't trust him," Tino says. "He stays up all night doing cocaine." Tino tells a story about how Mikey fell on a fat lady. "It was his own fault. His knee shaking so bad the whole rigging was moving. When I push off his shoulders, nothing, no support. He take a step back, misses the wire and goes into the net, pole and everything." In Vegas they use a net since they work directly over the casino. "He grabs on but his fingers rip off like nothing. Then he's swimming out over the people."

"And he lands on a fat lady?"

"Shit, yeah, she taking up two seats in baccarat. Black and white dress like a tent. He land on his head on her hip. A big pop. I know something broken."

"You thought it was his neck."

"No, I know it was her. She screaming like to make us deaf. Everyone trying to shut her up till the ambulance come. Six guys with a stretcher carry her out."

"Unlucky," I say.

"For her," he says. "Lucky for Mikey."

I ask how Mikey is working when he's in good shape. "Unbelievable," Tino says. "He does the double pirouette, the short rope with a full twist, the split real high like you used to do. His dancing is too much for the people, they can't follow it. At the end he does that fake trip onto the platform that you showed him and the people go crazy."

"He called from Canada," I say.

"Canada! With whores! He took off with whores!"

"He said they were strippers." I glance at my wife. She has the crowded eyebrows.

"He can't come back, that's why I need you, you were the best. I get you a grand a week." Tino has asked me out there before when he was in a jam, when Mikey was hurt, or they'd gotten into a fight. Always as if the interim years were to be dismissed, forgotten, like they hadn't changed anything. A few times I considered it, for the money, because my wife and I are struggling for money, and because she doesn't know how dangerous the job is, and because the job I have in Florida is not great. It's not even mentionable. I tell him I'm unemployed.

I tell him there are no jobs for ex-highwire walkers. No call to set up large tents. No one cares if I can drive to Poughkeepsie and back in record time without a map. Friends suggest I become a bridge painter, an antenna builder. People will not stop asking questions. Ben gets upset. I thought making it back to America was all I had to do, the place I was born, where I imagined I had some place, a home like I thought other people had. A regular life, no highs or lows. I found some old friends, some scattered family—"so that's where you were." I settled in a place near a place I used to think I knew. Settled down with a rolltop desk and a hatrack. And I met my wife, Emily, who likes a stable place with some land and a pony for kids and a garden to keep us safe. We work for that place, building it little by little, building a family, people to call us to breakfast in our old age, regular people we might go to the circus with. But I find no place is stable, not really; no place is permanent. I find myself alienated from the type of life I imagined regular people to have. I have no skills to bring to sedentary life.

"Why can't Mikey come back?" I ask. Tino tells a familiar tale. Words like words I'd heard before, could easily have told, had told even, at different times, in different places.

Tino and Mikey have been in Vegas long enough to earn

money booking acts other than their own into hotel casinos. Tino worked for weeks on a Chinese water buffalo act, was expecting a fat commission check. But the check never arrived, and Mikey disappeared with the wife and teen-age daughter of some big-shot hotel owner. Turns out Mikey had rented a suite in the guy's hotel and holed up there for days with the two gals, a hot tub, and a bag of cocaine. Tino says Mikey had been "messing with" these two before, though maybe not together. In any case they were caught because Mikey was inclined to piss off the balcony. He'd go out there stark naked and shoot a stream over the railing. It fell mostly onto the umbrella tables around the pool, but it also passed the lower balconies, and presumably people were sitting or standing out there watching the lights and enjoying the dry night air. But Mikey was lucky. When the manager used a passkey and found the two girls in the tub surrounded by piles of coke, Mikey was out on a booze run. I'd already heard Mikey's version of that story: "You should have been there, man. Those two, the mother and daughter, both like models. We had major rails laid out on the tiles around the tub. Rails like an inch high. I was chopping with a butcher knife. We had footlong straws like you get with a Mai Tai. I went out to get vodka. When I got back there were two unmarked cars out front so I took my party elsewhere."

"Lucky you noticed them."

"Never lack attention. You taught me that."

"I'm surprised you remember."

"I remember everything."

So do I. I know clowns do not remember my child. I take her to the circus when it comes round once a year. We live in a small town so we get to see the show in a tent, as it should be, with bouncy bleacher boards very narrow, or folding chairs of the hardest wood in the universe with loose slats that pinch. Once I saw Rudy Sabastian selling tickets and he asked my daughter's name—Isabel—and he let us in free. Rudy stood with metal braces on his arms. He walked by swinging his dead legs between two canes. Maybe he'd lacked attention, let his eyes wander, doubted his calling. I was not able to ask him about it. He seemed otherwise unchanged. Said he'd just had his third divorce. When I unwittingly mentioned that we were getting old he laughed at me. "I am not old," he said. "I may be disabled, but I am nowhere near old." Rudy moved on. Swinging his legs. Carrying his new rigging with him wherever he went.

I have to be careful what I say because Emily, though she appears busy, listens to my end of these calls from before her time. When we speak of the years before our marriage, or when she hears one side of a rare conversation, her eyebrows crowd together as if she is concentrating on solving some puzzle for which mere words are inadequate clues. When she asks me questions I find them hard to answer. She asks why I quit. I say I was homesick for a home I never had, the one we have now, and she thinks I'm just being sweet. It's hard to identify the past let alone the reasons why it became the past. It's as if my memory of it existed before the story happened, and the words needed to tell it were always there just waiting to be imagined, and maybe forgotten. Maybe that's the point of all this: to remember, so I know what to say goodbye to.

Once I saw Dean and his Polish girl doing an aerial act on a tentshow. She'd defected and they'd been married. They seemed happy. She was talkative, very good at English, gave me a can of Coke. They asked what I was doing there, here, in this place. I said this is where I live now. They said how can that be? I said it's not bad. It was awkward recalling things, as if we were talking about a third party, and in a way, we were. We remembered the day in Minneapolis when we saw Bob Dylan. I said that was the same day Cuts fell on his face in the unicycle act, but they didn't remember that. They remembered Cuts but had no idea what happened to him. They remembered Dave but couldn't remember his name. They told me Huffy died of heart failure. Easy to understand. His daughter Alberta became paymaster. They told me they'd seen Tino in Vegas. "He's doing good," they said, "but his partner's a maniac." We said we'd see each other again some day, which may be true, you never know.

I have walked above every state in America except North Dakota. I mean to take a special trip there. But I can't go any-place; I don't take family vacations, makes me jumpy, too much road time, too many miles. Dave was around for some of the time. Ben was there for the best of it. Black dog in the coach sec-tion of a Swissair plane, on a train through the Alps, in the beer garden in Munich, on the back of a motorscooter in Italy—a black dog smiling—drunken man driving, always the drunken man never stopping. Never a map. The road relentless, bringing places and not. People have been lost and I miss them. I miss my mother who died. Father buried in his own story. Grandparents dead. Yet, there is little to regret, only what cannot be remem-bered, and a few things that can't be forgotten. I've adopted a regular look now, at least, as near as I can identify it.

I show Emily photos, hundreds of them in boxes and books. Images of people in Spandex and plumes, tights and sequins, oddly fit people freeze-framed in actions incomprehensible to a standard-issue mother who tends house in the same town she was born in. She's never been to Biloxi, or Chicago, or Texas, or Timbuktu and has no need to go. Photos are static to her. They are like photos she might see in a glossy magazine, realize the type of picture, the type of people, and say, "My, how can people do such things?" Photos, old programs, newspaper clips, and words, especially my words, cannot bring to our living room the life I had then, any more than war pictures or the stories of sol-diers present the actual conditions of war. The words of Tino and Mikey on the telephone make miles of years condense smaller than any increment of time. Something from the past comes through the phone to touch a part of me that never changes, and frighten the part of me that has. Ben picks his head up off the carpet, releases a noisy sigh, puts his head back down. Ben, who will not be with us much longer.

Ben is a road dog and that's where he spent his time in our

new life. At first he stayed in the dirt road by our house day and night. Waiting and watching my truck, and when I came out he'd jump up, look at me, look at the truck, look down the road. When I didn't make for the truck he'd plop back down and wait. He waited to go. Because that's what he knew. Once we drove to the old winterquarters in Venice. He made the rounds, pissing on tentstakes, the electrical boxes, the strawbales, every single wagon wheel and elephant tub. Finally a workingman kicked us out. I asked him if he'd heard of the Tino Brothers. He hadn't.

Ben finally grew somewhat accustomed to staying in one place. My daughter helped. After Isabel was born Ben began sleeping in the house, but he never established a sense of territory that dogs have. He welcomes strangers to our place regardless of their intentions. If they want to walk off with the TV that's their business. He's gone gray in the muzzle since we've come off the road, grown stiff in the hind end as big dogs do, moves around the yard as rigid as a kitchen table. He lives much like I do, with no sedentary skills, the road receded into the background, but never completely gone. The names and places that we were always lurking behind us, pointing us out to strangers, calling in the holiday season.

Tino says the daughter of the hotel owner is pregnant, and the guy is walking around with a gun waiting to see Mikey. Mikey says he has it made in Canada with the strippers and he won't be coming back. My wife says if I don't get off the phone we'll never get these presents done.

"Remember," Tino says, "you are the best bottom guy I know."

"Right. I remember."

Tino says he'll send a plane ticket, and a contract. I say I'll think about it, hang up, and go back to the tricycle.

Emily doesn't ask what I will be thinking about, she knows I'm not going anywhere. But her eyebrows stay crowded together, her mouth clamped shut. Unexpectedly, she wants to know why a grown man is called Mikey. I am unable to answer. That we've all grown into men is as surprising to me as if I'd found myself back in the lot trying to walk a straight line in the dirt. When we stayed in the trailerpark that summer we had all the choices in the world. Mikey was just a kid, somebody's cousin, I think. He didn't have a real family. I don't remember the story on them. Maybe they lived in California or San Antonio. I think he came from a big family, too many kids or something. He lived with us, did what we did, practiced all day, went out all night, became what we were. Maybe I should have told him there were limits, that the lines we walked and roads we traveled easily slipped from view offering a rough landing in alien terrain. There wouldn't always be a fat lady to land on. You could count on growing old—but for how long? I tell Emily I don't know why we call him Mikey, if you call him Mike or Michael it just doesn't seem like Mikey. Maybe they call him something else now, whomever he knows, wherever he lives.

"Nostalgia is death," Bob Dylan says. Yet he's on a Neverending Tour. Dave drives up from Venice where he is a car dealer. We go to the show and sit in our assigned seats, two old farts that have given up even cigarettes. Dave drinks carrot juice, eats capsules with seaweed in them, tries to sell me freeze-dried vitamin powder. The house is full of college kids. I wonder what they see in this no-nostalgia man on stage not speaking to them, not one word the whole show, wailing out his old songs nearly inaudible one after another without break and spitting repeatedly onto the stage and walking in it. We decide he is obsessed with endings. He ends every song six or seven times, whumping his guitar once, twice, three times, and more, with the drums crashing in finale each time, each crashing chord anticipating the held last, but each one not the last, as if he is trying to get the ending just right but is never satisfied with what he hears so he goes on trying again and again to find something recognizable, whether sound or feeling, vision or memory, to make for himself an ending he can live with.

It's late. Things are as ready as we can make them. The tricycle is finished. Emily kisses me goodnight and goes to bed. I say goodnight to Ben, reach behind the presents, pull the plug on the tree, leave the window lights on. The small house on the dirt road lit only on the perimeter, dark inside, the windows black behind blue electric candles. In the tiny bedroom next to ours, Isabel sleeps in the corner of her crib, curled like a touched caterpillar. Her blankets balled up behind her head. I spread them over her and pick up the book lying open on the floor. Christmas stories we'd read till sleep. The Magi story. What a hard time they had of it on the road, following the star but basically lost in the dead of winter with lazy camels. Just the worst time of year to go calling. And when they found the place—recognizing all they'd found—my daughter is asleep so there's no point in going on. But I go on anyway, turning the page, and see no words there with the manger under the stars, no words on the page where my child sleeps. There are three trees low against the sky, the child in the straw surrounded by the animals, and the kings seeing their end and the new beginning.

Two weeks into the New Year Ben picks a spot under a bare sycamore tree and goes off the road for good. "He'll be cold," Isabel says, so we cover him with a blanket. I rise early and dress in the dark. I make coffee the way my wife likes it, and I sit in a chair by the window watching the light seek out shadows in the yard. I see him, a red hump in the frosty morning, the sun breaking over the horizon. I see him the day Elaine brought him to me, a handful of black fur, when I didn't know how badly I needed a dog. What was that, luck? Was that girl a genius? Or was the hole he filled so clear? It's the things you do not know you need that remain most valuable. Isabel comes into the kitchen rubbing her eyes with the backs of her hands. "I'm going to say good morning to Ben," she proclaims and goes out the door in her pajamas. Holding a mug of coffee in both hands I walk to the shed for a shovel, cursing the mess in there, the tangle of paintcans, fencewire, clippers, choppers, mowers. No shovel. A blot of hot coffee goes airborne and lands on my white canvas shoe.

I find a posthole digger and carry it across the yard to where Isabel sits in the damp grass with Ben. "How long will he stay dead?" she asks. Not still a baby at three, yet not much more, she does not cry for the dead. She understands that I am sad, but not my sadness.

"It's wintertime now," Isabel says.

"How do you know?"

"I see the leaves falling down on Ben."

"We have to bury Ben," I say.

"Why?"

We've been through the dead part. We've known for some time that Ben couldn't last and have tried to prepare Isabel for it. "Our dog is very old," she'd say to anyone bringing up the subject of dogs. "He's going to die." Who knows what she takes these things to mean, this old and dying business? She knows, at least in words, that because Ben is old he must do this thing called die. When Ben finally does lie under that tree and refuse to move, she knows, at least in words, that this dying has come. Burying is something else. Dying is an abstraction. Like memory, a mere word. But burying is here and now; it's a real thing.

"Why do we have to dig a hole?"

Repeatedly stabbing the ground with the posthole digger, or maybe her question, sends me to my knees. I must stand and bury my dog. I must answer my daughter's questions. I pull myself up by the handles of the digger and again begin hacking the ground, hitting roots and rocks, and finally throwing the thing down. I can no more bury Ben with a posthole digger than explain why I have to.

We drive to the hardware store for a short handled shovel, then choose a spot away from the tree and begin to dig. Isabel plays in the dirt with a plastic bucket while I dig. I dig a hole big enough to jump down into, a deep hole. I shave and shape the sides with the shovel then stomp the bottom flat. It will never be deep enough. I climb out and brush the dirt from my jeans, aware of Isabel's gaze, aware too that the burying question has

not been settled. Isabel is quiet; she's working up to something.

Together, we gather the red blanket around Ben and pull him to the hole. Afraid to stop even for a second, afraid to open my mouth and let everything loose, we roll him in. The blanket falls back. Dirt and leaves speckle his coat. "Ben needs a bath," Isabel says. It's a familiar thing for her to say, it's what she has worked up to so far. And when she doesn't get a familiar response, a response such as "that's a good idea," when her father just stands there, feeling like he might roll himself into the hole and pull the dirt down over him like a coffin cover, Isabel goes back to what she has been working on. "Is Ben going to stay in that hole?"

"Yes." I want at least that much said. "Ben is going to stay in that hole."

"You said Ben is going to heaven." True, I said that. Trying to prepare us for this day. Those are just words. I have no idea what they mean. They do not help me not miss my dog.

"Things change," I say. "Remember when you were little?" The unremembered past when Isabel was an infant is one of her favorite subjects.

"I couldn't walk or talk."

"Right. You've changed into a big girl. And you'll grow even bigger."

"Like you."

"Right. It's the same with Ben. He's grown to this place. Part of him will stay in the hole, and part of him will change into something else. People call it going to heaven. Maybe we'll just call it changing."

Emily comes out then, sleepy eyed and squinting in the early light, carrying a coffee mug. She sets it down on the ground, and we kneel, the three of us putting our hands together, and we push the dirt in on my dog.